COD of THUNDER

Antti Hakala is a Finnish actor, comedian and writer. He lives in England. www.anticomedy.net

Esa Hakala is a Finnish cartoonist, illustrator and game designer. www.esahakala.com

Also by them:

SVEN'S HERRING
SVEN'S BEAR
SVEN'S MOOSE
SVEN'S SEAL
THE LORD OF HERRINGS
SWEDISH WAR HEROES

COD of THUNDER

A.K. HAKALA

Illustrated by E. HAKALA

To Lipla Jolla

Acknowledgements

Many thanks to Bridget Gevaux for her outstanding editing services at ABC Proofreading, and a playwright Tony Leliw for his constructive feedback and great ideas.

I am grateful for my brother Esa, whose quirky illustrations and palindromes give this book a nice *Finnishing* touch.

Chapter 1

A RECAPITULATION

Beneath the surface of Lake Pihtamo there was submerged a small fishing town that used to bustle with hard-line ice fishers, their families and friends. A towering tsunami eroded the edges of the glacier on the north shore, causing the most destructive floods in the area's recorded history. Like a pyramid-shaped buoy left to rot in the middle, a lonely tip of an old church spire poked through the thinning layer of early spring ice, reminding everyone of the times before.

Both the rebuilding of so-called New Pihtamo and the relocation of the ones affected had begun. A decision was taken in the community to recreate the infrastructure further inland, near the fertile base of Saalamaa – the only active volcano in the region. For centuries, its rich soil had provided an ideal environment for the area to prosper in agriculture. In the past decades, though, fishing had taken over as the primary industry, as well as a pastime – a shift which had driven most of the population nearer to the coastline.

Not only had they lost an idyllic town centre, but the lake was no longer the same abundant fishing paradise it once was. Since the number of fish had dropped to equal that of the Dead Sea's zero, a retrieval back to the countryside had suddenly become a feasible option again.

The floods that followed were the last straw. The most privileged or courageous began to seek a better life and opportunities to work and fish near the surrounding lakes, like Mokkajaaka and Suolankala. Many who left couldn't see Pihtamo ever recovering. It was as if the region had experienced another wartime crisis, but this time with irreparable damages.

Those who couldn't afford the luxury to leave were forced to stay. Either lack of money or bravery, or both, prevented them from starting over somewhere new, where the surroundings didn't remind them of the past, supposedly so glorious.

The town and its dwellings had to be erected fast, as the cold climate gave no mercy. There was no extra time left for mourning or analysing the losses. All grievance had to wait until the work was completed – ideally, before the blooming of the first flowers in the spring.

Nevertheless, the urgency to recreate didn't make people forget the underlying suspicions and unanswered questions about the events leading to the disaster. Only a few fishermen involved knew the truth, or at least had their own perception of it.

This unexplainable disappearance of the lake's entire fish population was not caused by salinity levels or other impurities; it was a secret project orchestrated by just one man. Sixteen years ago, Roar, the all-time angling champion, and Carl, Roar's arch nemesis in the fishing scene, would go out fishing at the same time. However, their trips were cut short when, coincidentally, Wolferring, supposedly a half-wolf half-herring, simultaneously swam to both their baits. That was the most regrettable catch they would ever attempt to lure. With its spikey claws, sharp fins and razor-trimmed sideburns, Wolferring quickly demonstrated how they had met their match. The encounter turned into a lengthy struggle, which resulted in Roar losing a leg and falling unconscious, while Carl lost his life.

The next thing Roar knew was that he was being treated and medicated by a local indigenous tribe on the banks of the River Pihtamii, hundreds of kilometres away from the lake and the scene of the incident, where he had drifted aimlessly on Carl's durable Yolla rowing boat.

Soon after Roar had recovered, he noticed that something had changed. It was as if he was under a spell. He could move more swiftly across the lake, and fish anything and anywhere with his new 'magic' fishing rod, which he received as a gift from the tribal community.

He had become the Lord of Herrings.

As a nautical wizard, he decided to dedicate his life to safeguarding the fish of Lake Pihtamo from Wolferring's appetite for destruction. He began a mission stretching over a decade, during which he transported anonymously and single-handedly, on his clinker-built Viking-style vessel, the vulnerable fish into the safety of a secluded pond hidden in the midst of the dense, Arctic vegetation.

However, being spellbound, and immersed in his task all those years, Roar came to forget his own, real identity and the fact that he had a family waiting on the shore: a wife, Birgget, and a son, Sven, who was the current ice fishing champion. They both believed that Roar had drowned.

When Lake Pihtamo had started to become alarmingly empty of fish due to Roar's, a.k.a. the Lord of Herrings', actions, Sven decided to look for answers. He teamed up with Jaaku, his best friend in his shadow, and Viljo, the former ice fishing champion and Carl's grumpier brother.

Eventually, the three brave fishermen located the Lord of Herrings and held him at gunpoint. Years of relentless fishing in the wild, and uncontrollable hair growth, had made Roar unrecognisable, even to his own son.

Their long-awaited encounter, however, was interrupted by Mooses, the hunters' mythical leader.

Unbeknown to Sven, Jaaku had already grown interested in hunting. Jaaku had also been convinced by Börje and Kalle, two notable members of the hunters' community and the fishermen's worst nemeses, to prevent his fellow fishers from eliminating the Lord of Herrings, hence damaging the lives of the ones they despised: the fisherfolk. However, no one, not even the hunters, were aware of the Lord of Herrings' real mission, which was to rescue the fish.

Instead, Börje and Kalle wanted Jaaku to take down Mooses who, apparently, wanted to bring the hunters and fishers together in unity and make them tolerate one another. The majority of the hunters, however, opposed Mooses's progressive thinking, where representatives of these two very different disciplines could live and work in perfect harmony.

In the end, Jaaku failed to overcome Mooses. Sven and Viljo, meanwhile, totally unaware of Jaaku's conflicting agenda, failed to defeat the Lord of Herrings, as the powers the mortal fishermen were up against were beyond their imagination and skills.

The ultimate clash between the Lord of Herrings and Mooses caused a storm that eventually broke the edges of the glaciers. Gigantic blocks of ice crashed down, creating a tsunami. Mooses was believed to have drowned under a colossal wave that swept over him while standing on a small island, and his aide, Psalmon, a large preaching salmon, got sucked back into the depths of the lake, from where it had originally risen. The Lord of Herrings and the three fishermen ended up water-bound, fighting for their lives, clinging on to anything they possibly could find.

However, there was a calm after the storm. And another miracle happened: the men survived. The battle drained the Lord of Herrings' wizardry and powers. He was an ordinary man again, and Sven could have his father back.

Roar, Sven, Jaaku and Viljo were the only ones who knew exactly how the events had unfolded leading up to the disaster, yet they decided to keep the recent past to themselves. They feared the public would claim them mentally unstable if they were to start throwing names around like the Lord of Herrings, Mooses or Psalmon.

And yet, their encounters with extraordinary characters were far from over. While trying to navigate their way back home, they inadvertently discovered new species of fauna, such as: Yetilag, a tired monster on a long haul; Erm...ine, a hesitant stoat; Squirr-El, a rodent of steel; and many others. Each one of them communicated and formed comprehensible speech in ways no other animal had ever done before. Their traits were something revolutionary; yet, on the other hand, they could pose a threat to the superiority and uniqueness of human beings. The men were being introduced to a world that no one knew existed, and they wanted to protect it.

Only four other people, whom the men rescued from the roof of the flooded post office, knew some of the truth: Ida, Sven's pregnant wife; Marjukka, the manager of the post office and Jaaku's new partner; Christian, Ida's ex-boyfriend; and Birgget.

In the aftermath, Ida wasn't as lucky as Sven, who got his father back. Her father, Gustav, hadn't been seen since the storms developed. The last sight of him was by Sophia, his wife and Ida's mother. Like many other evenings, Gustav had taken his snowmobile and left their multimillion-mark estate in Örebröre to, supposedly, attend a Rotary Club meeting in Kihlava. A couple of hours later, the tsunami hit, and he was never to be seen again. It was concluded that he had travelled near to the shore and was taken by the wave, as he never reached the meeting with the Rotaries.

Ida's sadness of losing her father overshadowed Sven's happiness of reuniting with Roar. It was one of many examples of the world's mysterious ways of keeping everything in a bittersweet balance. Fortunately, however, her pregnancy was a consolation to her, bringing her renewed joy. *The generations come and go*, she thought.

Meanwhile, Roar was blessed – or cursed – with a priceless secret, which he had shared only with Sven. *Like generations, fish do come and go*, Sven reasoned, while studying the blurry phone image of a map leading to the pond that Roar had scribbled on a piece of a wrinkled paper. The elementary illustration didn't tell Sven much, except that the pond seemed at least a couple of days' boat trip away. He had sworn to Roar that he would never pass on this secret to anyone; it was to be kept only between the recently reunited father and son.

However, Roar continued to question his own role and responsibility. Why not share such valuable information for the greater good, he asked himself, since people were suffering and going through hardship after a disaster largely set by his own actions as the Lord of Herrings? Wouldn't the fish he had saved and kept alive in the pond help feed the struggling village population?

Obviously, he feared the public outcry, if he was to reveal that he was solely responsible of depriving so many livelihoods for years – even though he'd done it for everyone's best interests. Admitting the truth would have posed a threat to his own well-being, or even his life. He also knew the lengths the most vicious and greedy were prepared to go to reach the 'treasure pond'. His noble plan was to secretly, in gradual steps, reintroduce the fish back into the lake. But there was only one problem: Wolferring was still out there, swimming loose.

Chapter 2

ESSENTIALS FIRST

A thirsty mob persistently camping outside the relocated Arctic Bar generated enough pressure for Tomas – the owner of the previous bar that was now engulfed by water – to open this much-anticipated facility ahead of schedule. Dozens of volunteers, who gave their time away for the construction work that lasted only a record-breaking ten days, were also eager to redeem their liquid reward.

However, during the bar's first few weeks of operation, the sales had dropped drastically since its heyday in the old location. Some of the former customers couldn't afford to drink outside their homes anymore. Many struggled to make ends meet. After all, it was only three months since the disaster.

The interior was designed to reflect the original bar in every single detail. Purposely, no heating system was installed, thus allowing cold air to spread inside and frost to develop naturally all around on various surfaces, creating a naturally icy decor. Reindeer hides of various sizes padded the benches and furbished parts of the log walls. The latest edition of Arctic Wodka had been added to the usual spirit-heavy menu.

These somewhat minimalistic upgrades didn't impress the most seasoned drinkers, though. Change wasn't their best friend, like familiarity and comfort of knowing. They frequented the bar on a regular basis for one simple purpose: to consign themselves to oblivion.

Escapism helped to balance out the hard times of austerity. Those punters – for whom the bar had always been the only place to hide from an otherwise challenging life in this harsh environment – could find relief in front of a full glass or a bottle. Ideally, nothing or no one, apart from their favourite spirit, was allowed to invade their personal space. Strict social distancing rules existed by default. Hence, no pandemic of any sort or government interference that came with it, was needed; all unnecessary socialising and close contact was seen as a virus in itself.

Yet, something in the general atmosphere had changed – despite the relatively successful repeating of the old. The world was not like it used to be. The expressionless faces of the men and women in the bar, however, didn't give much of that real disappointment away, while drowning negative thoughts with every shot and pint they quaffed.

The bar was located on a focal point by a central crossing, next to a supermarket and Roar's fish restaurant – two less-essential facilities still under construction. In the most unlikely event of a tourist or an outsider ever visiting the area, they wouldn't have noticed any difference between the old and new towns. But the locals, who knew and cherished every stick and stone, thought the past was better than the present. Was it really so, or just nostalgia talking? These questions could never be answered, because their history lay at the bottom of the lake. The rebuilding conveniently distracted the locals from finding answers to questions about actual causes that led to the destruction. Yet, the uncertainty of the future was in the minds of everyone. When would the next catastrophe happen? What could it be?

The middle-aged and younger especially had developed a somewhat false, indestructible sense of being during the lengthy period of peace and calm – even though geological risks had always been present. The lake bordered glaciers on one side and an active volcano on the other. The weather conditions were harsh most of the year, with long winters and freezing temperatures. Even history books were crammed with major incidents, yet it was still unfathomable that such a large-scale disaster could happen on one's lifetime.

Admitting defeat to the lake and nature, however, was out of the question. Detecting any fear inside the bar was impossible. It was like the stage was set for those sensitive and insecure at home, but invulnerable in public.

Sven's expression was no exception, when he walked in looking deadpan. A few punters who recognised him exchanged low-browed, yet shy glances. After all, he was a local celebrity; the reigning ice fishing champion.

As if nothing has changed, Sven also thought, until raising his gaze and noticing the newly decorated walls. Even though he was far from being an interior designer, even he could tell that the dark grey hides were clashing with the shades of dark brown timber. A purposely chosen, dim ambience dominated the interior of the bar – the actual vibrancy was felt as a side effect from drinks the customers enjoyed.

'This is nothing like the old place,' Sven said to Jaaku, who was sitting at the bar.

Jaaku kept staring ahead, pretending he hadn't heard him. But he felt Sven's presence and his damp clothes that radiated more cold air to the room. Even Jaaku's thick, seal skin jacket, with its hood and fur collar, didn't stop him from getting goose bumps. 'Of course not,' he replied eventually. 'It's too... How should I say?' He picked up his full shot glass and smelled the liquid. 'Artificial.'

Sven parked next to him, and gestured to the barman. 'Tomas is trying too hard.'

Once Jaaku had downed the shot and brought the glass back down, he tapped the bar top with his knuckles. 'Even the materials are painted to look old. This is not even real timber.'

Sven slid his hand along the top. It certainly felt more like veneer that was only disguised to resemble hard wood.

He sighed and shook his head.

For a moment, the two stared ahead and comfortably enjoyed the silence between them. On a rare occasion, an inaudible word or two could be heard pronounced in the background. But largely, the other patrons' stance was very similar: less conversation, more drinking.

When people had to meet one another in any drinking facility at these latitudes, a common plan of action was to get drunk first and then, if absolutely necessary, socialise. The famous last words would then be pronounced privately to the toilet bowl and in 'Norwegian', which in Pihtamo was colloquial to 'spewing'.

The easy silence between the men was only broken when a gliding, empty shot glass clinked against Jaaku's bottle. The bartender at the other end winked, and went on serving other customers.

Automatically, Jaaku started filling both their shot glasses. Since he was a few steps ahead of Sven in lubricating his social skills, he also had the courage, finally, to say something. 'So... How is Ida coping?'

The personal nature of this sudden interruption baffled Sven. The men hadn't seen each other for months. Sven felt like there should have been a warm-up chat, or at least some small talk, as the sophisticated and worldly call it. He was hoping they would talk about simpler things, like ice hockey or fishing, and then slowly move towards more serious topics, once the bottle got a bit emptier. Pouring one's heart out created a void that should be filled with something, like *wodka* for instance.

'She has seen better days,' Sven replied briefly, and drank the shot Jaaku had poured him. When the liquid gushed down his throat and into his stomach, he could also feel the immediate effect in his brain. The bravery to communicate verbally slowly awakened. 'Not only that she's getting bigger by the minute... which, in her situation, is a healthy sign... but the loss of her father has really hit her hard.'

'You didn't really get along with Gustav, did you?' Jaaku asked bluntly.

Before Sven could even consider responding, he had to gesture Jaaku's bottle again.

Jaaku understood the hint and poured them another round.

After Sven's second shot, he felt his emotional floodgates beginning to open. 'Gustav never approved of me dating Ida. But, I do feel for her. I, if anyone, know exactly what it feels like to lose a parent.'

'Maybe you can help, then?' said Jaaku. 'Stand by her?'

Sven nodded subtly. 'This might sound a little bit selfish, but... her losing Gustav does take the shine away from me having just found my own dad. I feel like it's harder for me to be genuinely happy.'

Now, Jaaku started feeling uncomfortable. He turned the bottle around and examined the label. 'What are they putting in this new wodka? You've only had two shots and you're already opening up like a teenage girl.'

Still sober enough to feel embarrassed, Sven immediately wanted to change the subject to something more manly and less sentimental. He joined Jaaku in studying the label.

'Ööö... It has fifteen per cent more rye than in the last edition.'

'I can't really taste the difference,' Jaaku snorted, and served them more. 'The old saying, "He who has happiness, should hide it", applies perfectly to your current situation then.'

Sven sighed and raised his glass. 'For sixteen years, I waited for my father to come back to life, and now this has to happen.'

After these drinks, an opportunity to enjoy more silence was there, but Sven didn't let that happen.

'Enough about me. How are things with you and Marjukka?'

'We're actually... getting married,' Jaaku said in a melancholic tone – even though his genuine attempt was to sound as enthusiastic as any typical male from Pihtamo possibly could.

'That was quick.' Sven didn't portray much more enthusiasm, either. But he was happy for Jaaku, deep down inside.

'Why not?' said Jaaku. 'It's not like Pihtamo has that many options, anyway. Especially now, with so many leaving. And we're not getting any younger.'

'I think that deserves a toast.' It was Sven's turn to pick up the bottle and pour.

'Everything here deserves a toast,' Jaaku said, almost smiling.

'You didn't, by any chance, propose to her with... herring?' Sven smirked.

'I've learnt from the best how not to do things.'

'Well, things could be worse. Ida's due any day now.'

'Your parents must be thrilled. You must be.'

'They are. But I am terrified.'

'You'll do just fine,' Jaaku said encouragingly.

They raised their glasses and drank, enjoying how their confidence levels began equalling sober men in other, usually much warmer, cultures. Almost all the earlier tension was gone and their stiff upper lips were moving more freely now.

'That level of responsibility freaks me out,' Sven confessed. 'All I've ever had to worry about is how to get fish out of the lake. Nothing else. But now, there's gonna be another person in our lives. I'm just afraid that something might go wrong, like what happened to my parents.'

'But your father is back,' said Jaaku. 'And he was taken away from you, his family, against his own will. Otherwise, who knows what would have happened. Maybe he'd have stayed?'

'I don't think it was that simple. My mum and dad had their problems even before he disappeared. And I don't want that to happen to my own child, to grow up with just one parent.'

'Where would you go? It's very unlikely that some big fish would attack you, like it attacked your father.'

'Wolferring hasn't necessarily gone anywhere,' Sven said gravely.

'I know.'

Sven started muttering hesitantly. 'You know... all those fishes my dad caught when he was the Lord of Herrings...'

'He was catching a lot of fish, I remember. What happened? He ate it all?' Jaaku chuckled.

'He took them to... a hiding place.' Sven's slur may have just been the 'alcohol talking'. Or it may have simply been motivated by a common situation, where most of us have at least one person somewhere to whom we can pass secrets forward – even if we have promised to that one person sharing the secret in the first place, not to 'tell anyone'.

'All of them?' Jaaku became increasingly curious. 'Where?'

Sven took a deep breath, before fully breaking this unwritten rule that was almost meant to be broken. 'I believe so. To some small pond near the River Pihtamii, away from Wolferring.' His hand shook when he poured them both more. He had lost control over his sudden openness. He knew that what he'd done was wrong, yet he could not resist the thrill of divulging such classified information.

Jaaku's eyes widened as he stared at the glass being filled. 'The pond must be like a... goldmine!'

'Hush.' Sven glanced around nervously.

'*Hei!*' Jaaku grabbed the bottle from Sven's hand when the glasses began pouring over. 'You're wasting good stuff.'

'Sorry.' Sven wiped the spillage on his sleeve. 'You must not tell anyone.'

'Of course not,' Jaaku whispered. 'That's really amazing. So, he had a plan after all?'

'I think so. And next, we're going to transport the fish back to Lake Pihtamo.'

'That wouldn't necessarily be wise. What if Wolferring gets to them first?'

'That's exactly the idea. We wouldn't bring back all the fish, but only some as a bait to lure Wolferring. The rest we would save for later, when it's time to regenerate the fish population. It would also then give the others, the jobless fishermen, something to do. They wouldn't need to know how the fish got there in the first place. Maybe they'd believe that there were still some fish left in the lake, and that they began to procreate. Or something. There are lots of men out here with absolutely nothing to do. Not everyone wants to hunt or farm animals.'

Jaaku nodded doubtfully. 'You make it sound so easy. This wolf-fish, or whatever it is, has already done so much damage that, I think, we should let it be. If the lake is empty, it will probably just go away and leave us alone. Why can't we just fish straight from the pond where your dad left them? Wouldn't that be much safer?'

'Let it be?' Sven replied loudly. 'Are you serious? Fishing off the pond? This is not catch and release.' However, he soon realised he should keep his voice down. He saw a couple of heads turning. He moved closer to Jaaku. 'The pond is not big enough for the fish to grow properly. They suffer; start growing lice and all sorts. Eventually, they need more space. Besides, if we let Wolferring swim free, then it will go elsewhere and destroy someone else's lives.'

'It's not really our responsibility to get rid of it.'

'I need to fish! And I need to fish right here, in Lake Pihtamo. Do you understand?' Sven slammed his palm on the table, knocking the bottle to the side.

Jaaku quickly picked it up to avoid any further spillage, while Sven struggled to compose himself. He was portraying emotions rarely seen in this stern and stoic culture. He wasn't thinking about the staring eyes any more.

'I'm not going to fish in some pond like a three-year-old in a fish farm,' Sven said. 'This is my home and I'm a fisherman...'

'I know you are,' Jaaku interrupted calmly.

'What is your problem then?'

'Why are you telling me all this?'

'Me and Dad...' Sven lowered his voice again so that Jaaku could barely hear.

Hence, Jaaku had to move so close that they were now defying the unwritten rules of social behaviour set between two straight men in the Arctic. The tips of their noses could've easily touched one another, as if they were performing an Inuit kiss.

'We might need help to transport that fish to the lake,' continued Sven. 'It took years for him to get the fish in the pond in the first place. The job cannot be done by just the two of us, yet we don't want to share the secret with anyone, really. People would go crazy to have such information in their hands. It would be, as you said, another gold rush.'

Jaaku had to restrain himself from rubbing his sweaty palms together. 'Interesting.'

'Isn't it?' Sven pulled back to a more socially acceptable distance again. 'We were thinking about leaving tonight.'

'I can't,' said Jaaku. 'I'm busy. I'm travelling with Marjukka to Kihlava. She wants to visit this one exhibition. We are staying over there at her aunt's place.'

'I see.' Sven rolled his eyes, feeling like he had shared the secret for nothing. 'What is the exhibition about? Fishing?'

'Weddings,' Jaaku admitted, embarrassed.

Sven sneered. 'Well, I hope you find yourself a nice dress.'

Jaaku wanted to fire back, but nothing witty came to his

mind. Instead, he picked up the bottle and poured the last few drops into his empty glass, while doubting his life choices.

'Think about it. We may need to visit that pond more than once.' Sven stood up and walked out.

Chapter 3

IN SEARCH OF HERRINGS

An identical replica of Yolla – a popular plastic dinghy in the 1970s and 80s – replaced Sven's old wooden boat, which had been taken by the tsunami. He kept his new pinkish Yolla discreetly hidden on a marshy shore, sheltered by a batch of silver and curly birch trees, black alders and overgrown reed.

Springtime had arrived, wetting the snow in the ground, giving brighter hope for the future. The rebuilders welcomed warmer weather with higher efficiency, whereas Sven had mixed feelings about the looming summer season, which deprived him of two of his passions: ice fishing and kicksledding.

Impatiently, he took his phone out and checked the time. Roar was already five minutes late for their appointment. Sven peered at the dark forest, but saw no signs of his father. He became growingly agitated. Punctuality was a common behavioural trait of *Pihtamonians*. When the mutual agreement to meet at a set time was being disrespectfully broken without prior notice, all hell could break loose.

The first stage of this painfully unfair waiting process is *worry*. Has something happened to the person I'm expecting to meet? Sometimes, even little selfish thoughts can cross one's mind: *Why haven't I been notified about this unexpected delay?*

Frustration is soon to follow, when there are no signs of the culprit. Who has the right to ignore the fact that other people may have better things to do in their lives than just wait around and stare at their watches? The offender had better have a good explanation. The reasons for being late often varied between bad route planning and not giving oneself enough travel time.

The next step is *disbelief*. How can someone do this to me? I thought we were friends! At this point, the victim would have already made, or tried to make, contact with the tardy, or vice versa. Judging by the authenticity of excuses, the person being let down could determine whether to keep waiting longer or move to the next phase.

In the end, when all hope is gone and no excuse is sufficient enough – apart from serious accident or death – come *renunciation*. Usually, after about fifteen to twenty minutes of agonising waiting for nothing, it becomes time to abandon the scene of rejection. This drastic action should teach the tidsoptimist a lesson not to waste valuable human resources, ever again.

Some learn; the others never.

As the phone signal by the lake was non-existent, Sven couldn't receive any updates from Roar. He was in a complete blind spot. He had to only trust his instinct, while trying to put aside any negative thoughts about something bad having happened. The feeling of concern had been omnipresent in his life from the age of twelve, when Roar disappeared. Every day, for the next sixteen years, Sven had waited for him to return.

But now, he had done his time. No more waiting.

A fifteen-minute mark passed. Sven turned to stare at the calm lake. The idyllic sight didn't bring him the same feeling of serenity like in the past. He struggled to be in the moment. The temptation to take out his phone again kept growing. There was the entire universe waiting inside that tiny little gadget. Even though his Mokia smart phone wasn't the latest technology available, it did have a web browser – which was also fully accessible when nearer to urban areas. He couldn't resist the burning sensation the phone created in his pocket. However, as he pulled it out, the dimly lit screen didn't recognise the tips of his woollen touch-mitts, knitted by his mother, Birgget. She was a skilful artisan, yet clearly struggled to develop functional knitwear for the demands of such an advanced technology.

Thus, Sven was forced to defy the coldness and reveal the hand operating the phone. There was still no signal, but he could browse offline some of the latest news headlines from *Pihtamo Journal*, that positively stated 'Road to Recovery' about the reconstruction, whereas *Fishing Weekly* was not as optimistic with a caption 'Fishy Disappearance'. The latter article dramatically described the decline of the lake's fish population and analysed – without any scientific proof – the different, potential causes, such as thermal pollution and algae blooms, that could be behind this unfortunate phenomenon.

After reading through the latest ice fishing results from the sports section, Sven then opened the Coldfacebook app – a new social media platform that brought together largely isolated communities living above the Arctic and below the Antarctic Circles. When signing up for the app, the user profile only accepted postcodes from those two polar regions.

Sven was never big on social media. He had set a personal profile mainly to communicate with other fishermen in their own, private group. His role was more passive, though. He used the group to read and learn about new events taking place. Unfortunately though, the correspondence had stagnated after the lake got flooded and there was no fish left to talk about. A few remaining active members tried to keep the group alive by posting old photos of the catch they used to reel during the golden era. Some images with captions like 'The Good Old Times' or 'Where Have All The Fishes Gone?' further illustrated the bitterness and disappointment that could easily be read between the lines. Lengthy debates in the comments section from the most sociable participants highlighted the good and bad of the online community. Sometimes, the conversations turned heated and vicious.

Before such an advanced network existed, arguments were more locally concentrated and about simpler things, like the best fishing spots, equipment and techniques. However, after the birth of social media, many fishers developed political opinions and simple solutions to sociological or economic problems, globalisation or other wider issues, and their threshold to share them online was shockingly low. Suddenly, all that Arctic shyness disappeared when facing just a keyboard and a screen.

This new phenomenon of virtual openness also gave room for a few conspiracy theorists, who gained popularity and stirred already confused public opinion about the lake's status. The Arctic Wodka factory was being accused of water pollution, killing all the fish. Another thing they could blame was the recent implementation of a global 6E mobile network, which required thousands of new satellites orbiting the skies while emitting radioactive frequencies to the Earth, giving the population a tenfold stronger exposure than the equipment and infrastructure of earlier solutions.

One of the most controversial theorists, Marku Penttin-Veli, explained: 'As a result of this radioactivity beamed directly from our skies, all the fish had escaped it and hidden to the bottom of the lake, or to other lakes, or even seas, since no dead fish were seen floating on the surface of Lake Pihtamo.'

The situation within these somewhat rogue online groups – although shrinking in terms of participation, but not in feistiness – was becoming so critical that even death threats were being shared, when the virtual consensus between the argumentative parties could not be found.

Sven's introverted nature also reflected his social media behaviour. He tried to stay away from any lengthy, inconclusive conversations. He was more the observer and listener and tried to act based on his own intuition, and what he thought was the right thing to do, rather than following the most opinionated and, so often, the least knowledgeable.

It was a system he had always relied on, as well as in real life, which had somewhat worked for him and brought him relative success. Observing and learning from the two greats – first from Roar when he was a child and, later on, from Viljo – had helped him to become the ice fishing champion.

The controversy around his victory, though, had given him another reason to avoid any online rants. The disputable ending to the championship contest was frequently discussed in various forums. Still today, many disagreed with the results.

Unfortunately, Jaaku had to bear the brunt of most of the accusations as the main perpetrator in the competition. Hence, he had to delete all his social media accounts to avoid any retrospective abuse through the cloud. Accidentally, his breaking of the ice underneath many other competitors – including Viljo, who had been about to win the contest – was still seen as an act of sabotage to help Sven, who gained the victory in front of Viljo's drowning eyes. Jaaku thought it was better for him to keep a low profile from there on. In a way, the lake being empty gave him a perfect excuse to continue living a quiet life with Marjukka and concentrate on doing his own thing.

The preceding conversation at the bar was the first time Sven and Jaaku had met since the tsunami destroyed Pihtamo. Sven hadn't seen or spoken to Viljo at all since they parted after finishing the rescue mission. The three men, who departed on a journey together to find the Lord of Herrings, hadn't fully recovered from the aftermath. The unfolding events were things they'd rather not talk about. Keeping a distance was an easier solution, rather than facing one another and discussing what had really happened.

The rumours indicated that Viljo had to move to a retirement centre. In the floods overnight, he had lost his home of fifty years. For a strong, independent and relatively stubborn man, just the idea of life in the care home felt like the beginning of the end.

The last journey to the lake, where they had faced the storm, had worn him out. Rebuilding the old, or finding a new home, were not on the cards anymore. He was too demotivated to start all over again at eighty-something. Therefore, being looked after by the government became a feasible option – but with a minimal amount of service and care that he had specifically asked for. And he got exactly what he wanted. Due to his explosive and grumpy nature, the nurses only cared for him when absolutely necessary. Even the fellow residents kept a safe distance from him – except when watching television. That seemed to calm his nerves.

Nevertheless, the ones who knew the history of ice fishing well enough were able to understand the bitterness Viljo may have felt, for being overshadowed throughout his whole career by Roar's remarkable records. Viljo was left with one championship less than Roar, when the last chance to reign was stolen from him by Sven.

On the other hand, it wasn't the worst overall result, and a lifetime achievement for Viljo. Yet, seemingly, it was not enough for his ambitious character.

This debatably 'smart' communication device had cleverly distracted Sven from the present reality for quite some time now. Any unpleasant feelings of loneliness and frustration he had momentarily forgotten. As a side effect, though, his bare hand holding the phone began to freeze. Once the coldness prematurely drained the battery, the only remaining source of light was the half-moon in the sky, which made the tampered snow glisten under his feet. He heard a rustling sound in the distance. He looked up. Roar's silhouette came into view, bringing the agonising wait to an end.

'You're late,' Sven snorted.

'Nice to see you, too,' Roar's voice echoed from the darkness.

'What an earth are you wearing?'

'It's comfortable.' Roar described his grey, loose cloak, similar to the one the Lord of Herrings had.

'We were supposed to be discreet,' Sven sighed, and saw a ragged piece of paper in Roar's hand. 'Is that the map? I have it on my phone,' he said bluntly, took a key from his pocket and undid the padlock that had kept his boat chained to a birch tree. Once the boat was freed, he grabbed its edge and started lifting.

Roar dropped his bag to the ground and joined Sven, when the boat was already on its side. He felt Sven's frustration.

'I came as fast as I could. There was an emergency in the restaurant. The opening is in a few days and we are nowhere near ready. The oven broke and I had to find a way to fix it.'

'In the middle of the night?' Grunting, Sven lowered the boat onto its bottom.

'The oven is made in China,' Roar stammered. 'I had to make a phone call to Shanghai.'

'That must have cost you a fortune.'

'Getting involved in this whole restaurant business has. I'm learning the hard way.'

'So, someone from China came to fix it?' Sven smirked.

'Very funny,' replied Roar. 'It was a helpline. I managed to service it myself just by following their instructions.' He dropped his gear into the back of the boat. 'This reminds me of those old Yollas.'

'It is,' said Sven. 'Only a new version. It's even made of the same material: hard plastic. Ida bought it for me. I guess, she wanted to make me feel better after losing my old dinghy. Unfortunately, though, there hasn't been much use for it.'

'Much? It looks completely untouched.' Roar let his hand glide along its smooth edge.

'This is its virgin journey.'

'It'll be nice to row a fresh vessel for a change. That Viljo's motor-boat was one, giant piece of crap,' Roar snorted.

'Miraculously, though, it saved our lives.'

'Santa Claus saved us all.'

'Him, too,' Sven smiled. He picked up the oars and placed them on the loops on either side.

Meanwhile, Roar took another, careful look at the torn and crumpled piece of map he had crafted about fifteen years ago when he begun transporting the fish. 'It's slowly coming back to me...'

'There cannot be that many small ponds around here. Or are there?' Sven suddenly realised that he had never really been fishing outside Lake Pihtamo – apart from his and Ida's tropical honeymoon to Great Britain, where he ended up fishing, with great success, on a fish farm in the most exotic Lake District.

'I recall it wasn't far away from that tribal village,' said Roar, 'where I was being taken care of after Wolferring's attack.'

'And where was this village?'

'Near the banks of the River Pihtamii.'

'It's a long river,' Sven sighed. 'This is exactly why I wanted you to show up on time. You understand that it will take us all night to row there.'

'Twenty minutes won't make a difference.'

Sven glanced at Roar as if he was in the presence of an alien. He couldn't believe how their attitudes towards punctuality were completely opposite. Perhaps the situation would have been different had it been Roar who had to do all the waiting.

Fiercely, Sven pushed the boat to the water, while Roar tried to keep the conversation going. 'Have you told Ida?'

'She was fast asleep when I left...' As Sven replied, his boot slipped on the wet soil. He lost his balance, hitting his forehead on the edge of the bow. Quickly, he bounced back up as if nothing had happened. He shook his head a little.

'Have you been drinking again?' Roar sounded like that annoying inner voice that sometimes sits on one's shoulder.

As much as Sven loved his father and was happy to have him back, at this very moment he wasn't sure whether he was an angel or the devil.

'You sound like her now.'

'What's your excuse then, when she wakes up? She knows the lake is dead. You were... bathing your tackle?'

'I could say that... I was reminiscing about the good old times. Isn't that what everyone is doing here nowadays? Because that's all we have. The past.'

'You can still text or call her, can't you?'

'My phone battery just died.'

'You can use mine.' Roar pulled out his even older, foldable Mokia phone, which had stiff buttons, a tiny screen and a retractable antenna.

Mokia was a mobile phone brand originating from Kihlava – the nearest and the most notable population centre to Pihtamo area. The company was renowned for making moccasins, until they got drawn into the technology race of mobile phone development. They were specialists in the earlier versions – like the one Roar was still using – but later on, their stagnated production sites, poor decision-making and miscalculation of the upcoming market trends made them fall behind the major players in the industry. Even the word '*mokia*' in their native tongue translates as 'mistakes'.

'Sorry. No reception,' Roar grunted.

'Dad, you should really get a new phone.'

'At least I can still switch it on,' Roar smirked, and put the phone back in his pocket. 'The battery has lasted for two months.'

'Not really helping us now.'

'Do you still wanna do this, or not?'

'She is due any day now,' Sven said hesitantly.

'I understand,' said Roar. 'I can go on my own.'

For a moment, Sven thought about his choices. He looked at the vast and dark lake ahead. Only a faint howling from the distance – that could have been a wolf – broke the somewhat eerie silence. Having lost his father twice already, together with the fear that Wolferring may still be out there, made him stay. He simply couldn't let Roar go alone. 'Forget what I said. I will come with you. She won't give birth tonight. Not yet. I can feel it.'

Chapter 4

THE THIRTY-SEVENTH WEEK

Drenched in sweat and struggling to breath, Ida lay alone in the middle of their marital double bed. As an attempt to ease the agony, she pushed the blanket down to her feet and rolled to her side. With a slight delay, the full-grown foetus inside her followed this sudden manoeuvre, until slamming against the wall of her uterus. Ida let out a tired squeal, like an elephant seal that had just beached after a long journey across the Arctic Ocean. Their rougher-than-usual bed sheets – that Sven had recently washed in too high a temperature with too much washing powder – felt like grainy sand against her sensitive skin. Even though Sven's deed to participate in household chores was noble, the execution had poorly failed.

As Ida stretched her arm to the side, there was only emptiness beside her, and no one to complain to about her fraught condition. She lifted her head and saw the bright red numbers of the alarm clock radio displaying the time: 2:26 in the morning.

She reached out for her Andersson phone – a brand that had recently taken over the leading position from Mokia in the competitive market of mobile devices. Andersson's business model was better prepared and geared up towards popularity of touch screens, apps, and rising demands for more complex software.

There were no messages or missed calls from Sven, or anyone

else. She dialled him, but the call went straight to his voicemail.

'Here we go again,' she sighed, and dropped the phone next to her on the bed. She wanted to cry, but was too exhausted. She had nothing left to give. She couldn't fathom anything more difficult than what she had already experienced within the past nine months of pregnancy. And the worst was still ahead: the delivery.

Why is this taking so long? Her feet, ankles, fingers, arms and thighs were all swollen to their limits. She felt as if she could burst any minute. Also, her urge to go again was nearing. In the past weeks, the toilet seat had become her throne. Hence, she took the phone with her, pushed herself up and wobbled out of the bedroom. She plodded along the corridor, feeling like a stranger in their new home. Seeing her two cats and a rabbit, snoozing near the radiator, made her feel slightly more settled.

They could afford to resettle by borrowing cash from her affluent family. The property was situated on top of a hill on a former peninsula which, technically, had become an island. Promptly risen water levels had drowned Sven's previous lakeside cottage – the first place where the couple had actually lived together. This new residence was not necessarily any further from the new coastline, but on a higher altitude. The area had lost its landlinks in the floods. Though, when the surface was low, they could almost take a leap from their front porch to the mainland. To reconnect them permanently to the continent, the building of a pedestrian bridge was under way.

The frame of their two-bedroom house, with a large open-plan living room and kitchen, and a bathroom with a wood-burning sauna, was constructed of laminated round logs of natural pinewood colour. Sven's only wish was to maintain an uninterrupted view of the lake, which he got. Apart from that, he voluntarily left decisions about interior design, furnishing and colour palettes to her.

As Ida neared the bathroom door, she saw a reflection of herself in a full-length mirror. She knew stopping wouldn't be wise; but, out of curiosity, she did anyway. It had been months since the last time she'd checked herself out: a combination of baggy eyes, pale and flaky skin, messy hair and chubby cheeks made it seem like she had aged a generation. *But it's only temporary, right?* Even she wasn't immune to the ever-present glossy magazine gossip about how celebrities get their post-baby bodies back in shape in a matter of weeks after giving birth.

Shaking her head, she entered the bathroom, where the game of human Tetris began. The building seemed to be shrinking around her, when she, with great effort and having avoided obstacles, plonked herself seated on the toilet. Finally, she could rest her elbows on her thighs, bring her mobile up and ring her mother. The dialling tone clearly indicated that the phone was ringing – unlike Sven's earlier.

'Ida?' Sophia answered. She sounded tired. 'Is everything alright?'

Even though their mother-daughter relationship had its issues, Sophia's sleepy voice still soothed Ida. She knew that, when things got this serious, her mother, if anyone, would be there for her – one way or the other.

Chapter 5

A FISH IN THE OINTMENT

The oar handles rubbing against Sven's palms made his skin blister. He panted heavily, his back hurt and his mouth was dry. The past months as a house-husband had seriously thrown his physique to a decline.

'Shouldn't we be there by now?' he moaned in agony.

Roar ignored Sven's struggle, while thoughtfully observing the plain horizon ahead. To get a better overall view, he looked around a full three hundred and sixty degrees. There was only water in sight.

'I remember the estuary being on a low-lying land,' he said. 'The mouth of the river must have shifted dramatically.'

'What if the flooded lake merged with the pond?' asked Sven.

'That would be a disaster,' Roar replied hesitatingly.

Once Sven decided to stop rowing, he sighed deeply. He blew soothingly on his sore fingers. 'We can test it.'

'How?'

'By casting a bait. If we actually catch something, then the worst may have happened.'

Sven's exhaustion had become obvious to Roar, who thought his suggestion was only an excuse to get some rest. 'I guess a little break won't harm anyone.'

'Who said we needed a break?' Sven snorted, while proudly but poorly trying to hide his pain. 'We can troll. If you don't mind taking the oars for a change? I can release the bait.'

'As you prefer.' Roar shrugged his shoulders, and offered the backseat to Sven.

With urgency, Sven prepared his gear. Time was not on his side. Ida's critical condition was at the forefront of his mind. Once again, he was torn between two responsibilities: marriage and fishing. Part of him wished this adventure would be over as soon as possible, yet he was equally thrilled to be out on the lake after such a long break.

He tilted and swung the rod to the side, casting about thirty metres behind them. He then turned sideways, locked the line and waited.

While slowly rowing, Roar simultaneously and discreetly watched Sven. It was as if nothing had changed over the years – except that Sven had almost doubled in size since the last time they'd fished together, and his skill level was supposedly from another dimension. But the same feeling of familiarity and easiness was still there.

'This is like back in the old days.'

Sven nodded subtly, while keeping his eyes on the drawn fishing line. *It is and isn't*, he thought.

Not seeing a close family member at all for over a decade and a half was unavoidably a harsh reminder of the fact that time had passed. Sven couldn't really see or feel himself getting older, until Roar had returned with a grey hair and beard, and wrinkles on his forehead and around his eyes. Suddenly, Sven had looked into the mirror from a different angle, realising how this universal phenomenon of aging seemed to affect them all. He could already see the first dark circles developing under his eyes and his hair thinning – both, most likely, premature side effects of his upcoming fatherhood.

'You remember the time you fell off the boat?' Roar's smirk caught Sven's attention.

'When exactly? It happened so many times.'

'The first time? When you were five or six years old?'

Sven pulled a cheeky smile. 'Who would forget the first time? That's when I learnt to swim. Thanks to you, irresponsible father!'

'That's exactly how my dad taught me to swim.'

'By throwing you in the water, and seeing what happens?' Sven gasped.

'Those were different times,' said Roar. 'My father wasn't necessarily showing that much affection to us kids. But now, I understand he meant well, when he purposely rocked the boat.'

'I hope there was at least a life vest?'

Road nodded unconvincingly.

'There wasn't?'

'Don't be such a snowflake! Who wears a life vest in Pihtamo, anyway? Besides, if you'd struggle, I was there to rescue you. But you didn't need any help. You were like a natural-born swimmer.'

Sven shook his head, appalled by this controversial method of raising a child. 'That is just wrong.'

'Well, think about the time Mooses created the storm and you all ended up in the freezing cold water,' said Roar. 'You were the one keeping Viljo afloat, while Jaaku was barely able to cling onto that capsized boat. How do you think you managed to pull that trick off and not sink to the bottom?'

'Enlighten me.'

'Because of the training I gave you, you became very strong and confident in the water. You just never really explored that avenue, not since you became so focused on fishing.'

In disbelief, Sven stared at Roar. 'I never realised there was a purpose for you throwing me in the water. I thought you were just being mean. I always took it as a punishment of something I'd done wrong.'

'No. It's called "upbringing", my son.'

Sven scoffed and turned his back to Roar. He watched how the line stretched over the draft and wakes behind them. In his mind, the recent conversation caused him to worry about his own, yet unborn, child. *Is that what it takes to raise children? They have to be literally thrown at things for them to learn lessons of life?*

Sven's deep thoughts were cut short when the boat made contact with something underwater. It sounded as if the bottom was being scratched or swept.

Roar felt the oars becoming heavy. As he brought them

above the surface, spruce branches appeared to be wrapped around the blades. Both men peered overboard and saw a group of tree tops lurking right underneath them, submerged in the water. Ahead, in the distance, there were more trees rising from the water. Urgently, Sven began retrieving the line and tackle in an effort to prevent them from getting entangled in the midst of the sunken forest. He had reeled in about half of the line, when the mechanism got stuck and the rod began to bend steeply.

'Can you stop the boat?' he cried out.

Roar slammed the oars back in the water, bringing the boat to a halt.

Since the repetitive yanking motion didn't go away, Sven became most certain there was something alive and active at the other end of the oars.

'Maybe the lake and pond have become one and the same, after all.' He panted while struggling to hold the rod. 'This is a big one!'

'Do you need a hand?' asked Roar.

'I got it.' As Sven grimaced, he felt a mixture of pain and joy. It started coming back to him what he had been missing out on. Too much time had passed since he had caught anything.

Roar observed Sven supposedly doing what he did best. He had taught his son almost everything he knew. And now, the huge amount of work and practice Sven had put himself through became obvious from his confident stance, and smooth and eloquent handling of the rod. There were grips and movement patterns that Roar had never shown him, or didn't even know himself. He began to understand why Sven had become so successful.

His thoughts were interrupted by that one correcting step to the side from Sven that caused the boat to rock dangerously. Roar had to support himself by grabbing the edge of the boat with one hand, leaving the other hand vulnerable on the handle, ready for the catch. As Roar watched Sven's struggle, his strong faith in his son quickly reverted to concern. There was fear in Sven's eyes again. Hence, Roar stood up and tried to grab the rod off him.

'Let me.'

Sven pulled away, and regained his balance. 'I can handle this.'

The rear of the boat dived as they had both vacated the same end. Water poured over the edge, wetting the floor and their boots. Forcefully, Roar slammed his hands on the rod next to Sven's. Sven's hands were now bleeding, the blood running along his wrists.

'Get off! We're going to sink.'

'Yollas don't sink.' Roar tried to appear calmer, but failed.

Being the more sensible one, Sven renounced himself and let go.

'What are you doing?' said Roar. 'I need your help.'

'No, you don't. It's all yours.' Sven moved to the front, balancing the boat.

Meanwhile, the enormous strength pulling the boat from under the water made Roar question any earlier confidence he had in himself, or anyone else. He wished there were four hands holding the rod instead of just his two.

'Yes! Let's go near it!' he yelled in sudden euphoria, when the boat began reversing.

'I'm not doing anything.' Sven held his bleeding hands up in the air, as the boat involuntarily glided over the trees.

Their free ride took another sudden turn, throwing Roar onto Sven's lap. Sven could see how Roar's hands were bleeding, too.

'Dad! Are you okay?'

'Just lost my balance a bit.' Roar tried to shake Sven off, but Sven grabbed his waist and didn't let go. 'What are you doing? It's getting away!'

Never before had Sven witnessed Roar raging in such a manner. Apparently, his bad temper escalated during fishing contests. Gladly, Sven never had to compete against him. That was until now, as he became doubtful if this really was a fight against a common enemy anymore or a long-awaited bout between the father and son.

Without any intention to grab the rod, Sven carefully moved closer to Roar and spoke softly in his ear.

'That is not a fish from the pond, but something else. Let

go, Dad. Please.'

Roar heard the plea, but ignored it. He was not ready to accept defeat, despite having his arms nearly pulled off. He bit his teeth together. He had to press the soles of his boots to the backboard for more support, as the boat reversed even faster towards a solid line of tree tops. He lay almost horizontal on his back, Sven's lap as a pillow.

'Dad! We're gonna get wrecked!'

During all their fishing trips, Roar had never given up in front of Sven. He had created a flawless illusion of himself – apart from that one time as a wizard when he'd got beaten by Mooses on the lake. Admitting his loss again, and in front of his son, was the hardest bit to swallow.

'There's nothing left to prove.' Sven's hand moved to Roar's bag. He opened it and felt an axe – exactly what he wanted to find. He took it out and placed the blade in the middle point where the bend rod met the line. 'May I?'

With hopeless eyes, Roar glanced at Sven, and then nodded.

As Sven cut the line, the rod flew from Roar's hands, flipping over and landing in the water. The catch that got away dragged the remains of the line and tackle underwater. The boat gently thumped against the first, solid pine tree top.

Exhausted, Roar dragged himself onto the rear seat again. As he faced the front, his eyes lit up. He pointed ahead.

Sven looked over his shoulder. The daylight was making its first appearance. There was land ahead and a gap between the tree line. He took the oars and started rowing towards it. The only noise breaking the silence came from those underwater tree tops swiping the bottom of the boat. It was as if the men knew exactly what had been at the other end of the fishing line, but neither of them dared to talk about it.

Chapter 6

LIFE AFTER GUSTAV

The dawning sky painted a pale blue and bright orange canvas over the rich farmlands of Örebröre. Another growing season was near. Only a thin layer of snow covered the fields – barely keeping Ida's snowmobile going.

Elma, her white Dole Trotter, greeted her with a happy neigh. A steamy cloud in her wake, she skidded through the open gates of her family's estate. She passed the dormant water fountain in the front yard and the overgrown cypress trees of the maze garden, eventually stopping in front of the mansion. She rolled herself off the saddle and swayed towards the front door of majestic height, while her thick winter apparel hid any signs of the full-term pregnancy.

The exterior of the building had deteriorated since her last visit a couple of months ago. All the windows were blinded by thick curtains. The curtilage around was unkempt. Litter on the driveway poked randomly from under the snow. Any stranger visiting would've thought the house was either haunted, abandoned or vacated by squatters.

Since there was no reply to her knocking of the door, she decided to push it open herself. After all, it was the home where she had grown up, hence she believed she had every right to enter at any time.

The hinges needed some oiling judging by the way they squeaked. The air inside was nearly as cold as outside. She could see her own breath when she exhaled.

'Mum?'

'Over here,' came Sophia's faint reply from the darkness.

Ida removed her wet boots and followed the direction of the voice. The wooden floor creaked as she, in her woollen socks, walked towards the end of the hallway. She stopped by the arched doorway leading to the living room, where she saw Sophia sitting alone in the middle of a twelve-seater corner sofa. Her mother looked so small and insignificant in this room the size of a church hall. She was sipping red wine, a half-empty bottle left open on the coffee table in front of her. The expression on her face could've been a mixture of serenity and sadness.

'How are you?' Ida asked, while stepping out of the shadow.

'I think the question is, how are you?' Sophia put the glass down and turned to Ida. Her eyes widened. 'You are really big.'

'Thanks for the reminder,' Ida said sarcastically, and removed her overcoat.

'How did you get here? On a kicksled?' Sophia smirked.

'I've still got my snowmobile. I must admit that it makes life so much easier, especially now.' Ida pointed at her tummy, and took a seat at the other end of the sofa.

'It does, whether you're pregnant or not,' said Sophia. 'I just don't understand how you and Sven have the patience to live so... primitively.'

'Don't start now.' Ida shook her head in disappointment. It had to take less than a minute for her mother to start speaking disrespectfully about her son-in-law. As if Sven had a choice to live differently.

'Having said that, you really shouldn't be driving yourself anymore.'

'I just needed some fresh air,' Ida blurted out, while eyeing the wine bottle. She had stayed away from alcohol during the entire pregnancy – until now, as she felt an urgent need to find any cure to ease the awkward friction between mother and daughter. 'Sven didn't come home last night.'

'Wouldn't be the first time, right?' Sophia grinned, showing her wine-stained teeth.

Ida felt shivers, not only from Sophia's scornful attitude,

but also from the exceptionally low temperature in the room. She touched one of the wall radiators behind her.

'The heating's off.'

'I'll be fine without it. It's already April,' Sophia replied casually, and leant over to top up her glass.

'Are you crazy?' said Ida. 'It's still freezing outside, and it's going to be for another couple of months.'

The lump in Sophia's throat felt like it was about to burst at any moment. She needed to confess.

'The truth is... I have to save money. Maintaining this big property is neither easy nor cheap, since... well, you know...'

A moment of silence gave Sophia just enough time to swallow her tears. Losing Gustav had taken its toll on her, not only emotionally but also financially. She had to close down their small animal farm and the accommodation service that came with it.

'I can give you some money,' Ida carefully suggested.

'Don't be silly. I don't need any charity. Even though I've put everything else, all other activities on hold, I still have my Tuppervaara business.' Sophia swirled the wine in the glass, but she didn't feel like drinking anymore. She placed it down on the table. 'Would you like some coffee?'

Ida nodded in relief after hearing a more shallow question that was more in keeping with their somewhat formal relationship. Light-hearted chit-chat was usually much easier between the two, rather than any deeper or meaningful discussion about feelings or dramatic events that touched them personally, such as Gustav's disappearance – a topic that they had avoided until this day.

'Good. I can make you some.' Sophia stood up.

'You?' Ida looked confused. 'What about the housemaid? What was her name again...?'

'Cannot really afford her either. She's only doing part-time now,' Sophia said melancholically, and left the room.

That news made Ida worry over her mother even more. How was she going to cope with this reality check, if there was no one in the house to talk to? Sophia wasn't even that invested in the internet and social media, whereas Ida could always find ways to suppress negative emotions to oblivion by taking her phone out and escaping in the virtual world.

This time, though, Ida's trick to distract herself from reality didn't seem to work. While browsing photos of her Instakilo followers' salmon portions, her eyes kept wandering around the living room. Even though it was her childhood home and where she had lived most of her life, the usual familiarity of the place was suddenly gone. As if all the love, that had been the driving force decades ago, had evaporated. The kids had moved out and the father was recently deceased. The once vibrant and elegant colours of the interior seemed dull and dusty, not to mention the stuffy and damp air.

As distraught as she was about the loss, Ida similarly felt frustration and anger. She had witnessed first-hand Sven's suffering of growing up without a father. Yet, she found it harder to deal with her own situation and emotions. The distance between her and Gustav had always been more obvious. There were so many unspoken words she never got to say to him that could have potentially rebuilt and strengthened their relationship. Or completely derailed it. Who knows? Unfortunately, the realisation to open up came too late. She just wasn't prepared for a tragedy of this scale – no one was.

She didn't perhaps get the best father experience, but at least she was trying to forgive and understand that Gustav had tried to do his best with the tools and understanding given to him. He had grown up amongst the elite and it was not entirely his fault that he saw life through the pink lenses of wealth, prosperity and privilege.

Rather than spending quality time with his daughters, he had always instead opted to purchase and bribe his way to their hearts. Family meant business to him. In the beginning, his calculating method of parenting may have worked; but, eventually, a developing mind of a child was able to see through its weaknesses. Sometimes, Ida only needed an embrace from her father, or to have a genuine discussion with him, or for him to ask a simple question, like how was she really doing? But these warm gestures were not part of his repertoire, and now she was left thinking that they never would be, even if he was still amongst them.

On the flip side, experiencing a loss of this magnitude must have matured her – even though her choice to play Cod Crush, to suffocate any negative thoughts, wasn't the best example of personal growth.

'Where is he then?' Even Sophia's snorting didn't make Ida take her eyes off the flashing screen of her mobile. Until she heard the rattling of a silver tray with a white porcelain pot, two coffee cups, small jugs for milk and cream, and a bowl of sugar.

She finally put the phone away when she saw her mother carrying out work usually done by the housemaid. Sophia placed the tray on the coffee table and sat on a leather armchair next to her daughter.

'I thought there's nothing left to fish.'

Ida leant over to put four sugar cubes in her cup. 'What?' She felt Sophia's stare.

'Four cubes?' Sophia said condemningly. 'You should pay tax on those.'

'I'm pregnant!' Ida snorted. She added two more cubes, leant back and folded her arms over her belly.

Sophia sighed, then poured filtered coffee over Ida's dangerously high stack of sugar. She tried to reminisce what it had been like to be pregnant, three times - though her memories may have changed over time, as she couldn't remember being such a drama queen.

Meanwhile, Ida sipped her coffee, while staring absently in the distance.

'How's the coffee? Too sweet?' Sophia smirked.

But Ida was not paying attention. She bluntly ignored Sophia's wittiness. 'I even bought Sven a new boat right after the disaster. He had lost everything. I was hoping it would calm him down. A fisherman without any fishing gear and his boat is like...'

'A half a man?' Sophia suggested.

'Something like that. It's hard to tell from men here what they are thinking and feeling. No matter what happens around them, even if the world falls apart, they always have that same grave expression on their faces.'

'Tell me about it.'

'Was Dad like that, as well?'

'What do you mean? You can't remember? It's not that long ago.'

'I mean, what was he really like? I only knew him as his child; as his daughter.'

'You're not a child anymore.'

Ida gave her a subtle smile. 'I am. That's the way every parent treats their children, until the end.'

Sophia became more serene, as she tried to think. 'Gustav was different to many other men. He was sociable. The good upbringing and education gave him decent manners and etiquette. He was sophisticated.'

Ida rolled her eyes. *I wish he would have shown those sophisticated manners to his children as well.*

'Are you sure you like my coffee?' Sophia gathered strength, wiped the corner of her eye and changed the subject again to something more facile.

'It's fine,' Ida said bluntly, and took the conversation to another direction. 'I'm not sure if Sven's telling me everything.'

'Does that really matter anymore?' replied Sophia. 'I thought his fishing days were over, anyway, and that he was supposed to get a proper job, right?'

'I doubt that's ever going to happen,' Ida sighed. 'He tried that already before the lake flooded, but he just doesn't have any recognised skills or qualifications – apart from fishing. And now, after the disaster, the chances of getting hired are non-existent.'

'Finding a job right now shouldn't be as hard as catching fish, though.' Sophia leant over to Ida and gently took her wrist. 'Darling. Father and I warned you about this.'

'Please, don't call me that.' As Ida ripped herself away from her mother's patronising hold, some coffee spilled on the carpet. 'You tried to push me into the arms of Christian – who is, by the way, also a fisherman.'

'Yes, but he is...'

'...from a wealthy family.' Ida finished Sophia's sentence. 'I get it. I got it a long time ago. No need to explain.'

'Fine,' said Sophia. 'Let's assume Sven went to the lake, then. Why? To get some "me time"?'

'Enough about him, okay?' Ida took a couple of deep breaths, while holding her stomach. 'He will come back. He always does.'

'Are you alright?'

'Never better,' Ida snorted, and stood up slowly.

'I wasn't thinking that he wouldn't come back,' Sophia said apologetically. 'But I understand how you must feel. You must be worried to death because of what happened to his father.'

'Let's not even go there.' Ida shook her head, while trying to find the most comfortable way to stay on her feet – there wasn't any. Even the simplest things in life had become a struggle, like standing straight. All that extra weight of her belly strained her arched lower back. Like so many women, though, she was a master at dealing with pain and discomfort. Her eyes were fixed on the end of the room, onto the doorway leading to Gustav's office. 'Shall we begin then? That's what I came here for, right?'

Sophia took a deep breath, left her coffee cup on the table, and lead Ida through the open doorway, to another dark brown wooden door at the end of corridor. She pulled out a set of antique keys. The biggest and sturdiest of keys slid into the lock. She twisted and the door opened.

'Voila!'

Anxiously, the women stepped into Gustav's highly secluded office. In awe, Ida looked at the low ceiling and the dark furniture – as if they had stepped back in time a century or more.

'Have I ever been to this room?' she asked.

'Perhaps, when you were a little girl,' replied Sophia. 'Gustav rarely let anyone in here. He demanded to work in complete privacy. I didn't always understand why, but I didn't want to argue, either. Let him have his peace, I thought.'

Ida walked behind a large mahogany desk and, with her forefinger, wiped some dust off the top.

'I remember now. I was playing under this desk; in the gap where the feet go.' Her eyes lightened as warmer memories of her father resurfaced. Smiling, she leant over to examine the square space behind it. 'That's it. I used to tickle his feet when he tried to do some work. Sometimes, he even left me in this room by myself. When he went away, I used the opportunity to climb on the furniture. When he came back, I thought he'd shout at me.

But instead, he took me in his arms and told me off firmly, but politely.'

'His feedback was often constructive.'

'He was so tall and strong. I felt safe. I must have been six or seven years old then.' Suddenly, Ida's upbeat tone became more serious. 'It must have been around my teenage years, when he didn't quite understand me anymore.'

Sophia turned to Ida. 'Or, you both stopped understanding each other?'

'Why do you keep defending him?'

'Ida, you must understand that he was the man I married, loved and shared my life with. He wasn't as bad as you make him out to be. Really.'

Ida shrugged her shoulders. 'Well, that part will always remain a mystery to me.'

To change the subject, Sophia pointed at a stack of cardboard boxes in the corner of the room. 'I've already started going through his stuff. There's so much of it. He wasn't the most organised person.'

'Must bring back lot of memories.'

'It does.'

'I'm sorry, Mum.' Ida patted her mother's shoulder. The tragedy had at least brought them closer to each other – though, not quite as near as family members could be. How well Birgget and Sven got along, for example, was something Ida had always wanted to witness in his own family. A direct comparison to a mother-son relationship, however, may have been unfair, as they often tend to be less tense. Nevertheless, she remained hopeful that she could at least build a special relationship in the future with her own child.

'Don't worry,' said Sophia. 'I am sorry that he wasn't a better father to you. I always thought he was.'

'I think he meant well. I can see that now. But his way of showing it was... fairly unusual. Distant. And he always struggled to accept my lifestyle and choices; disappointed that I didn't want to live my life the way he had. He detested my marriage to Sven.'

Sophia looked away, trying to hide her guilt for sharing Gustav's opinion about the marriage. 'There's nothing wrong with how we have lived our lives, is there?' she said defensively, oozing insecurity.

'I am not saying what is right or wrong.'

'It kind of feels like you are.'

'I mean, for me, personally, the material things, wealth and glory, didn't mean a thing. I thought they did, but once I grew up and became more myself, I understood what was really important. Dad always tried to buy his way into our hearts. But all we wanted was for him to be there, share those moments with us, like a normal family.'

'That's the only life and reality he knew.'

'Privilege,' Ida snorted.

'It's not that simple,' said Sophia. 'No matter how much someone who is poor tries to...'

'Please could you not use that word,' Ida interrupted.

'Ah. Okay. I mean, when someone from a completely different background tries to explain to us about their values, it can be difficult to relate.'

'A clash of social classes,' Ida added.

'It's hard to let go of something you get used to. The same applies to material and wealth. It can be like a drug. Addictive.'

'It was never for me, even though it was all around us.'

'How can you be so sure?' said Sophia. 'It may have given you underlying stability and confidence, even if you don't really think about it. You know very well, whatever you do or try in life, you can always fall back on us. There has always been a safety net for you, whether you need it or not. Even the subconscious awareness of that, my love, can shape people in very different ways. And I'm only saying this on a positive note. Somewhere, deep down inside, you've always known that you have us, and your father's support, no matter what. He even came to your wedding.'

'Financial support, perhaps,' Ida sighed. 'Besides, he hated being at our wedding.'

'Well, to be honest, it was a very unusual ceremony...'

'I knew you would bring that up!' Ida grunted.

'Sorry.' Sophia took a step back. She then tried to make up for her previous comment by asking a proper question. 'How is the... marriage, then? Is everything okay?'

Ida questioned the genuineness of this sudden interest in her relationship, which she knew her mother didn't approve.

'Everything is great,' she hesitated, 'if only he wouldn't keep disappearing like he did last night.'

'I always thought that, if men are not really around anyway, then at least they should be...' Sophia stopped in the middle of the sentence.

'Rich?' Ida guessed the end of it. 'Is that really how you think?'

'Forget about it.' Sophia turned her back to Ida and started going through the items and books on the shelves. 'Let's just get this cleaning over with.'

Ida didn't want to let her mother off the hook, while simultaneously knowing that it was probably too late to try and change her opinions and views. Besides, they had just, in the last few minutes, conversed more than in the last year or so. They were both on the verge of an information overload.

In silence, Ida moved to the other end of the room to examine the overwhelming number of framed photos and certificates on the wall. There was also a vitrine bursting with medals and trophies. Even though Gustav had been taken prematurely, it seemed like a life fully lived – at least, in terms of business and social activities. Ida rolled up her sleeves and sunk herself into the past, a past that no one had ever told her about.

'He achieved so much,' she said in wonder, as her eyes scanning the wall that was covered in images summarising her father's most glorious moments. 'But, what about pictures of his family? Where are they?'

'Elsewhere,' said Sophia. 'The ones you've seen in the living room and our bedroom.'

'Framed by you?'

Sophia nodded.

Ida rolled her eyes, and took a step closer to the bookcase. The top shelf was filled with old photo albums. She pulled one out, and opened it. Inside, there were old newspaper articles of Gustav in various occasions, such as him opening the new ski slope, presenting the yearly agriculture conference in Kihlava, running a local charity event and so on.

'He did a lot of good,' Sophia said longingly.

'I never realised. I wish he'd told me.'

'Perhaps, he would have. He just wasn't sure you were interested. Or wanted to hear. Especially in recent years, he suffered from being estranged from you and your sisters.'

Ida slammed the album shut. 'I doubt it.'

'Trust me,' replied Sophia. 'He just didn't know how to close the gap. He was a man of his generation. But he was a human, after all.'

'All we wanted was for him to be there.'

'I guess, but that's the part he didn't do so well.'

'So well? He failed.' As Ida vigorously pushed the album back to where it belonged between two thick encyclopedias, the entire bookshelf shook. A couple of random editions from the top shelf fell on the floor.

'Carefully!' Sophia pressed her hands against the bookshelf frame to keep it steady.

Once the shaking had stopped, a section of the bookcase began rotating like a revolving door. A metre-wide doorway opened in front of them. Ida gave Sophia an enquiring stare.

'I have no idea,' Sophia said, astounded.

Chapter 7

THE RIVER PIHTAMII

The first rills and gullies of the Pihtamii River originated from the snowmelts of Äkän-Lierimo fells. Approximately halfway down the slopes the runoffs merged together forming the official starting point. From there onwards, the river wound its way in the midst of a dense Arctic forest, until the flooding lake stole a part of its total length of a hundred and fifty kilometres. How much exactly the estuary had shifted inland, was still unknown.

Roar couldn't recognise the river mouth anymore, whereas Sven had never been this far, so he couldn't tell the difference. The banks on either side, and the wet ground extending behind them, looked more like mangroves. Only alligators were missing, yet something equally dangerous may still be hiding below these dramatically changed tides.

The rising sun gave Roar just enough light to be able to read his crumpled map. 'First, the river should bend twice to the right, then one steep left, and then it's supposed to be fairly straight for another...'

'We've already been swiping tree tops for the last half an hour.' Sven rolled his eyes to the beat of the oars.

'Ah. Maybe we're near, then.' Roar took his focus off the map to look for any familiar landmarks.

That's what I've wanted to hear all night, Sven thought, and picked up the pace. His motivation suddenly spiked, despite his pain from rowing. He had squeezed the handles so hard that the blood had stopped dripping. The journey had already taken much longer than expected, but they'd gone too far to turn back.

Chapter 8

THE SECRET BUNKER

The torch on Ida's mobile phone dimly lit the secret doorway the women had inadvertently discovered. Thick cobwebs decorated the low ceiling inside the stony tunnel, leading to the spiralling stairwell that descended into darkness. A cold breeze and musty smell rose from the bottom, making the women even more hesitant to enter.

'What is this?' Ida carefully peeked in. 'A hidden wine cellar?'

'I guess there is only one way to find out.' Sophia gave Ida a gentle nudge in the back.

'No!' Ida resisted. 'You go first. I'm pregnant.'

'Again,' Sophia sighed, and grabbed the phone off Ida. 'You cannot use that excuse forever.'

'Only nine months at a time,' Ida smirked, and tucked her tummy away as Sophia tried to squeeze past.

At every step going down, the temperature dropped at the same rate as the humidity intensified. It was as if they were being transported back to the Middle Ages, as the rugged walls on either side kept narrowing. Sophia couldn't help but feel disappointed that, after so many decades, her home was still holding secrets like this. In frustration, she picked up speed, fearlessly racing ahead and out of Ida's sight, only the dim light in the distance giving Ida some sense of direction.

Fairly soon, though, their winding descent came to an end. As Sophia stepped on a flat concrete floor, she felt something soft underneath her shoe, followed by a high-pitched, echoing squeal. She quickly pulled her foot away and retreated to the stairs. The torch from the mobile, beaming downward on the slabs, revealed the long, thick tail of a giant rat that she had just stamped on. The poor rat, looking as frightened as the women, scurried into the darkness ahead.

'What was that?' said Ida, arriving behind Sophia.

'You don't wanna know,' Sophia panted heavily.

'You look like you've seen a ghost.'

Ida took her phone from Sophia's shaking hand. Then she pointed the light straight ahead and moved it from one side to the other, and up and down, revealing a dark, wooden desk in the corner; a couple of arm-chairs on the other side; a glass vitrine against the opposite wall; and a large, stuffed moose head erected over it.

The rats from the floor had gone into hiding, so Ida stepped cautiously towards the centre of the room. As she was doing so, she felt her face being caressed by cobwebs again. She erratically swung her arms around, accidentally catching a narrow string hanging off the ceiling. She closed her eyes and gently pulled it. The underground office became lit by one single light bulb, swinging above them from side to side. Now they could see everything. There were two stuffed moose or deer heads on the side walls and two rifles leaning against the wall in the corner, at the back of the room. The interior didn't seem that medieval anymore, but modern.

With careful steps, the women took their own sides of the room. Ida examined the used ashtray on the desk, with cigarette stumps and a used pipe on top.

'I didn't know Dad smoked.'

'Neither did I,' Sophia said, while staring at the large stuffed moose head right above her. 'Are we sure it's him, though?'

'Who else?'

Sophia shrugged her shoulders, and read the plaque underneath the wall mount. 'Fair enough. This one has his name on it. He caught it... eight years ago!'

'Well done, Dad,' Ida said sarcastically, and looked at the scattered photos around the ashtray. One of them was of Gustav proudly posing in front of a pile of half a dozen of moose carcasses. She couldn't hide her feeling of disgust.

'He had his silly hobbies,' Sophia said defensively.

'A hobby?' Ida snorted. 'He was a savage.'

'Well, he was hunting some moose. How does that differ from...'

'The men already argue enough about what is right and wrong: fishing or hunting,' Ida interrupted. 'We don't need to be like them.' She was determined not to engage in a debate that may never end. The ongoing battle between fishing versus hunting divided opinions of entire communities and no one seemed to find a common ground.

'Gustav hunted for many reasons, not only for our needs,' Sophia said, but felt like she needed to explain more. 'Because we already had everything, he did it for the community. He always thought about the greater good. You see, the moose are also a pest.'

'Now I understand why we always had elk and moose on the table.' Ida realised how the excessive consumption had put her off eating red meats. Later on, the lack of fish in the region and, most recently, having met intelligible fauna, were the other factors making her lean towards vegetarianism, or even veganism – two lifestyle choices that were still difficult to follow through in Pihtamo, where plant-based products were scarcely available.

Nevertheless, tonight wasn't about delving into her dietary choices, but about sorting her late father's belongings. She continued the detective work by pulling open a drawer underneath, which revealed a hand-gun together with some ammo, rolling around it. She grimaced and quickly shut the drawer. The next drawer was filled with random papers and documents. The Moose Hunting Association certificate, with Gustav's name printed on it as the honorary member, was on top of the pile, and underneath was a stack of completed hunting permits, all signed and approved by Gustav. She raised her gaze to her left, where the rules of moose hunting were framed on the wall. The document was also signed by Gustav. In disbelief, she turned to Sophia.

'What is all this?'

Sophia shook her head. 'What scares me the most is that I don't know about any of this, and haven't known for over thirty decades while living under the same roof with him. I thought he just liked to hunt every once in a while.'

'Everyone has secrets.'

'But to this extent?'

Ida noticed a common feature in all the photos of Gustav. She picked one of them up and showed it to Sophia. 'Why does Dad wear a massive set of antlers on his head?'

Sophia leant over to get a better look. 'Indeed, he does. Antlers growing out of a helmet?'

'And a long cape?' Ida said, dumbfounded. 'He's like some religious figure from a fancy costume party.'

'He looks like an old fool,' Sophia snorted, and cleared all the items on the desk to the side, revealing a large sheet of paper spread out underneath. 'A floor plan?'

Ida brought the torch closer, trying to make sense of the scribble and drawings. 'It says... titanium and tungsten on the walls and roof; own air supply...'

'It cannot be.' Sophia scratched her chin in awe. 'The renovation of this house about twenty years ago.'

'I used to play on the scaffoldings. They covered the house like... forever.'

'The builders were here for almost five years,' said Sophia. 'It seemed a very long time for just a basic renovation. It was supposed to cover only some painting work, new drains and floors.' She looked above at the pitch-black ceiling. 'Of course. Floors! He was building this bloody dungeon. Or whatever this place is.'

'But, why all these elaborate, expensive materials?' Ida pondered.

'Gustav always wanted everything to be top notch, the best in the market and the latest technology available.'

'A titanium roof sounds a bit much, though.'

'But it would explain why the work cost a fortune,' Sophia sighed.

'Like he was getting ready for a nuclear war,' Ida smirked, until her eyes lit up. 'What if he somehow predicted the tsunami, and knew that we'd be safe here?'

'If that was the case, then the least he could have done was to tell us about this place. Finding it like this doesn't really help anymore.'

'Maybe it will help us to get to know him better,' Ida said with a positive tone.

'Not sure if I want to,' Sophia hesitated.

'Well, if you do want to, have you noticed there's another door right behind you?' Ida pointed at the pair of camouflaged hinges painted to blend with the back wall.

Sophia turned around to face a metallic vault, taller than her.

Ida stood beside her and grabbed the handle. 'Shall we?'

The door didn't move, though, until Sophia came to push with her. They managed to open it just enough to have a peek inside. It became clear that they hadn't seen the entire space. Only Sophia was slim enough to sneak through the gap they'd created, while Ida couldn't, no matter which angle she tried.

'Do you need light?' Ida passed her phone to the other side.

'Ah, thanks.' Sophia grabbed it and pointed the beam to one element at a time, first capturing a long meeting table made of hard-wood, set in the middle of the room. Three wooden chairs were on each side of the table and one throne-like seat at the end, with a cushion that had a small dent pushed down, as if the chair had been recently used. The walls around were decorated with more framed photos of strangers meeting in peculiar gatherings and ceremonies.

'What can you see?' Ida queried through the gap.

Sophia thoughtfully examined the findings. 'This room is very much about moose hunting again.'

'Dad must've been quite devoted to his passion.'

'That's a mild way to put it. Obsessed, I would say.'

Sophia leant against the backrest of the throne. She stared down at the cushion and tried to imagine whether the dent could have come from the shape of Gustav's bottom. But she could only think of a behind belonging to an aging man, all wrinkled, hairy and flat, which in no circumstances could have filled the entire area. It must have been there for much longer, perhaps from the time when Gustav's bottom had more meat around. Or, perhaps it had been created by someone else; a guest to their house, who knew about the secret meeting place long before her, his wife of thirty years.

As Sophia moved to the other end of the room, she accidentally kicked her foot onto a tin of paint. A used brush resting on top fell to the floor. Some loose cables, hanging from the ceiling, brushed her ear.

'Is everything alright?' Ida called worriedly.

'This place isn't quite finished yet. You can still smell fresh paint.'

Next, Sophia spotted a kitchen corner with cupboards and two big fridges. 'Not sure if I want to know what's inside those.'

'What?'

'Nothing. Just speaking to myself. There's a small kitchen here, and another door beside it. This place is never-ending.'

Sophia's pulse accelerated when she grabbed the fridge handle. Fortunately, there were no moose heads, only water bottles. Then she went through the cupboards, which were filled with about a dozen cans of tuna, six jars of peanut butter and about twenty packets of crackers. *Quite unusual catering for business meetings.*

Disturbed by the size of the basement, Sophia then walked up to the next door. Her frustration and disappointment were peaking. She held her breath and ripped the door open, with reservations.

The beam of her torch revealed another room, with a king-size bed covered in red fabric. There were candles on the wall racks, and dark brown antique bedside tables upon which sat old lamps, with baroque-style shades. The backboard and the bed frame were made of cast iron. The cover seemed untouched. Yet, she couldn't stop grinding her teeth together, as the first thought that came to her mind was Gustav enjoying this secret love nest with someone else.

'What is it?' Ida's question echoed faintly from the distance.

'Looks like... Dracula's bed and breakfast,' Sophia grunted, while holding back her tears and anger. Strangely, the bedroom had more character and romantic features than their own marital equivalent upstairs.

Feeling overwhelmingly defeated, she turned around and trudged back towards the front room. 'Some husbands have their little sheds in the garden where they can hide from the family, whereas Gustav had his titanium bunker,' she murmured ironically. She swung past Ida and went up the stairs. 'This was just too much. Too much.'

Without having seen the pinnacle that was the bedroom, Ida could share her mother's feeling of disappointment. She took one last look at the photos of his father wearing the helmet with moose antlers, and randomly decided to take one of them with her.

Chapter 9

A TREASURE POND

Roar could hear rumbling sounds coming from up ahead. It all came back to him, when he began to recognise most insignificant of the trees, plants and rocks around them. Years of having regularly visited the area had ingrained the final stretch of the route deep within the corners of his memory.

'We are near.'

They came to a crossing, where the river branched out to a narrow creek. Roar turned the boat towards it, picked up speed and allowed the boat glide underneath the tangling canopy of branches. As they ducked down and pushed through, a heavy fall of pine needles rained on their necks and backs.

'You really hid the fish well,' Sven muttered, while whacking the most intrusive wilderness off his face.

'I can't remember it being this difficult.' Roar had to bring the oars near as the channel constantly narrowed. The blades dragged reed in their wake. The vegetation above retrieved upwards and they could sit tall again.

The creek eventually led to steep white-water rapids. Roar glanced over his shoulder.

'This is it! The pond is at the bottom of that slide.'

'Slide?' Sven gasped in terror. 'This is not an amusement park!'

'You're gonna love it,' Roar replied enthusiastically.

'But, we cannot fit through. The boat is too wide.'

'Don't worry. I've done this many times!' The oars kept knocking against the banks as Roar tried to speed up.

'Why go faster?' said Sven anxiously. 'Aren't the rapids enough?'

'I know what I'm doing.'

'Are you sure? Maybe your Viking boat was narrower, and you had no oars.'

'Let's put them away, then, and let the rapids do the job.' As Roar raised the oars up in the air, one of them accidentally hit a spruce tree and flew out of his hand, disappearing in the thick bush.

'Well done, Dad,' Sven replied sarcastically.

Embarrassed, Roar lay the remaining oar carefully back on the benches beside them. 'Everything's under control. I've been here hundreds of times.'

'Under some bloody magic spell,' Sven muttered under his breath.

'What was that?'

'Nothing.' Sven grabbed the oar and, from the rear of the boat, smacked it in the water. 'At least, now we have a rudder.'

'Not sure if that makes any difference.'

'What have we got to loooooose...' Sven was unable to finish the sentence as the rapids grabbed them.

The ride started steep, like in the most extreme funfairs. In this particular carriage, though, any health and safety measures were non-existent, as the boat twisted between rocks and floating logs. There were neither seatbelts nor safety bars, but only the men's solid grips and individual stamina holding them down. Their knuckles turned white from squeezing the sides, while butterflies filled their stomachs. For a brief moment, their journey slowed down when they reached a flatter surface, until another, even steeper downhill began.

'You did this every time?' Sven shouted, before gulping a mouthful of foamy water.

'This was the best part of it,' Roar replied excitedly. He could see the bottom of the ride. 'And, that's the pond.'

'We're gonna sink!' Sven adopted the brace position; it was something he had learnt from watching closely the Rye'n'Air flight attendants' safety demonstration on his only ever flight to London, or anywhere in the world, while on his honeymoon with Ida. Even in his wildest nightmares he couldn't have predicted that, one day, he would have to use these extreme precautionary measures in the most bizarre situation: while crash-landing to a pond on a small dinghy in the middle of a forest.

One can never tell when, where and which of our skills will be put to the test. This was a valuable lesson he would take home with him – *if* they were to survive. He looked like a foetus sitting so comfortably that Roar, noticing him, decided to follow suit and roll himself into a ball as well.

As they reached the end of the slide, first the dinghy nose-dived and then glided underwater like a fast-moving torpedo, until shooting back up again. During that short stint under the surface, the boat had scooped itself full of fishes of all sorts and sizes. The men had just unintentionally conducted the easiest form of fishing imaginable.

Gradually, the fishy ride slowed down and came to a halt in the middle of the pond. An overwhelmingly miraculous sight was all around them. This Arctic haven, hidden by lush and dense vegetation, held thousands, if not tens of thousands, of fish, protected from the dangers of the outer world. It was a wet dream for those lazy fishermen who were after an easy catch rather than a challenge.

As much as the fish must have appreciated having been rescued by the Lord of Herrings, they also must have wished to be freed and settled in their usual habitat, away from these crammed and temporary conditions. They were like those many immigrants, who had to compromise on their living standards and quality of life, to gain change or peace in return. Or like goldfish, who were kept in captivity for the entertainment of the people.

Yet, would migrants or goldfish live their lives differently if they had a choice? Abandoning the safety of the 'fish bowl' can lead to other problems. For the fish, in this particular pond, so-called freedom would mean being faced by Wolferring, as well as the baits of hungry fishers.

'I have never seen anything like this,' Sven said in awe.

The memory of the adrenaline-filled slide was already in the distant past. The constant sound of splashing fins and tails was like music to his ears.

'The rich bounties of Lake Pihtamo, all in one tight space,' Roar said proudly, and looked down at their feet. The boat was filled, knee-high, with fishes. 'I guess our job here today is done. All this can be our first load to be reintroduced to the lake.'

Sven hesitated, as he observed the fishes tangled and rolling on top of one another. 'They look like they are suffering, though.'

'Look at you. Our champion, caring about the well-being of the fish!' Roar smirked.

'You still think we couldn't catch Wolferring without using fish as bait? Wolferring wouldn't come only after us?'

Roar let out a long sigh. 'I believe, ultimately, that Wolferring's after the fish, not us. We may simply be standing in its way, like Carl did, and that cost him his life.'

Sven took a careful look at the busy pond around them. 'I just don't think it's a wise thing to sacrifice all this fish. Instead, we should keep protecting and saving them for the fishers who need them the most.'

'It's gonna take us a lot of time and many trips to transport all this fish, anyway,' Roar pondered.

'But you understand the risks?' said Sven. 'We might end up losing all of them, which would be a disaster. You spent years saving them.'

'We'd just have to be really fast. The problem is that no one has ever really stood up and fought against Wolferring. Maybe it was a mistake to take the fish away in the first place.'

'No, Dad. You did the right thing. Wolferring would have eventually eaten them all, otherwise. In hindsight, you saved our fishing industry – even though we first feared the opposite.'

Roar gave a modest nod. 'I appreciate what you just said. But how should we solve the problem? I cannot sleep at night knowing that Wolferring is around, possibly already causing havoc and destruction elsewhere.'

'What if we only use some of this fish as a lure? We can leave most of them here in the pond, and then reintroduce them to Lake Pihtamo once we've gotten rid of Wolferring. We don't have to sacrifice them all in one go.'

Roar contemplated in silence for a moment. 'That's not a bad idea. We could call them our "little assistants".'

'I guess so,' Sven replied hesitantly.

'What's wrong? You are still the top fisherman in the region. Since when were you so protective over fish?'

'You know the time we met Psalmon?'

Roar's face turned grave. 'Psalmon tried to kill me.'

'Yes, but only because it thought that you were evil. We all thought you were.'

'Fine. Go on.'

'Encountering Psalmon changed my thinking a lot. Before, I only saw fish as soulless objects fulfilling our egoistic needs.'

'And filling our stomachs, and our need to survive,' Roar added.

'But does it have to be that way?' replied Sven. 'What if they are all "special" like all those animals we discovered from the forest: Links, Yetilag, Erm...ine...'

'What are you saying? That we should all become vegans now?' Roar chuckled.

'No. I'm saying that we have to start protecting our nature and its animals. We must promise to ourselves that, if we were to use these fishes as baits, we must be ready and alert before Wolferring gets them. We must anticipate its attack to minimise the number of casualties and the loss of innocent fish.'

'Now you sound like some crazy politician; a world leader.' Roar smiled subtly, but soon became serious again. 'But, the fishing won't stop.'

'Of course not. I didn't say that we wouldn't still fish for ourselves and our needs. Sure we will, until our last breath. But Wolferring is wasting our time, our fish, and that is something we must prevent. It's a pest that we must eliminate.'

That's my boy talking, Roar thought.

'But we cannot do this on our own,' Sven added. 'There are just too many fish in here. We need help.'

'We cannot tell anyone about this pond. Who else would you trust?'

'Well... I sort of told... Jaaku,' Sven said sheepishly.

'Sort of?!' Roar gasped. 'Of all the people?'

'Who else?' Sven spread his arms. 'Viljo is too old. You wouldn't wanna work with him, anyway. And I wouldn't ask Christian in a million years.'

'There must be other decent fishermen in Pihtamo willing to help.'

'But I don't know them, or trust them.'

'But you trust Jaaku, the moose hunter, who almost got me killed, too?' Roar grunted.

'Please. He was after Mooses. Besides, there were quite a few angry people in Pihtamo at the time who wanted to get rid of the Lord of Herrings.'

Roar gave Sven a suspicious look. 'Even yourself?'

'Let's not talk about this again,' Sven snorted, and grabbed the one remaining oar. He started paddling, switching sides like on a canoe. 'We must find the other oar. We have to get out of here. We have been away for who knows how long and Ida is... you know... And I'm soaking wet and cold.'

Roar pointed at a sturdy pine tree by the shore. 'I can use my axe to carve us an oar out of one of those thick branches.'

Sven nodded, and paddled them by the lonely pine. Roar hopped off and let the axe swing. The old method of taking such a heavy-duty tool on a fishing trip was something he had learnt from Carl, and again it was paying off. They got themselves a replacement oar, although a slightly disproportionate and uneven one, but sufficient.

Apart from Wolferring's looming presence, everything else seemed to be falling into place. Despite the recent cold plunge, Sven felt warm from inside. It was just him and Roar again. The boat was crammed with fish, even more than in the good old times. Pihtamo was largely rebuilt. The lake would soon have fish. Ida was about to give birth to their first child any day now. It was as if things were slowly returning to normal. *Could life get much better than this?*

Chapter 10

TOO MUCH INFORMATION

All eyes were glued to Ida as she entered the Arctic Bar. Never had anyone in such an acute prenatal condition been seen in this male-dominated serving facility. She felt the judging glares as she squeezed through the scarcely vacated seating area.

Most of the town's folk knew her as the wife of Sven, and the privileged heiress from Örebröre, who got introduced to the world of fishermen in the most embarrassing way possible – by receiving herring on the altar. What the two, Ida and Sven, saw in each other was a question often asked. People just couldn't help but gossip. Was he only after her wealth? And was she trusting him to become subsequently wealthier through his success in ice fishing? Or was it not about money at all, but just simply true love?

No one had ever become rich from ice fishing. A slightly above average angler could secure just enough lakefood on the table for the family. Even the prize monies available for the competition winners were insignificant, like supermarket gift vouchers or free yearly subscriptions to Gillnetflix, an online streaming platform specialising in marine-related entertainment and aquatic content.

However, not all looks thrown at her were unfriendly; there was sympathy as well. She was expecting a baby with a man whose two fundamentals, his only source of income and personal pride, had been deprived from him. On top of that, the future of the fishing industry didn't look bright, either.

Ida didn't care what the others thought of her, since she was on a mission. She spotted Jaaku alone by the bar. The strangers nearest to him suddenly vanished when she approached. He wiggled uncomfortably when he noticed her.

'Ida? You're here? But you're...'

'I know exactly how pregnant I am,' she sighed, while observing the room in disdain. 'So, this is what the fuss is all about?'

'Well...'

'Ida!' Tomas called out from behind the bar, while polishing a pint glass. 'Surprised to see you here.'

Ida didn't like being recognised immediately by name, yet she managed to force a smile. 'Tomas. Well done for opening the bar so quickly.'

'It's been fantastic. On the first day, the queue stretched around three blocks.'

'How impressive,' she said sarcastically. 'All men, I presume?'

'Actually, we've had more women coming in lately.' Tomas looked at her from head to toe. 'So, when is the baby due?'

'Was yesterday,' she sighed.

'Maybe you shouldn't be drinking then?' Jaaku snorted.

'Don't worry. We have this new version of non-alcoholic wodka,' Tomas intervened, afraid to lose a customer. He pulled out a fresh bottle.

Jaaku wasn't convinced. 'That sounds disgusting.'

'Does it come in any flavour?' Ida asked.

'Yes, flavour of... wodka,' Tomas muttered, while pouring a glass. 'This one's on the house. After all, your husband saved my life. Without him, none of us would be here.'

'Please. It was a team effort.' She gave Jaaku an acknowledging nod. 'There were others involved.'

Jaaku looked down at his shoelaces, struggling to hide his guilt.

'Whatever you say,' Tomas hesitated.

'Tap water is fine,' Ida said bluntly.

'Seriously?' Tomas smiled uncomfortably, while being annoyed at wasting a bottle which, most likely, no one wanted to finish.

'Be careful,' Jaaku smirked, and raised his shot glass. 'He's probably got real wodka running down the tap.'

As Ida rolled her eyes, a half a pint of water appeared in front of her.

'There you go. Freshly pumped directly from Pihtamo's own natural springs,' Tomas said. 'It's probably better for the baby.'

'Thanks for coming to your senses,' she smirked, and looked at Jaaku who was already down to half a bottle. 'It would be better for all of us.'

Jaaku downed the shot and wiped his mouth on his sleeve. 'That's not why you came here, though? To criticise our drinking habits?'

Tomas felt the tension, and thought it was better to leave the two alone. He disappeared in the kitchen. Whether he was really needed there, no one knew.

'I want to talk about Sven,' Ida admitted, while a part of her wanted to keep lecturing about the men's alcohol consumption. 'He has been away since yesterday and I can't reach him on the phone.'

'And that's a surprise for you?' Jaaku snorted. 'After all these years?'

'But he hasn't been anywhere for months,' she said worriedly. 'What is it with you fishermen? I'm due any day now and...'

'Look,' Jaaku interrupted. 'Sven may have his own issues, but don't drag me down with him. Or with you. We are all very different. For example, I genuinely like to spend time with Marjukka.'

'I know you do,' Ida said apologetically, and finally took off her woollen hat and mitts, placing them on the bar top. 'How is she? I haven't spoken to her since our Christmas dinner on the post office roof.'

'She's fine. And strong,' Jaaku said bluntly, and started pouring himself another shot. 'I haven't really seen anyone else since the disaster. I only met Sven once before...' He stopped halfway through the sentence.

'Before what?'

He took a deep breath and moved closer to her. 'You must

promise not to tell anyone.'

She nodded anxiously.

'Before he went fishing.'

'But the lake is empty?'

He looked over his shoulder. 'He hasn't told you?'

She shook her head.

'The fish are still alive and well,' Jaaku whispered her the secret he'd promised not to share with anyone. 'Roar rescued them and took them to a secret pond. They went after them.'

She held her stomach. 'I don't believe it.'

'Are you okay?'

She nodded, even though she seemingly wasn't feeling well. 'I know about the pond. But why did it have to be now, when I needed him the most? They've had all these months.'

Jaaku filled his glass again. 'Everyone warned you about this. Fish will always be his number one priority.'

'Tell me something I don't know,' she grunted. 'What about you? Why didn't you join them, or go instead of Sven?'

Jaaku drank his shot in silence.

'It's fine if you don't want to fish anymore,' she continued.

He coughed, nearly choking on the liquid. 'He told you?'

'Everyone knows. You can't hide forever.'

'I don't know what I want.' As he grunted, a few heads turned in their direction. Jaaku had to speak quietly again. 'Everything has changed. Part of me wants the old Pihtamo back, but part of me doesn't.'

'Tell me about it,' she sighed, and had a sip of water. 'Sven's still living in the past.'

'Yesterday was good for him.'

Her eyes became teary. 'Well, at least he got his father back.'

Ida's sentimental reaction made Jaaku freeze, both physically and mentally. He was still too sober to be witnessing someone expressing such a negative emotion. Slowly, he raised his mitt and was about to pat her shoulder. But he couldn't. If he was to touch her, the extreme physical closeness between the two would have broken all those unwritten Arctic rules and boundaries of acceptable social interaction. In the end, his gesture looked like an awkward wave.

'Are you sure you don't want anything stronger?' he asked.

As Ida was wiping her face on her sleeve, she mumbled thru the fabric, 'Okay, then.'

Hesitatingly, Jaaku gestured to Tomas to bring them another shot glass. Seemingly irresponsible, yet pleased to see them wanting more, Tomas fulfilled Jaaku's wish.

'Welcome to the club.'

Jaaku didn't react, but simply took the bottle off him and poured Ida a shot.

At least now they can't blame me, Tomas thought, and walked off again.

Looking gloomy, Ida grabbed the glass. 'My father is the real reason I came here to talk to you. I know you've hardly met him, but...'

'Just once, at your wedding. The first one.'

'Right.' She wondered if they'd ever stop talking about that particular wedding. Probably never, because almost all their friends and family had witnessed the failed attempt, whereas the second, more successful one, was a private event. 'So, what's the stupid thing you guys say here to cheers again?'

'*Hölöökynkölöökyn!*' Tomas intervened from the distance.

Ida rolled her eyes, yet repeated the phrase in a slightly mocking tone, and clinked her glass with Jaaku's. As they downed the shots, the patrons observed her in horror. Her face immediately turned sour, and she started coughing.

'How can you drink this poison?'

'Another?' Cheekily, Jaaku shook the bottle in front of her, while she made gagging sounds. 'It's years of practising,' he confessed proudly. He put the bottle down, and became serious again. 'So, about your father... What happened to him? It wasn't the floods, was it? Örebröre wasn't really that affected.'

Ida cleared her throat before she spoke. 'With my mother, we found a secret entrance through a book-case in my dad's office, in our house in Örebröre. It led to a basement that was filled with his belongings. The place had been there for who knows how long, and even my mother didn't know about it. All his stuff had something to do with hunting, like moose heads, rifles, photos of game and so on.'

Jaaku's face turned grave. 'And, that's why you wanted to talk to me?'

'Well... I thought you might know something,' she stammered.

'I'm sorry, but I really can't help you,' he said bluntly, and was ready to pour some more.

But Ida grabbed his wrist and looked deep into his eyes. 'Jaaku, my dad was heavily involved in hunting. If you know something I should know, please tell me. This is very important.'

He nodded nervously. 'Okay. But can I have this shot first?'

'Fine. As long as you can still talk.'

Meanwhile, Ida rummaged through her purse, that typical bottomless handbag holding everything one needs to survive a day out. Jaaku even thought that he saw a herring's tail popping out at one point. He couldn't tell whether it was the drink making him see things, or if she truly carried a fish with her – perhaps the same one Sven gave her at the altar.

In the end, she revealed a photograph that she put it in front of his tired eyes. 'I found this picture from my dad's secret basement.'

'So?'

She pointed at the photo. 'That's him, Gustav, dressed up in a very odd fashion, with facial hair I've never seen on him before.'

Jaaku leant forward to get a closer look under the dim lights. He immediately recognised the cloak and the helmet with moose antlers. His jaw dropped.

'Oh, deer.'

'What?'

'That's... Mooses!' He bounced up, and took a step back, while rubbing his forehead.

'You mean the same Mooses that...' Ida stopped in mid-sentence.

Jaaku dropped his head down. 'What exactly has Sven told you? What do you know about Mooses?'

Now, her eyes were filled with tears. Suddenly, the hope of her father returning was gone. She held her stomach and grimaced. She was breathing heavily.

'Ida? Are you okay?'

With her last strength, she composed herself and grabbed his lapels. 'What did you do to my father?!'

'Ida, please.' Jaaku gave apologetic looks to Tomas and the patrons staring at them, as she hung on his collar. He whispered his response. 'He was out of control. I mean, Mooses was.'

'Just tell me the truth!' One big gasp came from their audience, as she went on pounding his chest. 'Did you kill him? Or was it Roar?'

'It was his own fault,' he said nervously.

'I don't believe you.' Her voice lowered to desperate whimpering. She began to lose her strength. She grabbed a hold of the bar. 'Don't tell me it was Sven?'

'No! Your father, or whatever form or powers he had adapted, divided the lake and...'

'I know the story!' Ida raised her voice again. 'But I need to hear, how did he really lose his life? Who is responsible?'

'But you must understand that he had powers unimaginable to all of us. Somehow, don't ask me how, he managed to split the lake in half that eventually caused the flooding, and that also sealed his own destiny.'

'Are you blaming my father for the destruction of Pihtamo?'

'I'm sure that it was not his intention,' he whispered.

While they had been squabbling, their eavesdropping audience was growing. Hence, Jaaku forcefully escorted her behind a slot machine to gain more privacy. A couple of curious necks stretched from around the corner. He turned his back to them, blocking their view. Two tall men stood up at the other end of the bar and started making their way to the arguing pair.

'Perhaps he couldn't understand or control the potential he had.' Jaaku spoke faster when he saw the men coming. 'Once he brought the divided lake back together, the tidal waves collided, causing the floods. He may have miscalculated the damage the merging water masses would cause, such as his own drowning, together with the island where he was assumed to be keeping base. That is the only truth. He caused his own drowning.'

'But, he was trying to protect himself...' she sobbed, '...from you lot.'

Jaaku grimaced and looked away. 'It was us or him.'

She shook her head in disbelief. 'That is so unfair. Sven got his father back... and I lost mine! At least Roar is hailed as a hero, a good man, whereas my father... was a monster.'

'Don't say that.'

Ida began shaking. She sought support from the slot machine, but soon her legs gave up on her and she collapsed to the floor on top of her belly. Her head hit a door frame. She lay on the wooden floor, bleeding.

'Ida!' Jaaku knelt beside her. He felt her pulse racing, but her eyes were closed. She didn't react. She was unconscious.

Suddenly, he felt a force pulling him upright. The two large men had reached him. One held him still, while the other spoke. 'What do you think you're doing to her?'

Before Jaaku could respond, his lights went out.

EVERYBODY LOVES IDA

Sophia barged through the double doors of the Kihlava General Hospital intensive care unit. Jaaku sat slouched in the waiting area by the reception, pressing a piece of red-stained cloth against his face. She vaguely recognised him from a distance. After all, he had been Sven's best man at the failed wedding – the disastrous ceremony she also remembered so well, yet wanted to forget. She still strongly believed that Jaaku was behind the herring prank, which ended up staining her daughter's reputation.

She ignored him and headed straight to the reception desk. 'I'm here to see my daughter, Ida Gustavsdøtter.'

The young receptionist, fresh from nursing school, studied her computer screen. 'And you must be... Birgget?'

'What?' Sophia gasped. 'I'm her mother, Sophia.'

'Ah. I see.' The receptionist looked at her. 'Have you got any identification?'

Frustrated, Sophia pointed at herself. 'Anyone at my age should be exempt from carrying ID. Can you not see any resemblance to my daughter?'

'It's the hospital policy. We cannot allow anyone to visit our patients without checking them first.'

'But, you rang me?'

'I'm sorry, madam. You need to be able to prove your identity.'

'I cannot believe this! I and my husband donated money to

build this hospital.'

'I can confirm that she's the mother.' Sophia's remonstration was convincingly interrupted by Jaaku, who had dragged himself up and stood behind her. He lowered the cloth and ice pack to reveal his black eye and bruised right cheek.

'Fine,' the receptionist concurred, and turned to Jaaku. 'How are you feeling, by the way? It looks like you've stopped bleeding.'

'I've seen better days,' Jaaku smirked painfully, and pointed at the corridor. 'I can show her the way.'

Sophia stared at him from head to toe, and then turned to the receptionist, who nodded agreeably. Why all this friendliness towards him, but not her? It seemed that visible injuries and bruises were required before one could receive any decent customer service in this particular institution.

'Come.' Jaaku started walking towards another set of double doors.

Once Sophia had caught up with him, she asked, 'And what happened to you?'

'It was me. I asked the hospital to ring you. I got your number from the Tuppervaara website.'

'So, you were here just by coincidence, when Ida was admitted?'

'No. There was a minor incident in the bar. Ida was involved, too.' Jaaku pushed through the doors and disappeared on the other side.

Confused, she followed him to the next corridor, and grabbed his shoulder. 'Why was she in the bar? Did you talk her into going there? Or did Sven?'

'It was nothing like that.'

'I knew it was a mistake when she started spending time with a bunch of fishermen...'

'She went there of her own will,' he interrupted. 'She wanted to talk about... hunting. But then a fight broke out.'

'Between you and her?' Sophia tensed. 'Did you hurt her?'

Jaaku sighed. 'She was upset about losing her father, and that set off complications. She fell unconscious. And then these big blokes attacked me, for no apparent reason. I'm sure she can

78

explain more once she recovers.'

'Where is she, then? I need to see her.' Sophia's voice had rarely directed any compassion and genuine worry towards the youngest of her three daughters. She had always viewed Ida as a bit of a rebel and different from the rest of the family. Ida had moved to Pihtamo and married a fisherman, unlike the two older daughters, who both moved far away to bigger cities to pursue their dreams, to build careers and to marry affluently. After losing Gustav, Sophia had to start patching things up with Ida, who suddenly was the only remaining family member within easy reach.

'Through those next set of doors and second room to the left.' Jaaku pointed ahead, before clearing his throat. 'I tried to call Sven, too, but he doesn't pick up the phone.'

'Surprise,' Sophia replied sarcastically, fully aware of Sven's disappearance. She was already tempted to blame the two friends for causing this incident. Jaaku's story didn't make sense to her. She couldn't trust anything that had to do with Sven, and Jaaku was too close to the periphery of his influence.

'Well, I... have to get going.' Jaaku sheepishly avoided eye contact. 'Good luck.'

She rolled her eyes, and continued walking along the corridor, while he staggered in the opposite direction towards the exit.

Following his instructions, she found her way to a room where a male nurse, in his early thirties with a short, blond hair and striking blue eyes, greeted her.

'And you must be Birgget?'

'Sophia. Her mother,' she replied promptly, and then saw Ida over the nurse's shoulder. The heart-breaking sight made her forget how the hospital staff had just confused her with the mother-in-law. Right now, none of that mattered. Peacefully and with eyes shut, Ida lay in bed under a turquoise cotton blanket. She was connected to a ventilator. An intravenous line fed fluids into her bloodstream.

'Ida!' A panting female voice from behind Sophia interrupted them.

Both the nurse and Sophia turned to look to the door.

'And you are?' the nurse asked.

'I'm her mother-in-law,' Birgget said, breathing heavily. 'I came as fast as I could.' She pushed past them, kneeled beside Ida and softly touched her forehead.

Sophia realised that she should be doing something similar, but she hadn't been fast enough. Hence, she took to the other side of the bed and touched Ida's arm that was connected to the intravenous drip.

'How did you know she was here?' Sophia asked Birgget.

'I got a call from the hospital.'

'That's interesting.' Sophia gave the nurse a doubtful look. 'How did they know to call you?'

'They automatically ring the next of kin,' the nurse said.

'But I'm her mother,' said Sophia indignantly.

'We rang her husband, Sven.'

'Who's gone fishing!'

'...and Birgget,' the nurse added.

'Yes. That's me,' Birgget nodded.

'So, my name is not on the list?' Sophia gasped in frustration.

'Since she's married, the husband's name will pop up first,' the nurse explained. 'And the second name, she must have added that herself when she registered.'

'I see,' Sophia sighed disappointedly.

The nurse thought it would be wise for him to move to the foot end of the bed, with one of the ladies on either side. He stood there like a referee.

'Would you like to hear how she is doing?' he asked. 'According to her friend, Jaaku, who was hurt in the same incident in the Arctic Bar...'

'Why was she with Jaaku?' Birgget interrupted. 'In the bar?'

'Nothing good can come from spending time with fishermen,' Sophia quickly fired.

Birgget responded with a look that could kill.

The nurse had to intervene again. 'Apparently, they were talking and she started feeling dizzy. She collapsed on the floor on her stomach and hit her head.'

'Just like that?' Sophia asked, baffled. 'She wasn't drinking, was she?'

The nurse studied the forms he was holding. 'When she was admitted to the hospital, her blood alcohol concentration was only 0.013 grams per hundred millilitres, which means she had been drinking alcohol, but only had one or two units.'

'Only? Why was she drinking in the first place?' Birgget looked enquiringly at both of them.

'I don't want to repeat myself,' Sophia snorted, and then sympathetically turned to Ida. 'Whatever Jaaku did to you, he will pay for it.'

'Jaaku wouldn't do anything to anyone,' Birgget said defensively.

Sophia shook her head. 'These things only happen when my family interacts with people of your likes.'

The situation was ready to escalate out of proportion any second. The nurse remained vigilant and clenched his muscles – in case the two women should start physically hurting one another and he would have to pull them apart. However, just before Sophia and Birgget were about to jump on each other's throats, the door slammed open again.

Sven came in first, followed by Roar, both soaking wet and stinking of fish. Sophia had to take a step back and pinch her nose between two fingers to block her air passageway.

'Where on earth have you been?' Birgget asked the men, with mixed emotions. She still felt awkward in the presence of her long-lost husband, but was glad to see her son exactly where he should be.

'There was something we had to do.' Sven's first words came out calmly, until he saw a glimpse of Ida over Birgget's shoulder. 'Oh, my God!' He rushed to kneel beside her, and gently caressed the bruises on her head. He saw her belly rising and lowering as she breathed slowly. She was connected to so many tubes and cables that he didn't even dare to ask about the purpose of them all.

'I don't want to know where you two were, but this is the trip you shouldn't have taken,' Birgget stared gravely at Roar, who was wracked with guilt.

Meanwhile, Sven's weepy eyes were fixated on Ida's motionless body. 'How is she?'

'She has suffered some minor brain injuries,' the nurse shyly intervened the family drama. 'She has fallen into a coma.'

There was a communal silence, until Sven raised his sad gaze. 'What about the baby?'

'The foetus seems to be fine. We know that she's due any day now. Depending on the length of her coma, if we have to, we may start the birth even if she is unconscious.'

'You cannot do that,' Sven insisted. 'She must be awake for that to happen.'

'Her situation is critical, but steady,' the nurse said calmly. 'We doubt she will go into labour yet, but we must be prepared. Therefore, we will be asking you, as the closest relative, to give us permission to use a C-section procedure, if necessary.'

Sven couldn't believe what he was hearing. He pulled a chair next to Ida's bed and sat on it. He rested his elbows on his thighs, letting his heavy head hang low. He couldn't feel the wetness or coldness anymore. Another drastic change in his life had happened so suddenly and unexpectedly, bringing him to his knees.

When they had discovered the bountiful pond, momentarily he thought things would only get better. Wolferring would get caught, the lake would be filled with fish, he'd become a father, and they would all live happily ever after. Yet, another punch in the face waited for him in the so-called 'real world'.

Sometimes, he wished he could just remain alone on the boat, in the middle of the lake – which seemed to be the only environment he really understood and was able to cope with. He could gut, scale and slice open any kinds of fish, of any size. He could easily choose which fishing gear he'd need and the spots where the fish would bite. But, to be the chosen one responsible for giving the green light to critical actions impacting Ida and their baby's life was beyond his comprehension.

Birgget slowly moved behind Sven, and rested her hands on his shoulders. 'I want you to know that we'll support you in any way we can.'

'If you'll excuse me.' The nurse seized the moment and moved nearer to the door. 'If there's anything you need, just press the alarm button next to the bed and a nurse will be with you.'

Roar nodded, being closest to him. 'Thank you so much for your hard work.'

The nurse found it hard to accept any credit – after all, he was only doing his job. 'And you, sir, should get some dry and clean clothes.'

Another awkward silence followed once the nurse had departed. Roar, for the first time since he'd arrived, paid more attention to Sophia and Ida's resemblance. Quickly, he connected the dots.

'You must be Ida's mother? I'm Roar, Ida's father-in-law.' He offered his hand to Sophia.

Sophia judgementally scanned Roar's scruffy appearance. Unfortunately, his scent had left an unforgettably disgusting first impression. Reluctantly, she offered him a brief, limp handshake.

'I have heard many things about you.'

'I hope not all bad?' Roar replied modestly.

She scoffed, and turned to Sven. 'Ida was drinking in the bar with Jaaku. Something to do with you?'

'What are you talking about?' Sven grunted.

'You left her alone again when she needed you the most.'

Sven seemed genuinely confused. 'I have no idea why she went to the bar.'

'No wonder you don't know, because you're always away.' Sophia had to sit down as well. The conflicting energy in the room was exhausting, not just for her but everyone.

Sven feared this conversation wouldn't lead to anything good. Therefore, he kept quiet and rested his hand on Ida's tummy. However, he already felt guilty – even without Sophia and Birgget reminding him about being constantly absent.

Roar didn't want to intervene, either, as he'd had no part in all the problems the people involved had developed with one another over the past years. He felt like he'd been ripped away from the comfort of their fishing trip to another dimension, or parallel universe that couldn't be more complicated. He hadn't properly seen or spoken to Birgget in nearly seventeen years, and had only ever vaguely heard of Sophia and her family, who all came from another social spectrum.

Sophia's disapproval of fishermen was ubiquitous. She attended Sven and Ida's first wedding attempt only for Ida's sake. This time, the prospect of her becoming a grandmother gave her a reason to stay, even beside people she would normally despise.

On the other hand, Ida's suffering brought out the best in all of them, and forced them to push their own personal issues aside. In spite of all their family disputes, different backgrounds and toxic chemistries, everyone wanted to stand behind Ida and wished her a fast recovery. The latter was at least that one positive thing they could all share.

Chapter 12

SUSPICIOUS MINDS

Thoughtfully, Sven's eyes wandered along a string of ice that created a transparent frame around the bottle display behind Tomas. For the first time ever, Sven couldn't decide whether to drink or not. He had only come to the bar to escape the silence of their home – even his longing for solitude had its limits.

'What can I get you?' Tomas carefully asked, sensing Sven's mood to be even more downbeat than usual.

Since most men in the area seemed depressed by default, detecting any change in their emotional state required great attention to detail – which was a skill Tomas had developed over the years in the hospitality industry. He wanted to know his customers inside-out so that he could offer them the right cure.

Sven stared blankly at the wide selection in front of him. 'What did she have?'

Tomas pretended he didn't understand who Sven was talking about.

'It's unbelievable... drinking when nine months pregnant!'

Nervously, Tomas picked up a random glass from an empty sink and started wiping it with a cloth – even though the glass was already perfectly dry.

Sven sneered at Tomas's futile task.

Tomas sighed, and put the glass away in the rack above. He had promised to himself not to share information about his patrons, unless it was law enforcement interrogating him.

Otherwise, what happened inside the bar, stayed there.

'You can tell me,' Sven said in a friendly tone. 'We know each other so well. I've been coming here since I was sixteen.'

'Sixteen?' Tomas gasped. 'That's illegal.'

'I was tall for my age.' Sven looked around. 'Do you think everyone here tonight is old enough?'

'I'd sure hope so.'

Sven laughed. 'Not busy enough, eh? You need to fill the gaps with minors?'

'The opening week went really well... but then it got a little bit quiet,' Tomas admitted.

'People can't afford to drink as much.'

'Hope the economy will bounce back.'

Tomas put a shot glass in front of Sven and started pouring wodka into it. 'This one's on the house.'

Sven looked at him suspiciously. 'You give out too many freebies.'

'Only to a selected few.'

'Was Ida one of them?'

Sven's questioning distracted Tomas, making the glass overflow. 'Sorry.'

'And you have to learn to minimise the waste,' Sven smirked.

Tomas put the bottle down, and started wiping the top. 'It was the first time ever I've seen her here.'

'Did you serve her?'

Tomas hesitated. 'It was Jaaku.'

'Since when has he worked here?'

'I mean, she drank from his bottle,' Tomas muttered, while feeling the guilt from breaking his oath of secrecy.

'Bottle?' Sven gasped. 'You could have stopped her. Like now, you could eject those kids from the table in the far corner.'

Tomas didn't have to look, as he knew exactly who Sven was talking about: the three suspiciously young-looking teenagers, sipping their gin and tonics and pretending to be adult-like with their cottony moustaches and oversized blazer jackets.

'I guess, I could... have.'

'I'm just telling you as a friend that you could lose your licence.'

'Honestly, I don't know why she was here. And I didn't hear their conversation. It was very loud that night.'

'Loud? Here? Give me a break.'

'It really was, until the scuffle began.'

'Scuffle? Between them two?'

Now, since the floodgates were open, Tomas didn't see the point in keeping secrets anymore. 'I couldn't see clearly. They were arguing behind the slot machine. Then, suddenly Ida was on the floor, and Jaaku got beaten up by these two big lads.'

Sven's blood started boiling, like lava getting ready to erupt from a volcano that has been dormant for centuries. His hibernating temper was hidden so deep inside his gut that it took a moment to become familiar with this rarely occurring sensation. Now he understood why Jaaku hadn't joined him in the bar.

'Will you excuse me?' Sven got up and headed towards the exit.

'What about your drink?'

'Give it to the kids!' Sven yelled from the doorway, before stepping out. Immediately, he took his mobile out and tried ringing Jaaku. It took five attempts before he finally picked up.

'Who is this?' Jaaku's voice had an echo, as if he was in a cave. In fact, it was his igloo's acoustic properties that created this unique sound quality.

'I need to talk to you.'

'I'm not buying anything,' Jaaku replied bluntly.

'Can you not hear me?'

'Sven? I'm sorry. I thought it was one of those cold callers again. They seem to ring up here on the glaciers almost every day, asking how cold it is, and offering tropical beach holidays to places like Scotland, and all sorts.'

'You haven't saved my new number, have you?' Sven enquired.

'Ööö... Of course, I did,' Jaaku muttered. 'But my old SIM card is frozen.'

Sven couldn't make sense of his stuttering. 'I thought we were supposed to meet up in the bar. I wanted to talk to you about Ida.'

'Ah. Sorry. I was... ' He coughed a couple of times, got up from beside Marjukka on the sofa and quickly sneaked to the bedroom, leaving her alone to watch the end of an old musical classic, *Sound Of Moose-ic.*

'Are you still there?'

'Yes. I'm actually feeling a bit rough, so I decided to stay home.' Jaaku closed the door behind him. 'So, how is Ida then? Is she okay?'

'You tell me?'

Jaaku didn't know how to respond, as he sensed Sven's anger.

'Why didn't you stay with her in the hospital?' asked Sven.

'I thought it was better to leave her with the family.'

'You are part of the family.'

'I'm sorry,' Jaaku muttered.

'What happened in the bar? Did you make her drink?'

'No! She wanted to drink.'

Sven shook his head in disbelief. 'But she never drinks. Until now, when nine months pregnant? It makes no sense.'

Jaaku took a deep breath, while gathering courage. 'Now, listen. This will blow your mind. Are you ready?'

'Make it quick.' Sven could feel his bare hand holding the phone beginning to freeze in the cold.

'Her father was... Mooses.'

'What? The man with those antlers? The man we...' Sven stopped there after realising what had happened to Ida's father.

'The same one,' said Jaaku. 'Ida came to show me a photo she'd found in her father's secret bunker under their house. She didn't know where you were at the time, and she had to speak to someone. She knew I would, most likely, be in the bar and that maybe I'd know something. She was aware of my... connections to hunters. When I told her the breaking news about Mooses, it really upset her. I've only seen Gustav once, and that was at your wedding, that first one, so I couldn't tell whether the man in the photo was him or not. But, apparently, she recognised him.'

'I can't believe this,' Sven gasped. 'I just got my own father back and she...'

'That's exactly what she said.'

Sven felt so dizzy that he had to seek support from someone's kicksled parked next to him. 'I never got along with Gustav, and he didn't like me, either. But I wouldn't have thought...'

'I guess this explains his sometimes hostile attitude towards fishermen.'

'But him being Mooses? Is that a bit too much? Was she one hundred per cent sure it was him?'

'You would think anyone would recognise their own father?'

'Well, I didn't, when we met the Lord of Herrings for the first time.'

'True.'

'We must go and visit this bunker.' Sven sounded determined. 'Did she tell you anything else? How to access it?'

'There should be a hidden entrance behind the bookcase in Gustav's office. She didn't say much, until she... well, you know... collapsed. The shock was too much for her to handle.'

'I can only imagine,' Sven said thoughtfully, remembering the time he'd first heard about Roar's disappearance. 'Well, I'm free tonight to go and find this basement. Or every night, in fact, until Ida recovers.'

'Sophia wouldn't let us in, would she?'

'I doubt it. But we'll find a way in.'

'I'm not so sure about this.'

'Just this once. For Ida's sake,' Sven pleaded. 'And besides, aren't you curious at all?'

'Of course, I am,' Jaaku said, while listening with his other ear through the bedroom wall. The television was still on in the living room. He took a couple of steps back, and then whispered a list of excuses. 'But... I've just moved in with Marjukka, we got a lot of things to do in the igloo and...'

'Can't those wait?'

'Sorry, but... I like to do stuff at home and... spend time with her.'

'What's that supposed to mean?' Sven grunted. 'Ida's lying in the hospital in a coma. What do you want me to do? Sit at home alone and wait?'

Jaaku hesitated. 'I guess... we could go tomorrow morning, after Marjukka goes to work. Though, it's a long journey to Örebröre. How do you think we'll get inside the house?'

'We could try when Sophia is visiting Ida in the hospital or something.'

'So, we need to break in?'

'Technically, yes.'

Jaaku sighed, not keen to get himself into any further trouble. He was still being accused of fiddling the end results of the last ice fishing championship contest. He was one of the three fishermen suspected of having to do with the floods. Ida had just blamed them both for the loss of her father, and, as a consequence of that, he'd ended up in the middle of a bar fight. And now, he was expected to enter someone else's property without permission. Clearly, his journey to vindicate his name, and be a law-abiding citizen, had become a long and winding one.

Chapter 13

A MONOLOGUE

Sven spoke next to the comatose Ida, wishing she could hear him. They were alone.

'Jaaku told me what had happened... Gustav? Of all the people? I cannot believe that both of our fathers were somehow... special. Or cursed.' He sighed, and took her lifeless hand. 'I hope you can forgive me, but I have to go and find more answers. I'm sure you'd do the same if you were in my shoes. The thing is, that... we need to be fully certain. For your and your mother's sake. If your father was truly involved, you must trust me when I say that, what happened at the lake that night was... an act of self-defence. Mooses was out of control and wanted to get of rid us all. That is the fact.'

Sven peered over his shoulder to make sure no one was listening. Despite the slight hesitation in his voice, he felt the most comfortable speaking up when no one else conscious was nearby.

'It is very difficult to describe the situation we were in; and, I fear that people wouldn't really listen to us. And we haven't spoken to anyone. They would think we're crazy, and probably hold us accountable for the destruction of the entire Pihtamo.' He dropped his head low. 'I don't know. Maybe I'm going too far; overthinking. But I'm scared, you see. I wish I could put those events into words. Everything happened so fast, and there were many factors we had to take into consideration. Our boat had capsized. We were in the water, in the middle of the lake. We had just come face-to-face with the Lord of Herrings. Then Mooses appeared. It was just too much for us, mortal fishermen, to deal with. Whereas these two larger-than-life "characters" were something else, from another world. We truly believed that, if the wizard wouldn't kill us all, Mooses would. I wish I could put it nicer, but I can't. I'm sorry.'

She breathed softly during the spiel, while being supported by the machinery on the bedside. He gently stroked the top of her hand.

'The bottom line is that… we always have hope. Right?' He stood up, leant closer and whispered, 'Can you hear me? I'm sure you can. I love you so much.'

Then the door behind Sven flew open. Sophia entered. She immediately took a step back. 'Don't let me disturb you. I can come back later.'

Sven composed himself, then picked up his coat from the backrest of the chair. 'No. I was just leaving.'

As he swung past her, Sophia said with a hint of mockery, 'Is it the lake calling again?'

'The lake is empty,' he snorted, and stepped out into the corridor. However, before he slammed the door shut, he needed to say the final word. 'I genuinely want you to spend time with your daughter. I know how she always wanted your attention, but never got it.'

'Look who's talking!' Sophia lashed out.

With no riposte left up his sleeve, his last response was the slamming of the door.

Sophia wasn't sure if he heard her last remark, nor did she care. She knew they would meet again, because they would have to. They were family now.

Chapter 14

WINNING ICE FISHING

Two kicksleds wound through the dense spruce forest, both forced to follow the narrow remains of wet snow. Sven led the way, while Jaaku struggled to keep up. They would remain in that formation until they got into a steeper decline, that gave Jaaku the advantage as the heavier one, enabling him to catch up. Their wooden steering bars made contact when he squeezed past Sven. By the time he reached the bottom, Sven was still halfway at his descent.

'Come on then!' Jaaku gave a cocky glance over his shoulder, knowing this was one of those rare occasions when he had been ahead of Sven at anything.

However, Jaaku's celebration was short-lived once they were on an even surface again. A wider and thicker strip of snow ahead, that had congregated in the valley, gave them enough room to ride more amicably side by side. The tension and nervousness caused by their planned deed, however, was palpable.

'When was the last time you went to Örebröre?' Jaaku tried to break the ice.

Sven's only visit was still fresh in his memory. He had caught Ida in the house with her ex-boyfriend, Christian. Technically, Sven and Ida were on a break from their relationship at the time, even though they never really had 'the talk'. She just disappeared from sight after being humiliated by him at the altar.

'Can't remember,' Sven vaguely replied.

'Interesting,' Jaaku said dumbfounded. 'And you two are married?'

'I know this sounds messed up, but I've only been there once. And even then, I had to break in.'

'Glad you have experience, then,' Jaaku smirked. 'Are you sure that Sophia won't be there tonight?'

'Definite. I just saw her at the hospital. She arrived to visit Ida when I left. She probably thought I had to go fishing or something.'

'She must really think you're the ideal son-in-law,' Jaaku said sarcastically.

'The feeling is mutual.' Sven glanced at Jaaku, and took the lead.

Their long journey also brought back other, more pleasant memories, when the men passed Lasi Vekasi – an idyllic chapel where Ida and Sven had finally got married. The old, petite wooden structure hidden in the dark forest was lit up. They could hear the organ playing a familiar wedding tune. A ceremony was underway, bringing another new couple to holy matrimony.

As they passed the church, a melodic singing began to echo through the thick walls of the chapel. Sven's musical ear wasn't that developed, yet he could definitely recognise the deep baritone voice that belonged to Lumbardi Martello – the Italian singer-sensation and heartbreaker who had taken Pihtamo by storm decades ago. He was also the same man who had sung at his and Ida's wedding.

Not only was Mr Martello known for his magnificent voice, but also his honed womanising skills. Birgget, for instance, was one of many who had an affair with Lumbardi while being married to Roar. After hearing about Birgget's eye-opening adventures, Sven, who had already recovered from such revelations that Tooth Fairies and Easter Bunnies didn't really exist, was again forced to digest another, more cringing fact of life, that his own mother was also a woman with biological needs. It all felt like a part of some step-by-step induction to the complexities of adulthood. Only the most recent meeting with the supposedly real Father Christmas had brought a glimmer of hope and trust to some of those remaining magical elements in life. Not to mention all that mythical fauna they had discovered, whose existence would've been easily denied by even the most naïve and childish individuals. Nevertheless, Sven's trust in marriage as a lasting and reliable institution was wavering due to his parents' infidelities.

But, as the singing faded, so did Sven's negative thoughts. He tried to focus on what was important right now, and that was Ida's healing. And, once she had recovered, he wanted to be ready with more answers about her father.

As they reached the edge of the forest, a flat terrain of hard soil opened in front of them. For another two to three months, only microbial life could enjoy the frozen richness of these barren fields, until the first swede seeds were to be sown. In the horizon, the dark corrugated iron gates of Ida's family home stood as a proud sign to welcome visitors from all over the region.

However, the neglected condition of the estate became apparent the closer they got to the entrance. Sven raised his forefinger and stopped to listen to the silence. The guard dogs made no sound. The gates had been left slightly open. The security booth was empty. The hinges made a creaking sound as he pushed the gate wide open.

'It's disturbingly quiet. I cannot remember entering being this easy.'

The house, perching on top of a hill, at the end of a long driveway, looked haunted, as if from a scene from an old, black and white horror film. The heart-melting Italian love ballads were far behind them, replaced by the distant howling of the wolves.

They walked their kicksleds up the rest of the icy driveway. As they reached the front of the house, there was not a single light on. The building looked eerie and lifeless – exactly the way they preferred to find it. Only a garage door was left wide open to reveal its emptiness.

'I was expecting something more glamorous,' Jaaku said with a hint of disappointment.

'It used to be,' replied Sven. He stared in shock at the poor state of repair the estate had fallen into in such a short period of time. He thought that squatters might take over the place any time soon. 'We should hide our kicksleds.'

'But, we won't be long, right?'

'Just in case.' Sven pulled his kicksled to the shady side of the house, behind a cranberry bush and the last remaining pile of packing snow that had fallen off the roof.

Even though it felt like a pointless exercise, Jaaku decided to follow suit rather than take any risks. 'So, how do we break in?' he asked impatiently.

'With these.' Sven put his hand in his pocket and took out a set of keys.

Jaaku nodded, impressed. 'I thought you didn't get along with the family?'

'The keys are actually Ida's.' Sven returned to the front yard, Jaaku right on his tail.

'Does she know?'

'What do you think? She's in a coma.' Sven didn't feel particularly proud of borrowing from his unconscious wife, yet he resolutely began fitting the keys to the front door lock. 'Let's get this over with quickly, so I can return the keys to her before she wakes up.'

Only the third and the biggest of the keys disappeared inside the lock, and turned correctly. While holding his breath, Sven pushed the door open. The dampness and more cold air greeted them as they entered. The wooden floor creaked, breaking the silence. Both men walked on their tiptoes. The room temperature dropped the further inside they went. The moon shining through the windows gave them just enough light to locate the living room.

'Does anyone even live here anymore?' Jaaku could see his breath as he spoke.

There was a coffee table in the middle of the room covered with a few empty whiskey and brandy bottles. 'Someone does,' Sven replied in disdain.

Jaaku admired the decorated walls on either side of the room, with artworks that could've been from any private gallery. 'Who are all these people in the paintings?'

'Their relatives or friends, I think. She came from a very affluent and privileged family.'

Mesmerised, Jaaku could only nod. It was clear to him how Sven had struck a goldmine by marrying Ida.

'I can see that now.' Jaaku walked to the end of the hallway, where a door left ajar shed more light. He peered through the gap. 'She said something about an office.'

Sven caught up with him when he was already inside the room, staring at the towering bookshelf in front of him. Jaaku observed, from left to right, at hundreds of editions of the most well-known classics, as well as some more experimental works of unknown writers.

'Do you think he read all these?' Jaaku pondered in awe.

'Even if he did, there are certain things you don't learn from books,' snorted Sven, who had only read two publications in his life: *Winning Ice Fishing* and the Bible. After a brief examination, he couldn't spot either of those titles on the shelves.

Jaaku moved his hand along the vertical dark wooden frame of the bookcase, and then gave it a gentle push. Sven took the other end, and did the same thing.

But nothing happened.

Next, they prodded random books on the shelf, dropping some of them accidentally on the floor. Coming this far had to bring them results, at any price. Momentarily, they forgot how this was meant to be a discreet, yet unlawful, visit to someone else's property.

Finally, however, their vigorous effort paid off when the last section of the bookcase at the farthest corner started rotating, bringing an even colder and dustier breeze into the room. The hinges of the old mechanism squeaked, until the secret door came to a halt. The men stared in awe at the large gap in the wall.

'The bunker?' Jaaku concluded.

Sven shrugged his shoulders, took out his phone and used it as a torch to light the tunnel ahead. In careful steps, he entered the stony stairwell.

'Are you coming?' he said, looking back at Jaaku.

'I'm going to put the books on the shelf first. Looks less suspicious.'

'We can do that afterwards.' Sven continued to descend the stairs, while Jaaku soon followed after he had cleared the floor.

As they reached the bottom, they could see all the hunting-related memorabilia, photos and trophies, untouched, the way Sophia and Ida had left them.

'Amazing.' Jaaku tried but couldn't suppress his excitement.

'I always knew there was something wrong with Gustav.' Sven went to shuffle a stack of items on the desk. There was a photo of the hunters' meeting, where Gustav spoke on the podium; and another, with him standing on a tree stump.

In each picture, he was like the leader of the pack, and dressed in a similar fashion to how Sven remembered Mooses presenting himself. He was like the head of some cult, spreading his arms wide in front of big crowds, who all seemed transfixed by this extravagance. *Why did he leave all his stuff lying around? Did he want people to discover everything? Or was he caught off guard?*

Meanwhile, Jaaku's investigation was bringing more results. He had come across an eloquently written document in the vitrine, next to a collection of trophies. He took out the old scroll and started interpreting it.

'Mooses is predicting a fish exodus arising on land...'

'What is that nonsense.' Sven's snorting interrupted him.

'It says here, in this... manifesto,' said Jaaku, reading from the paper, 'The fish would crawl out of the water, adapt a superior form and enslave the entire humankind. The end of modern Pihtamo is near, if the hunters and fishermen won't unite and take action.'

'That's a bit outdated,' Sven chuckled. 'The fish came from the sea millions of years ago. Gustav must have lost his mind.'

'He's talking about modern times.'

'Depends when that piece was written.'

'Can't be that long ago. In his lifetime?'

Sven pondered. 'Fish exodus, eh? You think he is referring to Wolferring?'

'I would prefer Venezuelan Herring,' Jaaku said with a hint of a smile.

'I just can't see fish living on land.'

'Well, after what we saw before Christmas, when the disaster unfolded, I feel like anything is possible,' said Jaaku. 'Hairy

monster flying a plane, a big salmon doing magic tricks, a lynx using a computer...'

'And them all talking,' Sven added.

Jaaku sighed. 'And now, her father was Mooses. Unbelievable.'

'She's gonna blame me, or all of us, for the rest of our lives for what happened to him.'

'It was not any of our fault. Gustav fought for his own cause, ended up in the wrong place at the wrong time and eventually the accident took his life.'

'Accident? I guess we can call it that. Try explaining that to Ida.'

'Besides, the battle between Mooses and the Lord of Herrings was only a matter of time. It was unavoidable. It was either your or her father.'

The way Jaaku put it made it sound like the harshest choice no one would like to make. Discovering this unfortunate truth about Gustav took the last shine away from beating Mooses.

'I think we've seen enough,' Sven said bluntly. 'My dad's opening the restaurant at eight. I wanna be there early.'

'Tonight?'

'Didn't you see the invitation?'

As Jaaku shook his head, a roaring sound of an engine coming from outside grew louder.

'Ida's mum!' Sven gasped, and looked up to the ceiling.

Jaaku sighed. 'She's riding a snowmobile?'

'I know. They move slightly quicker than kicksleds,' replied Sven, rushing to the stairwell.

Quickly, Jaaku tried to place the manifesto back in the glass vitrine, but he missed the opening. Instead, he punched the document through the glass. The vitrine came down from its wall brackets, smashing against the floor into hundreds of tiny shards. In the same instance, the noise from above died down. They froze, listening to the silence.

'We have to get out of here,' Sven whispered.

The front door on the ground floor opened, then slammed shut. Loud footsteps tapped the wooden parquet above them.

Jaaku chucked the manifesto on the desk, on top of other documents. Then, on tiptoes, he followed Sven up the stairs, where the bookcase was still wide open. They saw flashes of Sophia swiping past the corridor. They heard a fridge opening, followed by a rumbling of an ice cube machine.

'We have to close this bookcase.' Sven started pulling the heavy door shut.

'With us inside?' Jaaku remonstrated.

'Where else can we go?'

The approaching steps made the reluctant Jaaku join the effort. Only a fraction of a second before Sophia walked into the office, the men had sealed the entrance to the basement.

From her point of view, everything seemed normal. Accompanied by a glass of whiskey on the rocks, she sat on Gustav's leather chair. She took her high heels off and threw her feet on the desk. She took a large sip from the glass and wiped her mouth. 'Ah, darling. My Gustav. What have you been up to behind my back?'

As she leant against the backrest, a single book fell from the top shelf, exactly where the secret door was situated. Her heart started pumping faster. As her eyes scanned the bookcase, it seemed to her that a few encyclopedias and volumes were randomly placed, not in their usual numerical order. Anxiously, she pushed the whiskey glass further away on the desk, as if to blame the alcohol – which, to be fair, she was consuming increasingly lately.

She got up and moved closer to the bookcase. Spending time alone in the house for the past few months hadn't helped. It had made her fearful and highly sensitive; almost paranoid. Anything this ghastly was the last thing she needed in her life right now.

She stroked the row of books that stood exactly between her and the men hiding. The men held their breaths as she picked the fallen book up off the floor and flipped it around to see the cover.

The book was *Winning Ice Fishing* by Rauno Kolumpio – a former ice fishing specialist, who reigned in the 1940s and 50s.

Chapter 15

FRESHWATER FISH AND
NEW POTATOES

The new town of Pihtamo was finding its shape, centring a small square on a slightly tilted plateau against the east side of the volcano. A modern version of the church became the village's most dominant building, with its pyramid-shaped timber spire rising above the flat skyline. A modest police station and supermarket were also established.

It was as if nothing had changed from the previous. Entrepreneurs were not keen to take unnecessary risks or try anything drastic since the old system and layout had functioned sufficiently. The community was insular, where not only success stories but especially mistakes were duly noted. No one wanted to be a target of ridicule due to a failure.

Despite the uncertain times, Roar's Freshwater Fish and New Potatoes Restaurant and Take Away Service was one of the few, brave start-up businesses going against the trends, ready to celebrate its grand opening on the outskirts of town. Since the lake had apparently dried out of fish, already with its ironic name the diner generated controversy. The main battle, however, was against popular home cooking, that had always been highly regarded and widely practised in the area, whereas takeaway food and eating out were seen a bit nonsensical and a waste of money and time – a challenge that Lumbardi Martello, the former owner, also struggled with before his karaoke restaurant, Martello's Arctic Pizza Buffet, in exactly the same facility, went bust.

However, Lumbardi had his time in the limelight, not necessarily because of his culinary skills, but because of his appeal to the opposite sex, combined with his mediocre singing talent. And long before anyone in Pihtamo had even heard of this exotic flatbread called 'pizza', he was partly the reason for the downfall of Roar's marriage to his now ex-wife, Birgget.

Some thirty years later, however, it seemed the hatches had been buried, when Roar bought Lumbardi's dying business and got a hold of his poor accounting. The transaction settled their accounts, once and for all. *What goes around, comes around, one way or the other*, thought Roar.

There were times in the past when Roar felt inferior to the magnificence and versatility of Lumbardi. As the years went by, though, he began to realise the fragility of this mysterious Italian showman. In the end, when the good looks had worn out and everyone had heard all the songs, Roar believed that life was more about hard work, persistence and consistence. These were the few qualities Lumbardi lacked when managing the business, as well as his game of numbers – which also led to his eventual bankruptcy.

Roar taking over the business wasn't that straightforward, but a combination of many factors. A coincidence and great timing played their parts. He enjoyed the conquest and saw this as a minor revenge on the old times. Him buying off Lumbardi was also an example of how small the circles in Pihtamo really were.

However, Lumbardi's decline didn't happen overnight. After the relatively successful first few years, natural demand for pizza in the area turned out to be limited in the longer term. In desperation, he even tried to draw customers in by experimenting with more local and familiar toppings, like reindeer meat and herring. But, his exotic cooking style, with too many hot spices and mixed flavours, never attracted the masses. Traditionally, Pihtamonians liked tasteless food, and Lumbardi's menu was far from it.

Eventually, not even his fading celebrity status could help Lumbardi to keep the clientele. The natural disaster before Christmas was the last nail in the coffin. He was forced to sell the business for a bargain price – which Roar could afford, largely with government support for new entrepreneurs, and with an additional relief fund released to help rebuild the disaster zone. Roar had no savings or assets as such, since he had been officially deceased for over a decade. Yet, his secret pond was available as an abundant and free source of fish for months to come – an opportunity he decided to exploit in moderation and discreetly.

To his advantage, the competition in Pihtamo in the catering businesses was non-existent – apart from Jaaku's parents' pie shop, which temporarily operated from home and only as a delivery service after their previous shop drowned in the floods.

The opening night was monumental for Roar in many ways. It was the first time he'd be meeting so many of the town's folk after his disappearance. The event was not only a celebration of his new business venture, but also his coming back to life.

As he shovelled gravel on an icy pavement in front of the restaurant, he looked easily ten to fifteen years younger than the night he appeared as the Lord of Herrings. He had trimmed his beard and combed his longish, white hair. He was all suited and booted, oozing satisfaction and confidence – like many fresh business owners who hadn't yet opened and didn't know the outcome. However, his biggest fears were: seeing so many old faces and the variety of questions these people might present to him.

Once the first kicksled appeared on the horizon, he stopped gritting, went back inside and took his position in the foyer next to Ronja, Ida's best friend, who stood behind the reception desk studying the guest list. Behind them swiped Irmeli, the top fisherwoman in Pihtamo, whose livelihood had also been affected by the lack of fish. Hence, she had to get a job outside her area of expertise. She was the head and the only waitress. She went off to make finishing touches to the dining area, pouring champagne into glasses, folding napkins and so on.

Ronja leant over to Roar. 'Looking very smart, sir.'

Roar glanced nervously outside, while twitching in his

dinner jacket. 'I haven't worn anything like this since my wedding.'

'I was meaning to ask if she's coming? Birgget? I can't see her name on the guest list.'

'She knows about the opening' replied Roar. 'But I doubt she will turn up. It's still a bit awkward for us to be in the same space.'

'Ah! I think there are our first guests.' Ronja swiftly moved away from this uncomfortable topic, and welcomed Jaaku's parents, Siimiuut and Aajamaak.

'Glad you two made it.' Roar formally extended his hand.

'We have plenty of time now, since our sales sunk, literally speaking,' Siimiuut said ironically, and shook hands with Roar.

'But home-cooked food is what people want, right?' Roar said on a positive note.

'Yes, but people also want to cook themselves,' Aajamaak added. 'Besides, our kitchen in our igloo is not quite up to restaurant standards.'

'Anyway, enough about us,' Siimiuut intervened. 'We're here to celebrate your new creation. You were lucky to get a hold of this property. You've done some great work here. It does look very cosy.'

Roar glanced proudly at the compact seating area. There were five tables and an open-plan kitchen. 'We've worked really hard to transform it. The place was quite run-down when I acquired it. Feel free to look around, and sit wherever you like. Ronja here can take your coats, and Irmeli over there has some welcoming drinks for you.'

'Thank you for inviting us.' Aajamaak handed her and Siimiuut's coats over. 'We thought Jaaku was coming with us as well, but we can't get a hold of him.'

'Jaaku?' Roar seemed caught off guard.

Meanwhile, Ronja's eyes wondered through the guest list. 'But I can't see...'

'Yes,' Roar interrupted. 'He's probably coming with... Sven.'

'Ah. I would have thought with Marjukka?' Aajamaak said, confused.

'Always the same with those fishermen. Disappearing into

thin air,' Siimiuut smirked.

'Better than Finnair,' Roar chuckled uncomfortably, and looked past them. 'Will you excuse me. There are some more guests coming. Please make yourselves at home.'

Once Roar stepped outside, he immediately rang Sven.

But the call went to voicemail.

After Ronja had escorted Aajamaak and Siimiuut to the dining area, she joined Roar outside. 'You didn't invite Jaaku?'

'I... forgot,' Roar said unconvincingly, and put his phone away. 'Can't get hold of Sven, either.'

'Just relax and enjoy,' said Ronja, smiling. 'It's your big day. I'm sure everyone will come, including Sven.' She went back inside.

For the most part, Ronja was right. Within the next half an hour or so, the restaurant filled up with almost all the people that were invited, except two: Birgget, whose absence wasn't a big surprise, yet to Roar's biggest disappointment, and Sven.

Once the opening drinks had been served, it was Roar's time to step in front of the crowd. The pressure was laid upon him as the guests expected to hear a speech. Weirdly, he was being treated like he had already won something, even though this was only the beginning. More than anyone, he knew what winning felt like, and this wasn't it. For him, the most important family members were missing, who were the real reason he woke up in the mornings, did things and wanted to achieve.

As before any contest, he had butterflies in the stomach and felt like he was going to faint. He started clearing his throat, when Ronja walked up to him.

'I still can't get a hold of them,' she whispered.

'Just keep trying,' Roar replied discreetly, grinding his teeth together. He didn't have a good feeling about both Sven and Jaaku being unavailable. He knew exactly where the mobile network coverage was non-existent, and that there was plenty of fish available in the pond – the latter being classified information, which had now leaked who-knew where. And he could already anticipate how curious some guests in the party would become if his only son wasn't present.

Ronja stepped aside, giving the stage entirely to Roar. He

turned to face the audience of about two dozen people. He felt the nerves kicking in. He was far from being a public speaker, but only a hard-working fisherman. Also, he had been away for too long. It was like showing up to a school reunion after not seeing anyone for the last twenty years or so. The names and voices of the people made more sense, whereas the faces were only distant memories from the past.

He pulled a stack of crumpled papers out of his pocket, the top one being the map leading to the pond. Quickly, he stuffed it back in his pocket, and then started reading from the next sheet in his hand.

'I would like to... welcome you all to... this modest creation that can also be called a "restaurant".'

There was a chuckle from the audience before he continued.

'It has been so long since I have stood in front of you all. So much has changed. Everything.' He looked down, hiding his feeling of guilt. 'But there is always hope, even when the hope is gone... Pihtamo has transformed within recent months, and I thought it was time for me to change with it. Fish have always been the greatest passion of mine, as many of you know. And the best way for me to give back to the community that has lost so much is to serve you... the best fish in town!'

There were a couple of claps from the audience, which quickly died down.

'Thank you... The lake has suffered so much, but I'm confident it will bounce back. Until then, we're forced to source our fish from further afield...' Like some of the best politicians, he was unable to share the whole truth of the matter.

The speech was interrupted by the opening of the front door, and a breeze of cold air that came with it. Everyone turned to look how Birgget apologetically entered, and sat on an empty seat in the farthest corner near the reception desk.

'Okay... I believe I have said enough,' Roar stuttered uncomfortably, as Birgget's surprise entrance had taken the last edge off his already flat performance. 'Welcome to you all and enjoy your stay.' He raised his glass, and promptly stepped out of the spotlight.

The audience gave another subtle applause, and then begun

chattering amongst themselves. Occasionally, random people came to flatter Roar about the great work he had done. Yet, his distracted eyes always wandered off to Birgget, who kept signalling and miming back at him. *Where is Sven?* he read her lips, but could only respond by shrugging his shoulders.

Despite the complex nature of their relationship, seeing Birgget there delighted Roar. Apart from Sven going missing, everyone else was there, the speech was over and it was time to party. In his opinion, the event could have gotten a much worse start.

Until Irmeli went to serve at Birgget's table.

Chapter 16

EXTENDED STAY

Sophia slouched back in the arm chair, the book resting on her lap. Contemptuously, she opened a page somewhere in the middle and began browsing. Ice fishing was the last of her interests and, in her opinion, only practised by the lowest classes. It baffled her how such an insignificant book had ended up on their majestic bookshelf filled with academic literature. Why anyone would sit, frozen on the ice hour after hour, chasing miniscule prize monies, was never clear to her.

The title page was decorated with an illegible signature and 'Merry Christmas' wishes to 'Gustav'.

Was he secretly ice fishing, too? she thought, and let the book fall out of her hand and onto the floor. Feeling melancholic rather than frightened of the ghost, she asked herself, 'How did this happen?' She couldn't yet fathom how her adolescent dream, to share a life with a successful husband and have three beautiful daughters by her side, had gone by so quickly. Suddenly, she was left alone to live in an unlawfully spacious mansion, accompanied only by the skeletons Gustav had left in the closets – more so in the basement.

It was truly the first time Sophia had realised how lonely the empty house could make her feel. For the past few months, she had only used a fraction of the entire space reserved for her. No matter how many social events and Tuppervaara parties she hosted, the late evenings, nights and early mornings would often painfully drag. She hadn't yet found a solution how to fill the gaps in her life. Whether she would have the motivation and interest, in her late fifties, to find someone new, only time would tell. What she did know for certain was that no one would ever take Gustav's place – no matter how dark his secrets would turn out to be.

Perhaps, though, a companion might be nice for sharing everyday chores – when the time was right. *Maybe a puppy*, she thought. *But no more scary guard dogs.*

While Sophia couldn't find enough reasons to get off the chair, behind the bookshelf Sven and Jaaku tried not to breathe so as not to get caught breaking into her house.

'What do we do now?' Jaaku whispered.

Sven pointed at the stairwell. 'Go back down?'

'What about the restaurant opening?'

'It's too late for that.' Disappointed in himself, Sven sneaked downstairs. Sophia's whimpering faded as he descended into the darkness. And he didn't dare to switch the light on, until she had left the office for sure.

Jaaku waited and waited, until he finally gave up and joined Sven in the basement. Sophia didn't leave; instead, she poured herself another whiskey. She was determined to drown her sorrows – like every other night since the disappearance of Gustav.

Chapter 17

THE LAST GUEST

Sven, vigorously propelling his right leg, gave his kicksled powers equivalent to an output of a horsepower or two as he dashed towards his father's restaurant. While nearing the doorstep, the rails hit the gravel on the pavement, bringing him to a sudden halt and sending his body flying against the shop façade. Luckily, though, the durable triple-glazing kept him from smashing through and straight into the dining area. Instead, he smacked flat against the window, and then slowly slid along the glass to the ground – as the characters often do in slapstick cartoons.

Irmeli, who was alone cleaning the floors, raised her head after hearing a loud thump. The window frames were still shaking, but she couldn't see a thing; only hear painful groaning. Just then, a staggering figure rose behind the window.

'Sven?' She took a step back.

'Did I miss the party?' His light-headed panting made the window steamy.

She could barely hear his voice through the glass. 'Your father was asking for you.'

He was able to read her lips. 'It was not my fault. I wish I could explain to him.'

Irmeli came to open the door and poked her head outside. 'Roar is still here if you want to give it a shot.'

Feeling dizzy from the collision, Sven wobbled into the foyer. It was the first time they'd met since the last ice fishing championship contest, where Irmeli had been one of the victims of Jaaku's misconduct that had sent her, amongst many others, plummeting through the ice. Even though Sven had nothing to do with the incident, he wasn't convinced she knew or wanted to accept this fact. After all, Jaaku's accidental help had secured him the victory, not her.

'I was just finished, anyway,' she said briefly, and put on her overcoat. 'He's in the kitchen. Good luck.'

As she walked away, Sven could relax again – although Roar might not let him off so easily. Clunking and banging noises from the back caught his attention. He passed through the pristine clean dining area to the open-plan kitchen, where Roar, totally oblivious to Sven's presence, was leaning over the sink washing pots and pans.

'Dad?' Sven projected his voice over the burble of running water.

Roar turned off the tap, but kept staring ahead to the wall. He was breathing heavily.

'Would be good if you had a washing machine?' Sven tried to lighten the mood.

'It's broken. Therefore, I am the washing machine!' Roar grunted, and turned to face him. 'What are you doing here? The last guests left three hours ago.'

'I'm sorry. I really wanted to be here and I would have called, but...'

'It really doesn't matter anymore,' Roar interrupted, and started erratically wiping the kitchen top, like a frustrated husband or a wife.

Sven felt the urge to do something; to help. He randomly picked up a stack of dirty plates from the kitchen island. But the slippery plate at the bottom slid from his grip and smashed to pieces against the floor. The leftovers of mashed potatoes and lingonberry sauce spread all over the floor, splashing both of the men's trouser hems.

'Please. Don't touch anything!' Roar gasped. He wanted to discipline him, but didn't know how. Sven wasn't even his employee, but just another grown man now.

Apologetically, Sven took a kitchen cloth and knelt down to

pick up the pieces. He tried to wipe the stains on Roar's trousers, but Roar pulled away.

'Did you go fishing with Jaaku? Or to the pond? Without telling me?!'

'No.' Sven stood up. 'I went to Örebröre with Jaaku. We were meant to be back for the opening. I swear.'

'Why would you go there in the first place?' Roar interrupted. 'And today, of all the days?'

'This story will blow your mind, if you let me explain.' Sven raised his voice over Roar's. 'Before Ida ended up in hospital, she and her mum had discovered this secret bunker under their house. No one else, except Gustav, knew about this place. So, me and Jaaku paid it a little visit...'

'Sophia actually invited you two? She wanted to see you?'

'Well, we sort of... went there without telling her,' Sven sheepishly replied.

'You broke into their house? Is that what you've become now?'

'I am not a burglar!' Sven grunted. 'It's true that she would not have let us in. So, we just had to wait until she was not there, and go when the house was empty.'

'Sounds exactly what a burglar would do,' Roar snorted.

'But we didn't steal anything. We only... gathered information,' Sven muttered. 'And I'm glad we did. It seems that Gustav was not only a good hunter, but something more.' Sven dug out the photo of Gustav wearing the helmet and moose antlers, and dropped it in front of Roar.

'Mooses?' Roar's eyes widened.

Sven nodded. 'His bunker was like any hunter's wet dream: moose heads, guns, trophies, medals.'

'Does Ida know what happened to him?'

'She did go and see Jaaku the evening she got her complications. Whatever they discussed seemingly upset her. Whereas, I told Ida, months ago a vague story about Mooses confronting us, but I doubt she even remembered that. Back then, no one saw the connection between Gustav and Mooses. Usually, things become interesting to us only when they really touch us or the ones we love. She never questioned anything, until they found the bunker and she met up with Jaaku.'

'What about Sophia?'

Sven shrugged his shoulders. 'I doubt she knows about our involvement, as she has never brought the subject up.'

'True. I also ran into her a couple of times in the hospital. She just wants to avoid me.'

'So, I hope you can forgive me for being late,' Sven said. 'We were supposed to be here on time, but then Sophia suddenly came back home, got drunk and passed out right above the bunker we were hiding in. We couldn't call or text you, either, because there was no signal underground. We could only sneak out when we heard Sophia snoring.'

Roar thoughtfully re-examined the photo. 'I think you made an interesting discovery.'

'Do you think we should talk to Sophia about this?' Sven asked.

'Depends,' Roar hesitated. 'We did nothing wrong, right? Mooses would've killed us all?'

'I agree. But the loss of a loved one is always difficult to accept, no matter what the circumstances. I can say that from experience.'

'Can we even be a hundred per cent sure Mooses, or Gustav, is gone?' Roar pondered. 'We saw the tsunami washing over him. But considering the supernatural powers he had, there may be a chance of him having survived.'

'This may sound horrible what I'm about to say, but... would we even want to see him alive? I mean, Mooses.'

'Just don't say that to Ida,' Roar smirked.

'I won't, trust me. But we saw what a controversial character he was, and I wasn't convinced about the purity and goodness of his deeds.'

'Well, we must remember that, at that particular time, the Lord of Herrings was also seen as an evil figure. It could easily be me lying at the bottom of the lake and not Gustav.'

'I guess, we were lucky. But try explaining that to someone who wasn't there.'

'They only have to trust our word.'

'Or no words at all,' Sven said gravely.

'What do you mean?' Roar asked.

'I'd suggest we keep this to ourselves for the time being.'

'But, since Ida knows about Mooses, what's going to happen when she wakes up and finds out that we haven't even told her mother?'

'Maybe Ida... cannot remember?' Sven said hesitatingly.

'It still would be nice for her to make a full recovery, right?'

'Of course, you're right. How silly of me to even think that way.'

Roar sighed, and handed the photo back to Sven. 'Didn't really see any of this coming.'

'I didn't mean to ruin your big night.' Sven gave a subtle smile. 'How was it, then? What did I miss?'

'Considering that I have never done anything like this before, it went well, I guess. It was a full house. Even your mother came.'

'How did that go?' Sven asked, genuinely delighted.

'We barely spoke. It's still difficult.'

'I cannot even imagine.'

'By the way, when was the last time you visited her?'

'I saw her at the hospital when Ida was admitted.'

'But at her place?'

Sven tried to think, but couldn't remember.

'I know it's not my business anymore, but I don't want her to be alone,' said Roar. 'And she has never really been a socialite, anyway.'

'How do we know if she's alone? Times may have changed.'

'Unless, of course, she's seeing someone.'

'Me and Mum never talk about those things.'

'Anyway, my point is that you're her only child. Birgget might feel a bit lonely. I think you should go and visit her.'

'I will,' Sven replied. 'Tomorrow.'

Roar gave him a satisfied nod, and picked up the cloth. 'Let's finish the kitchen, then, so we'll get out of here before dawn.'

Chapter 18

BACK TO REALITY

Jaaku's journey home was longer and windier, yet gravel-free. The tundra, in which the subsoil was permanently frozen, was only accessible by vehicles such as snowmobiles or kicksleds like his. Not even the tsunami was able to thaw the ice underneath his modest igloo-like dwelling. The natural shift or flow of the glacier had been slow enough over the years, making it possible for Jaaku to live in the same spot for almost a decade. And now, with Marjukka there by his side, the place felt cosier than ever. Only rising average temperatures posed a threat to the young couple's future, who didn't look forward to those forthcoming summer months, when the glistening walls softened, and the floor underneath sank. Gladly, though, the cold winter always came, refreezing the parts of their home that were on the brink of melting.

Once Jaaku had parked his kicksled in the front, he then tried to sneak quietly inside, not wanting to wake Marjukka up. Instantly, though, in her fluffy white night gown and furry polar bear slippers, she stood greeting him in the front room.

'Where have you been?' she sleepily enquired.

'I stopped at the bar.' Jaaku tried to kiss her on the cheek, but she pulled back.

'It's two o'clock in the morning?'

'I know. It's early. They close at four.' His cheeky smile froze quickly, though, as the joke obviously didn't land well.

'You didn't pick up the phone.' She jabbed her finger into his chest. 'I tried to ring you like a hundred times.'

'The battery must have died.'

'Show me,' she grunted. 'Show me your phone!'

He sighed tiredly, rotated himself away from her fingertip and walked past her to the living room.

However, she followed, interrogating him. 'You are hiding something from me.'

Jaaku slouched on a pile of reindeer skins, took out his phone and swung it over his head. 'Have a look then.'

Hesitantly, she went to grab the phone off him, and tried to switch it on. But nothing happened. 'Fine. But you could have at least come home earlier. I was expecting you for dinner. I made salmon.'

'Where did you get that from?' Jaaku asked, dumbfounded.

'Supermarket. Where else?'

'We don't need to rely on their Chinese fish anymore. The lake has fish again. Sven and Roar have already retrieved some of it from this secret pond to lure Wolferring. The other fishermen are totally unaware of what's going on. They just think that the lake is somehow miraculously recovering.'

She came to sit beside him. 'You want to fish again?'

'What else would I do?' he said desperately.

'I don't want you to go out on the lake anymore. It's dangerous.'

'I don't know. I've been making these homemade pies now for three months and it's making me sick. I feel like this whole place stinks of minced meat.'

'It's good business.'

He shook his head. 'Life's not all about business or money – it's what you really enjoy doing.'

'You sound like Sven now. Doesn't he always go on about "Doing what you really love"?' she snorted mockingly. 'Just remember that you're not like him. Besides, we have to be realistic. We have bills to pay.'

'Sven and I are very different.' It was the first time Jaaku admitted that out loud. If the two things – enjoying the same wodka and an interest in fishing – were taken away, there wouldn't be that many other commonalities left.

'Why not try and find your own thing? What is it that you really want to do?' She realised she had never heard him say that directly, and neither she had dared to ask.

The question, however, silenced Jaaku. He had been asking the same question from himself for as long as he remembered; as long as he'd known Sven. He was so used to following Sven's lead that he lacked the courage to go and discover his own path. Was there one? There was only hunting, which was a passion he wasn't open about, even with Marjukka.

'Think about it.' She handed back his phone and stood up. 'Would you like to drink something hot? Or have you drunk enough?'

Jaaku grinned. 'Shower is what I need.'

'I'm sorry to tell you, but the shower stopped working after I had rinsed my conditioner off.' Marjukka gave him a sympathetic look. 'So, it's wet wipes until we get a plumber to come in.'

He took a deep breath, still smelling that stuffy and musty bunker on his clothes and skin.

'Actually, I've been meaning to bring this up, that...' She carefully phrased the sentence. 'Maybe we could start looking for a new place?'

'Why? What's wrong with this place?'

'It's an igloo, Jaaku! We have to think about our future. What if we ever have children? We can't raise a child in an...' She stopped, not wanting to regret what she was about to say. She knew that Jaaku had grown up in one himself.

'I see,' he snorted.

'I didn't mean...'

'It's fine,' he stood up, and moped to the bedroom. 'I need to think about that.'

She followed him to the doorway, while explaining. 'What I mean is, not just raising a family here, but also you can't really run a pie-making business from an igloo much longer, can you?'

He didn't respond to her last remark, but instead stretched out on the bedspread, still wearing his overcoat. He turned to his side, closed his eyes and wished that answers to his questions and doubts would arrive with the sunrise and the new day.

Chapter 19

BIRGGET'S REVENGE

Birgget put the last touches of parmesan cheese on top of a macaroni casserole, and then placed the tray in the cast iron oven. She felt Sven's stare as he sat behind her on a wooden kitchen bench.

'What?'

'Italian cooking?' he smirked.

'You know very well that I've done this same dish since you were a child. I got the recipe from... an old friend of mine.' She slammed the oven door shut. 'Let that bake for thirty to forty minutes.'

'Speaking of Italian food, how was the restaurant opening last night? Dad said you went there.'

Hesitatingly, his mother went to the fridge, but didn't take anything out. She stared at the half-empty shelves. 'What the Italians have to do with it?'

'It used to be Lumbardi's restaurant. You can still smell pizza in there.'

'Ah. I see.' Birgget sighed in relief. She took a milk carton out, which immediately slipped out of her hand and onto the floor. '*Cazzo!*' she cursed.

'Mum! Are you alright?' Sven jumped up and fetched a cloth from the sink.

'Yes!' She yanked the cloth from his hand. 'Don't worry. I've got this.' She knelt down to wipe the milk off the floor. 'So, about the restaurant... The pike was overcooked and he could have added a few more vegetables and other sides with the dishes.'

'Okay. But otherwise, it went well?'

'Surely, he wanted you to be there.'

'I know. I...'

'You were at the hospital?' she guessed.

'No.'

'It's not really my business,' she sighed, and placed the spilled milk carton on the kitchen top.

'I did make it to the restaurant, but really late. Dad was still there.'

'Alone?'

'With Irmeli. You remember, that old... I mean, sorry, not old...'

'She's about my age,' Birgget interrupted judgingly.

'You know what I mean.'

'Not really,' she grunted. 'So, she was still there?'

Sven sensed his mother's dismay. 'She works there.'

Birgget took a deep breath, then went to sit at the rustic table. 'Since you seem fairly grown up now, I wanna tell you something that I've kept inside for a long, long time.'

'Fairly?' he snorted.

'Thirty years old soon. Imagine. Where all this time went? I remember like yesterday how you were a little boy. You could barely climb on that bench. By the way, did you know we got this dining set from my great-grandparents?'

He shook his head and sat down opposite her, more interested to hear the essentials. 'Tell me what?'

'Irmeli, this "old" waitress, and your father...' She stopped to compose herself before finishing the sentence. 'They used to have an affair.'

Sven's jaw dropped. 'That's unbelievable.'

'It was a long time ago.'

'Before you two got together?'

Subtly, she shook her head.

'So, was yours... like a revenge?' Sven quickly connected the dots.

'What are you talking about?'

He then realised that she doesn't know that he knew about her and Lumbardi Martello's affair. 'Dad told me about you and... the Italian.'

'How convenient!' she gasped, and looked longingly out of the window. Her mind drifted away somewhere in the distant past; to a place unknown to others. 'You're right. Roar was first. Mine was the revenge.'

'So, Dad's been lying all this time?'

'Roar wouldn't lie to you. He just hasn't told you everything. He wants to be your hero. To appear better than he was; someone you can look up to. Parents do that. Unfortunately, he had his flaws, like all of us have. And some of the mistakes may partly be the reason he never wanted to come back from the lake.'

'You think so?' said Sven. 'You don't believe it was his "calling" as the Lord of Herrings that kept him away all those years?'

'As much as I want to believe in magic tricks, time has made me quite realistic,' Birgget replied. 'There is no hocus-pocus in this life; only cold facts.'

'But, we saw him with our bare eyes doing everything... flying up in the air with that boat, shooting laser beams...'

'Sometimes, people can see what they want to see,' said Birgget. 'We also know that you, Jaaku, and especially Viljo, must have had a few drinks that night.'

'Are you saying that we were drunk? That none of that really happened? The floods, fish disappearing...'

'I didn't mean it that way. I'm only saying that all we saw, the rest of us, was an aged and wrinkled man returning after having disappeared for sixteen years. He was like a sad shadow of the man I remembered him to be, and as far from a magical wizard as anyone can be.'

'I can't believe you don't trust me.'

'Of course, I do. But it's just... so much to take in. I hope you understand.'

'It is, for all of us.'

A brief silence followed before Birgget continued. 'But, looking at Roar now, and in the restaurant last night, he's clearly getting back on his feet. He looked quite smart, to be honest. But then that old trout... I'm sorry.'

She even shocked herself by speaking so outrageously in front of her son. Hence, she stood up quickly, and went to check through the oven glass the state of the macaroni casserole. The top part was getting a light brown coating from the grated cheese, which had melted into one, single layer. It was as if the entire tray was covered with a light brown blanket, hanging slightly over the edges on each side. She wore the mitts and retrieved the hot dish. The smell of basil, thyme and rosemary wafted around the room.

'Won't be much longer.' Birgget pushed the tray back inside.

Meanwhile, Sven had become slightly paralysed from the amount of new information he had to process within such a short period of time. Talking without any reservations, even to people of his own age group, like Ida or Jaaku, was sometimes an insurmountable task. Whereas now, it was his mother sharing details of such a sensitive nature, making him realise that even his own parents were human beings, imperfect, with their own weaknesses for all things immoral.

Out of the corner of her eye, Birgget saw him staring straight at the wall. Hence, she decided to ease the conversation. 'But it's all in the past now. None of it matters anymore.'

'Why are we having this conversation then?'

'I thought you oughta to know both sides of the story.'

'Well, now I know. Case closed,' Sven said promptly. 'So, you're fine with Dad and Irmeli working together, then?'

'Yes. Of course!' Aggressively swinging open the oven door, Birgget pulled out the tray and dropped the dish on top of the stove. Then she took a serving spoon and sank it in the middle of the casserole, scraping the bottom loudly. She chucked big lumps of half-cooked casserole on two plates, like frustrated prison caterers when they serve inmates.

'Are you sure it's ready?' Sven asked delicately.

'It is. We eat now!' She slid the steaming plate in front of him, while trying to restrain her emotions. She didn't fully understand what was happening to her. Her feelings towards Roar were supposed to have been buried and forgotten a long time ago. Yet, why did his behaviour bother her so much?

Chapter 20

UNWANTED SOLITUDE

'It's been almost two weeks, love,' Sven spoke softly by Ida's bedside. 'I miss you at home. It is too quiet. So quiet that I've started speaking to your pets, like I'm speaking to you now. It's weird. They haven't responded, yet. I mean, they have, in their own ways, but not like the animals in the sanctuary.'

He let out a nervous chuckle.

'Normally, I enjoy the silence. It's what I've always wanted; what I've always looked for in life. Until now. I've learnt that there can be too much of it. Without your presence, silence has become too much to bear. Solitude by choice can make a good friend, yet solitude by force can become your worst enemy.'

He stopped to wonder if the last sentence was a quote from someone famous, or if he was just making things up under pressure. Slightly embarrassed, he looked over his shoulder to make sure no one could hear him pouring his heart out. Even though the door behind them was firmly shut, he decided to shift away from such sensitive subjects to something lighter and more familiar. The redness in his cheeks began to fade.

'Apparently, the number of fish in the lake is in decline again. The fishermen are talking. They either fish too fast, or it's Wolferring's work. I don't know if we should just go after it straight away, or keep retrieving more fish from the pond. I've been trying to persuade Jaaku to come along, but I'm not sure about him anymore. Apparently, he's busy making those pies.

But I don't think that's the real reason. Marjukka may be the one stopping him. Or he's just simply afraid. I doubt Viljo wants to be involved, either. He's too old, anyway, somewhere between eighty and hundred. He has officially retired. And my dad, well, he's got the restaurant now. That's taking a lot of his time. Although, I'm not fully convinced that working in hospitality is what he really wants to do. But he's trying to reassure everyone that it is; that he gets close enough to fish and fishing only by running a lakefood restaurant. What a load of... crab!'

Experiencing such strong emotions – which he could never demonstrate in the presence of another, conscious person – exhausted him. He had to take a deep breath to calm himself down.

'It's weird, isn't it?' he continued. 'Everything has changed. And I think... I'm afraid, too. I really don't know what the best thing is to do. What do you think? Please say something.' He swallowed his sadness. 'We were supposed to be the lucky ones, right? We always were. But then something happened; only bad things.'

He shed a tear, while squeezing her hand tighter. 'You remember when I had just won the ice fishing championship and we were about to get married? Or when we drove away from Örebröre together on your snowmobile and finally got married in Lasi Vekasi? If there were any moments in life I could return to, those would be the two. Promise me, we'll have plenty more moments like that. Promise.'

Chapter 21

A PROPER JOB

After a successful opening week, Roar had to face the harsh realities of the hospitality industry. By Thursday the second week, one diner – a large, bearded man, wearing a lumberjack shirt and a cap – had come in. He sat in the farthest corner, drinking a cup of coffee, when Ronja came from the kitchen, carrying a bowl of hot salmon soup – the cheapest thing on the menu money could buy.

Then the front door opened, and someone entered the foyer. *Another customer?* Ronja thought excitedly. She rushed to serve the soup, spilling some of it on the table, in front of the only paying customer.

'Enjoy,' she said briefly, her eyes already glued to the entrance.

To her disappointment, though, the person stepping in was Sven, who stopped by the reception, obeying the 'Wait to be seated' sign.

'Good afternoon, sir. I'll be with you in a second,' Ronja said formally, making it seem as if Sven was just any normal customer. As she walked up to him, she kept up appearances. 'Where would you like to sit?'

Sven looked at her dumbfounded. 'I just needed to speak to my dad.'

She sighed, and leant over to whisper. 'Are you sure you don't want anything? It's been a very quiet week.'

He wiggled uncomfortably, like those vultures who visit the businesses of friends, relatives or acquaintances, but don't want to spend any money there because they automatically assume they will get things for free.

'Maybe some coffee, then,' Sven said under pressure, not knowing if he was expected to pay for it. He certainly hoped not.

'Great! You can take a seat here.' Ronja led him to the nearest and most draughty table by the window. Having him seated exactly there, in the most visible spot, made the place seem more popular to anyone walking past on the street – a common system used by many waiters in the industry to lure new customers in. However, the problem was that the streets in Pihtamo were empty most of the year, anyway.

As Sven reluctantly waited at the table, he discreetly glanced at the man slurping his soup. It was a common thing to do in a small town like Pihtamo. Since most of the population knew each other wherever they went, they always wanted to check if there was anyone around them they might recognise – not wanting to make it obvious, though, in case they made eye contact with someone unwanted. It was the complete opposite of what those living in bigger cities did, where avoiding eye contact was the norm. How big the population had to be for that change in behaviour to happen, no one knew. A hundred thousand? A million?

In this particular case, one of them knew the other. The bearded man immediately recognised Sven, and gave him a subtle nod. However, Sven looked away, not knowing who the man was. He had never learnt to deal with the fame his success in ice fishing had brought.

As Ronja came through the kitchen door with his coffee, some giggles followed through from the gap. It wasn't Ronja's voice, but some other female's. Sven stretched his neck to hear better, before the door shut behind her.

'Here's your coffee, sir.' Ronja, still pretending that Sven was a stranger, lowered the cup in front of him.

'Thank you, but you don't really need to call me that,' he said, while curiously peering through the kitchen hatch. He couldn't see anyone, but only heard a muffled conversation between a man and a woman.

'That's four fifty.' Ronja pulled out a card reader. 'Cash or card?'

Eyes widened, Sven turned to her, while tapping the side pockets of his jacket. 'I... actually didn't bring my wallet.' He stood up. 'Let me speak to my dad. He will lend me some,' he said and headed towards the kitchen.

Ronja anxiously followed him. 'It's probably better not to go in there. It's very busy in the kitchen at the moment.'

'Busy? For what?' Sven snorted.

The bearded man lowered his soup plate, while curiously observing how the scene developed.

'For... lunch hour rush,' Ronja muttered.

But Sven was already at the kitchen door, pulling it wide open. 'You think it's gonna get busier today?' he asked doubtfully, looking back over his shoulder, and entered.

The first thing he saw was Roar and Irmeli together, stirring a big silver pot. The pair immediately halted their intimate cooking session. Roar turned around and took a step away from Irmeli.

'It usually does,' he said with conviction, as if nothing unusual was happening.

Irmeli, with her blushing cheeks, thought it was better to leave the men alone. She swung past Sven, and away from the kitchen to the dining area, with Ronja right behind her.

'Come in.' Roar gestured to Sven, and then continued stirring the pot. 'People tend to eat their breakfasts at home, but around midday we should get a few regulars in.' He used the wooden spoon in his hand to taste their cooking. The aromas of cinnamon and honey spread in the air. 'This is nice. Irmeli really knows how to make a good porridge.'

'I bet she does,' Sven snorted.

'Do you wanna try?'

'I already had breakfast.' Sven shook his head. 'Are you gonna serve porridge for lunch?'

Roar had stopped stirring the porridge, while sensing Sven's discontent. 'So, how is the baby?' he asked, trying to steer the conversation away from what Sven just had to witness.

'Miraculously, the baby's doing fine. There were no complications during the C-section. But now, only time will tell. Ida's condition is more stable than mine. I had to get out of the hospital to get some fresh air.'

'I wish there was something I could do to help.'

Sven hesitated for a moment. 'There is actually one thing. I was wondering... if you need any help around here?'

'In the kitchen?'

'Or restaurant. I can do anything.'

Roar couldn't believe what he was hearing. 'You mean, like actual work?'

'Why not?'

'Well, I guess... you can always go fishing and supply the restaurant with some quality herrings. You know very well where to catch those, don't you?' Roar winked.

Sven smiled uncomfortably, and then looked down to his shoelaces. 'I was thinking... anything else but fishing, just to get my mind off from all the usual things. In fact, I have considered retiring from fishing.'

Roar dropped the spoon in the pot. 'You must be joking? You're too young and good to give up this early.'

'I'm not giving up.' Sven raised his gaze again. 'I just don't know if I want it anymore. I think, it's time to move on. Besides, I have to be realistic. I have a family to look after now...'

'So, did I,' Roar interrupted.

'Yes, you did. And look what happened,' Sven replied with a slightly judgemental tone.

Roar immediately got the message – that Sven was trying his utmost not to repeat his father's mistakes.

'Shoot yourself, then,' he said. 'As long as you realise that just any random, "normal" job may not fulfil your personal desires and ambitions. First, it can feel like a secure option with a comfortably steady income; but, in the end, it can be a helluva long road to travel.'

'It would certainly help with financials.'

Roar sighed. 'I can't really afford to pay you greatly, until the business is really booming. We're still in early stages and it's difficult to tell what the future might bring.'

'I don't mind.'

'Fine.' Roar gave himself a moment to think, before continuing, 'We always need someone to clear the tables, pick up finished plates, wash the dishes and so on. Like a kitchen hand. I know, it's nothing fancy or glamorous.'

'Sounds great,' Sven said without hesitation.

'Just be prepared for one thing,' said Roar. 'I'm not saying that this will happen, but there's a chance. Because you have this kind of a celebrity status in Pihtamo, people might think...'

'I don't care what people think,' Sven interrupted. 'I genuinely wanna do this. Hopefully, it will also take my mind away from Ida.'

'Okay, okay,' Roar replied doubtfully. 'So, if you're working, who's gonna look after the baby then?'

'I'll speak to Mum.'

'Did you go and see her?'

'Yes. She told me some interesting stories about the relationships different people in Pihtamo have had,' Sven said vaguely.

'Like what?'

'I'll tell you later. When can I start here?'

'When can you?'

'Tomorrow?'

'See you in the morning at five.' Roar picked up the spoon and returned to stirring the pot.

As Sven walked out of the kitchen, his nerves kicked in – even though the situation he was putting himself into wasn't supposed to be that unfamiliar. Early mornings and working with fish were exactly the two things he had been used to all of his life. What could possibly go wrong?

Amongst the many thoughts puzzling his mind, there was one thing in particular he was curious about. He turned around and returned to the kitchen door. 'Can I ask you something?'

'Depends,' Roar smirked, while tasting the porridge again.

'Is this restaurant business filling your ambitions? Do you feel like you're doing the right thing?'

Roar chuckled uncomfortably. 'Don't be late.'

Chapter 22

A RESTAURANT SOAP

Seconds after Sven had tied the apron around his waist for the first time, Irmeli was already eager to give him direct orders.

'Could you clear tables three and five?'

She had started working in the restaurant only a couple of weeks before him, yet seemed much more superior. She was over twenty years senior to him, which seemed to give her that extra amount of confidence to be this bossy, on this first day of his first-ever proper job. Anyway, at this early stage, he'd rather follow instructions than give them.

Filled with satisfaction, Irmeli followed from a distance, watching how he stumbled into the dining area, like a young Bambi trying to walk on ice. The tables had turned; the champion had become her subordinate.

A high stack of dirty plates and glasses was a completely new challenge for him. He tied the string of his apron tighter around his back, and rolled up his sleeves. He had seen how the most skilled waiters can carry three or four plates on each arm. Ambitiously, he attempted something similar.

Not taking any notice of the inquisitive looks from the guests, he took one plate in his hand and, with his other hand, put a second plate on the forearm, which he then tried to hold steady with his elbow pit. Already, some mustard and cranberry sauce dirtied his white shirt sleeve. When he tried to place the third plate directly on top of the plate already in his hand, the plate from underneath his elbow slid away and smashed, broken on the floor. As a consequence, the two other plates also slipped from his sweaty hands, ending up as shards on the same pile.

The loud noise drew the attention of two male diners sitting at the table at the opposite end of the restaurant. They whispered to each other while pointing at Sven. Discreetly, Sven looked in their direction. One of the men, who wore an orange cap and had a big, blond moustache, raised his arm up and clicked his fingers.

'Excuse me. Waitress!' he called out, grinning.

Sven bent down to clean the mess and pretended not to hear. He pulled out a wiping cloth from his belt. He glanced up to see if there were any signs of Irmeli or Ronja, who could come and save him.

But there wasn't. He was alone in the dining area with the two customers.

'Hey, I'm talking to you.' The moustached man kept pestering him. 'We want to pay for our food.'

Sven got up, but kept his head down. 'I'll get someone to bring you the bill.' Quickly, he turned away and headed in the opposite direction.

'You don't know how to use the card machine, champion?' the man chuckled.

With nothing to give back, Sven could only take the hit and retreat to the kitchen, where he found Roar talking to Christian by the back entrance.

Christian leant on the door frame, flicking his long blond hair. He looked at Sven from head to toe. 'I can see you have a new kitchen hand.'

'What the hell is he doing here?' said Sven.

'Christian... is supplying us with some... fish,' Roar stuttered.

Sven couldn't believe what he was hearing. 'He's fishing for you? For this restaurant?!'

'Will you excuse us?' Roar gestured for Christian to step outside.

'See you next week then, the same time,' said Christian. Before shutting the door behind him, he gave Sven an arrogant grin.

Once Christian was gone, Roar carefully approached Sven.

'Let me explain,' Roar started. 'You see, hardly anyone is fishing anymore. All my time goes running this joint. You said you might retire. And who knows what Jaaku is up to? So, I had to rely on Christian, since he's one of the only crazy fishermen still out there who's not bothered about Wolferring, or anything else.'

Sven shook his head in disbelief. 'You don't know him. He's doing this for only one reason; to get back at me. Don't you understand?'

'I would have asked you, but I thought you didn't want to fish anymore. You said it yourself. You want change. That's why you came to work in this restaurant, right?'

'Sure. This is what I want,' Sven murmured sarcastically.

'This is not so bad.'

Sven feared that what he was about to say next wouldn't turn out well. But he had the urge to say it, anyway. 'Is this what YOU want? To run a restaurant? You're the all-time fisherman. The greatest! You don't need to hide in here. What are you afraid of?'

Sven's outburst could be heard all the way to the dining area, where a new customer just entering the restaurant immediately decided to step out.

'Outside!' Roar grabbed Sven's arm and escorted him – like a child that was being disciplined – through the same backdoor Christian had just exited.

In the parking lot behind the restaurant, however, another unexpected surprise was waiting: Lumbardi Martello, standing with a cigarette in his hand and wearing a chef's uniform.

'*Eee...* What's the matter?' Lumbardi asked, and puffed up.

'Just having a father-son conversation,' Roar said, while feeling like he needed to explain to Sven even more about what was happening. 'Öö... Lumbardi is my new head chef. Just started today, like you.'

Sven's jaw dropped. 'Him? Of all the people?'

Roar sighed, and pulled Sven further away from Lumbardi. 'He's the best there is. His exotic cooking style is loved by all of Pihtamo.'

'Loved? Didn't his business go bust?' Sven snorted.

'*Eee...*' Lumbardi interrupted from the distance, before losing his train of thought.

Roar lowered his voice. 'It made no sense to leave him out of the restaurant business. I was supposed to work in the kitchen, but I can't. I am not a great cook, the restaurant is getting busier, and I have managerial duties to run. Besides, I have had to import lot of fish from far away, even from China. People in Pihtamo are very picky and they can taste if something is not local. That's why I need Lumbardi, to spice up the dishes so the customers wouldn't taste the difference.'

'*Si*. The best aromas straight from *Italia!*' Lumbardi added, while huffing his cigarette.

'This restaurant is like a bloody Temptation Island,' said Sven, moving closer to Roar so that he could whisper. 'You know damn well his spices are not the only thing he's loved by.'

'Please,' Roar said. 'That was a long time ago. Lumbardi and I have talked about the past and everything is fine now. We have buried the hatchet.'

'*Eee.*' Lumbardi interrupted again. He stepped closer to the men and offered his hand to Sven. 'Lovely wedding ceremony you had. How is your beautiful bride? *Bella!*'

His Arctic stiffness long gone, Sven ignored Lumbardi's gesture, and passionately rushed back inside, Roar on his tail. Sven was about to explode, but didn't know how.

'Is this really what you want? To run a restaurant with everyone's ex-lovers involved?'

'I knew you wouldn't understand,' Roar sighed. 'Pihtamo is a very small community. We have to rely on each other. It's better that way, rather than staying on bad terms, while doing poor business. You have to use whoever is available. You can't pick and choose.'

'Are you still on some magic mushrooms?' Sven said bitterly. 'Since when did you become so business-minded? Are you saying that you don't miss the waters, the smell of fish, the excitement of catching something, seeing the early sunrise in the horizon, hearing nothing but silence?'

'It's... complicated,' Roar said longingly. 'I really cannot see any other choice. You understand that now it's only us two. And

I'm not sure if you're completely... yourself... because of what happened to Ida.'

'Well, who would be?' Sven grunted.

'Yes. And that's why I think it's not wise for us to go out there right now. Whereas, Christian may keep on fishing since he has nothing to lose.'

'What have we got to lose? I thought I had everything when I found you and when Ida was fine. But now, suddenly, everything has turned upside down. Can it really get much worse than this?'

'Don't speak nonsense. You have a healthy baby. And Ida will come back soon. But being angry at me, or Christian, is not going to bring her back any faster. And as to my situation... well, I have a business to run here. If you think your heart is in the right place to go out there on the lake and get my restaurant some fish, please do it. I would prefer you doing it, of course. You're my son. But do it for the right reasons. And bearing in mind, that you may have to face Wolferring out there, and you may have to face it alone. And I would never forgive myself if something bad was to happen to you. Never.'

Roar paused for a moment, and changed to a softer tone.

'If I were you, though, I would rather concentrate on what is important right now, and that is, to stay beside Ida and the baby. That's where you'll need to be. If you wanna get your thoughts away from it all, you're always more than welcome to come here, work with me and talk – as we're doing right now.'

Sven's mind calmed the more he listened to Roar. 'So, hypothetically, if I was to supply you fish, what about Christian then? Would you keep him as well?'

'Well, the business seems to be picking up every day, so having two fishermen wouldn't be such a bad idea,' Roar carefully suggested.

'May I ask, where is Christian catching all the fish?'

Roar looked sheepishly to the floor. 'Well, you see, that's another thing. Because the business started so slowly and it was overly expensive to acquire fish from anywhere further afield, I thought it was easiest and the most economical to... share the location of the pond with him.'

'Have you gone absolutely mad?' cried Sven, his calmness

being just a thing of the past. 'You gave me grief for telling Jaaku, and now you tell my biggest enemy!'

'I had no choice. I have to survive.'

Sven untied his apron and let it drop to the floor. 'It's better you work with your new friends, then. I'm out!'

Chapter 23

FREE-FLOWING SUMMARY

'So, I got myself a proper job. Finally. Can you believe it?' Seemingly more nervous than during his previous visits, Sven strolled around Ida's hospital bed. 'I was helping Dad out in the restaurant. You should be proud of me.'

He paused by the window, and saw green grass making its appearance outside on the ground after a long winter. 'Unfortunately, my assignment didn't last long. A couple of hours, in fact... I just don't think I can work with him and the people around him. And the customers were just pure evil. A couple of diners from the ice fishing circuit recognised me. They were laughing their faces off when they saw me clearing tables. They mockingly called me the "champion" and all sorts. Who are they to tell me what I should do? I can do whatever I want, right? Right?'

He didn't let her unresponsive state discourage him from going on. 'I hated to be in that situation. For the first time ever, it sucks that everyone here knows each other. When you're doing great, people love you and pat your back. But when you're having a rough patch, they turn their backs to you. Now I understand why some people – like your sisters – leave this place and would rather be a small fish in a big pond.'

Clenching his fists in anger, Sven sat down beside Ida, still with so much left to say. 'Speaking about fish and ponds... This is actually what I wanted to tell you today: Dad is using Christian, of all people, to supply fish from the pond to his restaurant. The pond was supposed to be a well-kept secret!'

His frustration grew the more he spoke. 'And that's not everything. This is so messed up... He went to hire Lumbardi Martello as his head chef! You know, that has-been Italian singer and heartbreaker who also sang at our wedding, and who was the previous owner of the restaurant, until the floods sealed his bankruptcy. I never told you, but Mr Martello and my mum had an affair, way before I was born. Dad knows about it, but apparently has no hard feelings. He's just been so desperate to find a decent chef. To be fair, there aren't that many around. I mean, people here know how to cook, but not many bother doing it professionally. So, he had to settle for Lumbardi and his controversial methods. He always uses too many spices and herbs... Of course, I wish success for Dad's business, but I fear that people just don't wanna eat there. The menu is going to be too exotic again, which was the problem in Lumbardi's own restaurant. I just fear that Lumbardi will mess up Dad's life again...'

After taking a breath, Sven's tone became more serious. 'I don't think he really understands what he is doing right now. He also went and hired Irmeli as the waitress... I'm so sorry, honey. I'm blabbering on about this family drama. If you were conscious, I'm not sure how you'd take all this, because now it gets really crazy. It's been a very eye-opening couple of weeks for me. Apparently, Irmeli and Dad had an affair, a long time ago, even before Lumbardi and Mum. So, Dad's not an angel, either. And, as a result of his open-minded, yet peculiar, recruitment policies, both his and Mum's ex-lovers are working in the restaurant. I don't understand why he's doing it!'

Sven even shocked himself with this emotional reaction. Hence, he lowered his voice, as he didn't want the whole ward to hear about their complex family background.

'I know, Pihtamo has a shortage of workforce and sometimes you have to hire people you are already connected with in various ways, but do they all have to have such an intimate history with one another? It has even made me worry if we're gonna have these same problems one day. Or maybe there's a way to avoid them.'

He was hoping for any reaction or response from Ida, but in vain. 'Anyway, I don't think Dad quite understands how his actions are affecting the others around him. He has been away for a long time, and he has no clue how we all feel about each other. He must be lonely, as well. Maybe that's why he's gathering just anyone available around him, even old sweethearts. Most of his old friends and fishermen buddies have moved on. Or they don't quite trust him, because of what happened between him and Carl, and because he miraculously came back from the dead. Birgget doesn't really talk to him, either. It's been too long and difficult for them, and especially now after Dad's twisted staffing choices. I may be his only, real, friend. I guess I can call him that, a friend, even though he is my father. Hopefully, soon, he will have you as another friend. And his granddaughter.'

Just the thought of having the whole family, all generations, together, warmed his heart.

'I don't quite understand what got into me. I'm talking like a woman or a gay man. I've never felt this open, and I haven't even had that many drinks. It feels so liberating and easy to talk when no one is around. Well, of course, you are here. But you know what I mean. I hope I can talk like this even when you are awake. I love you so much and I miss you.'

He gently touched her cold cheek. 'By the way, Birgget has been so helpful with the baby. The baby has your eyes and my nose...'

Slowly, the door to the room opened, interrupting his flow of speech. The nurse stepped in. 'Mr Sven? I'm afraid the visiting hours are over. We have to ask you to come back tomorrow again, the same time.'

Chapter 24

YOU DON'T CHOOSE FAMILY; THEY CHOOSE YOU

'She really has your nose.' Birgget circled around her living room, with Sven and Ida's newborn baby in her arms.

'And Ida's eyes,' Sven said, while sitting on the green two-seater sofa. A wool rug made of thick red and yellow threads lay between them on the wooden floor. A ticking of a dark brown antique wall clock filled every quiet moment, until the baby gurgled again.

'A boy you could take ice fishing with you,' Birgget smirked. 'What's your plan for a girl?'

'Don't be ridiculous, Mum. There are female ice fishers, too.' Sven's innocent remark made his mother's face turn sour. Immediately, he knew who she was thinking about. Roar and Irmeli's affair wasn't necessarily buried in the past, after all. Hence, he felt the pressure to keep talking. 'As long as she is happy with what she will be doing. I won't be forcing her into anything.'

'Gladly, we don't need to worry about that for a while.' Birgget began to feel the weight on her shoulders, even though the baby was only at her tiniest. Yet, the decades had passed and grandparenthood suddenly arrived with new challenges. She remembered parenting a small child and how effortless it had seemed. 'They grow up so fast.' She offered the baby back to Sven, much sooner than expected.

Sven composed himself, while the baby's nostrils faintly whistled in his ear. The warmth and smell of a newborn made him think about Ida, and all the days and hours she was missing out on this pure luxury and joy.

Birgget clocked his downbeat expression. 'So, how does it feel to be a father?'

'A bit too early to say.'

'I really don't mind looking after her. You have so much on your shoulders right now. A new job, Ida in the hospital, the baby...'

'Actually, I quit.'

'You can't really quit parenting,' she laughed. 'That's so funny.'

'My job,' he added gravely. 'I resigned yesterday.'

'But... you only started yesterday!'

'It was too... complicated.'

Birgget sighed. 'I understand that you've been fishing all your life, and working elsewhere may seem difficult at first. But being a kitchen hand should be the easier of all those other "normal" jobs – as you fishers tend to call them.'

'The job itself was no brain surgery. The problem was Dad making the situation in the restaurant complicated. He is surrounding himself with all the wrong people.'

'Tell me about it,' she snorted.

'Apart from having Irmeli there, guess who else he hired? Christian and Lumbardi!'

'Why on earth?' she gasped.

'Who knows? He said that he had no options.'

She walked to the window and pushed a curtain to the side. Bright bursts of daylight shone through a gentle snowfall. 'Having Lumbardi there probably makes sense. You see, your dad is not much of a cook. And running a restaurant around here is a bit hit-and-miss, anyway. At least Lumbardi is one of those rarities who can make something special and out of the ordinary.' She touched the glass of the window with her forefinger, trying to capture a snowflake that was stuck outside.

Her reminiscing some old flames made Sven cringe. 'I bet

he does!'

His comment brought her back from the past. She quickly turned to him. 'But, why didn't he ask you to fish for the restaurant?'

'He kinda did... But I can't do it. Not now.'

'Because of Ida?'

'It's not just that. I think, I don't want to do it anymore.'

'Fishing? I don't believe you.'

'Maybe it's time to change, grow up, like Jaaku always says.' Sven stood up and turned his back to her. He pretended to look at something on the bookcase.

'Well, think about it. Don't rush into any decisions. I know exactly what fish means to you. Maybe now, going fishing could actually help to take your mind off Ida being in the hospital and all that. As I said, in the meantime, I can look after the baby.'

Sven nodded, even though he wasn't really listening to her words. He was instead mesmerised by the wide selection of books on the shelves in front of him. He had never really paid close attention to the spines of these works of art and intellect. He only recognised the Bible, but the rest of the titles he hadn't heard of. There was so much knowledge in the world he never knew about. Ignorance had been his bliss.

'Fishing used to be my escape from everything else,' he said. 'But now, seeing Ida the way she is, all I want is to be close to her. I would never leave her bedside, even if there was another natural disaster.'

'I'm proud of the way you express yourself,' said Birgget. 'Before, you've always been so economical with words. What happened?'

Sven turned away from the wall of books – just looking at them gave him a headache.

A sudden knock on the front door interrupted their deep conversation. Birgget sighed, as she would've been keen to hear more about her son's thoughts.

However, when another knock followed, she decided to get the door.

It was Roar, all windswept and looking tired. 'Is Sven here?' he asked bluntly, and tried to peek over her shoulder. 'I know his kicksled is.'

'We're kind of busy right now,' she hesitated.

However, Roar slammed his palm in the middle of the closing door. 'You could be a bit nicer, considering what happened to me.'

'Fine!' Birgget grunted, and led him in. 'But you can't use that argument forever.'

'For the next sixteen years at least,' he smirked, while following her along the corridor.

'He's there, in the living room with the baby.' She gestured ahead, and stepped aside.

'Thank you. I just want to apologise to him,' he said, and walked past her.

'Only to him?'

Roar stopped, keeping his back to her. 'Who else could I have hired? You?'

'Anyone else than her.'

'Does it really matter anymore, after all these years?'

'Does what matter?' Sven interrupted them as he appeared in the corridor, with the baby in his arms.

'Isn't she gorgeous?' Roar was immediately distracted by the baby's chubby cheeks and sparkling eyes. 'Unbelievable. Suddenly, my own son is a father.'

'That's how the world works,' Birgget snorted, and turned and went into the kitchen.

Sven, not impressed to see Roar either, returned to the living room.

Quickly, Roar kicked his shoes off and followed Sven. The baby chuckled at him, while being totally unaware of all the strange tensions the adults in the house had built between one another over time.

'It never crossed my mind that I'd get to be a grandfather straight away when I return,' said Roar. 'I still remember you as a little boy. It feels like yesterday. How did this happen?'

Sven gave him a blank stare. 'A lot has happened since. Many things have changed; much more than you realise.'

'On the surface, perhaps. But, apart from the younger generation growing and a few more wrinkles on the faces of the elderly, things seem pretty much the way I remember them to be.'

'Many of us have moved on.'

'I'm sorry about what happened in the restaurant, but...'

'No buts after an apology,' Sven snorted.

'I just wanted to explain.'

'Go ahead then.'

'Well, hiring people like Irmeli and Lumbardi are exact examples of how I've moved on. I had buried all those past experiences and I thought others had, as well. But I guess I was wrong. Being taken away for sixteen years helped me to put things into perspective. I had to lose everything to realise what is really important.'

'And what is that, then?'

'Family,' said Roar. 'And whatever happened in the past is past, and none of that matters anymore. We can only learn from our mistakes.'

'But still, working with all of them? That's just wrong.'

'If this is about Christian, I honestly wasn't aware of your relationship with him.'

'You shouldn't have hired him, Dad.'

'If I'd known, I would have used someone else. Not only because it was hurting you, but because he hasn't turned up for last three days to deliver fish. We are in trouble. I thought that I could trust him, but that was a big mistake. Most of the menu, obviously, has fish-based dishes and we haven't got enough stock. I can't get a hold of him. It's like he has disappeared into thin air.'

Sven wanted to smile, yet managed to keep the small sense of victory inside him for the sake of Roar and his struggling business.

'Christian is gone?' Birgget poked her head out of the kitchen. She couldn't help eavesdropping. 'Doesn't sound like him.'

'Sounds exactly like him,' Sven snorted. 'That privileged fool has had even fewer proper jobs than I have. What does he know about real life?'

Birgget stepped in, sounding defensive. 'I understand your

feelings, but Christian is a decent boy and would never disappear like that. He must have been honoured to work for Roar.'

'A peculiar way to honour someone,' Sven said sarcastically.

Birgget gave both men a serious stare. 'You must go and look for him.'

'Over my dead body!' Sven laughed. 'A grown man that has been away for three days is not really a national crisis.'

'I'll see what I can do,' Roar replied more diplomatically.

'You must need someone to fish for you, then?' Birgget pondered.

Roar sheepishly avoided eye contact with Sven. 'Technically, yes.'

'Is that why you came here?' Sven asked, disappointment in his voice. 'To ask me to fish for you, because you lost Christian?'

'I understand if you don't want to do it,' Roar replied promptly, and took sneaky steps towards the corridor. 'Anyway, it was nice to see the baby. She's absolutely gorgeous. Take my best wishes to Ida. I'm sorry about everything.'

He put on his shoes and walked to the front door. Sven and Birgget followed him. As Roar grabbed the handle, he looked back at them. 'By the way, Yetilag was asking for you, Sven. You haven't visited the animals since their sanctuary was opened. They miss you.'

With a sigh, Roar stepped out of the house to face the increasingly heavy snowfall. Bitterly, he tried to understand the emotions that human relationships can bring – something the invincible Lord of Herrings didn't have to deal with. As lonely as his life may have been out on the lake for all those years, at least he was under a spell that lifted him above all these energy-consuming controversies within the world of families.

Sven rushed to the window to watch his father leaving on his kicksled. As Roar pressed his head down, his upper back slightly curved. Tired and suddenly aged, Roar reminded him again of someone else: Sven's grandfather.

It struck Sven how he could not even comprehend what it was like to have missed out sixteen years of the modern life that moves on so fast. The most sensible way to catch up the lost time was to do it in good terms. But neither him nor Roar could see where to start and how to build that trust again.

Chapter 25

THE INTELLECT
ANIMAL SANCTUARY

When Erm...ine, the hesitant stoat, appeared from the dark forest and spoke words and language understood by Sven, Jaaku and Viljo, the men thought they were victims of some lousy prank. Soon after, the floods exposed more escaping animals who expressed themselves intelligibly, and the men never looked at fauna the same way again.

Creating a sanctuary on a no-man's land, about thirty kilometres north from New Pihtamo, was initially proposed by the same three men. They all shared a common fear: if the whole world was to find out about these unique species, the consequences would be catastrophic.

A discreet entrance at the end of a winding, private road led to the entrance gates that were camouflaged against the surrounding spruce forest. The impact of the volcano extended on this fertile haven, covering over five hundred acres of secure and protected land, and introducing nutrient vegetation that could be directly consumed by its most recent inhabitants. The discovery of about a dozen mammals and rodents portraying human traits was a highly sensitive secret within the community – only a few, carefully chosen individuals knew about their existence.

For most of these so-called animals, the likelihood of

becoming a lab rat or a victim of some sort of witch-hunt was high. Jaaku, who was one of the less desired of all the people aware of their existence, was another reason for them to go into hiding – which wasn't the most natural thing to do, but sensible if they wanted to stay away from the hunters.

Despite how well-equipped the sanctuary was, however, the residents couldn't help but feel imprisoned, one way or the other. The connection to the rest of the wildlife was being cut off, while, inside the gates, life was supposed to become the new normal. At times, that initial vocalising in the presence of human beings felt like a big mistake.

'We cannot accept any payment from you, Mr Birggetsson,' the security staff at the gate said to Sven who tried to offer him cash.

Sven hesitantly put the money away, with a feeling of satisfaction from being recognised more admirably and respectfully than before in the restaurant. The dopamine rush reminded him of the positive celebrity status he had attained as the reigning champion. However, due to the consequences and aftermath of the natural disaster, every future competition was put on hold for the time being. Rather than focusing on who was the best fisherman, people had other, more essential things to worry about, like the system's recovery and everyone's survival.

During this encounter, however, Sven's identity was obvious for other reasons. He was one of the saviours of the residents in the sanctuary. The staff members were well informed about who they could let in – although, even Sven's philanthropic status didn't exclude him from going through an X-ray scan in the security booth.

After successfully passing the first security procedure, his pockets and clothes were also searched as part of a normal routine.

'Have you had many visitors lately?' He tried to strike up a conversation, while the guard patted the top layer of his winter coat. In normal circumstances, Sven had no problems dealing with silence. Now, however, while being physically examined by a stranger, the awkwardness reached an equivalent level experienced during those frequent bathing sessions in a public sauna with a bunch of other naked men – that high-pressure social situation turning Pihtamonians into chattering magpies, or like Italians at a dinner party.

'You know very well that I cannot share that classified information with anyone,' the guard said firmly, and moved down to stroke Sven's inner thighs.

Sven subtly squealed from receiving more physical male attention in thirty seconds than he'd had in a lifetime. The guard's rough hands promptly ran along his trouser hems, down to his calves and ankles. Sven felt a tickling sensation, but his toxically masculine side couldn't let it show. His joyful eyes became watery, while managing to suppress his girly giggles.

The guard then stepped behind his desk, since the examination had revealed nothing suspicious. The intimacy between the two men was over, and Sven could breathe again.

'I still need your finger prints and eye scan,' the guard added.

After clearing all the security protocols, with his ink-stained fingers, Sven examined the map given by the security. It indicated each resident's approximate location. A narrow path ahead, between lush juniper trees, took him towards Erm... ine's territory. There were no cages or walls built to isolate the individuals from walkways, or away from each other's territories. The sanctuary was, instead, divided into sections, similar to, how people divide their residential areas, where everyone gets their own piece of land while maintaining their freedom to roam and visit one another.

The terrain dedicated to Erm...ine was mostly wet marshland, with a few scarcely growing pine and spruce trees where she could potentially hone her climbing skills. Even though stoats are mostly nocturnal, Sven spotted a white coat shining against the green moss. With a few twigs on her lap, she was seated on one of the horizontal logs placed around a flickering bonfire.

'I like your new home,' called Sven, waving from the distance.

'S-S-Sven?' Erm...ine said, bewildered. 'W-well, it's better than... no-no home.'

He heard hesitation in her voice, but wasn't sure whether it was just her usual way of communicating or if she genuinely felt hesitant.

'Better than nothing?' Sven replied. 'This is luxury.'

'I-I was comparing to wild n-n-nature. The past.' Erm...ine gestured Sven to sit next to her. 'P-please.'

Sven sat down on a log opposite her, only the flickering flames dividing them. 'I suppose, this environment is safer,' he added. 'And nothing is keeping you here. You're always free to go, right?'

'Do you want me to... go?'

'I didn't mean it that way.'

'I was... jo-joking.'

They both laughed.

'I must say that you sound... I mean... look well,' he noted.

Erm...ine gave him a cheeky smile, and went straight to the point. 'You must mean that I s-stutter less?'

'Hesitate less,' he corrected.

'That's... one way to-to put it. I've been taking e-elocution lessons from Links.'

'Great! And she can help you with some programming, too.'

They laughed again.

'How are the others?' Sven asked.

'Pole Vole's a-always practising. They've built g-good training facilities here... for voles to p-pole vault. Links is on the laptop all the time, still trying to avoid suspicious-looking links. Least Weasel is missing Less and More Weasel, who left... the sanctuary t-two weeks ago. They w-wanted their freedom back and to-to feel the e-excitement of wilderness again.'

'I hope they did the right thing.'

'T-hey were expecting to see you. Everyone has been.'

'I'm sorry.'

'I understand. You have your l-l-life to live. O-only those unfortunate c-circumstances brought us a-all together, anyway. O-otherwise, we would have never met.' She threw a twig on the fire, and stared thoughtfully into the flames. 'So... did Ida send you h-here?'

'No,' Sven replied promptly.

'That's fine. You're n-n-not obliged to come here. Only come... if you really want to.'

'I do. I did,' he hesitated.

'Really?' Squirr-El's suspicious voice interrupted them from the sky above. Also known as Squirrel of Steel, she pulled her red cape up before landing on a third, empty log circling the fire.

'Squirr-El! How good to see you!' Sven exaggerated his enthusiasm.

'I saw you walking in.' Under her brow, Squirr-El stared at him. 'What do you want?'

'Yaaaawnnn!' Another interruption, a loud but tired scream, echoed from the distance.

'Yetilag! And Pole Vole!' Now, Sven's voice had more genuine delight, as he spotted the odd-looking pair walking side by side towards them. Yetilag, with its enormity, baggy eyes and huge luggage, towered over the much smaller but friskier, Pole Vole beside it.

'Where have you been all these months?' Pole Vole bluntly asked, and came to sit next to Sven.

'It's been... quite busy,' Sven muttered. 'Rebuilding Pihtamo, Ida being pregnant, just lots of things going on...'

Sven's clumsy excuses made the animals glance doubtfully at one another. Squirr-El was the first to intervene before the situation grew any more uncomfortable.

'And how's Ida?'

The question forced Sven to become earnest. 'Not well. We discovered that Mooses, the hunter's leader who drowned, was actually her father. She took the news so badly that she's in a coma in the hospital.'

'That's terrible!' Pole Vole gasped. 'Is there anything we can do?'

'Keep yourselves safe and look after one another.' As Sven replied, he simultaneously spotted Yetilag's feet resting on the bonfire. 'Hey, you're burning yourself!'

'Yaaaawnnn!' Yetilag chuckled.

Pole Vole smiled. 'Nothing to worry about. Yetilag's fur is fire resistant and the soles of its feet and palms can bear enormous heat. While growing up in the eastern part of Kazakhstan, surrounded by hot springs and some minor volcanic activity, it is believed that its ancestors were exposed to unusual conditions and high temperatures, making the whole species evolve and adjust in this particular way.'

Sven watched in awe how Yetilag calmly stamped its feet in the snow to snuff out the flames that were scorching its ankle hair. 'That is... both so strange and interesting at the same time.'

'Would make a great fireman.' Pole Vole's comment made everyone laugh.

'I would have thought the opposite,' pondered Sven. 'That someone so big, white and hairy could withstand extreme coldness, but not heat.'

'Not everyone loves coldness, Sven,' Squirr-El smirked.

'I guess not,' Sven smiled. 'Even my and Ida's honeymoon in England was tough, because it was so hot all the time. British people think they're blessed with their warm weather, but I could never bear such high temperatures. It was a huge relief to get back home and feel the crisp Pihtamo breeze hitting my face again.'

The animals rolled their eyes in disbelief. Since their skins were more or less covered with warm, thick furs, they couldn't imagine how someone could even survive without one.

'And how's your f-father then?' Erm...ine's question brought the conversation back to a more serious level. 'You g-got him back. Congratulations.'

'We were both lucky,' replied Sven. 'He's running a restaurant now.'

The animals let out a terrified gasp.

Once Sven realised the reason for the unexpected reaction, he tried to soften the shock factor. 'He's specialised in fish.'

'Only?' Squirr-El asked doubtfully.

'And a little bit of lamb, beef, pork... and chicken.' Sven looked away sheepishly. He could feel everyone's disapproval, and how the general mood fell flat. The only sound came from the occasional sparks flying off the bonfire. 'What can I do? I can't make him stop. He has to live.'

'So do the animals,' Squirr-El grunted.

'H-how about a vegetarian restaurant?' Erm...ine suggested.

'Or vegan? Apparently, that's really trendy amongst humans,' Pole Vole added.

'In Pihtamo?' Sven shook his head. 'Not in a million years.'

'There's always hope...' Another feminine voice coming

from the forest interrupted them.

'...even when the hope is gone?' Sven finished the familiar quote, and excitedly turned to see who had spoken.

'Tell your father what a great man he is.' Links, the computer literate lynx, joined the ring of animals around the fire. 'What an unselfish act from Roar, to give his space on that boat to one of us. And from Viljo, for risking his life and sacrificing his boat in the hope of discovering land. You all did a fantastic job by bringing us to safety. We are forever grateful.'

'We did what anyone in our position would have done,' Sven modestly replied.

'I wouldn't be so sure about that.' Links gave each of the animals a judgemental look. 'It is unfair to give Roar any grief about his choices. He's only trying to survive by the common norms of society; the human society. Not that I'm defending his restaurant business, or any restaurant.'

'Y-you just did,' Erm...ine said.

'I can guarantee that he is not... serving any of your species.' Sven immediately realised how bad his statement sounded.

'Well, that's a relief!' Squirr-El grunted.

'Sven, please, we don't need to hear any details,' Links intervened. 'What happens in the kitchen, can stay in the kitchen. I genuinely believe your father wants us to be safe. He wouldn't have set up this facility otherwise. Unfortunately, though, there are so many others who don't want us to be happy.'

'The hunters?' Sven suggested.

'Them, of course. But also, since we've come out in public, so to speak, it's only a matter time before the media, scientists and powerful businesses come after us. Once the truth about our existence gets out, they will find us, put us into some lab and start sticking needles into us, and make us run on never-ending treadmills. Everything we represent would frighten those who cannot tolerate difference. We would always be seen as your inferior. You only need to look at the history of humankind: slavery, discrimination of the indigenous and immigrants, racial abuse, poor rights for women, gay and transgender. Recently, it hasn't been easy to be anything else than a straight white man.'

ERM
ERM

'I can see you've done your homework,' Sven said, feeling nothing but shame.

'Wikipedia,' Links smirked. 'Seems like you're a very complicated species, with a difficult history.'

'We've come a long way from the nineteenth and twentieth centuries.'

'You may have. But from our point of view, the society you've created wouldn't be ready for us.'

'That's why no one must ever find out about this sanctuary,' Sven said.

'N-never?' Erm...ine gasped. 'That sounds s-so... depressing.'

'The forests were our safe haven before the floods ruined it for us,' Squirr-El said.

Unfortunately, Sven couldn't even blame nature for the disaster – which was, again, caused by humans – even though with supernatural powers. 'Well, you all have the option to return to the wild,' he replied, 'and blend in with other animals that don't speak.'

'They all speak, one way or the other,' Links corrected.

Sven gave her a confused look.

'You just haven't dared to listen.'

'And, for us, s-speaking animals, the outside w-world is not the same anymore,' Erm...ine added. 'It h-has become even more dangerous. S-since we've "come out", we would be l-looking over our shoulders for the rest of our... lives.'

'Yes. So many people know,' Links said. 'Everyone from Viljo's boat and the post office roof, the sanctuary staff, the security, Jaaku...'

'You are mentioning Jaaku separately?' Sven asked.

'He's dangerous.'

'Well...' Sven started, but couldn't complete the sentence. He was truly uncertain about Jaaku's current interests and intentions.

'My last memory of him on the boat definitely confirms that he wants to hunt,' Links added gravely.

However, Sven tried to find ways to defend Jaaku. 'That was different. He was...'

'Hungry?' Links interrupted. 'I presume he was, as we all

were. Yet, we didn't start eating one another, and neither did you.'

Sven hesitated to say the following, but spurted it out anyway. 'Animals do eat one another in the wilderness. It's not like you come from a perfect place. Pie Polar Bears would have consumed at least half of you all, if we didn't bake those pies for them.'

'Fair enough. Yet, nothing compares to the distinction the humans have caused,' Links argued, while simultaneously thinking whether their debate would really resolve anything.

'What can I say?' Sven said, getting slightly frustrated.

'We just hope you understand our concern,' said Links. 'We are so different here and "creatures" like us are easily persecuted. We would never be equals to humans.'

'Not even in the circus,' Pole Vole added, and gave his pole a little twirl.

'Yaaaawnnn!' Yetilag's groan gladly broke the tension.

Sven gave Yetilag a subtle smile, even though its yawn always sounded more or less the same to him.

Links spoke more softly now. 'Nevertheless, we trust that you have a big heart, and that you can empathise. Although, it doesn't change the fact that you are privileged and that will always keep us separate from you. We must either follow humans, or hide from them. That's just a simple fact of our lives.'

'I'm on your side,' Sven said convincingly.

'Yaaaawnnn!' Yetilag replied on a positive note.

'We know you are.' Links smiled. 'Thank you so much for coming to visit us.'

'I'm glad I did,' replied Sven. 'It's nice to see you're all safe and doing well.'

Erm...ine reached down behind the log, to pick up a package from one of the pits she had dug in the ground. She offered it to Sven. 'Here's a little s-something from all of us.'

Receiving the gift made Sven blush. 'You shouldn't have. I've got nothing for you.'

'As we said, y-you've already done enough... g-good for our sake.'

Yetilag smiled. 'Yaaaawnnn!'

'But please, wait until Ida has recovered,' Links said. 'We want you to open it together.'

Sven nodded, and accepted the package, which was wrapped inside three large green lilac leaves and secured with brown strings of hay.

Chapter 26

DRUGS DON'T WORK

The door behind Sven opened, interrupting his private moment with Ida. This time he didn't even bother to look who it was – he only wished for the person to get the message and leave them alone.

'I'll be in the hallway, if you need me.' Roar got the hint, and turned around.

Sven waited for the door to shut completely before he was able to continue his monologue.

'So... the doctors have done more tests on you, since there were some complications. The results should be here any minute... I'm nervous. We are all very nervous. Dad just arrived. I managed to patch things up with him after I quit the job. Birgget's at home taking care of our baby. The baby's absolutely gorgeous, like her mother.'

Sven softly caressed Ida's cheek.

'Ronja should be here anytime soon. Your mum was supposed to be here an hour ago. She must have her reasons to be late. I must admit, it's still hard for all of us to be in the same space.'

He pulled her blanket up to her chin. Then he took the gift from his rucksack and put it on the night table. 'I went to visit our animal friends the other day. They gave us this present that we can open once you've opened your eyes. We talked about many interesting things. They reminded me how privileged us humans can be. The sanctuary is supposed to keep them safe, yet they are scared, probably more than they used to be in the wild before they got exposed. In the past, not so long ago, animals were just animals to us, and that's that. Whereas now, suddenly, they're something more...'

Then the door opened, interrupting him again.

'Could you just give us a minute?' Sven grunted, and looked over his shoulder. It was the doctor. 'Please, do come in.' Sven's tone quickly changed from anger to anxiousness.

As the doctor entered, Roar automatically thought he could as well. The doctor came to Ida's bedside and took a deep breath. 'We have got the latest test results. It has been four weeks since the incident and it seems that, unfortunately, Ida is not showing any signs of recovery. It is highly likely that her state will not change... ever.'

'What?!' Sven gasped. 'How highly?'

No matter how seasoned the doctor may have been, being a messenger of such negative news was never easy. He decided to look down and formally consult his notes. 'The last brain scan shows that all her brainstem reflexes have stopped. So far, we only know from experience that, in most cases, this is permanent. With ninety-nine per cent certainty, her state won't improve.'

'So, there is still hope?' Sven gazed desperately at Roar - who stood by the doorway - hoping his father would finish the famous quote he had come up with himself.

Yet, for the first time ever, Roar remained silent when he wasn't supposed to. His positive outlook in life had suffered a massive dent. The science had proven stronger than his made-up, famous quote.

'I am terribly sorry,' the doctor said, stepping back towards the open door. 'If you need anything, any more information, please don't hesitate to ask me or one of the nurses.'

It was as if the time stopped once the messenger of death had exited. Ida being admitted to the hospital may have felt like the beginning of the end. But this was the end of the end.

'So... unfair.' Sven dropped his face against her blanket to block the tears from falling. He mumbled against the fabric. 'There were so many things we had to do together. So many...'

'The doctors don't know a damn thing,' Roar muttered,

still holding onto that one per cent of hope.

'They must be wrong,' cried Sven. 'They have to be!'

While holding back his emotions, Roar pondered rationally. 'You know that time my left foot got bitten off by Wolverring and I fell unconscious?'

Sven raised his head, looking dumbfounded. 'What does it have to do with her?'

Roar started pacing around the room while reminiscing. 'I ended up drifting aimlessly around the lake for days. Not sure if I was officially comatose, though. But, in the end, I was brought back to consciousness by the indigenous tribespeople with their natural, alternative remedies.'

'We are not giving Ida any reindeer piss!' Sven remonstrated, while nasal mucus dripped downwards along his medial cleft.

'They also fed me herring, raw. That's the first thing I remember tasting when I woke up.'

'I cannot believe this,' Sven sighed, and wiped his runny nose with his bare wrist.

'What have we got to lose?' said Roar. 'The doctors believe that every method to bring her back has been exhausted. But I'm pretty sure they haven't tried this one.'

'Most definitely not,' Sven snorted.

'But we cannot tell the hospital about it, because I fear they will not approve.'

'Who would?' Sven said, and looked at Ida's lifeless body. Under pressure, he began warming to some parts of the idea. 'Herring we could try, even though it sounds ridiculous.'

'You almost gave her herring on the altar. This can't be much worse,' Roar smirked sensitively.

Sven sighed tiredly. Constant reminders about the wedding shambles had become an old joke. 'What if it gives her magical powers, or puts her under some spell? You still don't know where exactly you got yours.'

'Well, if that was an option, which one would you rather choose?' Roar replied. 'Comatose Ida you see here today, or Ida full of life like some... superwoman?'

The question was meant to be easy to answer, yet Sven couldn't immediately say the latter. She was already a strong character just by being herself. The idea of her having any supernatural powers on top of that, frightened him.

'It shouldn't take that long to reply.'

'Fine! But where should we get this herring, then? From the pond? Just any random herring doesn't seem to give anyone special powers. We eat herring all the time and I feel quite average. It needs to be some special kind.'

'The herring I was being given by the tribe members did taste odd,' Roar reminisced. 'It definitely had this peculiar yellow or orange marinade on top.'

'You don't say,' Sven sighed.

'I'm sorry, son. That method could be our only hope. And it's not like we're giving her chemotherapy or something. It's gonna be a... fully natural product.'

Sven shook his head in disbelief. 'And how are we supposed to feed her? She's in a coma. You can't fit herring through the nasogastric tube.'

Roar examined the equipment attached to Ida. 'Maybe in very small pieces?'

Sven started to realise how determined Roar was to get this plan through.

'Let me think about this for a second.' Sven leant over close to Ida's ear and whispered. 'I'm sorry, honey... If you don't open your eyes now, we may not have any other choice than to try this insane method. So, please, show any sign of life. Otherwise, I'm not sure if I can ever forgive myself for what I'm going to decide next.'

He pulled himself away and waited. And waited. But nothing happened. He dropped his head, and accepted the outcome. Frustrated, he got up and stormed out of the room.

Roar followed, and found him in the hallway, leaning against the wall.

'So, where should we get these... ingredients?' Sven quietly asked. 'Can we use any herring and reindeer?'

Since a doctor and two nurses were approaching, Roar had to move closer for more discreet conversation. As the staff passed them, they acknowledged the men with a subtle nod.

Finally, after a few beats, Roar could go on. 'I wish I knew.

Ideally, I would have wanted to visit the tribal village and ask them. But I cannot remember the exact location. It cannot be far from the pond.'

'It is still a big area to explore.'

'I can always get herring from my restaurant freezer and defrost it. And reindeers are everywhere.'

'Santa has reindeers. Pretty good ones, too.'

'We cannot...'

'I know exactly where he lives.'

'Arctic Circle. Everyone knows that.'

'He left his address when we met last Christmas,' said Sven. 'It's about three to four hour kicksled ride away.'

'If there's enough snow.'

'Or we walk.'

'How should we explain this to Father Christmas?' Roar asked.

'He knows us. He knows Ida. I'm sure he would understand.'

'I have my doubts. We can go there, but better not tell him about our motives. We should do it discreetly.'

'Break in after closing hours?'

'Of course, you're the expert,' Roar smirked. 'Let's see when we get there.'

Chapter 27

AN UNUSUAL REQUEST

In the foothills of lofty mountains, the dim lights of Santa's village glimmered like a mirage in the Arctic heath. The enchanting scenery could've been straight from any travel brochure with a few idyllic, snow-covered log cabins and timber houses of various sizes and shapes, together forming an entertainment hub, only half a day's kicksled journey south from Pihtamo. The resort included a toy factory, Mother Christmas's kitchen, husky rides, an ice skating rink, two restaurants serving traditional Christmas dishes, and so much more.

The low spring season seemed to keep the biggest crowds away. Yet, it was a well-known fact that the staff had to keep working relentlessly behind the scenes so that every gadget and surprise were ready for another festive period. Hence, the parking lot in front of the entrance was lined up with tens of kicksleds and snowmobiles. On the other hand, there were no queues to the box office, which motivated Roar and Sven to enter.

Once the men had parked their kicksleds, Sven walked up to examine a signage telling the opening hours. 'We have less than an hour left until closing. Maybe Santa will recognise us and let us in for free.'

'We can't let him know that we're here,' replied Roar. 'What would we say to him? We wanted to come and sit on your lap? Besides, he must be busy in the grotto with the kids.'

'It doesn't look too busy.'

A young male staff member sitting in a ticketing booth overheard the conversation. 'The grotto will close in fifteen minutes. But, you still have time to look around and visit a couple of rides.'

'Great,' Roar said, and casually strolled towards the gates.

However, when Roar was passing the booth, the young man popped his head out. He had a large pimple on his forehead and a smaller one on the tip of his nose. His voice was cracking, as if he was going through puberty. And he had two tickets in his hand.

'That would be a hundred and fifty marks, all together.'

'For fifteen minutes?!' Roar stopped advancing, and turned to him. 'That's a rip-off!'

'Unfortunately, we're not allowed to give any discounts. These are the rules from the top.'

'The top means: from Santa?'

The young man nodded.

'But, Santa knows us,' Sven added. 'He knows us very well.'

Roar shook his head.

'Of course, he does. Santa knows everyone,' the young man said sarcastically, having heard the same explanation hundreds, if not thousands, of times. Then he began turning the 'Open' sign around in the window between them. 'Would you like to go in or not?'

Apologetically, Sven patted the tops of his empty pockets. 'Actually, I didn't bring any money.'

Roar grunted to himself. 'I really hope this works,' he murmured and pulled out his wallet.

'Kids usually think this place is good value for money,' the young man added.

'Well, they have a very different perception of value and money.' Reluctantly, Roar gave away the cash.

Unintentionally, the young man deprived Roar's first business profits, only for the benefit of a large corporation. He was merely on minimum wage himself, while Santa's village was owned by Darkslab, an Arctic investment management company turning billions of marks yearly.

'If I could then quickly check your bags, please.'

Hiding the bag tightly behind Roar's back seemingly

hadn't worked. The men exchanged doubtful looks when they had to hand it over for examination.

As the young man sunk his hand inside the bag, first he felt the hard plastic bottle. 'No liquids allowed, unfortunately.' He pulled the bottle out. 'Ah. It's empty. That's fine, then.'

Both Roar and Sven managed to suppress their sighs of relief.

Next, the young man felt something hard and cold. 'A fish? I'm afraid this I have to confiscate. We can't let anyone bring food items to the park.'

'Why is that, then?' Roar grunted. 'So that you can sell your overpriced snacks?'

'It's a company policy.'

'But... that herring is frozen,' Roar started, not knowing where exactly he was going with this. 'We wouldn't eat it here. It's our dinner once we get back home tonight.'

'That's right,' Sven added spontaneously. 'It would take hours for the herring to defrost, and you're closing the place in about... half an hour, right?'

'Fine, then.' The young man leant forward and whispered. 'But keep the fish in the bag the whole time and don't show it to anyone.'

Roar gave a docile nod, and packed the contents back in his rucksack. The men were free to walk through the gates. Once they were safely inside, Sven patted the rucksack.

'Well done, Dad.'

'Don't get too excited. That was only the first hurdle.' Roar stopped to study a large map signpost at the beginning of their path. 'There's a reindeer enclosure right at the end, next to Santa's grotto and the gift shop.'

'We don't have time to do the whole tour.' Sven took a right turn, leading him towards the exit of the gift shop. 'Let's take a shortcut. Their security can't be that strict at this time of the day and year.'

Before Roar had time to disagree, Sven had already disappeared through the doors. Reluctantly, Roar followed him inside – only to find Sven immediately being questioned by a towering security guard.

'The sign says "Exit Only", which means exit only,' the

guard firmly advised Sven with his deep voice. He was one of those hench bouncer-types that leave no room for negotiations.

'Santa... forgot to give us the present,' Roar stepped in, stuttering another spontaneous response.

The security turned to Roar. 'The husky?'

Since Roar's reply took a couple of seconds too long, Sven had to answer. 'Yes. Exactly.'

The guard hesitatingly nodded, then released his grip. 'Let me escort you then, so you get your toy. Is it for your son?'

'Daughter,' Sven murmured.

'Fine. This way.' With his big hand, the security gestured towards the exit. 'I know a shortcut.'

'Wouldn't it be quicker through the shop?' Roar carefully suggested.

'Do you want the husky or not?' the guard grunted.

Sheepishly, both Roar and Sven nodded.

While being led outside, the men noticed how many of the little ones of the families visiting carried white plush huskies tightly in their embrace, or dragged them lazily behind, the dogs' sickle tails mopping the ground.

The security guard looked over his shoulder and pulled a cheeky grin, as if he wasn't fully buying the men's story. 'You'll get yours soon. Happy?'

Sven and Roar nodded uncomfortably, while constantly trying to think of a way out of the situation.

The winding path took them through a garden with many snow sculptures of angels, a mermaid, Christmas trees, Santa Claus, a couple of elves, reindeers and a sleigh. Where they had gotten the snow to build all these pieces of art, was a mystery to them.

'This way.' The security took a sudden turn, and pushed a metal gate open that said 'staff only'.

'Where are we going?' Roar asked worriedly.

'This path will take you directly to Santa's own private entrance to the grotto. I can grab a husky from there without us intervening with the general public going in and out.'

'That is so... helpful.' Roar struggled to hide the irony.

'We can't go in there.' Sven whispered nervously to Roar.

'You should have thought about it before you went your own way.'

'Look! Reindeers.' Sven's next whisper was too excited and loud for the guard not to hear.

'We have over two hundred in the village.'

'Amazing,' Roar replied bluntly, and slowed down his pace to lengthen the gap between them and the security. He grabbed Sven by the wrist and pulled him beside him. 'We have to get to the other side, where the reindeers are.'

'I can try, if you distract the guard.'

'With what?'

'What about... a fake heart attack? You're in the risk age group. It would be plausible.'

'I'm only late fifties, and healthier than ever,' Roar snorted.

'It's either you or me,' Sven said gravely.

The security looked over his shoulder. 'C'mon then. We haven't got all night.'

The men smiled innocently, and picked up their pace.

'Okay, then.' Roar took the bottle out and gave it to Sven. Then, awkwardly, he grabbed his own chest, while letting out weak groans. Once he dropped down to his knees, Sven wanted to disappear – not to the reindeer enclosure, but from embarrassment.

'What's wrong with him?' the guard asked.

'I don't know.' Sven tried to sound panicky. 'He's... old?'

Roar collapsed to the ground and started shaking vigorously. For a moment, Sven really thought he was in pain. And the more Roar kept faking it, the more he got into the character of a stroke victim.

'Maybe I could get him some water?' Sven waved at the empty bottle in his hand.

'Good idea,' the security replied, and urgently radioed for some help, 'Security to medic... An emergency. A man down near Santa's private entrance. Repeat. Man down.'

It was Sven's opportunity to sneak away. As he circled the grotto, he saw Santa through a window. Their eyes met. Quickly, Sven threw himself to the ground and crawled away. He made his way around to the front of the cabin, where the last family of five – hosted by an elf – waited for their turn.

'Have you lost something, sir?' the elf asked Sven, who landed on their feet.

'I was just... looking for a toilet,' Sven muttered, and quickly got up.

'It's not down there, unfortunately,' the elf said. 'By the gift shop, at the end of the tour.'

But Sven wasn't listening, as his focus was only on the reindeer closure ahead. He wiped the dirt and wet snow off his clothes and rushed past the family and the elf. Once he thought he was alone, he climbed over the lowest point in the fence and dropped down to the other side, landing on a pile of scat. Grunting, he got up and tiptoed towards three reindeers grazing the grass. He slowed down once he got nearer to them. He brought the bottle forward and approached from the side. He wasn't sure where the private parts of a reindeer were located, but assumed somewhere between their back legs.

Once he got within a reach, however, he heard his name being pronounced, with a thick German accent. 'Sven! Is *das* you?'

Sven stopped what he was doing, and looked up. An oddly muscular reindeer in front of him gave him a wide grin.

'Rhein Deer?' Sven promptly hid the bottle under his coat.

Rhein Deer rose on his back hoofs, while responding excitedly. '*Jawohl!*'

'Hush.' Nervously, Sven looked over his shoulder. He saw Roar in the distance being covered under a blanket and lifted on stretchers by two paramedics. 'I don't want Santa to know that I'm here.'

'But *vhy*? He'd love to see you.'

'Because... How should I explain this...?'

'Don't *vorry*. You can tell me *anyzing*. After all, you're a hero,' Rhein Deer said delightfully.

'Well, you might change your mind once you hear what I'm about to ask.'

'*Anyzing*, Mr *Swen*. *Anyzing*.'

'Alright.' Sven took a deep breath and revealed the bottle again. 'May I ask you to... release some liquid in this bottle?'

'*Was?!*' Rhein Deer gasped. 'Liquid?'

'Pee... I know, it's really weird and disgusting, but also a matter of life and death. You remember my fiancée, Ida?'

'*Ja.* Don't tell me she's into some golden *Zerman*...'

'No! Nothing like that. Something completely opposite. Something very serious, actually. She's in a coma in the hospital and the only cure may be... reindeer urine.'

'Ah,' Rhein Deer sighed with a slightly confused, yet flattering, tone. 'And you thought I could help?'

Sven hadn't thought about Rhein Deer specifically, but now it was better to play along. 'Yes. You, of all the reindeers.'

'Well, this is quite an unusual request,' Rhein Deer contemplated. '*Alzough*, whilst growing up in the outskirts of Berlin, I saw all sorts of scat going on.'

'So, you think you could...?' Sven gently shook the empty bottle.

'If it *vas* anyone else asking, probably not. Because it's you, *vhy* not? But please, look away *vile* I'm doing it. Stage fright, you'll see.'

Sven understood perfectly what Rhein Deer meant. It was a common problem many of us shared. Hence, he put the bottle promptly to the ground under Rhein Deer's belly, took a few steps back and turned away.

'Whenever you're ready.'

'You clearly don't know reindeer anatomy,' Rhein Deer smirked, and kicked the bottle back half a metre.

Please, just do your thing, Sven thought, while trying to get a glimpse of Roar across the fence. But the guard, the medics and Roar were all gone.

Chapter 28

ALTERNATIVE MEDICINE

'Just faking a heart attack almost gave me one.' Roar summarised his earlier performance to Sven, as they hurried through the double doors to the hospital ward.

'You did a great job.' Sven praised Roar's successful attempt to distract the workers in Santa's village, which gave him the opportunity, in the meantime, to collect a full sample from Rhein Deer. 'Now, let's hope Ida doesn't have any company, like Sophia. I doubt she'd approve of this method, either.' He went ahead to push the next set of doors open.

'Have you heard from Birgget?' asked Roar.

'She's looking after the baby.'

Roar stopped and sighed. 'Again?'

'Who else?' Sven stopped as well, right outside Ida's room.

'Maybe someone else could take care of the baby for a change and give her a break?'

'Actually, I was meaning to ask your help, but then opening the restaurant started taking up all your time. I didn't want to disturb you and put you in a difficult position.'

'That's what families are for.'

'Fine, then. You can have her, as soon as we've given Ida this... remedy.'

'I would appreciate that,' Roar said, delighted.

'Just don't throw the baby in the lake,' Sven smirked as he opened the room door. 'She's not quite ready to swim, yet.'

'Is that what it's about? Trust?' Grunting, Roar followed him inside.

'What is?' Sophia asked from the opposite corner of the room, where she was sitting. Her stingy perfume had reserved the entire air space. 'The visiting times are over,' she said bluntly.

'Why are you still here then?' Sven snorted, while struggling to breathe. It must have been the odour together with the fluff her fur coat spread that caused his sudden allergic reaction.

Meanwhile, Sophia also gagged in disgust by the foul smell of fish and some other unrecognisable substance the men brought with them. 'I was just about to leave.'

'Good,' Sven muttered, and impatiently tapped his finger to his thigh.

As Sophia swiped past them, she seemed genuinely distraught. 'Did you hear the news from the doctor?'

'We believe there is still hope,' Roar replied instantly.

'How? With one of your magic spells?' As she mocked Roar, Sven was showing no emotion – he just wanted her to leave. The level of coldness the men portrayed shocked her. In dismay, she stormed out of the room.

Once the door slammed shut, Roar revealed the full bottle and gave it to Sven to hold. Then he took out a plate and a gutting knife. 'The fish, please?'

Sven revealed the herring from under his shirt, where it had been tucked away, defrosting, skin against skin during their return journey. 'I hope it has melted enough.'

'The body temperature should do the trick.' Roar laid the fish on Ida's bedside table, which became his chopping board for scaling. He removed the fish's head, skin, intestines and, lastly, the bones. He put the waste in the bin. Then he chopped the tender and moist flesh into small pieces. Just by looking at the bright pink gills and bulging eyes, it became clear that this particular fish was an elite individual from the world of gill-bearing animals.

'Do you know what is the right amount?' Sven asked hesitatingly. 'Or wrong?'

The memories of the time Roar spent in the tribal village slowly came back to him. 'The herring was deboned, diced and then... fully marinated. Yes, that's it. And the pieces of fish should touch the roof of the mouth, which, apparently, has the most healing effect.'

'The problem is that she can't chew.'

'Well, then we could... feed her through the tube?' Roar randomly suggested, while examining the equipment in the room. 'Though the dices have to be smaller.'

The thought made chills run down Sven's spine. 'You cannot be serious?'

'What other options do we have left?' Roar picked up the knife and hacked the fish to even smaller pieces. Then he grabbed the bottle from Sven and poured the liquid evenly over every piece. Once the fish was fully marinated, he gave the plate a little shake. 'Now we have to let it sit for a few minutes.'

While waiting anxiously, Sven went to stroke Ida's silky hair. The last time he had offered her herring was at the church altar – that, now famous, failed event that had made him an object of ridicule amongst friends and family who had to witness the farce. How that herring had ended up in his tuxedo pocket, remained one of the many unsolved mysteries. Was it a silly prank by his best man Jaaku? Or did Sven catch the fish himself the night before during his stag do, and had left it in his pocket by mistake?

After the ruined wedding, Ida had completely lost her appetite for herrings. She still enjoyed other fishes like salmon, perch and pike, but never herrings again. Therefore, he could only pray that her body wouldn't reject this controversially prepared species. At least, she was unconscious.

Should we have gotten her another type of fish? What if I, not someone else, should've caught this particular herring? His hesitation and superstitious thoughts grew stronger.

'Just out of curiosity, where did you get this herring from?' he asked Roar. 'I know it's from the restaurant, but who caught it?'

'I doubt that would make any difference to the end result,' Roar said with urgency, while staring at the clock on the wall.

'Was it Christian?' Sven asked, increasingly agitated. 'You do understand that we can't use fish *he* has caught.'

Roar couldn't look him in the eye. 'It's her future we are talking about here.'

'Unbelievable! Of all the fishermen, you had to choose him?'

'Let's not go there again. Not enough time.'

Yet, Sven wasn't willing to lose this round to his arch-enemy. 'What if we buy fresh from the supermarket?'

'The supermarket has none,' replied Roar. 'I've checked. They have the same problem: only small, imported quantities that always fly off the shelves immediately. Besides, even if they had some, I doubt their quality would match Christian's.'

'Of course not,' Sven snorted.

'You must put your jealousy aside, this one time.'

Sven bit his teeth together. 'I'm not jealous.'

Suddenly, a shadow blocked the light coming from underneath the door. Roar slid the plate inside the bedside table drawer. The men held their breaths, until the footsteps passing faded in the distance.

Roar turned to Sven, and spoke softly. 'It's her life we're talking about here. Even if this herring was fished by God, you are the one who is here, feeding it to her.'

'Me?'

'Yes, you.' Roar took the plate out and offered it to Sven. 'That's all that matters.'

'But... this was your idea. You're the expert.' Sven tried to return the plate to Roar.

'But she's your wife. You know her better.' Roar pulled back and refused to accept the plate. 'Besides, I have only been on the receiving end. As far as I remember, no special tricks required. It's only a fish. The usual. Try not to give her bones.'

Indeed, it was just another strange task Sven had been asked to perform in the recent past. Hence, he reluctantly accepted the duty. First, he poked the fish with the tip of the fork.

'Can you at least help and open her mouth?'

Roar nodded. 'Remember to hit the roof.'

Hands shaking, Sven brought the first piece to Ida's lips. He carefully inserted the fork inside her mouth and wiped the roof.

'For how long?'

Roar shook his head.

'Right,' Sven sighed, and pulled the fork out. He repeated the action multiple times with different pieces, but without success. In the end, he left one of the pieces resting on Ida's tongue, and closed her mouth. But again, nothing happened. In frustration, he glanced at the nasogastric tube.

'What are you thinking?' Roar asked worriedly.

'This was your idea, then.' Sven started squashing the fish into mush, while staring at the giving set and the tube. He then took a forkful of mashed herring and inserted it gently into Ida's feeding system.

'Are you sure about this?' Roar didn't know whether to stop him or not. He didn't realise that Sven would seriously go for it.

Sven shrugged his shoulders, before manually pressing the pump, the way he'd seen the nurses doing it. The tiny particles of herring got sucked into the tube, that eventually transported them somewhere inside her digestive system. Sven's heart paced even faster, as he had no idea what he was doing.

Once about a half of the fish had gone down the tube, he stopped to wipe his sweaty forehead. He observed her stable condition on the monitor next to her bed. There didn't seem to be any change, apart from her heart rate picking up a notch.

'Did you see that?' He pointed at the screen.

Her lips began moving. 'Mmm...' she groaned quietly.

'Oh my God!' As Sven squealed, the fork fell off the plate.

'Give her more! In the mouth,' Roar encouraged him.

Sven didn't bother picking up the fork. Instead, he used his bare hand to scoop the remaining pieces of fish and stuffed them into Ida's mouth.

While she suckled his oily fingers, like a baby calf sucking its mother's nipples, the door behind them flew open.

'What on earth is going on here?!' the doctor yelled.

'Look! She's recovering,' Sven replied excitedly, his three fingers knuckle-deep down Ida's throat.

However, feeling distressed and betrayed, the doctor completely ignored Ida's improved condition. 'You cannot do that. Only the qualified staff can treat patients, not the visitors. This is a hospital!' Furiously, the doctor grabbed Sven's arm.

'But it's working.' Sven struggled against him.

Now it was the doctor's turn to sink his fingers in Ida's mouth. He tried to fish the remains of the herring away.

'What did you give her?'

'What are you doing?!' Sven screamed.

'We have strict policies about what medicine can and cannot be administered.' The doctor dug deeper in Ida's esophagus.

Meanwhile, Roar sneaked behind the doctor. He locked his arms around the man's neck and started pulling him away.

'I will have you both sued for this!' the doctor screamed furiously, while throwing kicks and punches in the air.

'No!' Sven firmly pointed at the doctor. 'We will have *you* sued for failed practices. Look at her. She's conscious.'

Indeed, Ida's eyes were open. She extended her forefinger and pointed at the plate.

'I think she wants to finish the fish,' Sven said confidently.

'What says the doctor?' Roar smirked, while holding him in an armlock.

The doctor whined in pain, while Ida reached out for the last big piece of mushy fish.

'She's a real fighter,' Sven said, admirably. 'My herring girl.'

Chapter 29

FISH, SVEN! FISH!

After weeks of lying flat and immobile, Ida could finally sit up against the headboard of her hospital bed. A couple of bulky pillows supported her sore neck and back. The chuckling baby resting in her arms made her teary.

'So... beautiful.'

Sven leant over to her and took her hand, while Birgget, Sophia, Ronja and Roar stayed at the back of the room, respecting the long-awaited gathering of the new family.

'I've been thinking... we can change the way we live. Really,' Sven said quietly, not wanting anyone but Ida to hear.

'I believe this little package will change everything.' She wanted to show happiness, yet smiling was still too painful.

'I'm sure it will. But, what I mean is that, if you don't want me to, I don't need to go after Wolferring. We've already lost your father and I almost lost mine. I doubt Jaaku is that interested anymore, and Viljo has retired. So, perhaps, it's time for me to stay away from the lake for good and start doing something serious. We have a baby to look after now. A responsibility. We are a family. I have to learn to look at things and life more... realistically. I should start doing something normal; get a proper job.'

'You? Working for somebody else?'

'Yes. In fact, I was already working in my dad's new fish restaurant, helping him out, collecting plates, washing dishes and all sorts.'

Roar couldn't help but overhear Sven's embellished confession. He tried to hide his smile, knowing how the beginning of Sven's career in hospitality wasn't quite as successful.

'I see,' Ida said doubtfully. 'Is that something you really want to do?'

'Well, not necessarily for all my life. But we have to be realistic. All I want is for us to be happy.'

'Come closer,' she said, and closed her eyes.

'What is it?' Sven did as he was being told.

Ida opened her eyes wide open, gave a subtle smile and whispered in his ear. 'Fish...'

Dumbfounded, he stared at her. 'You want some more? Because, we only brought that one herring, which is now more or less finished.'

'No.' She shook her tired head, and repeated. 'Fish, Sven. I want YOU to fish.'

This time, he understood clearly. He was shocked, as he hadn't seen that coming. Doubtfully, he pulled away from her. 'Seriously?'

'More than anything,' she said.

Roar, standing behind Sven, couldn't hide his excitement. 'Let's go then!'

Sven looked over his shoulder. 'Go where?'

'Fishing!' Roar exclaimed, and went to grab the door handle.

Ida pressed her palm on Sven's cheek, and turned him to face her. He looked confused, like a little boy in a candy store, when she spoke.

'Wolferring is the reason behind all the misery and downfall of Pihtamo and its fishermen. I know that nothing will bring my father back to life. But the least you can do is to... punch that shameful Wolferring's gills so hard that the next Wolferring body double will feel it.'

Sven's eyes widened. '*Vau!* Where did that come from?' Ida's motivational words clearly struck a chord with him.

'I live with a fisherman,' Ida replied, with a weak smile.

Sven moved closer and gently kissed the baby on the forehead. He embraced them both.

'I love you,' he said.

'I love you, too,' Ida replied. The warmth of the hug had an immediate healing effect. Momentarily, she felt no pain.

Chapter 30

NO PAIN, NO FISH

'Why are we meeting here and not by the lake?' Sven asked Roar, who was leaning against a pile of twenty-odd pine logs, lying flat in the middle of the forest. The blade of his axe was stuck deep in one of the trunks.

'First things first. Before we row anywhere, we have to get you back into shape.' Roar said with determination.

Scornfully, Sven stared at Roar's hanging gut and forward head posture. 'What about you, then? What have you done to stay fit, apart from waitering?'

'I'm in better condition than ever.' Roar oozed confidence.

Sven laughed.

The collective atmosphere felt in the hospital was suddenly a thing of the past. It was as if they were each other's fiercest competitors again. Forcefully, Roar yanked the axe off the wood and, with a subtle swing, sliced a thin piece of bark off one of the logs, demonstrating how sharp the blade was.

'You asked, why we are here? This one stack of wood should represent the approximate size of Wolferring.'

Sven lowered his fishing gear onto the wet moss, and took a closer look at the timber structure. 'So, that little stump resting on top of the pile is supposed to be its dorsal fin?'

'That's correct.' Roar offered him the axe to hold. 'I want you... us... to chop the entire pile into tiny particles, like sawdust. We'll time it. Then, we come here each day for a month and make sure you... we'll... consistently improve our time.'

'We haven't got a month. I'm ready now.'

'A month is the bare minimum. We're not ready yet. Trust me. We must be prepared. Wolferring is nothing like any other fish we've caught before. You know that yourself. We need to learn a completely new set of skills.'

'We'll be running out of time,' said Sven. 'I can't keep sitting around doing nothing.'

'We'd be doing more things than we've ever done before,' said Roar. 'I have such a training regime in mind that would make us not only much stronger, but also more able to compete and have a better chance to succeed in the next ice fishing championships. We are both currently undefeated. It won't be easy for either of us to defend our titles. For you, following the first victory is often the hardest, whereas I have been out of the circuit for so many years that I wouldn't know what to expect.'

'You've really thought this through.'

'That's the only way. All or nothing.'

'What about the lake, then?' Sven pondered. 'I fear it's getting empty again. The fishermen need fish.'

'You're absolutely right. Everyone will just have to find other ways to survive until we get to deliver the next batch. They can eat vegetables. Or go to my restaurant. Actually, that would be great for the business. The freezer is still full of herrings from the pond.'

'What about Wolferring? What is it going to eat?'

Roar sighed, getting frustrated by all these questions. Hence, he grabbed the axe from Sven and sliced another strip off one of the logs, like a knife cutting through butter. 'Once we've finished our training, Wolferring can eat this.'

'I'm so looking forward to that.' Sven's doubtful reply indicated that he wasn't fully convinced.

Anxiously, Roar wiped his forehead, that wasn't necessarily sweaty from that one swing, but rather from their tense debate. 'But, you need to listen to me, just like you did when you were a child. That's the only way we can succeed.'

'How did you come up with all these "methods"?' Sven asked doubtfully, while pointing at the logs.

'There is no instruction manual for what we're trying to achieve,' Roar replied. 'So we have to make one.'

The answer wasn't exactly what Sven wanted to hear, yet it intrigued him. Agreeing with Roar seemed to be the only option forward. Roar was adamant that this training period was required – which, as intended, made Sven question his own abilities and confidence. *Perhaps we're not ready yet after all*, he thought.

'I'll do this under one condition,' said Sven. 'I want you to start and show me "how it's done". You think that you're in great shape, but let's face it: a lot of time has passed. I may have been mourning over Ida for the past months, but all you have been doing is working in the restaurant – which is far from being the Lord of... you know...'

'Fine! I'll show you.' Furiously, Roar began swinging the axe. Thick wood chips began flying all over, as the log peeled thin in no time. The log split in half along its full length.

Sven took some distance, where he could watch and learn. Roar seemed deadly serious. Although, would he last long while maintaining such an intense pace?

Nevertheless, Roar's angry message became clear. Once the first log was in tiny pieces, he gave the axe back to Sven. Panting heavily, he pointed at the next log.

From there on, by taking even turns, the men gradually flattened the pile. Hours of hard work and sweat eventually paid off, transforming the logs into smaller pieces of wood that could be used in a fireplace or sauna oven. A fine layer of wood dust covered their shoes and the area around.

'That was amazing!' Sven radiated an unusual amount of positive energy. After the final swing, he dropped the axe to the ground, and then himself onto his knees.

'Not bad for first-timers.' Roar offered his hand to Sven. 'Same time tomorrow?'

Sven looked at his blistered hands, and hesitated. 'Anything else you had in mind other than axe-work?'

'Many things. You... I mean WE... need to hone our casting techniques, speed rowing, wrestling...'

'Wrestling? Against who?'

'We can practise on each other. Are you afraid you don't

have a chance?' Roar smirked.

Sven chuckled, thinking that Roar was either joking or utterly disillusioned about his capabilities. 'We should probably wrestle against bigger opponents, like Yetilag or one of Pie Polar Bears.'

'Let's take one step at a time,' Roar said modestly, knowing well how those bouts would end. 'There is one more thing: a weapon that we should consider bringing to the battle.'

'You really make this sound like the Third World War,' Sven laughed.

'It is, for us.' Roar became increasingly agitated again about Sven's relaxed frame of mind. Clearly, Sven hadn't seen what he had seen. As much as he had hoped that Sven's attitude had changed, he feared that the only way to understand the level of danger was to be there in person. 'Remember what I gave you for Christmas? Have you still got it? Or what was left of it?'

Sven nodded. 'Haven't dared to try it, yet.'

'Don't lose it. We may need it, once we're ready.'

The powers of the magic rod had never been tested after it got damaged and halved during the fight between the Lord of Herrings and Mooses. Just the thought of using it intimidated Sven, as he had seen the havoc it could cause in full capacity. Therefore, he had hidden it in the deepest of places: in his wardrobe, under his woollen socks and long johns.

Roar would be the only one to know the full potential of the rod, but he was operating it under a magic spell. However, no one knew for sure, not even Roar, whether the remains of it possessed any extraordinary powers. Whether he'd want to see it in full swing again, considering the horrific aftermath, was another big question mark.

Suddenly, both men were quiet, thoughtful and focused – exactly the state of being and mind they would need to successfully follow their training programme.

Chapter 31

FAMILY: A THREAT OR AN OPPORTUNITY?

The baby giggled on the sofa after another successful breakfast feeding session. Ida's mildly sore nipples reminded her of her current purpose. Seeing the baby happy, however, made the pain worth enduring.

Discreetly, Sven observed them from the doorway, feeling amazed and grateful how they had come this far. Not only the miracle of the baby being born, but the simple fact that all three of them were still alive and well after everything they had gone through.

Initially, Sven had been against having a family, fearing it would consume his valuable time to rehearse and ruin his chances of becoming the best fisherman ever. Even though his own father, the all-time fishing champion, had a family, too. What was debatable, though, was whether Roar had been the best parent he could be because of his obsession to his craft. 'Behind every successful man, there is a woman,' they said back in the old days. Birgget represented the generation of women who had stood by Roar the years he was present – even though he physically really wasn't. 'He was always fishing,' according to her.

In all honesty, Sven felt like Ida's support worker, rather than an equal parent – so attached the newborn baby was to her mother. Simultaneously, he stressed about the times ahead.

Once having reached motherhood, would Ida have the strength and interest to stand by and support him in his ultimate goal of becoming the greatest? So far, she had. Inspired by their love, this had secured him his first championship. But now, there was another person, a baby, in their life, and only time would tell whether the little package would suck out his will to live, or give him that extra boost that would take him to another level as a man and a fisherman.

Unfortunate for Ida, he was so focused on chasing his own dreams – just like his father was – that he didn't always show enough interest in her future aspirations. He simply thought having a family was one of Ida's biggest dreams – which was largely true. Yet, there was so much more that she had to give that he never thought to ask; neither did she dare to express.

As he saw the baby staring at him with her big, round eyes, he knew that fatherhood would have an impact on the choices he'd be making at the lake. Would he be more sensible and careful, hence weaker, in this so-called 'war' against Wolferring?

'It's time,' he said gravely.

When Ida turned to face him, she looked surprised. She wasn't aware that he had been standing watching them all this time.

'Okay. Be careful then,' she replied casually.

Her calm response disappointed him. He was expecting a more emotional send-off.

'By the way, I'm hosting a Tuppervaara party tonight, so no rush back,' she added.

'Hosting? Where?' he asked, baffled.

'In here. Haven't you noticed the big cardboard boxes in the corridor? They are my stock. My mum went around to do the "swede calling" on my behalf.'

'Is she coming here?'

Ida gave a thumbs up. She couldn't quite believe, either, that her mother had agreed to come to their humble residence.

'Finally,' Sven snorted. 'It took her years, a Tuppervaara party, and probably the awareness that I won't be here, to step foot into this dump.'

'Please, don't speak like that about our home.'

He nodded apologetically. 'Are you sure it's not too early for you to be working? You're still recovering.'

'If you're going to face the enemy of our lifetime, I don't think me hosting a handful of women is that a big deal,' Ida smirked. 'It's not really work per se. I've been watching my mum doing it for years and it's quite leisurely. And I get some social life, as well. This could be something to focus on more in the future before I get the husky farm up and running again.'

It wasn't exactly what Sven wanted to hear. However, he was pleased that she could have a life outside the family. Yet, his plan to become eventually a full-time fisherman again, while Ida would stay at home with the baby, or children – if they were to have more than one – was suddenly put in jeopardy due to her possible career goals.

Nevertheless, he realised that, right now, was the worst time to have a conversation about their ambitions. Therefore, as a distraction, he picked up on something else she had mentioned earlier.

'What is "swede calling"?'

Ida's eyes lit up when he showed interest towards her new passion. 'Basically, it means that a Tuppervaara party host will go around the houses of the invited guests, or potential new member candidates, who could join the sales network, meet them in person and leave them a free-of-charge Tuppervaara swede peeler and two swedes. Then, the customer in each household would be encouraged to peel one swede using a conventional potato peeler and the second swede using a Tuppervaara swede peeler. During this brief visit, they would also schedule the Tuppervaara party to be held in the host's house. The customers would then be asked to bring both peeled swedes with them, show the results to other guests at the party and there would be a general discussion about the whole topic.'

Even though he was slightly overwhelmed by her detailed business-like response, he made the mistake of asking an additional question. 'Why?'

'Well, fundamentally, the idea of these visits is to engage the guests in pre-activity that would, most likely, motivate them to join the event by demonstrating the functionality of

Tuppervaara products and their outstanding quality. Everyone taking their "swedes out at the party" would also be a great ice breaker.'

Still not fully understanding the concept of 'swede calling', Sven thought it was better to just smile and nod, as if he did understand. Then, hesitatingly, he had a last look inside his rucksack, where the piece of magic wand stood upright, tucked between his lunch box and another box containing his favourite tackle. There was also the wrapped gift given by the animals in the sanctuary.

'Ah. I got this from our furry friends,' he said. 'They insisted we open it together.'

'How lovely.' Ida accepted the present, letting the baby to caress the lilac leaves. She unwrapped the strings of hay, revealing a soft toy version of Yetilag. It seemed the baby was keen, without any reservations, to adopt the tired-looking plush monster as her new bedtime toy. 'That is so nice,' she added. 'Thank them for me, when you see them next time.'

Sven leant over to give a gentle kiss on the tip of the baby's head. 'Have fun then, both of you.'

'I wish I could say the same to you,' Ida said with compassion. 'Stay safe.'

He took his gear and walked out. It was not exactly the kind of goodbye he had expected. There were no fanfares, dramatic music or tears being shed to prepare him, but more banal conversation between a couple about everyday issues, such as work, mother-in-laws and swede peelers. He wished his sunken motivation to go fight the battle – as Roar described the event – would pick up soon. Otherwise, this war could be lost before it had even begun.

Chapter 32

PARTNERING FISHERMEN

'I still think we'd be better off without him.' Roar's voice came from behind like the devil on one's shoulder. His beard had grown longer. He looked more and more like a wizard.

Sven lowered his fist that was about to knock on the front door of Jaaku's igloo. 'Are you kidding me? We've come all the way here and now you're telling me.'

'I don't trust him,' Roar said.

Sven sighed. 'Is that why you didn't invite him to the restaurant opening?'

'I... did invite,' Roar stuttered.

Sven gave him a suspicious look. 'Well, he didn't know about it.'

'Maybe he forgot,' Roar added unconvincingly.

'There's one thing that Jaaku has that we don't. Something that could help us catch Wolferring.'

'We've been training like hell these past weeks,' said Roar. 'We could win any fishing contest on earth. We don't really need him.'

'But you said it yourself that this is not a contest, but war.'

Roar realised how comparing their mission to a large-scale international conflict may have been a slight exaggeration.

However, Sven had already taken his warning too literally. 'We need Jaaku's firepower. We can't take any chances. Within the past weeks, yes, we may have learnt very useful skills to fight

Wolferring in the most creative and vicious ways. Yet, whether we have all the tools to eliminate it, no one knows, not even you.'

Roar sighed. 'If there was a way to get his gun only, without the man himself.'

'We cannot just tell him to give us his rifle, while expecting him to stay at home,' Sven replied. 'How would you even phrase that sort of request?'

That instant, the front door opened.

'Gentlemen! What is the request?' Jaaku smirked in his reindeer skin slippers and a bathrobe, having seemingly overheard parts of their conversation. 'I thought it was *them* again coming to check TV licences. They must've spotted my antenna on the roof that I've now tried to cover under snow.' He stepped outside and closed the door behind him. 'Can you see it?'

Both Sven and Roar looked up, and shook their heads.

'What about when the summer comes?' Roar asked, immediately realising how he had never made a journey up to these glaciers. He couldn't tell how the seasons differed, if not at all.

'It never does. It's like this all year round.' Jaaku's lips began to tremble. He was good at tolerating coldness, but not when half-dressed. 'You two should've told me you were coming.' He noticed the men's kicksleds behind them all geared up for a full-on fishing trip.

'Nah. You probably would have thought it's just another cold caller,' Sven grinned.

As the two friends exchanged awkward chuckles, Roar meanwhile was losing his patience with this meaningless chit-chattering. 'We need something from you, Jaaku,' he blurted out.

'From me?'

'Your help,' Sven corrected. 'We are about to go after Wolferring and we thought that you are good... I mean... You can handle weapons.'

'Being good and being just-about-able are two different things,' Jaaku said modestly.

'Who is it?' A female voice echoing from inside interrupted them. The front door behind Jaaku opened, revealing Marjukka in her white bathrobe and elkskin lounge boots. She pressed herself against Jaaku's back and placed her hands on his waist. 'What a surprise to see you here.'

'We were just passing by,' Sven muttered, while sensing how their visit may have happened at the most inconvenient time.

'We would love to invite you inside, but...' Marjukka started.

'...we were just going to the sauna,' Jaaku added hesitatingly.

'That's fine. We were just about to leave,' Roar promptly replied.

Marjukka's eyes wandered to the ground and Roar's rucksack, where the axe was bulging from the side net. 'Well, I hope you... catch something big.'

Discreetly, Sven tried to kick the rucksack behind Roar's feet. 'Actually, we were thinking if... Jaaku would like to join us later?' he asked nervously, like a kid asking his friend's parents if the friend can come out to play.

'He's a big man. He can make up his own mind, right?' Marjukka smirked at this ridiculous question. To make the situation even more uncomfortable, she jokingly squeezed Jaaku's cheek. None of the men found her gesture particularly funny, though, which caused her to frown. One by one, she glanced at all three of them. 'What's wrong?'

Jaaku took a deep breath, and gently held her forearms. 'Honey, this wouldn't be just any fishing trip. Sven and Roar are here to ask me to join the hunt for...'

'Wolferring?' Something in Marjukka's expression changed when she said the name. 'I knew it!' Veins on her forehead bulged, as she turned to Roar and Sven. 'Do you two understand that we are trying to live a normal life here? You should try it for once...'

'We're sorry, but...' Sven stuttered, 'we're only here because Jaaku is the only one we know who has ever killed... wild animals.'

Embarrassed, Jaaku rolled his eyes. 'Well...'

'And killing fish doesn't count?' Marjukka fired back.

'Sven is talking about big animals,' Roar intervened. 'Mammals, like moose.'

'Actually, I've... never really properly managed to kill one,' Jaaku muttered, looking uncomfortable, not wishing to talk so openly about this 'other' side of his.

It seemed like they had put Jaaku in a difficult position. Hence, Roar decided to explain things in more depth. 'The bottom line is, we would require someone who's comfortable handling firearms, since Wolferring is beastlike – as strong as an ox. We are not certain if our equipment and conventional fishing techniques are enough to tame it.'

'You're talking about what *you* need,' Marjukka grunted, not letting Jaaku respond. 'What about what Jaaku needs?'

That was a question Jaaku had been asking himself all of his life, yet he was not prepared with an answer. Because he didn't have one. Instead, he put his head down and wandered back inside the house.

Marjukka was left outside alone with Sven and Roar. She raised her index finger and was about to say something. But nothing came out.

Roar sighed, and then spoke softly, 'This is not about him or us, but the whole community.'

'Is it so? Really?' She took a step closer to the men, and leant forward. 'I don't have a good feeling about this; about you two. Look what happened the last time. Pihtamonians have suffered enough. I lost my home, my job, my everything. I cannot afford to lose him. Jaaku will only leave this igloo and join you... over my dead body!' She turned around, went inside and slammed the door shut.

Sven and Roar dared to breathe again. 'Was it ever this hard when you and Mum were together?' Sven asked quietly. 'Did she let you go fishing and do your own thing?'

'Life was definitely easier before we had you,' Roar smirked.

Meanwhile, inside the igloo, Marjukka followed Jaaku to the kitchen. 'What was that all about?'

Jaaku bit his teeth together, until he managed to spurt the words out. 'Can't you let me make up my own mind?'

She came beside him. 'Tell me then, honestly. What do you wanna do? You want to go fishing?'

'I don't know. Maybe,' he mumbled to himself, while reaching out for a wodka bottle.

'Because if you go, I'm not sure I'll be here waiting for you.'

'What's that supposed to mean? You knew that I was a

fisherman.'

As he picked up the bottle, she took hold of his wrist. 'Were you? Are you? You haven't been fishing for as long as I've known you. When I met you, I thought you didn't want to fish anymore.' Slowly, she pushed his hand down. 'You don't need a drink now.'

'Yes, but...' Jaaku tried gently to resist, but eventually he allowed Marjukka to take the bottle and place it back on the table.

'Even if you wanted to do it, I cannot promise that I could wait alone at home for hours, days or years,' she said. 'Apparently, Pihtamo changed overnight when Roar disappeared. The partners of fishermen could never feel calm again.'

'How do you know?'

'I work in the post office. People talk.'

He breathed heavily. 'So, this is more about you?'

'No. It's about you. And us. I'm telling you clearly how I feel and what I want in life. You can do the same. I can tell you that, if I was with a full-time fisherman, the anticipation and fear would eventually tear me apart. I constantly hear these miserable stories from many partners of fishermen, and a few fisherwomen as well, about how lonely and afraid they are. I still don't understand how Ida does it.'

'Sven and Ida are different. They have a baby now. That's keeping her busy. She probably doesn't even notice Sven being gone.'

'What are you suggesting?'

'Nothing. Besides, Sven has always come home in the end.'

Marjukka sighed. 'You just don't get it. Perhaps Sven has been lucky, but Ida's father wasn't. Neither was Christian, nor Roar. Until, by coincidence, you ran into Roar. But he still lost sixteen years of his life, of his marriage, of Sven growing up, of everything. I don't want the same thing to happen to us. Do you see what I mean?'

'No. I mean... Yes,' Jaaku said, confused. 'So, what can I do?'

'As I said, it's completely your own choice. If you believe becoming a hunter is a more sensible and safer choice, then by all means. But I still cannot guarantee that I will be waiting for you if there are too many lonely nights.'

'I'm not a...'

'Don't bother,' she intervened bluntly. 'I've seen the rifles you've been trying to hide, the blood and mud on your boots. If there's anything else you wanna tell me, now is a good time.'

He took a deep breath. 'Okay. I'm gonna go and send them away.'

She smiled subtly. 'As you want. I'm going to the sauna now.'

As Jaaku went and opened the front door, Sven and Roar were already on their kicksleds, facing away and about to take their first strides.

'I'm sorry, guys, but... I think it's better I stay here this time,' Jaaku shouted from the doorway. 'I have lots of other stuff going on at this moment that I need to focus on...'

'But...' Sven stopped and turned.

'I hope you understand,' Jaaku continued. 'Maybe ask Viljo if he wants to join. Good luck!' He then closed the door.

'Don't worry about him,' Roar said calmly to Sven. 'I did expect something like this. Things change, people change.'

Chapter 33

THE ARMCHAIR ADVENTURE

The only retirement home in Pihtamo, Vakavanhankoti, was one of those few structures that avoided the floods due to its remote location. It was as if the elderly were purposely tucked away in the middle of the wilderness to prevent them from disturbing the hectic life of the young and restless. Yet, many of the residents actually preferred this quieter setting after having spent all their lives by the busier lakeside.

Viljo was not an exception. Lake Pihtamo had given him everything he could wish for. That being said, his heart and mind would always be there: rowing, casting a bait, netting, and living with Aune, his fiancée for over fifty years, who had now passed on.

Apart from hosting him, this aging and somewhat clinical council-run facility offered a home to two dozen men and women from all walks of life: a couple of farmers, a few fishermen, three hunters, a chef, a shop keeper, and land owners. Some had Alzheimer's, the others suffered with diabetes, high blood pressure, dementia, various forms of cancers, or a combination of any of these diseases. Offspring, grandchildren, even great-grandchildren and old friends – if they were still alive – popped by in various intervals. Some got more, some less visitors, some none at all.

'I'm surprised he allowed himself to be put into this dump.' Roar observed the dull grey corridor ahead, leading to the communal space.

'I guess this was the lesser of two evils,' Sven pondered beside him. 'If the floods hadn't destroyed his home, he'd probably be stuck alone in his living room, watching telly and drinking every day.'

'You need to promise me one thing: don't ever put me in here.' Roar grimaced, knowing his retirement days were less than ten years away, and a decade at his age can go in a flash. Relentless fishing of herring, without seeing his family and friends, and with controversial results, was a burden he would carry inside him for the rest of his life.

Roar's fears and agony only reminded Sven of how his father was suddenly older – which he couldn't yet fully accept. Sven struggled to find the appropriate comforting words.

'Viljo had a big house with a garden,' he said. 'He had to do everything by himself. It's more practical for him to stay here.'

'I haven't got anyone helping me either. Except you,' Roar smirked.

'He was almost ninety years old. There's a massive difference.' Sven overtook him, advancing deeper along the corridor, where the deterioration of the building became more apparent. The paint had scraped off the walls, windows on either sides were foggy and frames mouldy. The stench reminded him of those old pubs with stained carpets.

'The lounge is to the left,' said Roar, who spotted a sign on the dark turquoise wall.

Sven turned the corner and stopped. 'Is that him?' He pointed ahead to the communal lounge where half a dozen men, and a couple of women, sat and watched television. There was a canteen behind them.

The residents were brought together under the same roof either by circumstance or necessity. A similar social class was the most defining factor. The community wasn't large enough to boost injustice and inequality. Only the wealthiest who could afford private care – which was a rarity in Pihtamo – were able to keep themselves away from these types of institutions, whereas the majority had to adjust to written and unwritten rules of egalitarian society.

Each individual's background, life story, religion or political stance wasn't that different from the next person, since most of them grew up in the same surrounding area. Some had married young, others later in life, and some had more children, others less. There were always the rare exceptions who had left Pihtamo to live in bigger cities, some of them returning, whereas the others never looked back. Yet, none of that was supposed to matter anymore; after all, for everyone involved in this particular institution, the next destination would be exactly the same.

However, holding onto belief systems did matter, and till the end. It was not a kindergarten, where those first opinions were being formed, but the last destination filled with wisdom and where the 'truth' was being told.

'Viljo!' When Sven called his name, at least three other men turned their heads. But none of them were the Viljo that Sven and Roar knew.

'Yes. I'm Viljo,' a bald man replied delightfully.

'I'm Viljo,' a tall and skinny man next to him said as well.

'Me too,' one man, sitting in a wheelchair across the room, added.

Viljo happened to be one of the most common first names given to that generation of men in Pihtamo. Every fifth seventy to ninety-year-old male was called Viljo.

Sven shook his head and pointed at the fourth man, whose eyes were glued to the television. He was wearing a blue woollen jumper and a white captain's cap. 'What about him?'

'He seems to have better things to do,' Roar smirked.

Sven walked behind the man and gently tapped his shoulder. 'Excuse me.'

'Get your hands off me!' Viljo took his walking stick, stood up and limped to the canteen to pour himself a cup of black coffee. While facing the counter, he grunted with a raspy voice, 'What do you want?'

As hospitable as always, Sven thought sarcastically. It seemed to him that Viljo had aged dramatically since the last time they'd met. His back was hunched, making him look shrunken. His skin was paler and he was skinnier. He was far from being that strong character Sven had only recently got to know better.

'How are you?' Sven asked, and took a careful step towards the canteen.

The superficial question made Viljo cackle. As Sven was too near for comfort, Viljo grabbed his coffee and returned to the chair.

Roar was still standing behind all the other Viljos. 'Is this *The Funniest Home Videos?*' he said, trying to ease the tension by discussing something everyone could relate to.

Another Viljo, sitting nearest to Roar, chuckled like an old crow, while simultaneously pointing at Sven. 'You look like the idiot who gave his bride herring.'

All three Viljos broke into roaring laughter. 'That was so funny. That's definitely him,' the bald one said. 'Your wedding is the most ridiculous thing we've ever seen. What were you thinking?'

Even the giggling staff member clearing tables joined the mockery. Viljo, in the wheelchair, started coughing heavily when the level of joy became borderline lethal.

'It was not my herring!' Sven tried to raise his voice over the howling, but couldn't be heard.

Only one Viljo, the one they came to see, wasn't laughing.

'Why stress about it?' he said. 'She married you, anyway.'

Viljo's clever interference calmed Sven down. He could even laugh at himself a little. He must have done something right if a woman, after having totally embarrassed her in front of the whole family and friends, was still willing to spend the rest of her life with him.

'So, tell me, Sven, how can I help?' Viljo forced the question out. 'That's what you're here for, right?'

Hesitantly, Sven leant closer to Viljo, so that the other Viljos wouldn't hear. However, once he was near enough to recognise every single detail of the old man's wrinkled skin and tired, distant eyes, Sven had second thoughts.

'Go on, then. I haven't got all day. I might be dead soon,' Viljo grinned, while waiting for Sven to say something. The stalled situation was becoming uncomfortable.

Since Sven couldn't get a word out, Roar had to step in. 'We are going after Wolferring, and were wondering if you have any interest to join us?'

Without saying a word, Viljo got up, left the lounge and disappeared around the corner. His sudden swiftness surprised them all. Sven and Roar exchanged confused looks, before setting off a few steps behind him.

Viljo took the third door on the right, which led to his apartment. He sat down on the edge of a sofa, panting heavily. He gestured to two chairs under a small television set attached to a wall rack.

'Come on in. Have a seat.'

The flat was nothing like Viljo's house, which Sven got to visit once with Jaaku, for a very similar reason: to ask him to join their first mission. It was that journey which led them to discover the Lord of Herrings.

None of Viljo's personal belongings were there, or visible, apart from one framed photo of Aune. It stood on a small coffee table, beside the sofa. That was it. Otherwise, it could've been anyone's apartment. However, he was much more welcoming than the first time Sven had visited his home – he hadn't tried to shoot anyone, yet.

'The journey that destroyed Pihtamo was my last ever,' Viljo explained to the men who both still stood hesitantly in the doorway. 'I don't need that madness anymore. Just look at me now. I'm a human wreck. Old. And I almost lost my life the last time. We all did. What could happen now?' He leant over and lowered his voice. 'Of course, I would rather be out there fighting the biggest catch, or whatever monsters the lake is filled with nowadays. I'm not saying that I voluntarily want to stay in this place and surround myself with people who can't control their urine and thread of thought. But I have no choice. There's no one to look after me, except this... institution. A dump! They only take your last savings. To ask for one single sheet of toilet paper, they put that on the invoice. I can't even wipe my arse without them charging for it. It's a disgrace! My advice to you is: stay at home and stay fit for as long as you can. Or have lots of children and grandchildren and make sure you remain on good terms with them. That way – if you're lucky – they might even look after you when you're old and crippled. Otherwise, you'll end up like me: trapped inside this bloody prison.'

'This is not so bad,' Sven hesitated.

'It is!' Viljo grunted, followed by a series of coughs. He pulled back and tried to compose himself. 'Anyway, once you've finished your mission, do keep me posted. Who knows, maybe one beautiful day, I might get back into some recreational fishing. It will be nice to know then whether it's a safe thing to do or not.'

Roar subtly nodded in agreement with Viljo and his decision.

However, Sven wasn't quite as accepting. 'But, what you did last time on the lake with us was outstanding. There are many out there who owe their lives to you.'

'You want me to be honest?' Viljo gave them both a grave look. 'Already last time, we all should have died. I still don't understand why we didn't. So, to go out there again, knowing what is waiting, would be an obvious suicide. I don't need to take those same risks anymore.'

'I never thought that you, of all the people, could be afraid,' Sven remonstrated.

However, Viljo, being two generations older, could understand how inexperience can breed pointless remarks like that.

'In the end,' he said, 'I'm a human, if you haven't noticed. And the closer you think your time is coming, the more frightening the idea of losing your life becomes. People think it's the other way around. But it's not true. When you really have to face death and there's nothing you can do about it, then it becomes scary and relevant. Before that, life is just a game – like yours is. Besides, I have nothing left to prove to anyone. I have everything I need right here... except toilet paper!'

As Sven listened to Viljo's lessons of life, he could only bite his teeth together in frustration, as he couldn't come up with any more arguments to persuade him. The fear of having to face Wolferring with only Roar was becoming reality.

'I'm sorry to disappoint you, but that's just the way it is,' Viljo said melancholically. 'What about that crazy friend of yours? What was his name again?'

'Jaaku. He's not coming.'

'Well, at least you have each other.' Viljo grabbed his walking stick and pushed himself upright.

The men stepped aside and gave him space to walk out.

Then, like the detective *Kolumbia*, Viljo had that one more enquiry in mind he wanted to present from a distance. 'I'm curious, though. How were you thinking about catching this monster?'

'Lure it with a bait and then axe on the head.' Roar made it sound almost too simple.

Viljo chuckled. 'You reckon it'll be that easy? You need stronger tools.' He went back into the room and pulled open his wardrobe. 'I want you to take this.' He revealed a spear gun.

Roar raised his palms. 'We cannot accept that.'

'You can.' Viljo pushed the spear gun against Sven's chest. 'I've had this harpoon for over fifty years and it never failed on me. It might look like an antique, but it's also very lethal. My brother gave it to me as a wedding gift when I got married to Aune.'

'Makes you wonder what he was trying to tell you,' Roar smirked.

'Why are you giving this to us?' Sven asked in awe.

'Because you need it. You need all the help there is.' Viljo gave them an affirming nod, and walked out again. 'It's better to hide it when you take it out and through the reception. They don't particularly like the elderly bringing spear guns in here.'

Sven immediately began stuffing the weapon inside his jacket. It was so long that he had to push the tip of the arrow inside his trouser waist, which landed dangerously near to his crotch and the most sensitive parts of his body. He had to walk like he had a wooden or artificial leg – which, on the hand, Roar already had for real, yet no one could tell.

'Thank you. We will take good care of it,' Roar said to Viljo, who was already a few steps ahead.

However, Viljo didn't respond. He just continued back to the lounge with the other Viljos, and sat in front of the television to watch the end of *The Funniest Home Videos* – which, in the last clip, introduced a man who tried to fix an antenna on the roof of an igloo, but he slipped, fell off the roof and vanished inside a big pile of snow. All the Viljos cackled together with the canned laughter track from the TV. It was one of those rare remaining joys of Viljo's simple life that was fully lived anyway.

'That was funny.' One last time, Sven tried to engage with the elderly, as he and Roar walked past them.

Only that one Viljo they knew turned to look. And he seemed angry – exactly as Sven always remembered him.

'Now, get the hell out of here!' Viljo grunted, with a twinkle in his eye. 'Don't disturb us now. The next episode of *The Cold and the Passionless* is about to start.'

Sven could hear the half-irony in Viljo's voice. He responded with a subtle smile, while patting the spear gun under his jacket. Before he turned away, he gave Viljo a slightly longer look, the kind you give to someone when you don't know if you will ever see them again.

As Sven and Roar walked away, the opening tune of the longest-running Arctic television soap drama began to play in the background. *The Cold and the Passionless* had played a big part in Viljo's life. It was his late wife's favourite programme, and the show had never left Viljo alone since – even over twenty years after her passing.

Most likely, this particular soap drama's somewhat twisted plot lines would entertain him until his death. After all, for Viljo, television was greater than life and larger than any adventure Lake Pihtamo could have ever offered. Many stories lived forever, like their characters. The imagination of creators had no limits, the actors were like Gods, whereas a man like Viljo had faced his limitations. The arm chair had become his throne and the wide-screen in front of him his escape to the world he never fully understood, yet so much glamorised and looked up to.

Chapter 34

LITTLE LESS CONVERSATION

The three hunters stopped advancing when the bushes ahead began rustling. Both Börje and Kalle carefully cocked their rifles, whereas Jaaku doubtfully caressed his. He voluntarily stayed a step behind. None of them could see the target yet.

'There!' Kalle whispered, after spotting a glimpse of a small, triangular head, popping behind a mossy rock.

'What was it?' Börje asked.

'A weasel of some sort.'

Börje sighed and lowered his weapon. He turned to Jaaku. 'You can have this one.'

Jaaku's already rapid pulse picked up another notch. Reluctantly, he cocked his rifle and took a shooting stance. His nervous hands made the barrel shake as he searched for the target. His inexperience was obvious.

'What are you doing?' Börje grunted.

Eventually, the weasel had to reveal itself again. There was something familiar to it, like the ones Jaaku rescued from the floods with Sven and Roar. Hence, he couldn't pull the trigger; not even under pressure from his new 'friends'. He lowered the weapon.

The weasel, however, assuming it was going to be executed on the spot, gave them a last, hopeless look, as if begging for mercy.

'I feared this would happen!' Börje pushed Jaaku aside and

pointed his own gun at the weasel.

Jaaku knew he had about a split second to react. Instinctively, he pushed down Börje's barrel, so that the firing bullet ended up diving in the depths of the forest floor.

'What the hell are you doing?' Börje screamed. 'I had it right there!'

'I... I slipped,' Jaaku muttered.

Börje regained his posture and, this time, aimed at Jaaku. 'Why did you do that?'

Next to them, Kalle smirked, showing his gritty teeth. 'Yeah. What are you doing here with us, if not killing animals? Playing hide and seek with them?'

Jaaku glanced ahead, but could no longer see the weasel. First, he felt relief, until worry about his own well-being became a priority.

'Talk, Eskimo!' Racist Börje pressed the barrel deeper into Jaaku's gut. 'Ever since we've known each other, you haven't really caught anything, have you?'

'Sure, I have,' Jaaku hesitated. 'Many things, like... a bear.'

'You've killed a bear?' Börje asked suspiciously.

'I'm pretty sure it was... a bear.'

'You'd definitely know if it was a bear,' Kalle intervened. 'What did you do then? Did you eat the bear?'

'No. I just... left it there.' Jaaku feared his nose would start growing in length.

'On the ground? To rot?' Kalle shook his head in disbelief, while jealously thinking about all those brown bears he was yet to capture. 'That's disgusting. We are hunters, not barbarians.'

'Whatever,' Börje scoffed, unconvinced. 'How about this weasel, then? Why were you protecting it?'

'Yeah? Was it one of "them"?' Kalle added.

'Them?' Jaaku tried to appear dumbfounded, yet could already see what was coming.

'Did this weasel have some special skills we should know about?' Börje rephrased. 'Like, communication skills?'

Jaaku couldn't hold his poker face any longer. His eyes wandered, like he had just failed the lie detector test. 'You've heard?'

'Unbelievable,' Börje snorted. 'Just like Mooses. We should have gotten rid of him and his stupid antlers ages ago. Damned peacemaker!'

'Excuse me, but... what has Mooses got to do with any of this?' Jaaku carefully asked.

'Mooses did not only want peace between hunters and fishermen, but also to protect this new type of intellectual fauna, like your weasel friend here,' replied Börje. 'In the last-ever hunting board meeting in Mooses's cave, he even laid out a plan to build a sanctuary for these cursed creatures.'

'How noble was that!' Kalle snorted sarcastically.

'In a cave?' Jaaku asked curiously.

'It was more like a fully equipped underground apartment,' Börje replied.

'A bomb shelter,' Kalle added.

Jaaku casually nodded, as if this was the first time he'd heard about the place. 'So, what happened then?'

'Then you fishermen completed the mission and Mooses drowned. Am I right?' Börje looked Jaaku straight into his eyes.

'That's... correct,' Jaaku hesitated.

'And, thankfully, the sanctuary never saw the daylight,' said Börje. 'Yet, these talking animals are still out there. We have to shut their mouths for good. Who knows how many unflattering stories they have to tell about us, the hunters.'

A loud, high-pitched squeak interrupted their conversation. They could see a couple of trees tops swaying in the distance.

Grinning, Kalle started walking in the direction of the noise. 'We'll soon find out.'

With the tip of the barrel, Börje poked Jaaku in the back, ordering him to go in the same direction Kalle was heading.

After a short hike, they arrived at the scene where two weasels were trapped inside a net, hanging from a thick oak tree branch. The weasels were bundled on top of one another. They hissed in agony when Kalle began to swing the net back and forth.

'The trap worked! Well done, Kalle.' Börje took a step closer to the captured animals. 'Now, let's see if these specimens talk or not. I've actually never heard animals talk before; only heard stories of them.'

Nervously, More Weasel on top made a poor attempt to trill, while Less Weasel underneath added a few awkward whistles to their unconvincing repertoire.

'Nice try,' Börje scorned, and started prodding the entrapped weasels with the muzzle of his rifle. They squealed in pain every time he touched them, yet made no sounds resembling human voices.

Meanwhile, Kalle spotted, out of the corner of his eye, how Jaaku tried to communicate with the weasels and get his message across by miming.

'He's warning them,' Kalle revealed.

Immediately, Jaaku took a step back and spread his arms. Yet, he had no lies or explanations left up his sleeve that would enable him to get out of this situation.

'Alright then.' Börje became interested in Jaaku again. Frustrated, he pointed the rifle at him. 'Now, weasels, if you don't talk, you can kiss your best friend here goodbye.'

The weasels gave each other a look of terror, until More Weasel broke down. 'Please, don't...'

That was the show-stopping moment. Börje and Kalle's jaws dropped as they witnessed the little weasel forming understandable words. Everyone just stood still.

More Weasel wasn't sure whether he should say more or not. Would it make the situation better or worse? Could it get any worse? They were already trapped inside the net, in front of hunters ready to blow their or Jaaku's intestines out. The future prospects of all three of them couldn't look much more uncertain.

Kalle, being in awe, didn't remain quiet for long, though. He spit a small puddle of saliva on the ground. 'Let's shoot them, anyway. This is nonsense. Witchcraft!' He sought for Börje's approval, while simultaneously cocking his weapon.

'No, please.' Jaaku took a brave step towards the hunters. 'You can make better use of them.'

Börje lowered his rifle and grabbed Jaaku by the collar. 'What can be better use than shooting them?'

'Eat them alive?' Kalle smirked, and aimed. He was only

about a barrel length away. It was very unlikely he would miss.

'You can... sell them,' Jaaku spontaneously spurted out his last resort.

This unexpected suggestion, however, made Börje curious. 'Tell us more.'

'Don't trust him,' Kalle said under his breath.

'Shut up. I wanna hear this.' Börje let go of Jaaku's lapels.

'Well, our... your discovery, of talking animals, could make you a fortune.' Jaaku knew this was probably the only chance to save himself and the weasels from trouble – if he got it right. It was like his sales pitch of a lifetime, yet unrehearsed. He had to improvise the entire spiel. 'What if you keep them alive and sell them somewhere to scientific purposes? There must be labs everywhere dying to examine them. Whereas, if you shoot them, then you'd be just like any other hunter and nobody would believe what we've just witnessed. They'd be dead animals, just like the rest you've shot, and you'd only get a couple of meals out of them. Nothing more.'

Despite feeling nervous inside, Jaaku was able to elaborate convincingly. His speech made Börje ponder.

'There is one laboratory in Kihlava that does animal testing,' Börje said. 'Mostly with mice, though.'

'There you go.' Jaaku gave the weasels a subtle, apologetic look.

'You think you could lead us to other animals that speak?' Börje already felt the cash flowing in.

'I... I wouldn't know,' Jaaku muttered. 'I don't think so.'

'Maybe our two little friends here can help us?' Börje devilishly turned towards the net. 'I believe we have some serious interrogation to do.'

Looking disturbed, Jaaku thought it was better to remain a couple of steps behind. His slower-than-average brain cells worked harder than ever to come up with another, even better solution to get himself and the weasels out of the situation.

'So, tell us, little furballs, has anyone given you names? Börje asked. 'How should we call you?'

The weasels believed that they had come to a dead end. Pretending to be any less cognitive than they really were hadn't

worked, yet speaking words was probably not going to save them either.

'Did lynx steal your tongue?' Kalle snorted.

'Links?' Jaaku intervened worriedly. 'You know her?'

'*Her?*' Kalle laughed.

'Another one of your special friends, Jaaku?' Börje asked.

'No. I mean... since a lynx is a cat... and I would naturally call cats females... since they are girly... like, you know... dogs are... masculine,' Jaaku stuttered.

'What you just said doesn't make any sense at all,' Börje smirked. 'But we understand. There are more human-like animals than just these two weasels, and we will find them all. There's no one who can protect them from us. So, how is it going to be? One of you three is going to speak or bad things will happen.'

'Yeah. Really bad.' Kalle pressed the side of the net with his rifle. 'What do you think, boss? Should we just grill one of these weasels for supper?'

'Just wait a second,' Börje grunted to his impatient sidekick. Then he composed himself and addressed Jaaku. 'The question is, Jaaku – who do you want to save? You are not a stupid man. But you're hanging around with the wrong crowd today if you want to become an animal activist. The truth is, you could become a good hunter, if you'd start thinking more broadly. You have to understand that the world doesn't need more human-like species to control and consume the earth. There just isn't enough room for another intelligent life form on this planet. It's already difficult enough for mankind to work together in any sort of harmony. Throughout history, us humans have created a system that works in our favour, where we perfectly enslave and kill animals for our needs, and we should keep it that way. Until you start setting yourself above nature, you can never become a great hunter. If that is what you want to become.'

Whether Jaaku agreed with Börje's statement or not, was irrelevant at this point. He was up against two gun-savvy, unpredictable hunters with strong opinions, and he was all alone in the woods, apart from two weasels. If anything was to happen to him, no one would know. Therefore, he nodded submissively, while hoping for a miracle, like another tsunami or flash flooding, to come and rescue them. But there were none in sight. A light drizzle settled in, adding to the misery.

'Great.' Börje rubbed his palms together. 'Not the rain, but the fact that we have two weasels and a lynx. What else?'

'Yetilag,' Jaaku sighed, utterly defeated.

'We are not interested in hearing your travel stories,' Kalle snorted.

'Not jet lag, but Yetilag. A tired monster.' Jaaku felt another sting in his chest, while betraying the rare community of intelligent animals.

'Sounds dangerous,' Kalle smirked sarcastically.

'It is. It would rip your head off,' Jaaku snorted, while simultaneously trying to suppress his anger.

'Watch your mouth!' Börje smacked Jaaku with the stock of his rifle.

Jaaku groaned, holding his stomach. He dropped his weapon to the ground.

'Who else?'

'That's about it,' Jaaku whined.

'I don't think so.' Börje snapped his fingers, which resulted in Kalle immediately pressing the barrel on Less Weasel's forehead. 'What will it be? You can tell us everything you know, or your little weasel friend will end up in one of our lunch boxes.'

'There are many more.' More Weasel felt the need to intervene.

Börje gave Kalle a satisfied grin. 'Now the weasel's talking.'

'Jaaku is right,' More Weasel continued. 'Yetilag will come and tear you apart.'

'It must be quite a creature, then,' Börje scorned. 'Who else should we be afraid of? Just warn us, please, so we can be prepared. We have enough firepower to blast an entire herd of Yetilags, or some other tired freaks.'

'Yeah. Speak to the barrel, little monkey.' Kalle pushed the gun deeper into Less Weasel's soft fur.

'You can... kiss the tip... of my tail.' Despite the pleasure saying the witty remark gave Less Weasel, she also feared these would be her last words ever spoken.

Furiously, Kalle knocked down Less Weasel. Jaaku struggled to contain himself, while eyeing on his rifle.

Börje shook his head. 'It's such a pity. We are finally speaking the same language, but the level of conversation has to be this low. This is exactly what I meant, Jaaku. Not everyone or everything needs to be involved in a proper, intelligent conversation.'

More Weasel cleared his throat. 'The premise for any conversation to be intelligent or equal has already failed when the other party is being held hostage.'

The wittiness of the weasels began to infuriate Börje, whereas Kalle couldn't quite get More Weasel's clever remark. Yet, Kalle could read from Börje's negative reaction that the words were far from being a compliment. Therefore, he decided to punish More Weasel as well, and smack his snout.

'You little rat!'

That was when Jaaku reached his breaking point. He wasn't thinking clearly anymore. He had to do something, no matter what the consequences. Hence, he jumped on Kalle from behind and grabbed a hold of his rifle. The men fell and began rolling on the ground in their struggle.

'Jesus!' Börje stepped aside, finding it hard to aim as the men were all over each other. He was afraid Jaaku might shoot Kalle, who was on top blocking Jaaku underneath. Jaaku clasped his arms around Kalle like a digger in the soil. Every time Jaaku saw the gun pointing at him, he shielded himself by moving Kalle in between him and the barrel.

Meanwhile, Less Weasel returned to consciousness. In awe, both weasels could only follow the battle from captivity which, weirdly, was about them. While the scuffle kept the men distracted, More Weasel began to chew a hole in the net, giving them the path to freedom. As they lowered themselves to the ground, the weasels pondered whether they should help Jaaku, who was currently being sandwiched between the hunters.

'We trusted you.' Börje waited for that window of opportunity to shoot Jaaku. 'We should have finished you a long time ago.'

The moment came when Kalle managed to punch Jaaku on the chin. Kalle freed himself and rotated to the side, leaving Jaaku fully exposed on the ground. As Börje was about to pull the trigger, an agonising pain in his right foot threw him off balance. Less Weasel had sunken her teeth deep through his boot.

'Aarrghhh!' Börje screamed.

Simultaneously, More Weasel jumped on Kalle from behind and sunk his teeth into the man's neck. The agonising pain made Kalle throw his head backwards against a trunk of a pine tree. He fell unconscious.

Shaken, Jaaku had no idea what had happened, except that the roles of everyone involved had changed in the blink of an eye. Börje was hopping on his one foot, while Kalle lay emotionless on the ground, his face flat on the moss.

Jaaku yanked the rifle from underneath Kalle's limp body, which brought Kalle back to consciousness. When he opened his eyes, the first thing he saw was Jaaku pointing the gun at him. Blood gushing from his mouth, Kalle remonstrated. 'You wouldn't have the guts. You're just a failed fisherman...'

And Kalle was right. Jaaku couldn't do it.

Meanwhile, the weasels had disappeared into the forest. Jaaku decided to follow them, leaving the hunters behind, beaten and humiliated.

Gradually, Börje endured the pain. He picked up his rifle and limped in the same direction he saw the weasels and Jaaku escaping. Kalle was still on the ground, falling rain drops clearing the blood away from his face. He saw Börje vanishing behind the line of trees, but didn't have the strength to sit up and shout after him.

The thought of a potential monetary reward that would sort Börje out for life, kept him motivated. His knowledge of the forest was sublime as he had hunted in the area for decades. He knew every tree stump, rock and path. However, the weasels' agility and comfort in this familiar terrain was hard to beat.

Jaaku didn't have that advantage, except that his feet were fully functioning, unlike Börje's – and the fact that he was the one being chased, which usually makes us exceed our limitations.

Chapter 35

UNEXPECTED GENEROSITY

The downpour becoming torrential, however, didn't stand in Sven and Roar's way of executing their plan. After two unsuccessful attempts to lure fellow fishermen to go with them, they finally reached the coastline, where the spruce forest met the lake. Fallen branches and cones crackled under the men's boots as they tramped towards Roar's boat. The rain-drenched ground suddenly became clear of snow – a recurring event that always positively surprised everyone in the springtime, as did the very first snowfall every autumn repeatedly shock, creating confusion and traffic chaos. So short was the memory of an individual in the Arctic.

The path became narrower between the rough waters on one side and the vegetation on the other. The men had to form a single line, Roar taking the lead.

'You used to never want to leave the house when it was raining,' Roar called over his shoulder and smiled, not letting the poor weather bring him down. After all, during his years as the wizard, he had experienced any unpredictable condition this harsh climate zone had in store.

'Please. I'm not twelve anymore.' Having learnt from the most recent trips to the lake, where they had ended up diving to the pond or earlier capsizing Viljo's boat, it wasn't rain Sven worried the most. As a precaution, he had added an extra waterproof layer underneath his clothes. 'Do you think we are prepared enough? We have all these weapons, but...'

'But what?' Roar grunted, not keen to hear any negativity at this point. He picked up speed, also in an attempt to show the younger generation what he was made of. 'Personally, I have never been this ready. The fact is, somebody has to do something, with or without magic, and the dirty job landed on us. We can only do our best, not just for us, but for the whole fishing community.' He stopped and turned to Sven. 'But you must be careful, and stay back.'

Sven nodded casually. 'Sure. I can troll, if you want to row, and then we swap at some point.'

'I wasn't talking about our seating positions. I meant that, in any threatening situation, you must stay further away from Wolferring. Let me be the bait instead and the one who is the nearest. I want you to be safe. Or safer.'

Rather than just simply accepting Roar's natural need to protect the offspring, Sven took this supposedly thoughtful gesture as an undermining attack against his own skill-set and experience.

'We can't predict how this whole thing is going to pan out,' he replied. 'Wolferring doesn't just attack from one side or the other. Or does it?'

'I just don't want you to get hurt. If someone has to go, that would be me,' Roar declared unselfishly. Even though he did not want to die per se, his age had made him accept the limitations of mortality. For him, the end was supposedly nearer, one way or the other.

Sven, however, in his immortal youthfulness, hadn't even thought about the sad subject. 'We're in this together. I won't be hiding behind your back, if things get really serious. You understand?'

Roar sighed. 'I understand very well where your stubbornness comes from.'

'From Mum?' Sven smirked and gazed ahead of him, looking past Roar's shoulder.

The mist floating over the water was slowly vanishing and the expanded lake began to reveal itself. The falling rain drops left scattered marks on the surface, as if it was being punctured with thousands of tiny needles. A handful of fearless and optimistic fishermen, with their small dinghies and high hopes, broke the otherwise plain horizon.

'How far you've hidden the boat?' Sven asked.

Roar pointed ahead. 'Right there.'

Sven could only see a stack of reed between a group of birch trees. 'I can't see a thing. It must be quite small.'

'The smaller the better.' Roar went to swipe the loose reed off, revealing the boat's worn-out red paint on the bottom.

Doubtfully, Sven stared at it. 'Where did you get that from?'

'Actually, I found it,' Roar said with a hint of pride. 'After the tsunami, there were plenty of loose boats just floating around. And, so far, no one has come to claim this one back.'

'No wonder,' Sven gasped. 'Well, you can't blame me for being a burglar anymore.'

'What's that got to do with any of this?'

'You stole this boat.'

'No one needs it now, except us, for the greater good.' Roar bent down to flip the dinghy around.

Sven shook his head in disbelief. 'For the greater good' was a phrase that seemed to give justification for his father to do just about anything. 'But, that's *really* small. Wolferring will shred it to pieces.'

Sometimes I wish he was still twelve, Roar thought, while rolling his eyes in frustration. 'Being lower gives us a chance to reach the same level as Wolferring, and then we strike before it gets us.'

'If I'd known, we could have taken my Yolla again,' said Sven. 'They are built stronger. In the end, Carl's Yolla saved your life last time, right?'

'Son, I have to burst the bubble for you. Those new Yollas are not as good as the old ones. I have read many bad reviews about them. This boat here is probably as strong as yours, or maybe even stronger.'

Since Sven hadn't done his homework, he couldn't disagree.

Roar took the silence that fell between them as a sign of acquiescence. He pushed the boat into the water and gestured for Sven to sit at the back.

'I'll row.' Sven dropped his gear into the boat and jumped to the bow.

'As you wish.' Roar calmly kicked them off the land.

When Sven slammed the blades into the water, simultaneously a loud rustling came from the forest. They both turned to look, but saw nothing.

'A moose?' Roar suggested.

About a stone's throw away, a dark shadow dashed out of the bushes. Dusk had settled enough for the men to make out the silhouette of a person wobbling along the edge of the lake.

'Who is it?' Sven picked up the spear gun, even though he didn't really know how to operate it.

'Please, don't shoot!' The panicky voice sounded familiar. The man carried a rifle, which pointed unthreateningly to the ground.

'Jaaku?' Sven lowered his weapon.

The man took a step forward, his appearance becoming clearer under the faint moonlight. It was Jaaku, panting heavily. His face and clothes were muddy and dirty.

Sven picked up the oars again and reversed them back to the shore, where they could disembark. 'What happened? What are you doing here?'

'I... I...' Jaaku was out of breath. He couldn't get a word out.

'You look like you've just ran a marathon,' Sven said.

'Cross-country,' Roar snorted.

'Almost.' Jaaku carefully approached them, and offered his rifle. 'I just thought... you might want this.'

'You've come all the way here to give us your rifle?' Sven didn't know whether to be delighted or suspicious about this inexplicable gesture. He sought approval from Roar, who subtly shook his head. Sven turned back to Jaaku. 'Since you're here now, why not join us?'

'I can't,' Jaaku muttered. 'I just... wanted you to be safe. I know you've said that firearms are not needed for fishing, but maybe today's world is different.'

'We already have Viljo's harpoon,' Roar said bluntly.

Jaaku nodded and, over his shoulder, gave a nervous look to the forest.

'Are you sure everything is okay?' Sven asked, genuinely concerned.

'Do you want the gun or not?!' Jaaku grunted in sudden urgency. 'You can't imagine you can just simply catch Wolferring with a fishing line and a crawler.'

Roar and Sven exchanged confused looks after Jaaku's outburst. 'I guess some extra firepower is never a bad thing,' Roar hesitated.

'When did you become such a big fan of weapons?' Sven asked in awe.

'Maybe Jaaku is right,' said Roar. 'We can never be prepared enough. And we need all the help we can get.'

Encouraged by Roar's supportive words, Jaaku pushed the rifle under Sven's nose.

'Take it.' Roar nodded next to him.

With some hesitation, Sven accepted the rifle, exactly like someone who had never handled weapons before. His wrists were sloppy and his hands at the wrong places, as if he was holding a feather.

'Not like that.' Jaaku adjusted his grip, one hand on the barrel and the other on the trigger.

After Sven's stance had been improved, he gave himself a manly, affirming nod.

'Much better,' said Jaaku, thinking to himself that his work here was done. He took a step back and looked over his shoulder again.

'Are you in a hurry?' Sven queried.

'Yes, yes,' Jaaku stammered. 'Busy times.'

'Thank you, Jaaku,' Roar said promptly. 'We have to get going, too. Long night and day ahead.'

'Shame you gotta go.' Sven was still totally oblivious to the fact that Jaaku did not want to be there. He even felt slightly delighted for having unexpectedly reunited with an old friend that he had somewhat drifted apart from in the recent months. 'If you were to join us, this trip shouldn't take that long – especially with this heavy gun arsenal.'

Jaaku forced a subtle smile. 'Maybe next time. It's late. Marjukka is waiting for me at home. I just heard that she's pregnant.'

'Wow! That was fast.'

'I agree,' Jaaku replied flatly.

'Congratulations,' Roar said.

'Thank you, sir.'

'I understand,' Sven said, even though Ida being pregnant never stopped him from going fishing. 'Anyway, thanks for the rifle. And good luck at home.'

Jaaku nodded and started trotting along the coastline. He took a last glance at the men's boat, which he found somewhat unimpressive. Even though he was fully aware that the hunters were probably still after him, sending the men to the lake in such an old and weak-looking dinghy made him hesitate. In addition, the idea of tagging along with the fishermen and their firepower did make him feel safer.

Thus, he came up with two variable options: to keep on running, or help his friends. He went through a quick self-assessment in his mind. Unselfishly, and so unlike him, he chose the latter. Tagging along a little longer made him feel somewhat safer.

'One more thing.' He returned to interrupt the men's second departure attempt. 'If I were you, I wouldn't face Wolferring with that lousy dinghy.'

Even though Jaaku's opinions weren't always the most respected, this one gained Sven's attention.

'I told you, Dad,' he snickered.

'But, the lower edges of this boat give us a greater chance to lure sizable fishes, like Wolferring,' Roar said, defending his choice.

'With your own bodies?' Jaaku laughed. 'Why don't you take my boat?'

'Carl's boat?' Sven asked, intrigued.

'Yes. It's not a big boat, either. But, Roar, as you know well, Wolferring's teeth didn't manage to penetrate its hard plastic hull.'

Roar took a deep, nervous breath. The history really kept haunting him. He was being asked to use the boat of his worst ever competitor, and the same boat in which Roar had ended up floating aimlessly as an injured victim before he became the Lord. 'Yolla may have saved my life, yes.'

Jaaku took Roar's reluctant response as an agreement. 'It's not so far away. If you follow me, I can show you where it is and give you the keys.'

'Why not, then, take my new boat instead? It's Yolla as well,' said Sven, testing the waters, while climbing back onto the shore.

Jaaku chuckled. 'Your boat, I'm sorry to say, is only a cheap copy. It's nothing like the original.'

Now, it was Roar's turn to give Sven that 'I told you so' look.

However, Sven remained persistent, as there was something overwhelming in Jaaku's helpfulness. 'But didn't you lose your boat in the floods?'

'I did,' said Jaaku. 'But after one month of searching, I found it about twenty kilometres from its original position. I was lucky. It must have remained afloat due to its non-sinking qualities. Although, some dastard had used it and then just abandoned it. When I found it, it was full of old fishing equipment and the locks had been changed.'

Sven gave his father a disapproving glance. 'That's a disgrace – using someone else's boat without permission.'

'Fine! Let's use Carl's Yolla then,' Roar snorted remorsefully. 'At least Carl is not around anymore to blame us for stealing it.'

Again, Sven was impressed by Roar's ability to overcome past events and move forward – something he had already skilfully proven in the restaurant by hiring Irmeli and Lumbardi, the two most painful reminders of his bittersweet love life. Also, Roar reluctantly agreeing with Jaaku made Sven warm to the idea of changing the boat – even though he feared it might take some time. Ida had just recently resettled in their new home with the baby and was immediately being left alone there. Sven didn't want to extend this trip any longer than he had to.

'We don't want to lose any valuable time, then,' said Jaaku as he scurried ahead.

Reluctantly, both Roar and Sven began following his route to a soggier part of the coast where the signs of floods were even more devastating. The ground was soft, as in a swamp-like wilderness. It became harder to detect where exactly the lake began or ended. They were forced to leap over various newly formed creeks and use fallen trees and their branches as bridges to cross muddy streams.

After an hour of laborious trekking, they reached Jaaku's blue Yolla. Jaaku went to unlock the chain, and together the men flipped the boat around.

'I presume you don't need any further instructions?' he said.

Roar gave a long, perplexed stare at the original Yolla. He thought this day would never come. It was a reunion after so many years. He could still recognise the scratch marks. So many painful memories, yet, surprisingly, thankfulness was the sensation that surfaced above all.

Even Sven thought this was a much better option of the two, as he observed the strong edges of the boat. Roar's positive reaction reaffirmed their choice.

'Thank you for doing this,' said Sven. He was in awe of Jaaku's kindness, to the extent that even embracing him crossed his mind. Yet, he thought it wouldn't be appropriate in these latitudes, and in the dark forest between three straight men. Therefore, he ended up giving Jaaku an approving nod, which Jaaku perfectly interpreted – knowing Sven well enough – as a sign of gratitude.

'Should you be at home by now?' Roar intervened. 'You said Marjukka was waiting.'

Jaaku nodded calmly, while feeling safer and less paranoid about being chased. Perhaps he had managed to shake the hunters off.

'Have a safe journey.' Jaaku gave Sven and Roar a wave, and continued walking along the coast in the opposite direction they had just come from.

'Are you gonna walk around the whole lake?' Sven asked, baffled. 'That's gonna take a while. It's not a small lake anymore.'

'I just thought I'd need... a bit of me time,' Jaaku stuttered, and kept walking in the direction that wasn't necessarily the shortest way to get home, but could be better for his well-being.

Sven shrugged his shoulders, and climbed into the boat. 'I thought he was in a hurry to see Marjukka.'

'Well, anyway, how considerate of him to lend his boat,'

Roar said, while watching Jaaku disappearing into the forest. 'Maybe he's not so bad, after all.'

'This was a very noble gesture, indeed,' Sven replied thoughtfully. *Almost too noble.*

Chapter 36

LET THE PARTY BEGIN!

Two kicksleds reached the top of a hill. Birgget came first, with a stack of cardboard boxes taking over her entire seat, followed by Ida, with a cot in the front tightly secured with straps around the steering bar and the struts. Their scenic route was chosen by Ida, who knew the short cuts to her old home. The winds blew harsher on this open space that led to a ridge, with views overlooking the vast lake on one side and more forest down the other. The sun was setting behind the mountain range and the volcano, painting the sky with orange and red. From this high altitude, they could almost touch the shallow clouds.

'I'm so glad you decided to come,' Ida said, while keeping her eyes on the cot, like a hawk protecting its nest. 'It should be a fun night. You spent almost the entire time with the baby while I was in hospital. You deserve a break.'

'I only did my duty. What any grandparent would have done,' Birgget replied modestly, not keen to accept any credit.

'You did so much more. You always have,' Ida said melancholically. Her own mother's indifference towards the new grandchild kept bothering her.

Since the compliments made Birgget feel mostly uncomfortable, she wanted to change the subject. 'I hope your mother will appreciate this snake plant. She gave one to Sven, right?'

Birgget gestured to sword-like green leaves sticking out

from a paper bag that kept swinging back and forth on her steering bar. In their native tongue, the plant commonly known as *Anopinkieli* directly translated to 'mother-in-laws tongue'.

'To us,' Ida sighed, not pleased with the plant's unflattering and suggestive name. 'I'm the one looking after it. Sven's not really good with plants.'

'Like his father.' Birgget tightened her grip around the bag's handle. 'Me and Sophia are just so different. We've hardly ever spoken to each other.'

'It won't be just us there, but plenty of others,' Ida said. 'The whole idea of Tuppervaara parties is for the locals, usually women, to get together. Many of us just need another reason, or any reason, to get out of the house – like men when they go fishing or hunting, even if they don't really want to. Attending a party like this can still be the better out of two bad options.'

Birgget rolled her eyes in disbelief. 'Being at home can't be that bad.'

She never had to come up with excuses to leave the house, but the opposite. She sometimes had to create excuses not to accept every invitation which would have taken her away from the comfort of her own family – and, later on, her own private space.

'I like staying at home – even more if Sven would spend more time there,' Ida said longingly. 'But not everyone is like you and me.'

Birgget sighed. 'What about all that buying and selling of products tonight? Is that even important, then?'

'Of course. The products are always a good distraction, if the guests run out of things to say.'

Thank God for that, Birgget thought, while keeping an eye on the pile of boxes in front of her, wobbling from side to side. 'As long as we don't run out of products to talk about.'

'That would be a commercial success,' said Ida. 'But very unlikely, since my mother has got even more stock.' She was grateful for Sophia stepping in at the last minute and hosting the party on her behalf. Now, though, she had another thing to worry about: how Birgget and Sophia would get along. 'I genuinely wanted to organise this party at mine, but the earliest the engineer could get the boiler fixed was tomorrow.'

'It's still freezing outside,' Birgget gasped. 'How are you gonna survive until tomorrow?'

'I might stay the night in Örebröre. I'm sure you're welcome to stay, too.'

'Let's take one step at the time,' Birgget hesitated. 'What about Sven, then? Where is he going to stay?'

Ida knew that Sven wouldn't spend a night in Örebröre, even if the end of the world was in sight. 'He's been away all day and, most likely, will be all night. The men started the big hunt, so to speak.' She didn't sound as supportive of Sven's wish to go fishing, compared to the moment she woke up in the hospital. 'I know, I encouraged him to go. When I came to my senses after the coma, I wanted to give in; to reward him for being there for me, after all those weeks while I was lying as a vegetable. He looked after the baby... Well, you did. But he didn't disappear and never gave up on me. He stayed by my bedside. He even tried to change and get a proper job. So, I thought, he deserved a break from everything else, and have the chance to focus on himself.'

Birgget sensed regret in Ida's voice. 'Do you wish you'd acted differently?'

'Not sure if I could ever forgive myself, if I'd stopped him from going.'

'He gave you the option.'

Ida sighed. 'I would feel much calmer if there were more men helping them. Though, Sven always likes to do everything by himself.'

'Pihtamo has many capable men,' Birgget pondered. 'Roar will be there, for sure.'

'But, apart from him, not so many, if you think about it,' said Ida. 'Viljo has retired. Christian has disappeared. Nobody knows what Jaaku wants. And the rest, I don't know. There aren't many other fishermen who trust *our* men at the moment.'

'Or they are not willing to risk their lives for the cause,' Birgget added.

'It makes you wonder how lucky Sven and Roar have been.'

'Well, luck is subjective.' Birgget's tone changed. She couldn't see them being that blessed. Her own family had broken apart during a sensitive period when Sven was only twelve years old.

'Lucky in a sense that they are still here with us, alive.'

'If that's how low you want to set the bar,' Birgget smirked.

Despite Ida being modestly grateful, she did worry much more about Sven these days compared to the times they were only dating. Being a fresh parent had introduced a completely new level of sensibility and responsibility to her life. Before the lake's fish population vanished, nothing could keep Sven away from fishing. She knew how badly the men wanted that situation to return. Forcing Sven to stay at home wasn't an option either – the need to spend time with his own family would have to come from within himself.

On a more positive note, the amount of fish he caught in the past was more than enough to fulfil their needs as a couple. But now, having a child to support, Sven would either have to catch even more fish or get another job. Somehow, Ida wasn't confident the riches of the pond would last forever. Hence, she feared she'd have to rely, again, on the support from her wealthy mother.

Birgget understood how she and Ida shared a very similar kind of burden. 'Trust me. I know exactly what you're going through. I was once married to a fisherman.'

Ida started running out of breath from simultaneously conversing and riding a kicksled. She was forced to slow down. Being comatose for weeks had taken its toll on her physique, and she was still recovering.

'Can I ask you something?'

'Depends,' Birgget smiled, and kept to the same speed beside her.

'How did it work for you and Roar? When Sven was little, I mean?'

'Times were different back then. I stayed at home while Roar made sure we had enough fish on the table. To be fair, we had only one child. I know people with four or six children and they do just fine. The only downside was that having one child takes all your attention. You can't distract them with other siblings. Gladly, though, Roar took Sven fishing quite a lot, so I could have "me time". Or, I tried to have. I wasn't really good at it, staying on my own. I always wanted to have the family around.'

'Even more kids?'

Birgget's face grew serious. 'We tried a few years after Sven was born, but I had a miscarriage. And then, well, Roar disappeared.'

'I'm sorry. I didn't know.'

'You can't have it all. Everything is fine now.'

However, Ida wasn't fully convinced that Birgget was completely over it.

Nevertheless, Birgget pointed ahead and, again, smoothly changed the subject. 'Is that your house?'

Not even looking to the bottom of the ridge, Ida replied. 'That's it. You wanna race?'

'You've got the baby and I've got the products. Not a good idea...' Before Birgget could finish the sentence, Ida was already going down the slope.

Birgget let her go, instead taking her time to admire the grandeur of the mansion. As she began her slow descent, the house grew in size and became more intimidating the closer she got. It could have been a royal palace. Suddenly, she regretted her decision to join the party, while feeling herself shrinking. All those luxurious fur coats and expensive jewellery she had seen Sophia wearing at the hospital and the wedding made sense now; and they were probably just the tip of an ice-berg of wealth and glamour.

Birgget couldn't quite comprehend how such a modest and down-to-earth person like Ida could come from such a privileged and exclusive family. And why on earth was she married to *her* son: the poor, uneducated fisherman without any fish? *Love does make people do the craziest things.*

The bottom of the slope, however, revealed some unwanted gravel underneath the snowy path. As the surface suddenly changed, speed-loving Ida's fast ride halted, as if she'd hit a brick wall. She flew over the handlebar. The cot shot off the seat and landed on the snow beside her.

Meanwhile, Birgget managed to skid away from danger due to her slow speed. She stopped smoothly, went straight to the cot and took the crying baby in her embrace.

'Oh, hush,' she said gently. The baby's sobbing muted in the confident and soothing arms of her grandmother. 'I think she doesn't like speed quite as much as her mother.' Birgget finally paid attention to Ida on the ground.

'My ankle,' Ida grunted in agony, while trying to drag herself up against her kicksled that had been knocked on its side. 'You wouldn't mind helping me out, too?'

'Ah, sorry.' With her free hand, Birgget helped Ida onto her feet. 'I thought, let's take care of the youngest first.'

'I probably would've done the same.' Ida grimaced in pain, and lifted her fallen kicksled. 'Let's go then. We're almost there.'

However, the sprained ankle couldn't hold her full body weight. Riding a kicksled imposed a particular challenge, because one foot had to stay firmly on the rest while the other kicked and kept it in motion. But she couldn't do either of those.

'Why don't we make a train?' Birgget suggested.

'I haven't done that for years,' said Ida. 'Are you sure you can push us all?'

'We can try. It's just a short distance.' Birgget started reorganising the kicksleds, while Ida took a careful step aside. 'You sit in the front.'

Birgget interlocked the kicksleds with one another. Once Ida was seated, Birgget put the cot on her lap, while the supplies stayed where they were on the front seat of her own kicksled – which had now become the back seat of this tandem arrangement.

'Where's the plant? The bag isn't here.' Birgget slid her hands across the empty steering bar. She looked over her shoulder to the hill they had just descended. 'I must have dropped it somewhere.'

'Do you wanna go and get it?'

Birgget kicked the train of sleds into motion. 'I'll bring one next time.' Although, she thought it was unlikely there was going to be another visit. 'Do you always have to ride so fast? There will be plenty of chances for the baby to enjoy rollercoasters when she's older.'

'She's absolutely fine. It was a soft landing.' Ida knew she had done the wrong thing, yet didn't let the guilt show. 'She's so calm and sleeps well. I always thought the babies would just cry all the time.'

'She sleeps like Sven when he was a baby. Nothing used to wake him up.'

'Really? He sleeps so poorly nowadays.'

'His sleeping patterns changed after we lost Roar. Some of his dreams became quite vivid – so much so that he used to talk about them.'

'Tell me about it,' replied Ida. 'I remember, once he dreamt about a steam train full of king prawns, avocadoes and salmon.'

'I guess we all have those,' Birgget chuckled.

'Really? About a life-size sushi buffet train?' Ida laughed.

'Irrational dreams,' Birgget replied seriously. 'Have you found that Sven has changed, while you were in the hospital? Become more open?'

'I haven't really spoken to him much, since then. Has he said anything to you?'

Birgget wanted to avoid being the gossiper. 'Better you ask him, then. All I can say is that he loves you very much.'

Those heart-warming words made Ida momentarily forget the pain in her ankle. 'That's our driveway.' The gates in front of them were left open for the arriving guests.

More like a highway. Birgget rolled her eyes, yet vocally expressed herself more diplomatically. 'How lovely.'

Ida wasn't fully convinced about the genuineness of Birgget's monotone response. Yet, she let it pass.

Panting heavily, Birgget pushed the train up the lengthy driveway, finally stopping by the main entrance. There were a few snowmobiles parked sporadically around the front yard.

As Ida looked around her, it seemed the house was less gloomy compared to her last visit. It was as if parts of the building had been brought back to life by the visiting guests, and their chattering and laughter, which faintly travelled through the exterior walls. The light shining from the ground floor windows reinstalled some of that lively ambience lost with the passing of Gustav. Ida became hopeful that her mother was really getting back on her feet.

'Are you okay with the boxes?' Ida asked, while picking up

the cot.

'Of course.' Birgget nodded calmly, not letting her exhaustion show.

'This way,' Ida said, leading the way, whilst limping on her foot.

Birgget's vision became completely blocked by the wall of cardboard in her arms. Somehow, though, in the midst of carrying the heavy load, she still had strength to worry about her choice of wardrobe. 'Are you sure my dress is suitable enough?'

'Please. It's just a Tuppervaara party.' Before Ida had a chance to knock, the door opened.

'Don't speak nonsense, Ida. It's not just like any party,' Sophia blurted out and, without any reservations, went to tickle the baby's belly. 'How's my little granddaughter?'

'The trip by kicksled took a bit longer.' Ida limped inside, pulling the baby away from Sophia's reach.

'What's wrong with your leg?'

'Just some... post-hospital symptoms.' Ida didn't want to dive into details about her guilty pleasure: her need-for-speed.

'Is it serious?' Sophia enquired, while Ida pretended not to hear the question.

Then Birgget tried to enter with the boxes, grabbing Sophia's attention. Having to greet all three generations at once, all of which Sophia had very variable opinions of, was a situation confusing enough to deal with. However, she took Ida's coat, while ignoring Birgget.

'You should have told me. I could have arranged someone to pick you up with a snowmobile.' In normal circumstances, being a cloakroom assistant was something Sophia would never do – to lay her expensively manicured hands on other people's dandruff-ridden overgarments – but today the extra service was part of the show. She wanted to appear as hospitable as possible in front of any potential buyers and paying guests. 'Isn't she lovely? The baby?' She made an effort to connect with Birgget, without really seeing her face.

'A gift,' Birgget's muffled voice carried from behind the boxes.

Sophia turned to Ida again. 'You shouldn't have brought all

your stock. I have plenty here for everyone.'

'And now you're telling me?' Ida snorted.

Sophia, not used to doing physical labour, waved the housemaid to collect the boxes from Birgget. In no time, the housemaid did her duty, as well as removing Birgget's coat. Sophia was finally forced to acknowledge her, face to face.

'So, is this your first time to a Tuppervaara party?'

'Yes. Any party plan, actually,' Birgget replied.

'You've missed out on a lot. These are great opportunities for networking, learning about trends and meeting new friends.'

All three things Birgget wasn't bothered about. Yet, she tried to keep an open mind, when Sophia escorted them to the living room where the other guests were congregating. Now, Birgget became convinced that she had been brought into some royal palace free of charge – apart from any cost that may accumulate from shopping Tuppervaara. If she felt like shrinking earlier outside, now she wanted to disappear. She had never felt so small and insignificant. The guests were all wearing shiny, high-end cocktail dresses, whereas hers was a simple charcoal-colour calf-length crinkle dress she had sewn herself from a double-layered cotton weave.

Ida, on the other hand, wasn't even paying attention to the luxury on show around them, since she had been brought up in the middle of it. If nothing else, she was slightly embarrassed by it. However, the sudden cleanliness and liveliness of the place positively surprised her.

'What have you done here, Mum?' she whispered. 'The house looks so different, and I only gave you a few hours' notice to host the party.'

Sophia winked at her. 'I hired a last-minute decoration and catering company. They did miracles.'

It was the first time Ida had seen her mother this positive, almost glowing, since Gustav went missing. Socialising brought the best out of her and seemed to help with the recovery.

Sophia was in her element at these types of situations, like now, when she turned to face the crowd in the living room.

'I would like you to meet our new guests. This is Ida, my daughter. And, this is her mother-in-law, Birgget. And my granddaughter, who doesn't have a name yet.'

'Aw!' The guests, about a dozen elegantly dressed women, reacted in perfect harmony to the latter. Apart from one guest, Irmeli, who was unable to express joy as her eyes were locked onto Birgget's.

'What is she doing here?' Birgget grunted.

'Irmeli? The fisherwoman?' Ida replied.

Birgget bit her teeth together. 'Used to be. But now she works in Roar's restaurant.'

'Really? So nice of Roar to hire her,' Ida said, genuinely delighted. 'Irmeli has been a great example to many young women. She has shown to the world how everything is possible. There are still not that many women ice fishing, but the numbers are picking up – because of her.'

'She was good at many things.' Birgget struggled to hold back her emotions.

'Is everything alright?' Sophia interrupted, with a grin on her face.

Birgget gave a subtle, yet sour nod. *This is gonna become the longest party ever.*

Meanwhile, Ida began to fear for the worst. They were only in the first minutes of the party, yet Birgget's discomfort was beginning to show. As Sophia went to mingle with other guests, Ida thought it would be best to address the issue with Birgget.

'Could we just try to do this for my mother's sake? She's been having a hard time.'

The housemaid slowly cruised past them with a tray filled with champagne glasses. Birgget grabbed one for herself.

'This has nothing to do with your mother. Absolutely nothing.' She emptied the glass in one mouthful.

I thought she didn't drink? Ida pondered.

'I believe everyone is here,' Sophia announced enthusiastically. 'So, let the party begin!'

Chapter 37

THERE IS ALWAYS TOMORROW

Despite each other's support, the weapons they had with which to defend themselves, and Jaaku's protective Yolla, none of these factors made Sven and Roar any calmer. Normally, they thrived on solitude, but tonight the silence at the lake felt somewhat ghastly. The last few fishermen trying their luck were gone and out of sight. The land behind them was only a thin line on the horizon. The journey was becoming more like seafaring as the roughening waves pounded and rocked their small boat.

In the midst of battling the strong currents, Sven decided to say something for the first time since they had left the shore; something that had been bothering him since.

'Jaaku was behaving very strangely.'

'Is that something new?' Roar smirked, but felt immediately guilty for always mocking him.

However, Sven understood the perception some people had of Jaaku's controversial character. 'He is like a different person to the one I used to know. Or I thought I knew.'

'Life is long. Friends come and go.'

Sven sighed thoughtfully, and rested the oars to the side. They hadn't paused once since they'd departed. 'What about you? Who is, or was, your best friend?'

Roar began slowly retrieving the line. 'Me and your mother met when we were both quite young. My life revolved around fishing, family and marriage. I think, she was my best friend.'

'Really?' Sven sounded disappointed.

'There's nothing wrong if your wife is also your best friend, is there?'

'What about, then, all those years you were gone? Did you... spend time with anyone?' Sven asked.

'You mean, someone more than just a friend?' Roar was surprised by Sven's sudden desire to have a grown-up conversation. Their exchange was becoming like one of those man-to-man private conversations some fathers and sons have at some point – ideally a bit earlier in life than this. The delay was largely caused by Roar's long absence. Though, it was better late than never; some families couldn't even be this open and honest.

'Either way,' Sven replied. 'It was such a long time. You must've run into someone?'

'My task to save the fish took all my time and concentration. The devotion and purpose to help the community outstripped many of my individual needs and desires. Somewhere, deep down inside me, I felt lonely.'

'You were under a spell.'

'I guess we can call it that.' Roar faced the direction they had come from. His interest to delve into the past suddenly dropped when topics became too personal. 'Could you start rowing again?' he pleaded, and gave the rod a gentle pull. He felt resistance. He stood up and yanked it harder. The boat rocked, taking some water in.

'Careful,' Sven gasped.

'I know what I'm doing. The bait must've grabbed some weed, as we were not moving fast enough to catch anything else.'

'Why don't you row, then?' Sven grunted.

'Maybe I should,' Roar said under his breath, while balancing on his feet. He thought he must've ripped the tackle free, as he could no longer feel its weight.

'Could you please sit down?' Sven patronised. The stressful situation was getting to them both.

'You sound just like your mother,' Roar fired back.

'When has she ever instructed you in fishing?'

'She did, a couple of times,' Road said more calmly, while reeling again. 'You had a terrible stomach flu and my mother, your grandmother Wilma, was taking care of you. You were in bed for four days. Before you got sick, we had just laid those big nets across the lake and I couldn't check them myself. I had to take someone with me and that someone was your mother.'

'I remember,' said Sven. 'Grandma was washing the windows, taking carpets out, cleaning the whole house.'

'She had a way of making Birgget feel like a failure.'

'How was fishing with Mum, then?'

'We got along reasonably well at home, but fishing with her was a disaster. She had never fished before, yet she was trying to give me advice all the time.'

'Telling someone to sit down on a stormy lake is not a bad advice, though.'

'You're always taking her side.' Roar's grunt made him slip off balance. Yet, he managed to seek support from the gunwale.

'See. I told you,' Sven smirked.

Why is he such a snowflake? Roar thought, trying to contain himself. He was beginning to understand, more and more, where Viljo's bad temper came from. Perhaps it wasn't the old age making us grumpier, but the realisation of how frustrating some other people around us can be, especially the youngsters, yet we have to keep living with them.

Nevertheless, Sven, being clueless about Roar's suppressed fury, kept asking more questions. 'And then you disappeared soon after that?'

Those words made Roar stop reeling. He finally sat down. 'Arguing about some meaningless fishing techniques were the last moments I had with her.' The bitterness in his voice was easy to detect. Only minutes earlier, he had tried not to talk about the past, but now his mind was drenched in it. 'Once Birgget and I got back home from the lake, we didn't speak to each other. We went to bed upset. Then, early next morning, I left again... and never came back.'

'I'm...'

'Don't!' Roar interrupted. 'You've been sorry enough. Everyone's sorry. But there's nothing we or anyone else can do, except to pick up the pieces. The hardest thing for me is that those sixteen years felt like a blink of an eye, yet so much happened here – in your life, in the lives that I was supposed to be part of. Everyone has moved on, but I'm not sure I have.'

'But, it has also been a painfully long sixteen years,' Sven added. 'Every day I waited for you to return. I looked for signs at every fisherman and their boats. I tried to imagine what you'd look like a little bit older. Maybe you'd grown a beard.'

'You got that bit right.'

'But the rest, the magic was too much – even for my imagination.'

'Gladly, it was ONLY sixteen years,' Roar said. 'We just have to go on, enjoy the time that is left and look at the positive side of things. And there is still time – not for me and Birgget to get back together, for that boat has sailed, so to speak – but to see you and your children grow.'

Sven felt a touch of sadness. In his most childish fantasies, he wanted to see his parents together again, one way or the other.

The fishing line becoming heavy again alerted Roar back to the present. He yanked it a couple of times. 'It doesn't feel like a fish. There's no motion.'

Sven reversed the boat to the point where the line met the surface. They both glanced at Jaaku's rifle on the floor.

Roar nodded. 'Go for it – if you know how to use it.'

Sven's heart beat faster as he reached out for the rifle. He felt equally uncomfortable and awkward with it, like when someone's trying to play a musical instrument for the first time ever. In addition, when wrongly handled, this tool could kill instantly, which was much harder to achieve with a clarinet or oboe.

His shaky hands pointed the barrel to the water's edge, while Roar pulled up muddy leaves and reed that the tackle had scraped off the bottom. There was a sigh of relief from both of them. Sven could lower the weapon.

'Somehow, I feel like this lake is dead empty again,' Roar pondered, while clearing the dirt off the bait. 'Wolferring has been faster than expected. We should have come here much earlier.'

'Yes, but you wanted us to train,' Sven muttered.

'What did you say?' Roar bent down for his rucksack and

pulled out a small cooler box. He opened the lid, revealing a stack of half-frozen herrings. 'I took these from the restaurant. We could use them as a lure.'

However, Sven was more interested in their origin. 'Another batch of Christian's great work?' he snorted sarcastically.

'Please, don't make it a problem again. They've been searching for Christian for weeks. No sign of his boat. Nothing.'

'I'm sure he is fine. He's always been so lucky.'

'Can you show just a little empathy? Maybe he was born rich, but it hasn't always been easy for him either.'

'Why are you taking his side?'

'The man has just disappeared, for God's sake. I got to know him a little bit and he seems like any young man with high hopes and dreams.'

'Christian, the golden boy,' Sven grunted. 'It was enough that Ida's mum was head over heels for him. But now you as well.'

'Ah, dear,' Roar sighed. 'What I'm saying is that Christian hasn't always gotten what he wanted. He didn't get Ida, but you did. He hasn't won any ice fishing championships, but we have. I do understand if you feel that he's a threat, but he's still just a contender, and that's exactly how they are supposed to make us feel: threatened. They want what we have. But always remember that you have won, everything, even if you don't always feel that way.'

Sven, with his low self-esteem, still felt far from the winner Roar had just described him to be, yet he accepted that there may have been some truth in this spontaneous motivational speech. Lifting him up was always something Roar was good at, and he did it again.

'And don't get me wrong, I like your modesty,' Roar added. 'If possible, try to stay that way. But don't let your humility stand in the way of feeling worthy. You've done very well in life, and I just want you to acknowledge that. There's nothing wrong with being proud of yourself and showing confidence.'

'I'll try to remember that,' Sven replied, humbled by his father's knowledgeable words.

However, Roar wasn't finished yet. 'You also have to accept the fact that Christian is not my personal enemy. I don't have a past with him; only the present and future. He was my employee and a good one, who I have now lost.'

'Okay, okay.' Sven was beginning to regret opening his mouth in the first place. Normally, a fishing boat wasn't the most common place to delve into deep discussions. At least a steaming sauna, nudity and enough wodka were amongst things required, until conversations between Arctic men could become open and personal.

Roar understood that he had said enough; maybe too much. 'So, shall we test these herrings? Or continue to the pond to get some more?'

Sven yawned, and checked the time from his phone. 'I'd say we call it a day.'

'What do you mean?'

'You see, I kind of thought that I could still make it to... Ida's party.' Sven's cheeks began to blush.

'A party?'

'Tuppervaara,' Sven said so quietly that Roar could barely hear.

But he did hear, and didn't know whether to respond with laughter or to cry. 'Hold on. This is the moment we both have been waiting for. We have all the tools, fishing gear and firepower. We are finally together... and you wanna go and shop some kitchen containers?!'

'I... made a promise to spend more time at home,' Sven said apologetically. 'But, we have time. Since we've already spent a month training, a few more days are not going to hurt anyone. We can come back at the weekend, if you like.'

'Not hurt anyone? Except Wolferring's next victim!' Roar remonstrated. 'We've just lost Christian.'

'We're not really sure it was Wolferring, though. Besides, I doubt those herrings in the box are enough to really lure anything.' Sven spotted the branding embossed in the plastic. 'A box that is also made of Tuppervaara, by the way.'

Roar sighed. 'You really want to go to the party?'

Sven nodded subtly. 'Well, us staying here as baits is not really that intriguing.'

'You're right. Let's go back, so you can go shopping with

the girls.' Roar swallowed his bitter disappointment. 'I can row.'

Even though the situation had tensed dramatically, when it was time to swap seats, they both sensibly followed the advice from the only female member in the family, Birgget, who supposedly knew 'nothing' about fishing. The men kept their bodies low and passed the middle seat right at the same time – exactly the way Birgget had always instructed them.

Chapter 38

CONNECTION ISSUES

The diagonal antique coffee table, placed in the centre of the seating area in Sophia's living room, was covered with volcanic soy wax candles of many types: short, tall, thick, scented and shaped. Most of them were still wrapped in cellophane, but a few were available for the guests to examine. Each of the wax pieces featured ancient lava stones and moss collected from the soil around the Saalamaa volcano.

An archway separated the living room from the dining area, where the actual Tuppervaara Wood product line was displayed on a lengthy marble table. Again, the essentials were unwrapped and ready to be tested, whereas some were still sealed in their earthly, environmentally friendly packaging made of one hundred per cent recyclable materials. The assortment comprised anything from fishing knives to chopping boards, swede peelers, barrel-shaped shot glasses and wooden sauna ladles. Overall, the mood of the colours – whether candles or kitchen items – was creamy, darkish and modest. The designs were elegant and stylish, yet straightforward and practical.

The party was in full swing.

Meanwhile, Sophia had navigated herself to the middle of the room. 'May I have your attention, please,' she announced.

The women scattered around the space stopped chattering and sipping their champagnes

'Some housekeeping first. In case of an emergency, there are two exits: one in the front and one at the back.'

She made the guests laugh by gesturing her arms like an air hostess before the take-off. Even Ida gave a little chuckle. She never knew her mother had a sense of humour. It was a perfect ice breaker from Sophia to ease the tension amongst so many competitive females – a tactic she had learnt in Shotmasters, which was a local club gathering weekly to promote communication and public speaking.

'About what you see here today,' she continued, 'I am proud to say that we have managed to acquire a record number of items. The general quality is better than ever. We have one completely new supplier from Kihlava who produces our lovely wooden Christmas decorations. Those items are all minus thirty per cent off their original prices. I know, it's a little bit too early to think about Christmas. On the other hand, it's always surprising how quickly the seasons change.

'Since we're coming towards the summer, Tuppervaara kitchen and household items are more relevant. You can find them all in the dining area. Please, take your time to explore, see if there is anything you're interested in. Then, in about an hour's time, we can start talking business. Meanwhile, help yourself to more drinks and snacks. If you do want to become part of the sales network, come and talk to me, and I can explain how to join and get started. I have to warn you, though: running a Tuppervaara business is not necessarily easy. It's hard work, but eventually pays off. What's better than earning by doing something you love, and you can do it at home with a bunch of people you love!' Sophia finished with a high note while raising her glass.

The guests applauded enthusiastically, followed suit and had a sip of their drinks. Gradually, the chattering began again and the women congregated in their own little groups to various parts of the house that each found most interesting.

Apart from Ida, who couldn't hide her disappointment at the welcoming speech. She stormed up to Sophia and took her aside.

'I was supposed to be hosting this party.'

'Well, I thought since we're here, it would be more natural if I did the introduction,' Sophia said quietly.

'But now they all think you're running the show again,' Ida grunted.

A few of the nearest guests turned to look. Sophia gave them a quick, polite smile, before turning her back to them. 'Why don't you be responsible of charging people when they start buying?'

'I've always done that,' Ida sighed, tired of being her mother's cashier.

Across the room, Birgget sat on a sofa with the baby. She observed Ida and Sophia's heated conversation. Ida waved her arms, and started walking towards Birgget, who didn't want to get caught staring. Hence, Birgget quickly turned to examine the products on the table next to her. The variety and number of items rivalled any actual physical shop in the area.

'Not sure if I can afford any of these,' she sighed to Ida who arrived beside her. Then she whispered, 'I don't think this is really my thing.'

'You don't have to buy anything,' Ida replied, frustrated. 'Get some snacks. They are free.'

Just then, Sophia arrived, smiling pretentiously. 'So, Birgget, are you enjoying yourself?'

While Birgget tried to come up with the most diplomatic of responses, the baby in her arms opened her eyes and interrupted with her sobbing.

'Mum! See what you did.' Ida took the crying baby and walked away, leaving Birgget and Sophia together.

Sophia looked longingly at her daughter, who was being so overbearing. 'It's always like that with the first child.'

'I wouldn't know about that since I only have one,' Birgget replied bluntly.

Sophia realised how the grandchild could be a perfect bridge for them both to attempt an actual conversation. 'The baby does bring back lots of memories, don't you think?'

'True. Those were simpler times. Not financially, but spiritually and emotionally. Went by too fast, though.'

Sophia didn't know exactly what Birgget meant, yet she nodded. Due to the financial stability throughout her life, times of real hardship had been impossible to recognise. The media may have reported about austerity, poverty and struggle of the masses, yet for her this was alien terminology with a very different substance. 'Austerity' may have meant something like not being able to buy the third house, another fifty acres of land, or the latest Kanaali fashion dress every day, but only once a week.

In terms of the spiritual side of Sophia's parenting, she blindly believed she had always been there for her children – even though Ida would dare to disagree. However, the word 'spiritual' Sophia despised and avoided using, due to its connotation to something alternative and not tangible. She applied a similar approach when talking about emotions, which she didn't encourage.

However, she could agree with one thing: that years had gone by too fast. Yet, she did not reflect that experience through her children growing up too quickly, but in her own current life situation, in which she had suddenly lost the man who had always been beside her. Simultaneously, there was no beauty treatment sufficient enough to hide her aging.

Financially intact, Sophia's suffering had to come through tragedies, like self-infliction, serious illnesses or a close family member's death. Unfortunately, the most dramatic, latter event had to happen, crumbling the sand castle she had been building for decades. Suddenly, life was no longer plain sailing, nor was she emotionally bullet proof. With Gustav being gone, she faced a new challenge that no money or back-patting acquaintances could fix. No matter how many Tuppervaara parties she organised or whiskeys gulped, the pain took its indefinite time to heal.

Nevertheless, she was determined to keep up that façade of perfection to the outside world and not let her weaknesses show – at least, not today. One of the best ways to escape any negative emotions was to keep the conversation neatly superficial.

'These parties really divide us. Some people observe, some spend fortunes, whereas others only come here to make friends. I prefer the ones who spend a lot,' Sophia smiled jokingly. 'Which one are you then?'

'I'm still here,' Birgget smirked.

'Indeed,' Sophia snorted.

'Like that ice fisher.'

'Irmeli?'

Birgget nodded, grinding her teeth. 'I didn't expect to see any fishermen in here.'

'But she's one of a kind.'

'She's a woman?'

'Exactly. She has been paving the way for so many young, hopeful girls out there, to take part in such a male-dominated industry. That I respect. I couldn't care less about ice fishing.' Sophia leant over the table and picked up a wooden rolling pin. 'Let me introduce you to some of the items. This rolling pin was hand-carved by another innovative woman I look up to, Kataarina Finskabogadotter, a fourth-generation artisan from Örebröre. She has had her own workshop for over thirty years. She has won many international awards. Normally, these pins sell for ninety-nine marks each. But today, we can sell them for seventy-nine marks.'

She handed the pin to Birgget.

'It does feel... light.' Birgget tried to force an opinion about a product she knew she could buy ten times cheaper from Marksqueezer, a discount store in Kihlava town centre.

Sophia grabbed the pin back, unimpressed by Birgget's unsophisticated analysis. 'Tell me: what do you normally use to roll the dough?'

'A bottle, mostly.'

'A wine bottle?' Sophia laughed.

'Wodka,' Birgget corrected.

Sophia frowned. Of course, she'd never had to do any baking herself, since all that type of work was done by their housemaid. However, using an empty bottle as a baking aid sounded odd and primitive.

'Aren't they square?'

'The bigger ones are round.' Birgget immediately felt ashamed and the urge to explain more. 'It's not me. I don't drink. But Sven sometimes brings me empty bottles.'

The already lousy reputation of the son-in-law crumbled in Sophia's rolling eyes. 'Wonderful,' she replied sarcastically, and shifted the discussion to a more comfortable direction again. 'I hope you both brought your swedes with you? Soon, we'll be talking about the peeling results.'

Relieved, Birgget gently patted her purse. 'I have them right here. Looking forward to it,' she said, even though she really wasn't.

Sophia responded with another fake smile, and moved on to entertain the next group of guests. Birgget's tense body relaxed as Sophia went away. The contrasting energy between the two women, both from opposite worlds, was palpable.

Birgget looked around the room for anyone else to engage with. Not that she was desperate to socialise, but she felt exposed and alone in the middle of the room. She spotted Irmeli standing by the buffet table, munching a slice of raspberry pie. The women's eyes met again. While Ida was occupied calming the baby and Sophia busy chatting to other guests, Birgget and Irmeli were the missing pieces of the puzzle. They were the only individuals without any company. Yet, even if the world was about to end, they would probably let it end first, rather than engaging in any conversation with one another.

Chapter 39

SALSA AND SWEDES

Despite the surrounding noise and chatter the guests created, the baby managed to fall asleep on the sofa, Ida beside her. Sophia caught a glimpse of her tired daughter. She made her excuses to the women she was mingling with and walked up to her.

'Having a good time?'

'Maybe you did the right thing,' Ida sighed. 'It's better you host this party. I never realised having a baby could be this exhausting.'

'You have to cut yourself some slack.' Sophia carefully sat beside them. 'I thought about what might cheer you up. After I've shown these people how to make salsa, would you like to run the results of the Swede Peeling? I can stay with the baby while you do it.'

'Thanks, Mum. I'd love to,' Ida said, delighted. Immediately, her hand wandered inside her bag to check that her two swedes were still there.

'Great. I'll call you then.' Sophia stood up, then positioned herself in the middle of the room. 'Hi again, everyone. I believe you all have had time to initially browse some of the products. I hope you've found something you like. As I said before, we've got plenty of stock today, so things shouldn't run out. If that happens, though, just let me or my daughter, Ida, know and we can deliver directly to you after the party. This event tonight won't end any time soon, though. You have time to shop until the last woman is standing.'

While the laughs came, Sophia moved to the dining area to fetch a food processor. As she returned to the living room, she continued the speech.

'In each party, I always want to pick an item and give a brief introduction on how to operate it, and explain more in-depth one of the many things the product can be used for.' Her voice got a bit raspier for this next, more personal, sequence. 'As most of you know, I recently lost my husband, Gustav. After his passing, I learnt a lot of things about being alone – for the first time in my life.'

There were two variable reasons that made Sophia share her personal life in front of such a large group. The first was that she was being genuine, and speaking openly about the loss helped release some stress. However, she knew there were also a couple of other widows amongst the guests. Hence, she calculated that her touching example could appeal to those – even to Birgget – who had recently experienced something similar.

Nevertheless, Sophia's admission of her grief did somewhat unite the women, helping Sophia to catch Birgget's attention – even though Roar had returned.

'Again, I cannot thank you all enough,' Sophia continued. 'These parties, and your presence here, have helped me immensely to move on. My newly born granddaughter has shed new light on our lives. As they say, when one generation passes away, the new has come.' Her deep words changed the general mood among the guests. Some empathetic looks were exchanged. Even Ida felt the caring energy – which was a rare sensation to experience in the otherwise lifeless mansion.

However, Sophia's intention was not to turn the sales event into a memorial service, but rather to uplift the atmosphere again.

'Nevertheless, being single for the first time in over thirty years, I have already learnt that men in the area cannot master salsa that well.' Her sudden twist was welcomed with a few awkward chuckles. 'So, I have decided to show you how to do salsa properly.'

The women exchanged confused looks, wondering if there

was a dance number coming.

'Edible salsa,' Sophia added, which gained her more laughs, and the party was back to normal.

Sophia pulled open the lid of a wooden container beside her, which had peeled onions and garlic, and a few tomatoes and one lime. She chopped the lime in half.

'Making salsa with Tuppervaara food processor could not be easier and faster. You simply open the lid, drop the ingredients in, one by one, and let the blades do all the work. You just plug it in, press the button, and mixed salsa should be ready in about thirty seconds. And you can wear open shoes and your toes will stay intact, unlike on the dance floor.'

The curious crowd gathered around her as she pulsed the appliance.

'There we go: homemade salsa.' Sophia opened the lid and passed the container around. 'The food processor is one hundred and forty-nine marks, if you buy it today. We only charge the shipping costs on top, if you want it sent over. But remember, this offer is only valid until the end of the month. If you have any questions, or you want to make a purchase, please come and talk to me or Ida.' She received the container back, and handed it to Ida. 'Could you help me to pour this to the serving cups for tasting?'

Ida sighed, disappointed to be her mother's little helper again. Yet, she had to do what she was told, since there were too many judging eyes on them.

However, this time Sophia remembered her promise to Ida. 'Let's give them some time to taste it, and then it's your turn to introduce the swede.'

The butterflies awakened inside Ida's stomach. Swede peeling was one of the most anticipated single events in the entire Tuppervaara party plan concept. Not only did the organiser examine and judge each participant's peeling results, but also a speed contest was held in which the fastest swede peeler was rewarded with a one-year free Tuppervaara party plan membership. This was the first time Ida was given such a notable responsibility. Her mother's long hosting experience had set the bar high. In the past, Ida had only helped out with minor chores, such as laying out the products on display, opening doors to incoming guests, or, like now, serving salsa.

'You'll do just fine.' Sophia saw how nervous Ida was.

Ida gave her a subtle smile. She never realised how preparing to speak in public could be so agonising. She tried to remember phrases and vocabulary her mother had used in the previous years while hosting the contest, but none came to mind. Her respect for Sophia's work grew instantly; her mother was always so comfortable being the voice of the party, whereas she felt just the opposite. Ida was more the observer and critic; this time, however, she was throwing herself in the deep end in front of a demanding crowd.

Sophia sat down and rocked the cot soothingly. Momentarily, she wasn't thinking about Gustav; instead, she stared, mesmerised, at the baby's long eye lashes. Ida, watching her mother showing such hidden grandmotherly qualities, stopped worrying about her own performance. The gesture revealed a softer side to Sophia that had been hidden for a long time. It reminded Ida of earlier years when she was just a toddler and when her mother had been more present in her life. Once Ida grew older, they became distant, making her teenage years difficult. Then, mother and daughter continued for years hardly communicating, but only grunting to each other, while Gustav was constantly away on business. In the end, Ida was mostly brought up by her grandparents and older sisters. Later on, she reached adolescence together with her first boyfriend, Christian. Sophia had been living proof of a parent whose first excitement and interest towards her own newborn babies faded relatively soon once the novelty had worn off. Nevertheless, Ida remained hopeful that her mother would cherish *grandmotherhood* in a more mature and humane way, and see it perhaps as her second chance.

'Whenever you're ready,' said Sophia, giving Ida an approving look to start the show.

Ida scanned the room, listening to the loud chattering of the women. Her pulse began racing. She somehow had to get their attention. As she had seen Sophia do many times, Ida took a spoon and softly tapped a half-empty champagne glass.

'Harder,' Sophia said, since the guests didn't react.

Ida doubled the force, breaking the glass into pieces. The shards bounced off the table, while champagne sprinkled on the products and plates with half-eaten slices of sandwich cake. The guests stopped talking and turned to her. With only the stud of the glass left in her hand, she had at last got everyone's attention. She smiled, embarrassed. 'So, the next I would like to run is... the Swede Peeling sequence.' She put the remains of the glass away, and went to her bag to take out a couple of swedes and her Tuppervaara peeler. 'Did you all bring your swedes with you?'

With some hesitation, some of the women went to their purses, but most were not convinced by Ida's insecure opening.

'I'm sorry. I left mine at home. My husband. He is Swedish,' one woman heckled.

The guests laughed – even Sophia chuckled a little.

Ida, however, was the only one not laughing. 'Ööö... Okay. But did you bring your... swede?' Her clunky response showed no ability to think on her feet, and bounce back from unexpected responses and heckles. At this very moment, she wished to be anywhere else than making a fool of herself in front of this tough crowd.

'If I repeated myself, it wouldn't be that funny anymore,' the heckler snorted.

A sudden ringing of the doorbell came as another distraction to Ida's poor opening. On the other hand, it may have been exactly the interruption she needed to save herself from completely losing her reputation.

'The housemaid will open it,' said Sophia. 'You just get on with the show. You're doing very well.' She smiled, managing to conceal her true opinion.

Ida couldn't detect whether Sophia's supposedly encouraging last sentence had some irony hidden in it or not. As she turned to face the demanding audience again, she was greeted with a horrified gasp. *What now?* she thought, her remaining confidence sinking down the drain.

She then realised that no one was looking at her but the corridor leading to the front door. Turning to the direction the others were facing, she saw Christian standing in the doorway with his clothes ripped apart. He was shaking, and his body was covered in bruises and blood stains. His eyes found Ida's the second before he collapsed on the parquet.

'Christian?!' Ida dropped the swede peeler and rushed beside him. She knelt down and took his limp hand. He was unconscious, but breathing. She touched his blood-covered face with her shaky fingers. Some of the bravest and the most curious of the guests gathered tightly around them.

The housemaid was left standing alone by the doorway, looking apologetic for having let Christian come this far. 'I'm sorry, ma'am, but he forced his way through.'

Sophia rushed into the middle of the action, trying to appear as if she had everything under control. 'That's fine. He is... a good friend of ours.'

'Please give him space to breathe.' Ida tried to usher the most inquisitive guests away, while simultaneously not following her own advice.

Everyone else followed Ida's request, apart from Irmeli. 'We have to get him out of those wet clothes.'

Irmeli's supposedly innocent and thoughtful suggestion made Birgget see red. *Why am I not surprised hearing that from her?*

For the others, Irmeli's words made perfect sense. Sophia intuitively jumped to Christian's feet. 'But not here. In the bathroom.' She felt the weight as she grabbed him under his knees. 'Ladies, we need a few more.'

Instantly, Irmeli took one side of him, while Ida went to support his upper body. Ida gave Birgget an enquiring look, hoping she would take the other remaining side, opposite to Irmeli. But Birgget stubbornly shook her head.

It was the housemaid's time to react and be the fourth woman they needed to hoist Christian off the floor.

As the women carried him away from the living room, his dripping clothes left a reddish brown trail behind them. When they reached the doorway, Sophia, at the feet end, turned to the remaining guests.

'Sorry about this... minor interruption,' she panted. 'This shouldn't take long. Meanwhile, feel free to keep browsing the products… and help yourself to some more coffee and snacks.'

The baffled guests gathered in groups, as the rescue committee exited the room. Everything had happened so fast. Some of the newbies wondered if this was normal in Tuppervaara parties, whereas the more seasoned ones were prepared literally for anything.

Meanwhile, in the corridor, Ida used her backside to push the bathroom door open. They took Christian inside and rested his heavy body on a piece of a moose fur carpet – which was perfectly warmed by the underfloor heating. His bleeding stained the golden brown hairs of the rug.

Sophia couldn't be bothered about the mess created, however. As much as she wanted to help Christian, she was equally worried about the comfort of the guests. The house could always be cleaned, but the reputation of her parties wasn't that easy to restore.

'It's probably better to remove his wet clothes,' she prompted Ida, while making her way out of the bathroom.

'Why are you looking at me?' Ida asked, knowing quite well why.

'Well, you're the only one… you know.'

'And you haven't seen a naked man before?' Ida snorted.

'I have to be with the guests.'

'I can help,' Irmeli keenly intervened.

'Me too,' the housemaid said, intrigued to be part of something more dramatic than her daily mundane errands of cleaning the house, doing laundry and cooking.

'I don't think so,' Sophia said firmly. 'I need you two at the party. I don't want the guests to worry too much. Besides, Ida knows very well what she's doing.'

Ida sighed. 'Can you at least help to hoist him to the bathtub? I think he needs a little rinse.'

Without need to be asked twice, the other three women took their original positions and swiftly shifted Christian over the edge of the bath.

'Good luck, then.' Sophia was the first to let go. She gestured to the reluctant Irmeli and the housemaid to follow her.

'I won't be long,' Ida said.

Sophia let Irmeli and the housemaid exit first. 'Take your time.' She winked at Ida, and shut the door behind her.

Christian's neck rested uncomfortably against the golden taps. Ida wiped his long, wet blond hair off his face. It seemed as if all the moisture and dirt had given him highlights, making every fibre feel firmer and look more vibrant. She went to undo the laces of his muddy hiking boots. As she pulled them off, one at a time, with them came his soaked woollen socks. There was dirt between his toes and under his nails.

Ida moved upwards to his waist and undid his belt and zip. Carefully, she removed his ripped trousers. He was still unconscious, though his breathing had become more tense. She unbuttoned his torn shirt, revealing a white vest top underneath. She used all her strength to bring him to a seated position. His limp upper body leant to the side. She felt like she was undressing a tired, non-cooperative child.

He had a shoulder tattoo that she couldn't remember seeing before. It was a flying reindeer with wings drawn inside a circle or a globe. She pulled the vest top over his head, before removing his underpants. As she did so, she looked away, not understanding why. Perhaps for her loyalty to Sven. Then she went to the cabinet over the sink and took out some antiseptic cream and cotton pads. Fortunately, Christian couldn't feel a thing when she cleaned his open wounds.

As she turned the red knob to the west, the warm water began flowing. Soon, the tub underneath him began to gurgle. She harvested the underwater, accidentally discovering it was his bare bottom that was blocking the drain. She gently pushed him to the side, found the drain and inserted the plug. The water level began rising, creating more steam. Apart from his bruises and unconsciousness, she somewhat envied his pampered condition. She couldn't remember the last time she had been bathed by someone.

Once the water covered Christian's naval area, Ida took some lavender soap from the wall rack and rubbed it on her left palm. While keeping her eyes firmly on the ceramic tiles opposite her, she began rubbing the oily soap on his rough skin. She let her fingers run along his firm thighs and calves. The blood from his cuts had mixed with the bath. She had to dive deeper again to unplug and dispense the tub of dirty water. As she rummaged below the surface, her hands passed right above his groin, gently caressing his abdomen. She could clearly feel all six or eight firm lumps flexed underneath his skin – even though he was not even awake.

Her soapy hands glided further up to his broad, pectoral muscles. She had forgotten how intense and intriguing a truly athletic male body can look and feel. Some long-lost sensations awakened in her, as she took a deep breath.

With a soft sponge, she patted his face clean from all the blood stains. She no longer avoided looking at his body – it seemed like a natural thing to do. Christian, meanwhile, was unaware of everything happening around him, whereas she kept explaining to herself that a proper wash like this was good for his well-being.

A soft knock on the door interrupted her, when only one part of his body was yet to be washed.

'How are you doing there? Can I come in?' Sophia's voice travelled through.

'Just a second.' Ida quickly showered the rest of the soap off Christian, grabbed a white towel and patted his body dry.

'I have a few options here for him to wear. Can I show them?' Sophia asked.

'Clothes?' Ida looked at him longingly, before covering him with the towel. *What a shame to hide such a perfect creation with any fabric.* Nevertheless, she understood this moment wouldn't last. 'Come on in, then.'

Sophia brought in a pile of trousers, shirts and underwear. 'Seems like you've done a good job.'

'But... those are Dad's clothes! They are... for old men.'

'Do you think Christian would care what he's wearing in his condition?' Sophia dropped the items on the floor in front of Ida.

Critically, Ida browsed the selection the patient could potentially wear. 'There wasn't anything more youthful?'

Sophia laughed, and pulled out a suit bag from underneath the pile. 'What about this dinner suit? He only wore it once, at our wedding. In fact, most of this stuff he never wore. I kept buying him so many clothes, but he was always too busy to even try them on.'

'An old tuxedo?' Ida sighed.

'It feels like brand new.' Sophia retrieved it from the bag. Seeing the garment again brought back the warm sensation of being a newly-wed.

'Isn't that a bit much?' said Ida. 'He didn't come here to meet the president.'

'It is a party, though. We could dress him accordingly.' Sophia improvised answers to her liking. 'This tux cost Gustav about fifteen hundred marks. Christian would look darned good in it.'

Ida caressed the eloquent, silky materials and the work of fine tailoring. 'You're right about that, for sure.'

'Did you see that?' Sophia's eyes wandered over to Christian. 'I'm pretty sure he moved his finger.'

'Christian?' Ida squealed.

Christian's head dropped to the side, facing the women. His eyes and mouth opened a little. 'Where am I?'

Feeling gratitude, Ida kneeled beside him and put her hand on his chest. 'You're safe... with us.'

'Ida... Sophia... What happened?' Christian mumbled in agony.

'You're in Örebröre, at our house,' Ida said calmingly. 'You arrived here an hour ago, bruised and battered. Then you fell unconscious. You were away for such a long time. We thought we'd lost you.'

Christian coughed a couple of times, before grabbing the sides of the tub and attempting to sit up. But he couldn't. He looked down at his body that was merely covered by the towel and bubbly water.

'Ah. We had to... remove your dirty clothes and give you a wash,' Ida stuttered.

Sophia put the tuxedo hanger on the towel rack above them. 'We have here some clean clothes for you to wear.'

Ida stood up. 'We'll give you some privacy. Take your time to dry yourself and get dressed. Let us know if you'll need anything. I'll be right outside.'

'It's nice to have you back,' Sophia smiled, and left the room.

As Ida was about to follow her, Christian grabbed her wrist.

'Please, stay. I might need help,' he said with a quivering voice, contradicting the strength of his firm grip.

She couldn't move, nor did she necessarily want to. 'Fine.'

'You look well. What happened?' he asked.

She had to think for a second what he meant, until it became clear to her. 'Ah. The hospital? Yes. Thanks to you.'

Puzzled, he let go of her arm. 'What do you mean?'

'I'll explain later.' She went to close the door that Sophia had left open. 'Let's get you sorted first. Can you stand up?'

His lungs and head hurt whenever he took a deep breath. 'I can do this.'

Panting, he tried again, but failed.

This must be what it's like to be really old. He felt double or triple the age he really was.

While facing away, Ida could hear him struggling. As he finally stood straight, the towel covering his body fell off. Out of the side of her eye, she could see his whole silhouette in the mirror. The sweet smell of the lavender foam covering his loins filled the entire room.

Chapter 40

ANOTHER SURVIVAL STORY

The housemaid scrubbed the blood stains off the living room carpet. Meanwhile, Sophia's desperate attempts to calm the guests went to waste. Not even promises of further price drops and free memberships helped the majority to stay. Only the closest friends and the most devoted pyramid-sellers were loyal to the host. When the few remaining women saw Ida finally returning to the living room, they hesitantly pulled out their swedes again. There was still a pinch of positive anticipation left in the room.

Yet, hosting a contest was the last thing on Ida's mind right now. Neither was she keen to share openly any details about the aftermath of the incident they all had to witness.

'Doesn't he look great?' Sophia pried insensitively.

'What kind of question is that?' Birgget gasped.

'In the tuxedo,' Sophia added.

Ida glanced at Sophia before responding. 'He's resting, Mother, in your bedroom.'

Sophia's expression suddenly changed. '*Our* bedroom?'

'What difference does it make? It's nice and private,' Ida replied bluntly.

'Why not any other room? There are plenty to choose from.'

'I'm not going to ask him to move. Besides, aren't you sleeping on the sofa nowadays?' Ida knew how her mother had avoided the master bedroom since the passing of Gustav, as it had become more like a haunted shrine to her.

However, Sophia was determined to keep up appearances until the end. She was supposed to be the strong and fun host, not a grieving and devastated widow.

Birgget, if anyone, could see through her. From the beginning, she had spotted the sadness in her eyes. She knew the anxiety that having lost a beloved one brings. She empathised with Sophia, probably better than Ida could. Ida was much younger, with more optimism left in her, and with less experience of the disappointments and setbacks that life had in store for her.

Whereas Sophia couldn't see any light at the end of the tunnel. Gustav was gone forever – although 'showing up from nowhere' and 'returning from the dead' had become common occurrences in the recent past. One living example of these miracles was resting in her marital bed upstairs. *Could Gustav come back as well, like Roar and Christian did?* she wondered. *Can this happen not only to two, but three men they all knew?*

She doubted it.

Meanwhile, Irmeli saw her opportunity to approach the sofa. Immediately, Birgget bounced off her cushion and reluctantly chose Sophia, who was the lesser of two evils.

'You're neglecting the guests,' Birgget said.

'Indeed.' Sophia snapped back to the present, surprised by Birgget's friendly advice. 'Would you care to join me?'

Birgget glanced over her shoulder, and saw Irmeli getting closer. 'Sure.'

Sophia put on her trademark smile and led them to a handful of ladies across the room – who all seemed to be chattering more about the recent incident, rather than focusing on the products they were supposed to be buying. Sophia approached them with only one goal in mind: to get the party back on track and sell.

Ida, to her disbelief, witnessed how the times may have really changed, as Birgget voluntarily sought her mother's attention. She wished Sven was there to see this. She couldn't hear exactly what the two mothers were talking about, but at least they were laughing together and, from a distance, seemed to enjoy each other's company.

Since Birgget was conveniently out of the way, Irmeli had the courage hesitantly address Ida.

'I was actually thinking that... we should probably tell Roar about Christian's return, as soon as possible,' Irmeli said. 'He has lost a lot of business lately, since Christian was his only local supplier of fish to the restaurant. He even had to cut down my hours. I only did ten last week.'

'Why don't you start fishing again?' Ida immediately realised how inconsiderate the question was; telling some complete stranger what to do. 'I'm sorry. It's just that it's been so inspiring to follow your career. You've been a great example to many aspiring, young fisherwomen out there.'

Irmeli smiled. 'Thank you. Hopefully, I will start again, one day. But, until then, I need this job in the restaurant to get back on my feet. And, to be fair, it's nice to do something different for a change. I've been fishing all my life – for over forty years.'

It always amazed Ida how someone could stay so focused and dedicated doing the same thing most of their lives. It was early for her to say, but she never wanted to end up in a similar situation. Even though she was married now with a child, she still had desires to work in different industries in the future, and perhaps even live somewhere much further – just like her sisters did.

'Roar went fishing with Sven,' Ida said. 'Let's tell them when they're back.' She already knew that one of the men would be more delighted than the other to hear this breaking news.

'Fishing? Where?'

'I mean... they went... to look for Christian,' Ida muttered lies, not certain anymore who was supposed to know and what.

'Well, that mission has been accomplished.'

'Speaking of which, if you'll excuse me, I need to go and check how he's coping.'

'Enjoy.' Irmeli winked at Ida. 'He's quite a catch.'

Irmeli's unnecessary remark made Ida cringe. *What's wrong with the women here?*

'Darling!' Sophia's pretentious voice interrupted Ida when she was just about to step out of the room. 'Would you like to run the swede peeling contest now? Everyone's waiting.'

Ida anxiously looked over her shoulder. The guests impatiently fumbled with their swedes.

'Yes. I won't be long. I'm just gonna... change her nappy first.' She rushed back to the sofa, picked the baby up and pulled a disgusted face, as if the little one had pooped herself. All the women gave her sympathetic smiles. Unexpected problems with babies and children always seemed to pass as credible excuses that no one dared to question.

'Meanwhile, ladies, keep your swedes out, because when my daughter is back, we're going to run... the Swede Calling!' Sophia announced like some overly enthusiastic, American television game host.

The night had been long, however. The tired guests saw through Sophia's clumsy attempts to make things larger than they really were. The responses were a couple of gasps and yawns, followed by silence.

Apologetically, Ida disappeared with the baby. She ascended the spiralling staircase to the first floor. A large double door, with a dim light shining from underneath, loomed at the end of a long corridor. The walls on either side were adorned with golden-framed paintings of Ida's ancestors and other nobilities.

The distant chattering of the guests downstairs gradually faded as she reached the door handle. Gently, she pushed the door open just enough to see through. The emperor-size bed with four oakwood posters was positioned against the back wall. Apart from a few living candles on wall brackets on each side of the room, a starry night sky shed some additional light through the window. The floorboards creaked underneath her feet when she stepped inside. The issue to get them fixed was not about money, but Sophia and Gustav wanted to keep the rustic and antique feel in the house. In the master bedroom, the feature was seen as somewhat romantic. Occasionally, however, like now, it was borderline eerie and annoying.

Christian rested peacefully over a turquoise bedcover, his hands crossed on his stomach. He was wearing the tuxedo trousers, white shirt and a bow tie. The black jacket hung on the back rest of a white wooden chair next to a white, French-style dressing desk.

His eyes were closed. His hair was still moist from the bath, spreading evenly on the pillow on either side of his head, as if each fibre had been placed there by hand. His complexion had some colouring, as if he had already been exposed to the first rays of the spring sun. There was no dirt anymore – she had washed him so well.

The colour combination of his skin tone and smart clothing created a picturesque contrast against the aquatic-style bed linen. His chest went slowly up and down with calm breathing. His tall frame filled the length of the entire bed, from the head to footboard. It was like finding a tanned version of Dracula himself resting in his own castle, or an adult-sized dressing doll in a life-sized playhouse.

Ida stopped beside the bed and stared at him admiringly and with relief. It seemed as if a boulder had fallen from her shoulders. She was lucky to have gained someone back with whom she shared a special bond. They were each other's first love. They had supported one another when the tsunami almost took their lives. Together, they survived the floods and extreme conditions that followed. Even though Ida was married to Sven, Christian had played a crucial role in the person she was today, and vice versa. She felt a warmth and satisfaction to see him safe.

However, his suffering also reminded her of the concern she felt for Sven. *Could I really take this kind of lifestyle in the long run – to be the concerned wife of a fisherman?*

'I really like this suit,' Christian whispered with a creaky voice.

Ida pulled back. 'I… I thought you were asleep.'

He slowly opened his eyes. 'I believe I have rested enough.'

'A couple of hours,' Ida replied, delighted. 'The party is coming to an end. Almost everyone's gone.' She dared to take a step closer to him. In fact, that was what she really wanted; to be near to him.

'Tuppervaara, eh?' He gave a painful smirk.

'How did you know?'

He responded with a cough. Some blood and brown liquid dripped from his mouth on the white satin linen. 'I'm sorry.'

'I'll clean it up for you.' She rushed to get a tissue from a paper box on the bedside table. 'You're not well.' She wiped the stains off the fabric, while simultaneously holding the baby near to him.

His and the baby's blue eyes met, both expressing curiosity. 'So, this is your creation?'

She gave a pleased nod. 'Isn't she beautiful?'

'A future fisherwoman?' His attempt at being witty indicated some recovery.

'Only time will tell,' she replied, and went to drop the wet wipe in the bin under the desk. 'She can do anything she wants.'

'Anything? Even hunting?'

'Does it always have to be one of those two? There must be other professions in this world.' She wanted to avoid becoming one of those controlling parents who guided their child towards something very specific. Having been surrounded all her life by fishermen and being constantly concerned about their safety, she wouldn't mind her child finding interest in any other field. Gladly, though, she didn't have to worry about that right now.

'Maybe somewhere else, somewhere bigger, there are more opportunities,' Christian pondered. 'But, in Pihtamo, I don't think so. Unless you want her to became a cashier or a cleaner.'

Ida could detect a hint of disapproval in his tired voice. 'Those are completely respectable professions.'

He rolled his eyes. 'Well...'

She sighed disappointedly. Their reunion seemed to have started off on the wrong foot. 'Can we talk about something other than my daughter's career prospects? Like, what happened to you?'

Her direct question made Christian serious again. He grimaced in pain as he slowly brought himself up to a seated position against the headboard. 'I saw Wolferring, eye to eye.'

That was the worst news Ida needed to hear right now. Her thoughts drifted to Sven again. 'Eye to eye, like... Roar and Carl saw it?'

Christian nodded gravely. 'Except that I'm back now, not sixteen years later.'

'But how did you end up here, of all the places?'

'That's a longer story,' he said thoughtfully, and looked out the window. As he gently touched the bruise on his forehead, the pain took him back to the recent events of terror. His heart began racing. 'It was like any other day within last few weeks. I went fishing to get supplies for Roar's new restaurant. He had shared with me the location of this so-called "secret pond". But, before I got there, I cast a bait a few times in the River Pihtamii. I was impatient and curious, even though I knew it was probably pointless. However, I did catch a couple of herrings. Everything seemed fine; almost back to normal. Well, the fish weren't really biting, but otherwise I felt safe. That was, until the last time I casted, which turned out to be my biggest mistake. Wolferring caught my bait.'

Ida squeezed the baby tighter as she listened. 'What happened then?'

'The obvious: I couldn't keep up, or wasn't strong enough to reel. My rod didn't snap, though, when Wolferring pulled me along the river, and turned my boat into one big water ski. Every time it surfaced, it looked fierce and dangerous, like a fast-moving torpedo. Then, after about a couple of kilometres, I was wise enough to let go. We reached the entrance where the white-waters lead down to the pond.'

'Where did you get all those scars and bruises, then?'

Slowly, Christian attempted to stand up. He needed to be on his feet for his head to function better. 'The rod hit my face when I let go. And Wolferring didn't stop there. It came back, attacked my boat and started chewing it. It looked exactly the way it had been described in the legends, or by Roar: big sharp teeth, evil reddish eyes, clean-cut sideburns. I took one of the oars and smacked it. But I lost my balance and fell. I rolled in the river for ages. My lungs filled with water. Until another huge fish, or something, intervened. I couldn't tell what happened, since I was nearly drowning. I only heard a rumbling of a thunder, followed by an ear-shattering howling. After a while, it became completely silent, and I could climb on what was left of my boat. But the oars and all my gear were gone – exactly what happened to Roar, when he ended up drifting alone. I was soaking wet, cold and bleeding. There was no one else around. Gladly, though, the river bank was not that far. I could use my arms to paddle the boat to the shore. Then, my only option was to start plodding through the vast forests. I had to live like a primitive cave man, hunting with my bare hands, eating everything raw, berries, plants. I learnt how ridiculously urban we had become. But, somehow, I survived. Once I realised I had wandered near to Örebröre, I immediately came here to seek help.'

In awe, Ida listened. 'But there's no water near here? You must have travelled an enormous distance.'

'You must remember that the shorelines have shifted,' Christian replied. 'Besides, I ended up spending weeks in the forest. I had to stay moving, which took me here in the end. I am so lucky to be alive.'

'What an amazing story,' said Ida, unaware that she had been holding her breath.

'Most of all, I'm blessed to have you in my life.' His eye became watery.

'You're safe here.' She gently touched his shoulder. Simultaneously, though, the concern over her husband's well-being was increasing. 'Do you think this Wolferring is still around?'

'I certainly hope not.'

'Sven and Roar went after it.'

'Just them two?' he gasped worriedly.

'It would've been the more the merrier. Or none of you, if you ask me.'

'What about Sven's... *Eskimo* friend? He wasn't available?'

'Jaaku? He's an Inuit, by the way. You shouldn't use the E-word anymore,' Ida said judgementally. 'Jaaku doesn't want to fish anymore.'

'Then, I hope they have a strong boat and some top-notch equipment. That beast is evil. Roar knows.'

'As far as I'm aware, they took Sven's new Yolla boat. And I think Roar has an axe.'

'What?! That's an obvious suicide,' Christian gasped, knowing well how weak and soft the plastic of the new edition was.

The baby started sobbing once Christian raised his voice. She opened her little eyes and looked appallingly at her mother.

'I'm just being honest with you. They have no chance,' he continued bluntly.

'Baaaaah!' the baby screamed louder.

'Okay, okay. We get the message,' Ida snorted, and focused on hushing the baby. She went to the window and showed the baby the stars and constellations. They saw a shooting star. 'Make a wish.' Ida tried to sound excited, even though she was filled with worry.

'I'm sorry,' said Christian as he moved behind her and put his hands on her waist, 'also about calling Jaaku an Eskimo.'

'You did it again.' His unexpected touch made her disorientated. She pulled away, and walked quickly across the room.

Christian read the signs, and thought it was better to focus on the new life. He gave Ida and the baby a gentle smile. 'She's so beautiful, like her mother. What's her name?'

'She doesn't have a name yet, but we call her *Swede*,' Ida replied formally.

He found this slightly hilarious. 'As in "Swedish"?'

'The root vegetable.' Ida was embarrassed to admit the origin of the nickname, which obviously required more of an explanation. 'They've always been an important source of income for our family. We started growing them over a half a century ago.'

'Can I hold... Swede?' Christian chuckled, and took a step closer to her again.

Ida sighed at first, but softened the nearer he got. She had already forgotten how tall he was and how big his hands were. She took a deep breath, before nervously handing the baby over to him.

Swede almost disappeared inside his palms. Immediately, the baby gave him a shy smile while staring at his striking eyes again.

You know, what if I am... Just before Christian could finish his wild thought, the door behind them creaked opened.

'Ida, I have to...' Birgget stepped in, pausing mid-sentence, 'go.'

Quickly, Ida grabbed Swede from Christian, making her cry. 'Birgget, please. Don't you know how to knock?'

'I just wanted to say goodbye,' Birgget said apologetically, before turning to Christian. With mixed emotions, she looked at him from head to toe. She should have rejoiced for someone, anyone, to return after being lost. Yet, she also knew that seeing Ida and him together wasn't always the best for her son's interests. 'Christian, I can see you're recovering.'

'He was attacked by Wolferring,' Ida intervened dramatically.

'The same fish Roar goes on about?' Birgget asked.

Christian nodded gravely, but sounded grateful when he spoke. 'But I'm feeling much better now.'

'I bet you do,' Birgget snorted under her breath, while giving Ida a judgemental glance.

'A special thanks belongs to all of you.' Christian remained calm and refused to let Birgget's attitude aggravate him. 'Actually, I wish I could have helped Sven and Roar to catch it. I'm surprised they didn't ask anyone else to join them.'

'I don't think asking you was an option,' Birgget replied bluntly.

'I mean, anyone else in town,' Christian added.

Birgget realised that her confrontational approach wasn't in her nature, nor did it bring any desired results.

'What I gathered was that, it wasn't easy to get others involved,' she said. 'People haven't been that understanding after Roar's return. Even though, us, the family, may have celebrated, yet the conditions surrounding and preceding both Roar and Carl's disappearances caused a lot of controversy. Many people don't fully trust Roar anymore. Some are blaming witchcraft, magic and all sorts. We all believed that he was dead. We had his funeral. But now, he's miraculously back to life with his amazing story – while Pihtamo lies at the bottom of the lake. Don't get me wrong – it's wonderful to have both him and you back, but sometimes these survival stories can be too much for normal people, like us to comprehend.'

Christian began to worry about how well, or poorly, his miraculous return would be received and perceived in the community. 'Do you believe Roar and his story?' he asked both women.

They quietly hesitated a couple of seconds too long, which

made Christian dubious. Birgget replied first.

'I believe that my son witnessed something unusual. We're dealing with events and powers that are larger than life.'

'I agree,' Ida added. 'There are so many things we don't understand about this world. Let the conversing fauna be one example of these recent discoveries.'

'Of course. Them!' Christian snorted. 'I can see now why the town folk may not be that convinced.'

'You met them all, can't you remember?' Ida said.

'Briefly. I remember the ark sinking,' Christian replied ignorantly. He wanted to forget the embarrassing details of how their survival from the post office roof had unfolded.

'I'm surprised you do, considering how drunk you were,' Birgget snorted.

'Please,' Ida said.

'That's fine.' Christian kept his cool. 'Christmas can be a tough period sometimes, and that one was the rock bottom.'

The women couldn't but agree with his statement.

'I understand that we're dealing with something bigger here.' Christian took the conversation back to the supernatural. 'I have just seen Wolferring. And I have always been ready to help Sven and Roar to catch it. They just never asked me.'

Ida remained quiet as she knew the reason why. Hence, Birgget decided to speak up.

'I can imagine Roar wouldn't have a problem with that, but Sven...' She turned to Ida.

Since Ida had vaguely thanked him in the bathroom earlier, she decided to reveal the whole story.

'Christian, a herring that you had caught saved my life in the hospital. Roar knew about this old alternative method that could bring me out of the coma. Sven agreed to it; to feed me your herring. You are the reason I'm still standing here today and being able to mother my own child.'

Christian fell silent from a mixture of astonishment and pride. 'It could have been... anyone's herring.'

'No,' said Ida firmly. 'There were hardly any fish available. The lake is empty. Only you had access and the courage to go to the pond and defy Wolferring. Even Sven wasn't fishing at the time.'

Birgget wanted to defend her son's less heroic actions for not going fishing. 'Sven couldn't go because of Ida's condition. He had to stay by her side in the hospital.'

'So, if Sven has accepted your help already once, why not again?' Ida asked Christian.

That thought was a bit too much for Birgget, though. *Sven and Christian working together? Not in a million years!*

Chapter 41

THREATS OF DIFFERENT MAGNITUDES

For some time now, Sven and Roar hadn't said anything to each other. Utterly disappointed, Roar let the oars rotate in full circles, whereas Sven had lost all interest to troll. He slouched on the backseat, like a frustrated teenager again. They were nearing their starting point, when someone appeared on the shore, directly at Sven's eyeline. He sighed in relief, as they could finally shift focus away from one another.

As Sven pointed ahead, Roar looked past his shoulder. The person waved his arms. A waterfowl, most likely a goose, sat next to him.

'At least someone's happy to see us,' Roar snorted.

Once they got closer, Sven could recognise him. 'It's Jaaku again. Why is he still here?'

Roar sighed. 'That's weird.'

'Maybe he wants his stuff back?'

'Absolutely. No use for any of this. We might as well return Viljo's spear gun, too.'

'Dad, please. We will come back. I promise.'

'Whatever.' Roar began rowing even faster.

'Glad you two are back!' They were near enough to hear Jaaku shouting.

'You've been waiting for us here the whole time?' Sven yelled his reply.

'I had second thoughts. I would like to join you.'

Roar leered at Sven. 'Did you hear that?'

Sven felt equally confused. 'I don't understand.'

After a few more powerful strokes, Roar lifted the oars up, letting the boat glide the last remaining stretch, before docking itself in the grassy section purposefully dug for disembarking. As soon as the bow touched the land, he picked up his gear and hopped off. He chucked the rope to Jaaku, expecting him to tie and lock the boat to a tree.

'Thanks for lending your Yolla and the rifle,' Roar snorted. 'I'm sure they're useful... when the time is right.' He glanced at Sven once more, before randomly walking off towards the forest.

'You shouldn't go there,' said Jaaku calling after him. He chucked the rope onto Sven's lap, who was still sitting in the boat. 'You must go back. I mean, we all must...'

Roar stopped advancing. 'What are you talking about?'

'Not today, Jaaku.' Sven stepped off the boat and handed the end of the rope back to Jaaku, together with the keys and the rifle. 'We've had our share of fishing. We're gonna go home. It's a really nice boat, though. The rifle we didn't get to use.'

While Jaaku was reluctantly accepting his belongings, an ear-blasting shockwave threw all three men to different directions. Roar got pushed against a tree trunk, Jaaku fell on his face on a wet patch of lichen, and Sven flew on his back on the bottom of the boat. The goose took off and landed on the water, a safe distance away to observe the situation.

'What was that?' Roar grimaced.

Sven popped his head over the edge of the boat. 'An explosion?'

Beyond the forest, the horizon darkened. A moving shadow appeared from the bushes.

'I can see you!' Roar shouted.

Jaaku bounced quickly onto his feet. 'Please, Roar, Sven... listen to me. We must leave this place, not by foot, but by boat. Right now!' He chucked the rifle on top of Sven and jumped on the boat with him.

'Is someone chasing you?' Roar asked, looking at Jaaku.

'I'll explain later.' Jaaku kicked the boat off the grass and shallow waters.

'*Hei!* I'm not going anywhere!' Sven tried to stand up, but couldn't as the boat was reversing too fast.

'You are, if you want to survive,' Jaaku said determined, and took the oars.

Meanwhile, a cloud of grey smoke and dark ash rose behind the dark figure charging towards Roar. 'What on earth...?' he gasped.

'Saalamaa has erupted!' Jaaku shouted, as the ash cloud rose above the treelines.

'Ida!' Sven panicked, while staring at the darkening sky. 'I must get out of here.'

However, as Sven jumped on Jaaku, Jaaku launched his boot at his stomach, sending him back on his bottom.

'No, Sven! The safest place is out on the lake. There is no way back to Pihtamo. It's too dangerous. That's why I'm still here.'

Next, a bullet whistled past Roar's face, ripping bark off the tree trunk in front of him. Suddenly, it became easy to make up his mind. He jumped in the lake and waded in the knee-deep water towards the departing boat.

'We must leave this place!' he yelled.

'I can't stay here.' Sven tried to escape the boat, when Roar came and knocked him back in again.

'You can,' Roar grunted, and hopped in. 'Now, Jaaku, row!'

The mysterious man charging from the forest was Kalle. He reached the shore and aimed his rifle at the escaping boat.

'Duck!' Jaaku and Roar, being the two facing the coastline, shouted in harmony.

'Isn't that a goose?' Sven looked over his shoulder, when a bullet landed on the hard plastic of the backboard, barely missing him. He saw Kalle cocking the rifle for another shot. 'Ah. I see.' Sven dropped his head and upper body as low as possible.

The men were crammed on the floor like sardines in a can, as more bullets were fired at them. The brief moment of terror felt like an eternity – even though the rifle only made seven shots. Once the shooting stopped, they could hear some muttering, as if Kalle was swearing to himself.

'He may have run out of ammo,' Jaaku whispered.

'You wanna test?' Sven asked sarcastically.

'Or, he's waiting for one of us to sit up straight?' Jaaku added.

'Well, you know better. He's one of your friends, right?' Sven snorted. 'If one of us has to sit up, that will be you, Jaaku.'

Jaaku sighed, and yanked the rifle from underneath their bodies. He tried to cock it, but couldn't do it without lifting the barrel above the edge. Once Kalle noticed it, he jumped back and hid himself behind a thick birch tree. Slowly, Jaaku raised his head. He felt like a sniper in a duel situation. He observed the edge of the forest, but saw no one.

'There may be another one of them,' he said. 'We must go out further; much further. I can keep guard of the shoreline, if one of you can row?'

Both Sven and Roar, however, found it difficult to take orders at that very moment.

'I'm not going to row another centimetre today,' Sven scoffed.

'Please,' Jaaku said, sounding genuinely desperate. 'It's not just the hunters, but also the volcano. The safest place is at the lake and far away...'

'Fine then!' Roar grunted, and straightened himself just enough so that he could take the oars and insert them thru their loops.

'What are you doing? Get down!' Sven ordered, still hiding at the bottom. 'That's suicide.'

'Kalle wouldn't have stopped if he still had shots,' Jaaku explained, while keeping his eyes firmly on the forest. 'Most likely, he's loading his weapon right now, which should give us time to make distance. I'll just make sure he doesn't come out and start shooting. Once we're far enough, we should be safe. The hunters only stay on land. They can't even swim.'

The other threat chasing them, however, didn't necessarily stop at the waterfront. Even though Kalle hadn't made an appearance for a while, the densifying ash cloud began spreading over the lake. Even Sven, while still on the floor, could see it rising above them. He was wondering if the eruption had hit New Pihtamo. The town was purposefully built near the volcano, due to its rich earth and minerals. But now, the risk-taking and greed to exploit the natural deposits may have cost them dearly.

Up until now, the chances of the volcano erupting, and the population of this particular area experiencing another natural disaster in such a short period of time, were almost non-existent. The community had already suffered enough, yet somehow another nightmarish situation was becoming reality. It was like the ultimate jackpot of catastrophes.

The men had two options: to face the threat on the land, or to escape on the water. Neither of them felt like the right thing to do. Sven understood that running away from Kalle's bullets was the best solution in the short term, but once the time was right, they should look for another, safer place to land the boat and start looking for their loved ones. Finally, he dared to inch his head barely above the edge to get a glimpse of the retrieving coast.

'He cannot stay there waiting for us forever,' Sven said.

'I know he's crazy, but not that crazy,' replied Jaaku. 'Especially now the shore is entirely covered by the cloud.'

Eventually, Jaaku calculated that they had reached a safe distance from Kalle, and that his visibility had become poor. Jaaku lowered the weapon.

'But we still need to get even further away, just in case.'

Roar kept pulling on the oars. 'I'm working on it.'

Sven sat completely straight. He made eye contact with Roar. They said nothing, but they could read each other's thoughts. *Here we go again.* As much as they cared for one another, sometimes men like this, who thrived on solitude, needed their own space more than the average man. And, finally, when they thought they were going to get some privacy, Jaaku, together with the nature, decided otherwise.

Their desired 'me time' was postponed for the unforeseeable future, as they scurried towards the middle of the lake, away from two dangers of different magnitudes.

Chapter 42

SOPHIA'S CHOICE

The remaining guests glued themselves against the large bay window, all staring in terror at the ash cloud violently spreading into the atmosphere. A round-shaped trail rising over the treeline resembled a nuclear explosion, with its enormous force pushing the natural clouds away.

'Saalamaa,' Sophia said gravely. Nature had taken its course and decided to spoil the party – despite Sophia's relentless efforts to keep everyone engaged.

Another unexpected interruption halted Ida's presentation. She discreetly slid her swedes and the peeler away in her purse; the others followed her example. *Sven and I are always apart when these horrible things happen.* As she took the baby in her arms, she immediately thought about someone else.

'Birgget.' Ida's worried whisper created steam on the window. She saw Elma, her horse, jumping over a fence and galloping away. 'We must leave, immediately.'

Sophia responded with a subtle, nervous smile. 'Nothing to worry about. We should be far enough.'

'We're right next to it,' Ida gasped. 'That's exactly why we live here; because of the volcanic ground.'

'Yes, but...' Sophia muttered, and pulled Ida closer. 'I don't want to upset the guests.'

'There's hardly anyone left here, anyway,' Ida grunted.

Fully suited, Christian rushed downstairs and joined the

group. His poorly condition was a thing of the past as he parked himself next to Ida.

'We should get out of here,' he said urgently.

'I'll stay here and finish the party,' Sophia said to everyone. 'We are safe here.'

'That is total madness,' Ida cried. 'We might be on higher grounds, but the estate is still in the valley, which is a perfect funnel for lava to travel through. This is the worst place to be.'

'Where should we go, then?' Irmeli asked.

'We must find Birgget.' Ida hesitated. In reality, she wanted to go where Sven was, if she had only known his location. 'Towards Pihtamo?'

The other guests who were still there – three blonde women in their forties, Emilia, Silja and Karoliina – swung past them.

'Don't know about you guys, but we are out of here,' Emilia said firmly.

'Which direction you're heading to?' Ida asked.

'Kihlava. That's roughly where we all live, and it's directly in the opposite direction from the volcano. It feels like the safest bet. You should think about heading there, as well, rather than towards Pihtamo.'

'How did you all get here?' Christian asked.

'I took a snowtaxi,' Silja replied.

'But she can hop on our snowmobile,' Emilia added. 'It should be able to carry all three of us.'

As the trio walked towards the cloakroom, the housemaid scurried ahead to hand them their coats.

Once they'd left, only Sophia, Ida, the baby, Irmeli, Christian and the housemaid remained. They heard the unhealthy whirring and grinding of an engine coming from outside. Irmeli rushed to the window overlooking the driveway. Three-on-one on a snowmobile was definitely a crowd; however, the women managed to ride away, slowly but surely.

'Can you hold the baby?' Ida pushed her onto Sophia's lap so that she could get her phone.

'You know well that there's no reception at the lake,' Christian said.

'Sven could be anywhere,' Ida replied and dialled, anyway.

Meanwhile, Irmeli smoothly continued her way towards the exit. 'I should also go and... check on my cat,' she muttered.

'You wanna go to New Pihtamo, too?' Christian sighed.

'We don't know yet which direction the stream will take, if there will be one,' said Sophia, trying to remain calm.

'I'm not sure if I want to wait and find out,' said Christian, who turned to Irmeli again. 'The forest path from here to New Pihtamo winds very close to the lake at times, but keeps away from the volcano. If the worse comes to the worst, you can always seek shelter from the water.'

'Maybe borrow someone's boat, if I need to get off land?' Irmeli suggested.

'Not a crazy idea.' Christian impatiently waited for Ida to put the phone down.

'There's just one problem,' Irmeli said. 'I came here by kicksled.'

'That's exactly why I'm so worried about Birgget,' Ida said, and tried another number. Again, no answer. 'She doesn't pick up the phone, either. When did she leave – about half an hour ago?'

'There aren't too many paths you can travel on snowmobiles,' Sophia intervened. 'The snow is scarce. It has to be either the direction of New Pihtamo or Kihlava.'

Christian tried to offer a solution. 'What if Irmeli rides with Sophia and I'll sit with Ida?'

'Actually, I came here by kicksled, too,' Ida added.

'How on earth do you people commute here?' Christian snorted in disbelief.

'Look who's talking,' Ida grunted. 'The man who came here by foot.'

'You can take my snowmobile.' Sophia turned her back to everyone, and stared outside at the darkening sky. 'I will stay here. I won't leave my house. I have been here for over thirty years and nothing is going to chase me away. I have nothing to lose.'

'You're talking nonsense now,' Ida said, shocked.

'I doubt your snowmobile would carry five?' Christian pondered.

'Five?' Sophia said bluntly. 'I'm not coming.'

One by one, Christian pointed at each potential escapee, ending up with the housemaid, who was still waiting by the cloakroom, ready to assist those that were leaving.

'Ah. Her?' Sophia gave a firm look to the housemaid. 'She will stay here with me.'

The pensive expression of the housemaid could've been interpreted in many ways. Did she have a real opinion about her own destiny? Did she feel like she had a choice? Nevertheless, she remained quiet and nodded submissively to her employer – exactly the way she had done all these years while serving her masters.

'It's suicide to stay here,' Ida intervened. 'If the lava reaches this far, or even anywhere near, the heat will burn this whole place to ashes. The house, the window frames, everything is made of wood. The roof is thatched. The garden around is filled with flammable vegetation.'

With a blank expression on her face, Sophia turned to Ida. 'Well, then, I'll just hide myself in the basement. That titanium bunker, or whatever it is supposed to be. I would finally get to find out if it really is nuclear proof.'

'Mum! This is not a nuclear war, but a volcanic eruption.'

'Which one is worse?' Sophia questioned, with a soft and calm voice. 'Please, honey, try to understand. I have no interest to run away. No volcanic eruption is going to disrupt my party.' She went for her pocket and handed Ida the keys to her snowmobile. 'Take good care of it. I got it as a twenty-fifth wedding anniversary present from Gustav.'

While Ida reluctantly accepted the keys, Christian felt the urge to interrupt this emotional farewell. 'About this bunker... Where is it?'

Sophia pointed down to the floor. 'Underneath the house. There is a secret doorway through Gustav's office.'

'And, what did you say the place was made of?' Christian asked curiously.

'The building plans said something about...' Sophia gave Ida an enquiring look.

'... reinforced titanium and tungsten-insulated ceiling and

doorway, and steel support pillars,' Ida completed the sentence.

'Titanium and tungsten, eh?' Christian pondered. 'Those are two highly heat resistant materials.'

'How highly?' Suddenly, Ida sounded a tiny bit hopeful. 'Enough to withstand the heat of lava?'

Christian shrugged his shoulders. 'I couldn't tell, but we can Google that.'

'C'mon! You have to get going.' Sophia started escorting them towards the door.

Irmeli was already there with her coat on, holding the door handle. As she exited, the rising heat from outside took her in its warm embrace. Tiny dust particles floated in the air, spreading indoors.

'Please, hide in the bunker then,' said Ida. Bitterly, she had to accept her mother's insane decision to stay behind. 'Take plenty of supplies with you. Empty the fridge. Look after each other.'

Sophia took Ida in a tight embrace – something they hadn't done for years. 'Take care of yourself,' she whispered into her ear.

'I love you, Mum,' Ida replied, saying the three words she couldn't remember uttering since she was a little girl.

But Sophia couldn't get a word out. However, Ida was able to read her mother's lips, as she mimed her response. Ida gave her a serene smile when they separated. Sophia closed the front door and, together with the housemaid, went into hiding, not knowing when they would see daylight again.

Chapter 43

A HUNTER'S CONFESSION

Kalle had reduced to the size of a fingertip in the round lenses of Jaaku's pocket binoculars. He wasn't making attempts to fire anymore, which could've meant one of the following things: he had run out of ammo, the men escaping by boat were outside his shooting range, or both. There were no signs of his friend, Börje, either. Or the goose.

'Kalle's walking away. He's giving up,' said Jaaku in relief.

'It's about time.' Roar stopped rowing, while panting heavily. He truly was a shadow of the great Lord he used to be, since the second trip to the lake in the same day was already taking its toll. 'Why don't one of you youngsters take over?'

Since Sven only stared at him and didn't show any initiative, Jaaku reluctantly got up and swapped seats with Roar.

'Actually, could I sit all the way at the back?' Roar suggested to Sven, who was now opposite to him. 'I can try if the fish bites, since we may be stuck here for a little while.'

Those were not the words Sven wanted to hear. 'I'd say, rather than fishing, we start looking for a safe place to land.' Longingly, he gazed at the cloudy shore and the boiling volcano in the distance. He tried to predict the direction the eruption was going to take.

'Where's Ida?' Jaaku asked.

'At home, I think,' Sven replied. 'She was meant to be hosting her first Tuppervaara party tonight. Mum was invited, as well.'

'The party you so desperately wanted to go to,' Roar smirked.

'I wish I had made it on time,' Sven grunted. 'I wouldn't be stuck here with you!'

Biting his teeth together, Roar looked down at the water.

'What about Marjukka, then?' Sven asked Jaaku, while ignoring Roar. 'Or your parents?'

'They should be safe. The glaciers are far away.' Jaaku hesitated. 'Unless that's some sort of a super volcano.'

'Marjukka is strong,' Sven added. 'I'm sure she'll be fine.'

Jaaku started rowing, but said nothing. He was the master of hiding his emotions, anyway. Overall, it was sometimes impossible to tell what men in this part of the world really felt. The faces remained serious, and speech patterns and intonations monotone, no matter what the topic of discussion or how grave the situation was. 'Ida is strong, too,' Jaaku finally replied.

'The thing is that, it's not just her anymore,' said Sven. 'We're a family. New Pihtamo is dangerously close to the volcano. But all we can do is just sit here on this bloody dinghy and pray. I have never felt more useless.'

Roar, meanwhile, had gotten out his fishing rod. He wasn't expecting to catch anything, but by doing something he could perhaps extract himself from any more serious conversations. His input would have been limited, anyway. He had less to lose in life. His son, that he loved the most, was there with him. Of course, he empathised with Sven and Jaaku, and could feel their concern over their own families. Mostly, Roar worried over Birgget. And his restaurant business, but that was more financial stress rather than emotional.

Sven and Roar swapped seats. They were positioned exactly like they were hours ago, with the only exception that now the dry land had become a no-go zone. Roar cast his line, demotivated. He only did it to fight the feeling of helpfulness. Another lengthy stretch of silence took over. Yet, there were so many questions rushing through Sven and Roar's minds. *What was Jaaku still doing on the shore? Why didn't he fire back at Kalle?*

Sven wanted to open his mouth and ask, but wasn't sure

he could bear any more of Jaaku's clumsy excuses. He no longer knew if Jaaku was speaking the truth. Therefore, he approached the subject from a different angle.

'By the way, Jaaku, did you see the volcano erupting before you saw us?'

Jaaku hesitated. 'Yes... I was on my way home when the smoke and ash started to appear. My first thought was to head back towards the lake. It felt like the most sensible thing to do.'

But we saw him like hours ago: Sven pondered. *What was he doing all that time?*

Roar felt the urge to intervene. 'Interesting, because we couldn't see or hear anything when we approached the shore.'

'I think... it's perfectly normal,' Jaaku stuttered.

'That we didn't see anything?' Sven smirked.

'For volcanoes to behave that way. It can all happen very quickly.' Jaaku tried to focus more on rowing than answering these difficult questions.

Sven shrugged his shoulders. 'I have never experienced one, but you seem to be the expert.'

'You can tell us the truth.' Roar put his rod down, while biting his teeth together. 'What were you doing in the forest all this time?'

'Ööö... What do you mean?' Jaaku stuttered. 'I can't stay up so late? You're not my father.'

Roar was on the verge of losing it. 'Please, Jaaku. It was obvious that you had a reason to stay in the forest and it wasn't to help us. Just tell us.'

Unconvincingly, Jaaku looked up to the stars. 'The truth is...'

'Here we go again,' Roar snorted impatiently.

'Dad! Give him a chance to talk,' Sven interrupted. 'We don't need another Viljo here.'

'Another Viljo?! Where did that came from?' Roar grunted, and turned to Sven. 'His boat saved us all from the floods and he just lent us his spear gun. You should be grateful for what Viljo has done to you – to all of us!'

'A-absolutely. I was talking more about his bad temper,' Sven muttered.

'There's nothing wrong with my temper!' Roar shouted, and turned to Jaaku. 'I just cannot trust anyone who is... a hunter.'

'Is that what you were doing?' Sven asked Jaaku, deciding it was better to take Roar's side, after all.

There was a slight anticipation, until Jaaku confessed. 'Some minor hunting, perhaps, yes.'

'Hunting minors?!' Roar's strong reaction rocked the boat from side to side. 'What kind of person are you?'

'No! I mean, hunting just a little bit, but not much,' said Jaaku, correcting the misinterpretation, but looking pleadingly at Sven. 'What else could I do? I wanted to stop, but I didn't see the lake and fishing as having any future for me. I had to keep doing something to survive, anything else than making those pies. I'm sick of pies. Even Marjukka approves of my hunting. She only finds it a little dangerous, I guess.'

'Isn't it?' Sven asked bluntly.

'Well, that again, is debatable,' Jaaku suggested carefully, trying not to cause more controversy. However, he couldn't stop his opinions from surfacing. 'If you think about fishing and where it has led us. That is not a completely safe activity, either.'

Roar couldn't beat Jaaku's argument, whereas Sven disagreed. 'At least the fishermen are not hunting each other. I thought you were friends with the hunters?'

Jaaku pondered for a few seconds before replying. 'We were never friends. More like colleagues. Are you best friends with all fishermen?'

'The whole concept of fishing is different,' said Sven. 'We can do this alone, whereas hunters always seem to gather in big groups in log cabins with their four-wheel drives, right?'

'I wish,' Jaaku sighed longingly at Sven's unrealistic assumption about the life of the hunters.

'Somehow, I feel like you don't genuinely want to hang out with those guys.'

Roar smirked. 'Yes. The fact that they were chasing you with a rifle perfectly proves Sven's point.'

'They're not the easiest to get along with,' Jaaku sighed.

'That's a mild way to put it,' Roar laughed.

'There has been some mistrust between me and the hunters

after the tsunami incident,' said Jaaku. 'Even though they were pleased to hear that Mooses was no more, it all came at a high price, for both us and them.'

'Especially for Ida,' Sven added.

'Yes. Also, lots of forests were flooded, which was their hunting ground. Naturally, a bigger lake serves fishermen better and a bigger forest serves hunters. The hunters suspect the floods were caused by the fishermen on purpose, and so they are not sure which side I'm on. The fact that I hang out with you two, doesn't help.'

'You don't hang out with us that much anymore,' Sven said.

'Enough, though. We've been seen drinking together in the bar. Everyone knows everyone in Pihtamo and people talk. Even rumours about the secret pond have spread and the hunters suspect I have some involvement in that. As far as I know, no stranger has found it yet, am I right?'

Roar's face grew angrier once he heard about the classified information being leaked. His eyes turned to Sven. 'See! Jaaku has told everyone.'

'It could be Christian,' Sven grunted, equally upset.

Jaaku intervened. 'Don't worry. I haven't admitted anything. I don't even know the location of the pond. The only thing I know is that you two have retrieved some of the fish back to the lake.'

'Speaking of which,' Roar squealed, as the line underneath his boot began extending on its own. 'I think we have caught something!'

Chapter 44

INTO THE FIRE

The overloaded snowmobile roamed through the misty forest contaminated with sulphuric acid. Ida was on the handlebars, Christian in the middle, tucking the baby between him and her, while Irmeli clung at the back, her arms wrapped tightly around his waist. Repeatedly, the skis hit tree stumps and rocks hidden under the marshland. Ida had to trust her sense of direction as she steered them through the low-lying ash cloud. The visibility was poor. Every once in a while, though, glimpses of Lake Pihtamo appeared on their right.

They passed an abandoned kicksled. Ida slowed down. 'Is that Birgget's?'

'Has she continued by foot?' Christian said. 'That's madness.'

'Why are we stopping?' Irmeli said impatiently.

A figure appeared from behind the curtain of smoke, at the end of a path where snow met the barren ground.

'There's no way through!' Birgget shouted, dashing towards them. The dust cleared enough to reveal one side of the volcano behind her on the horizon. The lava stream was bursting over the rims and rolling towards them. It ploughed trees and set fires on its trail of destruction.

'But what about Pihtamo?' Irmeli said faintly.

Ida tried to think quickly whether there was an alternative route. She was determined to reunite with Sven and not remain separated from him again due to another natural catastrophe. *It just doesn't happen to the same people twice.*

'There's no way forward,' continued Birgget, panting heavily as she finally reached them. 'Trust me. I tried. There's no snow.'

Ida looked to every direction. 'We took a different route to Örebröre earlier today. We travelled closer to the volcano...'

'...which, now, is inaccessible,' Birgget added.

'Right,' Ida sighed, and started manoeuvring the snowmobile to the direction they had come from. Once they had done a full three-sixty, however, the engine died. She tried to restart immediately, but nothing happened. 'We have a problem.'

'We should push,' Christian suggested, but did nothing about it. Irmeli, however, had already jumped off.

'What about you, mister?' Birgget snorted to Christian, who was still comfortably seated.

'But... I have the baby,' he muttered.

Ida turned and ripped the baby off him. 'Not anymore.'

Sheepishly, Christian jumped off and joined Irmeli and Birgget at the tail end. They gave the snowmobile a push, while Ida, with the baby dangling on her lap, tried to ignite.

'I'm so sorry you have to go through all this,' she whispered to the baby. The engine coughed a few times before, all of a sudden, it started again. 'Hop on, then! Let's see how this beast can carry four.'

'That's five, if you count the little one.' Christian reclaimed the baby and sat behind Ida. Irmeli took a firm grip of his waist again, and Birgget grabbed the last place, half of her bottom clinging on the edge of the seat and the other half on a tail light.

'Everyone in?' Ida asked.

'Let's go!' Birgget shouted, while the rising heat caressed her backside.

All five bodies interlocked themselves tightly on one continuous leather seat, as if they were pieces of some four-dimensional puzzle. However, even though Ida twisted the throttle as hard as she could, they could barely reach the top speed of a giant centipede on skis. Sophia's new snowmobile was being put to an extreme test that no rally had performed before.

'It would be faster to run,' Irmeli snorted.

'Go for it,' Birgget smirked. Even this near-death experience wasn't enough for her to bury their bitter past.

'Okay, kids at the back, behave,' Ida grunted sarcastically.

A glimpse of water appeared again, this time on their left.

'We could still head towards the lake?' Irmeli suggested.

'Why?' Birgget asked, dumbfounded.

'We'd be safe in the water.'

'No, thank you,' Ida said firmly. 'I like coldness, but not that much.'

As they reached the slope, their combined weight functioned as an ideal, natural accelerator. The only problem was that the flowing lava followed similar physics of motion, although slightly slower. Their speedy descent resembled a rollercoaster or bobsleigh ride. However, that exhilarating, sinking feeling was short lived when a low-flying goose flew threateningly straight towards them.

'Duck!' Ida screamed.

On the very last second, the women managed to crouch down in different directions, apart from Christian.

'Where?' he asked, before the bird flew into his pretty face.

It was exactly like what happened to another gorgeous creation, Fabio Fitness, in the famous rollercoaster incident a few years prior. However, this goose survived and flew away, leaving a few of its feathers in Christian's mouth, that he tried to spit out.

The next incline brought their overweight ride to another halt. The magma stream behind them was still rolling downhill, nearly catching Birgget's hem. This time, everyone, including Ida, jumped off and began pushing the vehicle up the steep hill. Their boots kept slipping against the icy surface. Every once in a while, Ida rushed to the front to keep the handlebar straight. Eventually, their efforts were being rewarded by the views overlooking Örebröre.

'Great job! We're almost there,' gasped Ida as she hopped back on the driver's seat.

'Almost where?' Birgget asked, confused.

'Back to our house.'

'We're not going back there, are we?' Birgget remonstrated. 'We should keep going to Kihlava and beyond.'

'Look behind you,' Ida said gravely. 'There's not enough time. The lava is catching up with us.'

All heads turned to witness the façade of black and orange volcanic mass that had rolled the forest flat behind them. The dark wall of destruction was almost reaching the peak they had just climbed.

'The bunker,' Ida said to herself, but loudly enough for the others to hear.

'That may be our only hope.' Christian, bringing the baby with him, came to sit behind Ida.

Birgget and Irmeli weren't convinced, yet there was no time to take a vote. They had to join the majority – if they included the two who remained in the house.

As they began the final descent towards the estate, however, the snowmobile's engine died again. Ida put it in a neutral gear and let them glide freely, while simultaneously attempting to restart. But the motor gave no signs of life. The extra weight helped them through the gates and on the lengthy driveway, where the slight incline brought them to another halt.

'No time to push. Let's run!' Ida bounced off the stationary snowmobile, took the baby from Christian and dashed towards the house.

The others followed suit and began the race of their lives. As they passed the corner of the building, the magma stream began to push through the estate gates, into the vineyard and the hedge maze in the garden, setting fire to the trees, bushes and the shed. Any wooden structure would not remain intact for much longer.

Ida pulled the house door open and led them through the living room and into Gustav's office. 'Mum! Where are you?'

But there was no response. All they could hear were the loud knocking and rumbling noises coming from outside. The chandelier shook above them.

'The lava has reached us,' Birgget said gravely.

In panic, Ida started randomly pulling books off the bookcase. 'Are you in there?'

The housemaid appeared behind them, holding a set of towels. 'She is down there.'

'Why are you still here?' Ida gasped. 'Why aren't you with

her?'

'Madam wanted me to get these towels,' the housemaid said.

'Towels?!' Ida grabbed the housemaid's arm. 'Now we go down, all of us. Mum! Open the bookcase!'

The lava stream reached the windows, breaking them to pieces and setting the curtains alight. Then the magma began to crawl through each frame. The sulphuric smoke filled the room. The wallpaper curled and caught fire. It became impossible to inhale. The parquet floor was melting. As their last resort, the group could only press their backs against the bookcase. Then, just before the lava engulfed them, the bookcase rotated, grabbing them all on the other side. Suddenly, they were in the dungeon, face to face with Sophia.

'Mum!' Ida squealed.

'Everybody downstairs! Now!' Sophia ordered the rescued, and sealed the entrance to the stairwell with a thick titanium door. Once they all reached the basement, there was another similar vault that Sophia closed behind them.

Panting and shaking, they all huddled under the light of that single bulb. Violent rumbles of the outer world took to the stage. The eruption tore apart the remaining pieces of the centuries-old house. Everything that Sophia and Ida's family had treasured for hundreds of years was gone in a matter of seconds. So strong and cruel nature could be.

Chapter 45

DON'T SHOOT THE MESSENGER

The longer Roar fought against the fish, the more insecure he became. It had been an eventful day and he was tired. The last time he almost caught something this big was on their way to the river, until Sven decided to snap the line. But now, letting go crossed his mind. Losing Carl, in front of his very eyes, had irreparably damaged his confidence.

'Don't just sit there. Do something!' He took his frustration out on Sven and Jaaku, who could've used their dormant weapons that were going to waste.

The boat began reversing against their will. The fishermen suddenly became the bait for something larger and stronger underneath the surface. While Jaaku was already holding the rifle, Sven hesitantly picked up the spear gun. Neither of them knew where to aim, since nothing tangible had surfaced.

'It's moving very slowly.' Roar felt something wasn't right.

'There's three of us on the boat. A lot of weight,' Sven said.

'Look!' Jaaku shouted. 'It's coming to surface.' His pupils widened as he aimed at the dark, rising shadow.

'It's huge.' Roar could no longer feel any resistance. 'Shoot!'

Jaaku's performance anxiety kicked in again – like when he had to shoot Mooses but missed. This time, he kept hesitating.

Before Sven had even discovered the trigger of the spear gun, the creature had already emerged. Its dorsal fin towered from the water, followed by a wide, light pink back that had the shape and enormity of a submarine. Its fish-like tail, the size of the men's dinghy, flapped up and down, splashing water all over. Its body was roundish and smooth, as if it was filled with air, like a gigantic balloon or a puffer fish. Its head was bloated, yet the look on the face was somewhat approachable. It was obvious that the creature wasn't Wolferring, but something more familiar and less dangerous. The cross attached to the necklace around its almost unrecognisably thick neck, gave away its purpose; also part of its identity. From a distance, it could've been a whale, a fat seal or a rocky island; but the pinkish tone of its scales and skin gave away its true identity: an enormous salmon.

Roar rubbed his tired eyes. 'Is it... Psalmon?'

'What has happened to it?' Sven whispered.

'It's really big,' Jaaku said in awe, while keeping his finger on the trigger.

Psalmon's body was about quadruple in size compared to the last time they'd seen it. It didn't rise above the water, but stayed comfortably floating right on the surface.

Even though Roar himself once had supernatural powers, he didn't particularly enjoy running into anything or anyone else mythical. Previously, the encounter with the likes of Psalmon and Mooses had sealed the Lord of Herrings' final destiny.

'Ööö... Mr Psalmon,' said Sven with some hesitation. 'How are you today?'

Psalmon sluggishly flapped its fins. Its heavy breathing caused tiny waves, on top of the bigger waves that its moving body was already creating. It floated nearer to the men and gave them a depressing glare. It had bags under its eyes and swollen eye lids. Its jaws rotated slowly as if it was chewing gum. Solidified, porridge-like drool dripped out its half-open mouth.

'Burrrrp!' The raspy noise from the depths of its throat was accompanied by the foul smell of rot.

In disgust, the men covered their own nasal passages.

'That's revolting,' Roar grunted through the collar of his jacket.

'It looks so different,' Sven said, trying not to gag.

Psalmon spat Roar's tackle out of its mouth, so that it could say something. 'Brave fishermen, I have surfaced to warn ye about a great danger.' It accidentally gurgled water, making it sound slurred, like it was a little bit drunk. 'My good friend and fellow preacher fish, Cod of Thunder, has turned to Satanism. It will gather darkness to please it, before grilling with its lightning strikes. Beware!'

The last thing we need now is another deadly fish, Sven thought.

'What about Wolferring?' Roar asked suspiciously, not fully trusting anyone or anything anymore – especially fish that talk. 'Have you seen it?'

'Hah! A fish of the wastewaters,' Psalmon snorted.

A sea change in Psalmon's opinion came as a complete surprise.

'But the last time you spoke so greatly yet fearfully about it,' Sven said, and quoted, '"The Diving Destroyer who fears no fisherman and so on".'

'That was then. The world underwater is ever-changing,' Psalmon said briefly, and began diving. 'I shall return. It is time for fasting.'

'Really?' Jaaku said in awe, thinking how Psalmon must have recently gone through the opposite of fasting.

'Wait!' Roar yelled. 'What should we do about this... cod?'

'It can be beaten.' Psalmon's voice was already gurgling in the water. 'But you must believe. Have faith.'

'I hope I don't have to read the whole Bible again,' Sven sighed under his breath.

'Thy rod shall comfort,' Psalmon said. 'And worms, too.'

'We have both,' Roar said.

'In the River Pihtamii, Clash of the *Piscis* shall take place.'

'Clash? What does that mean?' Sven asked, worried that they might lose their valuable source of information.

'Where about? It's a long river,' Roar added.

But Psalmon wasn't paying attention anymore, as it went on blabbering about its future plans. 'Forty days of Lent leading to Easter. We must only consume vegetables and water to set ourselves apart for God.' Before disappearing in the depths of the lake, it did a sign of a cross with its pectoral fin. 'As I dive through the canyon of the shadow of death...'

The men raised their heads to get a better view. But Psalmon was gone.

Roar shook his head. 'I don't think I'll ever get over the fact that any other life form speaks, apart from us, humans.'

'But, what happened to it?' Sven pondered. 'As if it had bulked up in advance to survive through the fasting period.'

'You should know about that. You've read the Bible,' Jaaku smirked.

Sven shrugged his shoulders. He couldn't remember fasting being mentioned in the book, together with most other things.

'I don't know anything about fasting, either, and would never do it voluntarily.' Roar was taken back to his past again. 'After Wolferring's attack, all those days I drifted on the lake were enough of fasting for me. Since then, I've always appreciated a good meal.'

'Well, Psalmon had definitely enjoyed a few meals too many,' Sven sighed, as if he thought it was partly to blame for the fish exodus.

However, Roar was bravely thinking ahead. 'So, who's curious to witness this "clash"?'

Sven and Jaaku had also heard Psalmon mentioning the river, but avoided the subject. Neither of them were keen to make that lengthy journey. On the other hand, besides worrying about the Saalamaa's path of destruction, they could use this time doing something purposeful.

It was time to toss a mark.

Chapter 46

LOCKED DOWN

The stream of lava rolling over the survivors turned everything into charred ruins. Gustav's building plans were being put to the test with real-life participants. They had so many disconcerting questions. How long could this basement protect them from the heat and the pressure above? Had they just voluntarily dived into their own mass crematory, with an inevitable result of lava engulfing them all?

There were no quick answers, while positive thoughts were so few. They were still alive, and may have bought themselves some extra time. For how many minutes or hours, though, no one could tell.

We should have gone towards Kihlava, not New Pihtamo, Christian thought to himself, but didn't dare say it. Their choice had reunited them with Birgget, yet at what cost? If they had followed the three other women to Kihlava in the first place, they wouldn't be trapped, sweating, in this stuffy cellar.

'So, what are we going to do now?' Ida dared to ask the most relevant question everyone was thinking.

Nervous looks were exchanged, but no one replied.

'We just wait for someone to find us,' Sophia suggested eventually.

'But, that could take ages,' Ida replied.

'How quickly does lava cool?' Irmeli asked.

To everyone's surprise, the housemaid quietly intervened.

'It really depends on the thickness of the flow. The crust on the surface can form and cool quickly, yet underneath and towards the bottom it can take much longer.'

'How do you know all this?' Ida asked, surprised to hear the housemaid speaking so confidently.

'I studied seismology at the university,' the housemaid replied shyly.

'You did?' Sophia couldn't believe what she was hearing. She always assumed the housemaid wasn't that educated.

The housemaid nodded, knowing she had mentioned her qualifications at the job interview, and also that they were on her resume, when she applied to be Sophia and Gustav's housemaid. But she did not want to embarrass Sophia in front of everyone by reminding her.

'It's a shame you couldn't predict this disaster,' Sophia said mockingly.

'Actually, the threat level was raised to moderate,' the housemaid said. 'Everyone in the area should have been informed.'

'Now you're telling us,' Sophia grunted. 'And, why are you still here, then?'

The housemaid looked down to the floor. 'Ma'am, I need the work.'

'So, who else knows about this place?' Christian intervened, before Sophia would lose her cool.

Pleadingly, Sophia looked at Ida in the hope she would do the explaining.

'Not sure.' Ida decided to speak up when she saw the despair in Sophia's eyes. 'Me and my mother only found out about this place recently. It seems like Dad, Gustav, held some sort of hunters' meetings here.' She tried to engage with Sophia, hoping she would add to the conversation.

However, Sophia looked away in agony. Still, she had strength to feel stupid and naïve, even though all her earthly possessions were being swiped off the planet. The more she thought about the bunker, the more disgusted she felt about the idea of her husband hiding such a big secret for all these years. She hated that Gustav knew so many people she had never heard of, and some of these people had been to their house without her knowledge. A complete double-life was suddenly being exposed, and now she was expected to speak openly about this embarrassment, right in front of so many strangers.

Ida could quickly assess that her mother wasn't comfortable talking about the subject. Hence, she steered the discussion away from her and Gustav. 'Sven knows about this place. And Jaaku.'

That was when Ida and Sophia noticed the shards of broken glass on the floor and the metal frames that were left of the glass vitrine. *Someone has been here since?* they thought and looked at one another.

Meanwhile, Christian was both impressed and confused. 'So, this basement has been here all these years and neither of you...?'

'We know!' Sophia yelled at Christian's tactless remark, but soon regretted her overreaction. She tried to turn her back to everyone. But, since the space was so limited, even being properly upset was difficult to hide. She could still feel the staring eyes.

Since Christian lacked the skills to ease the tension, Birgget had to intervene. 'We just have to get a hold of Sven or Jaaku, then.'

'Or hope they'll realise to look for us,' Ida added, and then pointed at some pictures on the wall. 'Or maybe some of these people in the photos will come and find us. There are so many I've never seen.'

'Who are they?' Christian asked.

All eyes turned to Sophia again, whose back was to them.

Ida replied on her behalf. 'Hunters, obviously.'

Birgget had a closer look. 'Do we know any of them?'

Sophia took a deep, frustrated breath. 'The only thing I have learnt is that Gustav did not want his family to know about this place.'

'But why?' asked Birgget, pouring more water on hot stones.

'That's not really important right now.' Again, Ida stepped in to protect her mother's sanity. 'Can we talk about something else?' Hers was the question commonly thrown into conversations when topics got too heated for someone's taste. And sometimes, this interruption worked, killing many meaningful and progressive debates.

This time, however, the small group ended up talking about absolutely nothing. They could hear the house burning and its structures collapsing. Any conversation would have helped distract from those terrorising noises.

This complete standstill was too much for Sophia to bear. She needed more space to breathe. Hence, she swung past the others and grabbed the handle of the vault at the back of the room, revealing that there was more.

Chapter 47

THE MOMENT OF TRUTH?

Jaaku had to steer the boat blindly according to Roar's intuitive hand signals, who was beginning to regret ever having trusted Psalmon's advice. *I can't see a darned thing.* His vague guidance was fully based on his last, distant image of the river delta ahead, before the ash cloud had settled around them, blocking all visibility and taking over the entire air space.

'Shouldn't we be there by now?' Sven asked quietly, while shallow breathing.

'Actually... we may be.' Roar joyfully spotted land behind the curtain of mist.

The positive news gave Jaaku a reason to keep rowing. The sound of the treetops swiping the bottom of the boat was another good sign. The banks appeared on either side, while the waterway stretched ahead. 'So, what's next?' Jaaku asked.

'Cast a bait?' Sven said casually.

Roar looked at him anxiously. He feared that any casting could be the baneful one, hence he didn't want Sven to be in the frontline. Even though Sven wasn't that twelve-year-old boy anymore, yet, like any parent, Roar had a natural instinct to protect his son.

'I could give it a go,' he said, and reached out for his rod.

'I think it's my turn.' Sven did exactly the same.

Curiously, Jaaku followed this psychological battle between the two generations. He made sure his rifle was at arm's length in case one or the other, the son or the father, was to reel in something larger than life.

Since Sven remained determined to test the waters, Roar couldn't let him do it alone. Hence, simultaneously, they casted to opposite directions, while Jaaku anchored the boat with a heavy rock tied to a rope. Once the big splash had settled, everything around them was tranquil again. Only a peculiar smell in the air reminded them of the recent volcanic eruption. The ash cloud was thinning, though. Lava was probably making its last, destructive stretches in places unknown to them, and there was nothing they could do about it.

Immediately, Sven felt a soft pulling, followed by a gentle, continuous nibble. 'I got something.'

Roar dropped his rod to the side. 'Be careful.' His hand went inside his bag and grabbed the handle of the axe.

Reluctantly, Jaaku aimed the barrel at the water.

'This is not fighting back at all.' Sven reeled with ease. 'Probably just a tiddler.'

Roar's heart beat faster. 'I wouldn't trust it.'

Chapter 48

TRANSACTION DECLINED

Based on individual preferences and chemistries, the people in the basement divided into three smaller groups in the two rooms. Ida and the baby had followed Sophia to the meeting room, whereas Birgget and the housemaid went past them to explore the small kitchen unit tucked in the corner. Christian and Irmeli remained in the front room.

Birgget found some filtered coffee next to a coffee maker. She prepared a full load and switched the machine on. Sophia was partly underneath the long meeting table, rummaging through two polypropylene bags with *Nikea* labels branded on the side. It was surprising to Birgget how such an elegant and wealthy woman like Sophia, who only seemed to rely on luxury items from high end retail shops even owned shopping bags from an entry-level chain like Nikea. *Did she secretly shop cheap?*

Nikea was both famous and infamous for making and selling cheap trainers, as well as nearly-impossible-to-assemble wooden furniture. The synergy was unusual and complicated for the company to maintain, which usually resulted in poor product quality and problems with managing the distribution channel. The usual target shoppers were lower income families and young students, forced to sacrifice hours, or days, to interpret the complex instruction manuals of the furniture, and sometimes replace missing bolts and screws with random spare parts, like fish bones or even shoelaces from Nikea trainers, that they may have received as a part of a bundle deal.

To Birgget's disappointment, the contents of Sophia's bags were nothing more or less than Tuppervaara.

Meanwhile, across the room, Ida impatiently played with her phone, with the baby in her arm. 'No signal down here. Can't even connect to broadband. Way to go, Dad!'

A sudden, loud banging of the table made Ida raise her gaze. 'What are you doing, Mum?'

From the second bag, Sophia dug out more items and spread them on the table. 'Since we'll probably be stuck here for a while, I thought we could finish off what we started upstairs.'

'We're in the middle of a natural disaster, and you are thinking about Tuppervaara?' Ida's gasp echoed all the way to the front room.

Irmeli barged in excitedly. 'That's the best idea I've heard since we got down here.'

Birgget, however, was not pleased about Irmeli's entrance, which narrowed the physical gap they had purposely created.

'What else could we do?' Sophia replied casually, and handed one of the bags to Irmeli to explore.

'You two are crazy,' Ida snorted.

Sophia stopped unpacking and turned to Ida. 'It's the end of the world outside. We have nowhere to go. No one is going to find us until the eruption settles, and that can take a long time. A very long time. Until that happens, we must keep ourselves entertained. I know, I will.'

'Me too,' Irmeli added.

Ida sighed. This was just one of many times she struggled to argue against her strong-willed mother. The baby, who was resting in her tired arms, let out an uncontrollable chuckle, distracting Ida away from all these complex adult relations the bunker was filled with. She tried to enjoy to the fullest this brief phase in the baby's development before her daughter's willpower would develop and grow stronger. Like many fresh parents, Ida naively believed that she could somehow protect her child from becoming too complicated later in life. But the least she could do was to minimise the damage – though, she had doubts as to how it could be done, especially when surrounded by this bunch of broken souls.

Meanwhile, Birgget began serving coffee to her and Ida. She tried to look at the positive side of things. 'At least it's warmer down here than what it was last Christmas on that post office roof.'

'Very funny,' Ida snorted, and had a sip of the coffee. 'Now I know where Sven got his senses of humour.'

'Maybe there are some lamb chops hidden somewhere here, so we can cook a nice dinner,' added Birgget. With reference to their Christmas dinner on that same post office roof, she tried to brighten the atmosphere – even though she didn't even find herself that funny anymore.

'Of course. Eastertime!' In the midst of all the action and drama, Ida had forgotten the holiday period that was due the coming weekend. 'Unlike last time, we don't need to worry about coldness.'

'How much is the knife stand?' Irmeli's penetrating, high-pitched voice stood out, while she haggled with Sophia. 'Though I haven't got much cash left.'

It was a cruel reality and a wild nightmare, how Birgget and Irmeli had ended up in one, confined space.

'No problem at all.' Sophia went to her purse, totally oblivious to both Birgget and Ida's disapproving stares. 'Thankfully, I brought the card reader with me. It takes contactless as well.'

Irmeli delightfully offering her credit card was the final straw for Ida. She bounced up furiously. 'You can't seriously be doing that while lava is piling up on top of our heads?!'

Her outburst seemed to make time stand still. Both women at the mobile check-out froze on the spot. The only noise interrupting the silence was a chirping card reader that started spitting out a receipt from Irmeli's recent transaction. It felt like the longest ever feeding of the roll.

To Sophia and Irmeli's disappointment, though, the receipt read: Purchase Declined. Sophia examined the failed card reader. 'It doesn't connect to broadband.' She ripped the receipt off and chucked it on the floor.

'I told you,' Ida snorted.

'Are you happy now?' said Sophia, turning to Ida. 'If you

just prefer to stare at the wall and cry about our horrible destiny, there's one more room down there.' Sophia stuck her thumb up and pointed over her shoulder. 'You can write a diary there or something. Who knows, one day it may sell millions of copies. And, while you do that, I will be hosting my party, because that's what I decided to do today and no volcanic eruption, lack of internet or outburst from my daughter is going to stop me.'

'I hate you!' Ida screamed like a teenager, and swung past everyone to the next door, leading to the bedroom. Furiously, she pulled the door open and slammed it shut behind her.

Chapter 49

THE VENEZUELAN HERRING

A foot-long, elongated herring with a roundish body, tangled in Sven's bait. Its silver stripes narrowed and faded towards the rear, before reaching its forked tail fin. Non-threateningly, it didn't resist, but gave in to its destiny.

'Should I just let it go?' Sven pondered.

'It must be one of the many we returned from the pond.' Roar could let go of his axe, without even revealing it.

'*Ay, ay, ay!*' the herring let out a scream, as the hook yanked the side of its mouth.

As Sven lifted the herring above the gunwale, he stared at it in awe. 'It can't be...'

The fish became completely still – like a wet cloth, hanging in front of the men's very eyes.

'The Mexican herring?' Jaaku poked it with the tip of the rifle barrel.

'Wasn't it from Venezuela?' Sven said.

Jaaku shrugged his shoulders. 'It was definitely more lively than this.'

Carefully, Sven brought the sloppy fish over the boat and let it drop at their feet. 'Actually, the *Latino* was quite useful herring. It led us to Roar.'

'No. It was Spin the Herring,' Jaaku argued, and turned to Roar. 'We got the herring so drunk that it passed out. Then we spun it and followed the direction its nose pointed. The herring did absolutely nothing.'

'You played Spin the Herring?' Roar chuckled. 'That's a very old, traditional game. I'm surprised your generation has even heard about it.'

'It was Viljo's idea.'

Roar smiled. 'Of course.'

'The first time we saw you, the herring immediately escaped to your boat,' Sven said. 'I mean, the Lord of Herrings' boat.'

'As you know well, I don't have a clear recollection of those times,' Roar replied. 'Besides, I probably wouldn't have paid any particular attention to one single herring, while simultaneously my boat had hundreds of them.'

'Fair enough.' Sven looked at the lifeless fish. 'What should we do with it, then? Throw it back?'

'Why not spin it?' Jaaku suggested, and pulled out a pocket-sized bottle of Arctic Wodka from the inside of his jacket. 'A bit more guidance wouldn't hurt. Otherwise, we'll just end up aimlessly raking these waters.'

Sven nodded, hesitatingly. 'Jaaku has a point. Psalmon brought us here, but what next? Maybe the herring could show us direction?'

Roar hid his uncertainty behind his laughter. 'This is a river. We can only go one way or the other.'

'The river does branch out a few times, though,' Sven said seriously.

However, Roar remained unconvinced that Spin the Herring would bring the desired results. He only knew it as a drinking game with his friends during his bachelor years, before he met Birgget. All the 'lads' usually formed a circle with their kicksleds. Then, the herring was spun in the middle, on flat, icy ground. Whoever the herring's nose ended up pointing to had to have three shots of straight wodka, and then ride his kicksled, in his underwear, to that same direction indicated by the herring, until he was no longer visible to any of the participants in the circle. Every second felt like hours while looking for that place to hide in the freezing temperatures. Big rocks, fallen trees and piles of snow often gave the escapees enough shelter. The same routine was repeated over and over again, until there was no alcohol left.

'Should we?' Jaaku shook the half-full bottle in front of Sven. 'If mine isn't enough, I presume you brought some as well?'

'Actually, I'm trying to... cut down since... you know... the baby and all that,' Sven muttered.

Grinning, Jaaku twisted the cap off. 'It's your loss.' The spicy aromas spread in the air, like a genie had been released.

Even Roar became curious when he saw the updated label and bottle design. 'Is that the new edition?'

'Yes. Do you wanna try?'

'Why not? This could be our last drink together.' As Roar grabbed the bottle, however, his joke didn't go down well with the youngsters. The night had been too long for such a grave gag. They all understood too well that it really would be their last drink together before facing the aftermath of the volcanic destruction. At this very moment, they only knew the past, which was certainly better than what the future had in store for them and for New Pihtamo. Not a single scenario came to their minds in which things could have improved.

'*Hölöökynkölöökyn!*' In their native tongue, Roar broke the awkward silence. He raised the bottle up in the air as if to say 'cheers' to the world. Then he had a large gulp, and passed the bottle to Sven.

Without hesitation, Sven brought the neck to his lips and had a tiny sip. His throat was burning, but so sweetly. His eyes were wide open again. He felt a warm sensation.

Lastly, Jaaku took his share, leaving the rest for the herring. 'Let's see if we hear any more languages.' He raised the bottle high above, and poured the spirit unevenly over the herring's scales and head.

'Actually, can you save me a drop?' Sven nervously watched their favourite drink going to waste. His withdrawal symptoms started kicking in straight away.

Jaaku nodded, knowing well what Sven was going through. 'I tried once a whole weekend without it. It was like hell on earth.'

Once the herring was completely soaked, Jaaku stopped pouring, leaving about half a unit floating inside the bottle. The men attentively waited for the herring to react.

To their disappointment, though, it just lay on the floor motionless as if nothing had changed.

'That was a bottle well spent,' Jaaku grunted, and handed the leftovers to Sven. 'It definitely said something at the beginning.'

'Would a little scaling make it talk?' This time, Roar pulled the axe out and raised it above them. It was shining clean and still sharp enough to cut thin slices of cheese on toast.

Jaaku stared at it, both impressed and intimidated. 'You really came prepared.'

Roar wiped the blade with a cloth. 'This actually belonged to Carl. It was part of his gear he left behind.'

'I didn't know.' Sven was surprised to hear, after having used the axe for their training purposes. 'You've kept it all these years?'

'It was better to hold onto it,' said Roar. 'It's actually a really good tool for scaling and gutting fish.'

Sven shook his head. 'Unbelievable. It was such a big deal for you to sail his boat, yet you've been using his axe all the time. What a hypocrite!'

'I guess... I just... grew into it.' Muttering, Roar brought the axe above his head. In the recent years, he had grown to respect Carl's unusual skill set and methods more than when he was still alive. Glamorising the greatness of the ones that had passed on was a typical behaviour amongst many. In fact, Roar had often belittled and looked down on Carl, even though he was one of the most skilful fishermen ever – even matching many contemporary greats, like Sven.

However, Roar sensitively kept this comparison, between Carl and his own son, to himself.

Hesitatingly, Sven followed the execution that was about to begin. 'I don't think this is a good idea. But do as you wish.'

'As you *fish*,' Jaaku chuckled.

'Why not scrape the surface first?' Sven sympathetically suggested. He was still carnivorous, yet his ability to empathise with all living things had reached another level since they discovered animals that can express themselves humanely. The herring that Roar was about to slaughter did clearly master some basic communication skills, and the awareness of this uniqueness put Sven in the most awkward position. He was supposed to be a wholehearted fisherman and not the fishes' protector. In fact, all three of them were aware of the existence of such intelligent life forms, yet this random act of cruelty seemed to bother Sven the most. Perhaps, his bond with the intelligent fauna was the strongest.

Fortunately, Sven's thoughtful request softened Roar. *The new generation*, he thought, and lowered the axe, gently touching the skin of the herring. Then he dragged the blade back and forth along the scale.

The herring's eyes flew wide open. Pleadingly, it screamed at Roar to stop. '*No hagas eso!*'

'I guess, that'll do,' Roar smirked victoriously. He put the axe away, grabbed the herring by its tailfin and hung it upside down in front of them.

'*No más!*' It cried for mercy.

Roar chucked the herring onto Sven's lap. 'It's all yours. Feel free to spin it, eat it, save it.'

Sven's paternal instincts surfaced. Holding the tiny fish made him think about the safety of Ida and their little girl. He found himself sweet talking the herring. 'Don't worry. You'll be fine. We just need a little bit of your help.'

Roar shook his head in disbelief. 'I've never witnessed such a tenderness and connection between a fisherman and a fish.'

'Says the man who saved all the fishes of the entire lake,' Sven snorted.

'Yes, but... that was different,' Roar stammered.

'Wasn't the oldest one supposed to do the spinning?' Jaaku tried to change the course of the conversation.

'Who told you that?' Sven asked.

'Viljo.'

'He probably just made it up so that he could do it himself.'

Meanwhile, the herring poked its head up, and broke into a big smile. It pointed at Roar with its pectoral fin. '*E Señor de Los Arenques?*'

'What? *Señor?*' Sven was able to repeat one Spanish word.

'He s*ave* my life.' The herring joyfully stared at Roar.

'It remembers you,' Sven smiled.

The recognition made Roar feel like any confused celebrity

who had been too occupied and focused to pay any attention to the masses around him. Every fish knew him by face, whereas, for him, they were all just one and the same.

'I thought you'd have gone back to Venezuela by now?' Sven asked the herring.

'I tried,' the Venezuelan replied passionately. 'I was halfway across the Atlantic when that same external force dragged me back here again. *Otra vez!*'

'It's getting those signals again,' Jaaku said.

'*Si! Si!*'

Gravely, the men looked at one another, until Roar spoke out. 'Take us to Wolferring.'

'*Es el riesgo!* Too dangerous!' the herring gasped.

'I'm afraid you have no other choice.' Discreetly, Roar's hand searched for the axe again.

'You sound more and more like Viljo,' Jaaku smirked.

'Please, don't compare me to that old hag,' Roar grunted, and took the axe out. 'So, how will it be?'

Since one of its saviours suddenly became an oppressor, the herring turned pleadingly to its only hope: Sven.

However, Sven shrugged his shoulders, while trusting that his father was only threatening the poor little fish.

'*No...*' The herring dropped its head and spread its fins as signs of defeat.

Sven delayed the fake execution by sharing a few motivational words. 'You can obviously sense something we cannot. If you lead us, we can show you the pond, where you'll definitely be safe with all the other fish, until it's time for you to return to Central America. The water in the pond is warm and the vegetation around tropical – which you'll like.'

Roar and Jaaku glanced at one another, knowing that Sven was making things up.

'Pond? *What is?*' the herring asked.

'A bit smaller than a lake.'

'Ah! *El estanque.*'

Enquiringly, Sven looked at Roar and Jaaku. 'Should we do it then? Release the Venezuelan and follow it?'

'I'm not convinced,' said Jaaku, shaking his head. 'Last

time, its path was so winding that we ended up in the same spot that we started from. Besides, it's probably a little bit drunk right now. I'd suggest we spin it.'

'Dad?'

'Well, you said earlier, that eventually the Venezuelan led you to me...'

'It's nose. We spun it,' Sven added.

'Right.' Roar hesitated. 'Well, something attracted Mr Arenque back here. I don't know. You decide.'

Sven rolled his eyes in response to the most indecisive answer his father had ever given him. The only remaining, unheard opinion was that of the herring. He sought for any reaction, gesture or feedback. Eventually, the herring discreetly pointed its pectoral fin towards the river.

'Okay, then. Let the herring show us the way,' Sven hesitated.

After the release, the herring swam to the front and looked over its non-existent shoulder.

'What if it disappears, or swims away?' Jaaku asked.

'I want to believe that it has learnt its lesson. It should feel safer with us, rather than out there alone in the vast lake.'

'And how the world has turned upside down,' Roar sighed.

'It's moving, doing salsa again.' Jaaku dropped his face to his palms.

As they had expected, the journey began with a couple of unnecessary, three-sixty degree turns. Sven, who had the oars, struggled to follow the herring's irregular path.

'You don't have to imitate its every move,' Roar grunted.

'Do you wanna row?' Sven brought the boat to a halt. 'Let's wait until this cabaret show is over.'

'*Olé!*' The herring spun glamorously on the surface, like a solo synchronised swimmer.

Jaaku, however, believed that some immediate disciplinary action was required. He pointed the rifle to the dancing Venezuelan. Only the simple sound of the cocking of the rifle, and the awareness of being at gunpoint, made the fish finally swim on a straight and orderly line along the river.

Chapter 50

THE BUSINESS HOURS ARE OVER

Since Irmeli was the only remaining customer, and the card machine didn't pick up the signal, Sophia could start reducing prices on selected items. By making bargains, she could meet Irmeli's limited available cash funds.

'I'll pay any excess when we're out of here, okay?' Irmeli made a hesitant promise.

The concern wasn't about her being able to pay back, but more when.

'Don't worry about it,' Sophia said, and tried to think of other products she had always wanted to get rid of. 'What about these salad servers? They're made of oak.'

Meanwhile, Christian's dramatic entrance to the meeting room went completely unnoticed. 'We have a problem,' he said gravely.

Birgget and the housemaid were again examining the treasures of the kitchen corner. They were in the middle of an inventory of the items pre-stored in the cupboards and shelves for the use of potential survivors.

'Someone really thought about everything.' Birgget said, impressed by the large number of cans of tuna and beans, bags of pasta, bottled water and toilet paper. Lots of toilet paper. There was easily a few days' supply of various goods, if they were rationed equally between the seven of them.

'Not everything.' This time, Christian properly projected his

307

voice, grabbing everyone's attention. 'The front door is melting. The lava must have penetrated the bookcase and reached the stairwell leading down here.'

Immediately, Birgget and the housemaid stopped rummaging through the kitchen and came to listen. Sophia, on the other hand, continued serving Irmeli as if nothing had happened.

'That container is fifteen marks.' Sophia said urgently, while feeling Christian breathing down her neck.

'Please, listen to me!' Christian banged his fist on the table, making a couple of Tuppervaara mugs fall off the edge. 'We will burn alive soon, if we don't do something about it.'

Swiftly, Sophia pushed one more container under Irmeli's nose, and grabbed the last remaining money off her. The transaction was finally completed, and Sophia could focus on the real issue. 'Okay. What can we do then?'

'It's your bunker,' Christian snorted. 'What CAN we do?'

'We have only been here once, as Ida said. I really don't know more about this place than any of you.'

Christian looked pleadingly at everyone else, hoping for any ideas.

'Could we seal the door with...' Birgget hesitantly turned to the housemaid '...wet towels?'

Sophia's eyes lit up. 'Of course! We have plenty of them behind that bedroom door Ida just barged through. It's an en suite.'

'Great idea,' Christian said. 'We could also wet the floor.'

Birgget dashed back to the kitchenette. 'We have plenty of bottled drinking water. But I would use it sparingly.'

'Tap water?' the housemaid suggested.

'As long as it doesn't run out.' Birgget wanted to ask more questions about the place, but wasn't expecting Sophia to know. *Would the tap be linked to the main supply?*

'The extra towels are still in the front room,' said the housemaid, who headed off in that direction.

'I'll get the ones from the en suite then.' Birgget went to knock on the bedroom door. 'Ida?'

'Just go in. We have no time to waste,' Christian urged.

Birgget pushed the door open. She had seen Gustav and Sophia's master bedroom upstairs that wasn't to her liking, with its overly grandeur décor; this one wasn't much worse. What saddened her the most was the thought that Gustav had never shared the space with Sophia. The dungeon was only built for his secret plans, whatever they were.

She found Ida sitting on the bed, staring longingly into the distance. Ida didn't say a thing or look back at her. The baby rested quietly on the bed beside her, totally oblivious to her mother's worries.

Apologetically, Birgget trotted past her towards the bathroom. 'We have a bit of a situation in the front room.'

'Situation?' Ida woke up from her trance.

'The lava is about to melt our front door,' Birgget called out. 'We're trying to find ways to block it.' She grabbed two small hand and two large bath towels, both white in colour. She felt their softness and high quality against her palms; they were the type one would find in five-star resorts, and nothing like her old and raggedy towels.

'Let me know if you need help,' Ida said melancholically.

Birgget nodded, even though there was a wall between them. She soaked the towels under golden taps. She wanted to ask if Ida was alright.

But there wasn't enough time.

As Birgget returned to the meeting room, one of Sophia's Tuppervaara sauna buckets was already filled with water, and the housemaid had fetched more towels. Sophia and Irmeli were packing away the sales items from the table into those two Nikea bags. Christian grabbed the full bucket and threw all the water against the door leading from the meeting room to the front room.

'Why did you do that?' Birgget asked.

'It's too late to save the front room.' He rushed back to the kitchen to refill. 'The main entrance is gone.'

'Just don't use all the water,' Birgget said, and went to seal the bottom of the door with towels. She could feel it was hot down there.

As Christian joined her with another bucket-load of water,

he noticed the door beginning to bulge. 'It's coming through!' he squealed.

'We need to retreat again,' Sophia said gravely, and picked up her Nikea bags. 'Let's save everything we can. Empty the kitchen.'

'...and your Tuppervaara products?' Birgget snorted.

Sophia ignored Birgget's comment. There was no time to quarrel. She took the bags to the bedroom, where she found Ida lying on the bed. The baby was asleep on one side, and the letter she was reading rested on the other.

Ida sat up. She quickly slid the letter back in its envelope and casually dropped the envelope back in the bedside table drawer.

'Unfortunately, we all have to invade your privacy' Sophia said to her. 'This doomsday shelter is falling apart.'

The others made sure that the tuna cans, water bottles and toilet paper kept flooding into the bedroom. Once everyone was inside, they sealed the door gaps again with those few remaining wet towels, and then watered the doorframes. Apart from the bathroom, this was the furthest they could go.

Chapter 51

THE CLASH

The herring stopped advancing and popped its head up where the river branched out to a smaller creek. From their last visit, Sven vaguely recognised this narrow access point to the pond through the dense forest.

'*Vale!* This is it,' the herring said.

'This is *what*?' Roar asked, as if he didn't know where they were.

'I cannot feel it anymore. I can't hear the calling. *No hay señal!*'

'Are we near?' Jaaku nervously caressed his rifle.

The herring looked puzzled. '*No se!*'

'Show us the way 'til the end,' Roar insisted.

But the herring didn't move a muscle, apart from crossing its pectoral fins. '*No!* My work here is done. It's time for *siesta*.'

Stunned by the herring's arrogance, Roar decided to let it go. 'Alright then. If you follow that creek, you can find the pond at the end Sven was talking about. You'll love it there.'

'*Gracias!*' Gratefully, the herring began swimming towards the gap.

'Why did you let it go?' Sven stretched his neck, but the herring was already out of sight.

'I thought it deserved a break,' Roar said, while preparing his rod. 'What did Psalmon say about worms?'

'Or maybe you needed a break,' Sven smirked.

'So, what's the plan?' Jaaku asked tensely. 'More fishing?'

'Why not?' Roar said, while placing a worm in the hook. 'We've come this far.'

Sven and Jaaku gave each other that fearful look. *Here we go again*, Sven thought tiredly, and contemplated where to begin.

'*Ay, ay, ay!*' A blood-curdling scream carrying through the forest, however, alarmed them. 'Come, fishermen! *Rápido!*'

'The Venezuelan!' Sven changed his plan, took the oars and began steering them towards the mouth of the creek. 'We're coming!'

'Relax.' Roar calmly retrieved the line. 'It's probably just dancing bachata with the other fishes.'

Sven nodded, even though his gut was telling him differently. 'Whatever. I wanna see it.'

Forcefully, they had to push through the stiff branches and their thick needles. The wilderness around the creek had overgrown.

'The least we can do is to fill the boat with as many fishes as possible from the pond,' Sven added, 'and take them all back to the village for those who most urgently need them.'

Once they reached the chute of white-water rapids, the weight of the boat with one extra person made their descent quicker. From past experience, Roar and Sven knew exactly when to take the brace position, whereas Jaaku kept his head up, as they, almost vertically, dived straight into the pond. Jaaku gulped a mouthful of water while the boat ploughed the muddy bottom, until they surfaced, like a misfired squib torpedo. Eventually, the exhilarating ride came to a halt in the middle of the pond.

'That was even better than last time!' Roar shouted, soaked yet refreshed from the plummet. However, his excitement was short-lived once he looked down at their feet. The boat hadn't filled up with any fish; not a single one. The floor was only covered by reed and lily pads floating in ankle-deep water.

Sven couldn't get a word out. The silence around them was deafening. There were no fish jumping like before. The flat surface of the pond simply mirrored against their boat and the surrounding dense forest.

Jaaku noticed how Roar and Sven became uneasy. 'Is there

a problem?'

'Did Christian fish this place empty?' Sven snorted half-jokingly.

In disbelief, Roar stared at his own reflection in the calm water. The Lord of Herrings' hard work, that had lasted decades, became suddenly meaningless, and the future of every fisher and their families was again uncertain. In his mind, he tried to add up the total number of fish Christian managed to supply to the restaurant before disappearing. But, whatever estimate he came up with, none of them could explain the empty pond.

He tried to think of any scenario where things might have gone wrong. Did he miscalculate and overestimate the restaurant's need for stock? Did Christian also fish for his own needs – like Sven had just suggested? However, catching this many fish would have taken Christian a notable length of time which, realistically, shouldn't have been possible.

'It cannot be only him,' said Roar. 'There must be someone else involved. Or something else.'

'*Hola!* Venezuelan?' Jaaku shouted.

'You speak Spanish?' Sven asked, impressed.

'Just that one word. I've learnt from watching lots of interviews of the great, Ecuadorian footballer, Leon Él Messy.'

Once Jaaku finished explaining, the silence returned. There was no sign of the dancing herring, or any other fish or life forms whatsoever. The mist settled on the edges of the water – this time, a phenomenon not caused by volcanic activity, but naturally formed by moisture condensing into droplets that were suspended in the air. The tall and densely grown trees around them created a secluded pocket, where they couldn't see or hear the level of destruction the eruption was currently causing to their homeland. Despite the idyllic setting, it wasn't what they wanted to discover. It was a tragedy.

Only a dark brown pile of wood on the shore, like a boat wreck, broke the deep green colours of the land. Roar's eyes locked onto this unexpected sighting.

'That wasn't here before.'

'Let's go up to it.' Sven willingly took the oars, needing any excuse to keep warm after their recent dive.

As they got closer to the wreck, they noticed how its clinker planks were severely damaged and ripped apart. The remains of the vessel had similarities to an old, wooden Viking-style narrowboat.

Sven gave Roar an enquiring look. 'How is this possible? Your boat sank.'

'My boat?' Roar's heart beat faster, as he reminisced about his times as the wizard. He carefully observed every detail of the wreck – which seemed identical to the Lord of Herrings' boat.

However, he was not able to comprehend how it had ended up all the way here, hours away from the location where it had sunk in the middle of Lake Pihtamo. The wreck drifting by itself upstream, along the river and through the creek, down to the pond, was impossible. Someone must have brought it in here. Unless, the Lord's boat was not one of a kind.

They disembarked and laboriously plodded towards the wreck. With every step, their boots sank deeper into the soggy soil. The combined smell of tar and fish from the boat's remaining planks was another trip down Roar's memory lane.

There was an abandoned fishing rod and a grey carry bag inside the ruin. It was neither Roar's nor the Lord of Herrings' gear. The bag felt heavy. Roar let loose two soft leather straps and looked inside. A few nuggets of gold shone in the bottom. However, a stack of tri-folded brochures on the top caught most of his attention. He pulled them out and read.

'Roar's Fish and...' He stopped midway through the sentence, when it became clear that they were menu cards from his own restaurant. Anxiously, he rummaged through the bag again, and found one more piece of paper. 'Oh, no.'

'Dad? What is it?'

'It's the map I drew... for Christian!'

Perplexed, Sven kept staring back and forth at the map and the boat. 'But... that's not his boat, is it?'

'I don't know what sort of boat he had. Maybe he had several. He was from quite an affluent family.' Roar chucked Christian's bag and all his paperwork into the mud. 'We've seen enough. Or nothing at all. Let's just go home.'

As frustrating as the idea of giving up was, Roar was not

completely wrong. Apart from discovering the mysterious boat and some of Christian's belongings in it, the trip had clearly gone to waste. They had arrived too late; someone had got there before them.

'What if Christian had acquired some magical powers?' Jaaku playfully suggested while walking away.

'I sure hope not,' Roar snorted. 'But if somehow he did, let's all pray that he used his skills for a good purpose.'

'Doesn't look like it,' Sven grunted.

'Isn't it strange that all these things happen at the same time?' Jaaku added.

'What are you saying?' Roar asked, and followed Jaaku.

'What if Christian's behind all this, even the eruption?'

'Don't even start.'

Sven, however, didn't want to leave empty handed. He picked up the bag and the map off the wet ground – the only evidences of Christian's disappearance. They were a minor consolation compared to the men's original, ambitious plan for this trip; yet, it was better than nothing.

Disheartened, Roar and Jaaku returned to the Yolla and, without exchanging a word, took their seats. Jaaku abandoned his rifle and placed it by his feet, thinking it wouldn't be needed anymore. Then came Sven, chucking Christian's bag on the floor, next to his own.

As he kicked them off the grass towards the middle of the pond, however, a large head of a fish surfaced.

'Wolferring!' Roar screamed, immediately recognising the aquatic predator from the most dangerous spectrum.

A complete panic erupted. Roar reached out for his bag, while Jaaku and Sven reached for their weapons. Rather than achieving any results, the men only bumped and tangled into one another.

'Get out of my way!' Jaaku, as the heavier one, pushed Sven overboard.

Sven fell right next to Wolferring's face, looking straight into its dead eyes.

Meanwhile, Jaaku and Roar had gotten their tools out. Roar was waving his axe up in the air, while Jaaku pointed his rifle in the water. Sven tried to swim away, fearing he would get caught between Wolferring's razor-sharp teeth and the men's heavy armoury.

Somehow, though, it made no effort to chase him.

Nevertheless, Roar didn't care. He attacked anyway. This was the moment he had been waiting for. After years of agony and fear, it was payback time. His elaborate swing of the axe landed straight in the middle of Wolferring's forehead – exactly like they had trained for the past months.

'Way to go, Dad!'

But why didn't it resist or grunt in pain? Roar couldn't quite celebrate yet.

Suddenly, its whole skeleton body rose to the surface. Its head was intact, yet the rest of its skin, flesh and intestines were completely consumed. Only the long, thick spine was left.

'What on earth?' Roar panted, perplexed.

Sven stopped swimming away and Jaaku lowered the gun. They all stared in awe at the floating carcass. It had cuts on its lifeless, pale face, and its sideburns were literally burnt dark. Otherwise, it was just an enormous fishbone.

'Are you sure that's it?' Sven asked, while carefully wading back towards the boat.

'Definitely,' Roar nodded, filled with doubts. A weight falling off his chest was quickly being replaced by another. 'Sven, I think you should get out of the water.'

'I'm working on it. This bottom is just damn soft.'

Like a hawk, Roar kept scanning the water.

'Dad, it's all fine now. Wolferring is dead. We can go home.' Sven grabbed the edge of the boat and threw his leg over.

'But, what caused it?' Roar pondered. 'Where's all the fish?'

'Maybe it ate them all?' Jaaku intervened. 'Which is very sad.'

'Well, who ate Wolferring then?' Roar spurted out the question everyone was thinking. *Clash of the Pisces*, he remembered Psalmon's warning.

As Roar and Jaaku leant over to hoist Sven up, a sudden thunder rumbled from a clear sky. A section of the water began to rise next to them, like a big fountain. A large, greenish-grey creature surfaced, and jumped at them.

'Duck!'

By now, they knew exactly what Roar meant. They all hit the deck. There were neither waterfowl flying nor bullets whistling, but a colossal fish jumping up in the air and spewing lightning from its mouth. The strike hit the side of Yolla, shaking it vigorously, but was not able to penetrate the hard plastic. However, the men could feel the amount of electricity the impact contained.

'Cod of Thunder?' Sven whispered, while huddling on the floor between Roar and Jaaku.

Roar nodded gravely, and slowly poked his head up. 'It's gone.'

'I wouldn't count on it.' With trembling hands, Jaaku tried to shake his rifle dry.

Sven reached out for the spear gun, while Roar went for his rod. And worms.

'You think worms will be the solution?' Sven gasped.

'What have we got to lose?' Roar snorted, and placed one wiggly in the hook.

Meanwhile, grunting, Jaaku fired another showery blank. 'This rifle is useless!'

'Take this.' Sven offered him the spear gun. 'I can row; keep us moving. Otherwise, we'll just be an easy target for it.'

For Cod of Thunder's next attack, the men were as ready as they could be. Sven steered the boat in random turns around the pond; Jaaku was armed with the spear gun; and Roar's worm in the hook was flying high up in the air, perfectly attracting lightning strikes.

Although the poor worm got grilled, the men survived – this second round.

'The worm clearly distracted it!' Roar celebrated, retrieved the line and put another worm in the hook.

'How many you have?' Sven asked, sweating in the oars.

'About a dozen.'

'That's twelve rounds – like a pro boxing match.'

However, Cod of Thunder didn't play by their or any federation rules, when it jumped on the boat, landing in the middle, right on top of Jaaku and all their weaponry. This sudden attack rocked the boat, knocking Sven overboard to the shallow end of the shore.

The fish's wide open, growling mouth, sharp teeth and the lightning it was spewing, somehow missed them. It smelled like a fishmonger's after a long and hot day, or one of those elderly fishes that had been ploughing different lake and river bottoms for decades. It wasn't quite as large as some sea creatures, like the Great White Shark, but it had sharp teeth and fins, and a pointy barbel in the chin – the latter, a common feature of the cod family.

Jaaku remained trapped under its body – which was big enough to fill the entire boat sideways, with its tail and head spilling over both edges. Alive, but with minor burn injuries, the suave herring from Venezuela was tangled in its mouth, ready to be cooked. When Sven tried to compose himself in the waist-deep water, a thick and solid tailfin propelled furiously against his ribs, knocking him down over and over again.

Roar discarded his rod and was about to escape. *But where?* The oars were also squashed under the monster. He wasn't keen on joining Sven, either, since water was the fish's element and territory.

That life-changing split second, when Cod of Thunder's jaw wasn't fully locked, was the Venezuelan herring's opportunity to slip out and flick itself in the water. In fury, the cod shot more lightning towards the little herring. Still agile in its moves, though, the herring managed to escape upstream along the white-waters – like a salmon on its way to spawn.

Meanwhile, Roar was left with no other option than to start pounding, with his bare knuckles, on Cod of Thunder's thick skin. It was the least noble and most desperate way to try and win this *David and Goliath* battle. He never thought that this long-awaited fishing trip would end so primitively: him throwing weak punches at a large cod. Instead, he always dreamt of a *Grand Finale*, where guns blaze, arrows fly and rods bend.

All the while, the equipment was there, but out of reach.

It didn't take Roar long to realise that his every strike must have felt like an insignificant sting of a mosquito. Once Cod of Thunder began to take an interest in Roar's poor attempt to fight back, it stopped waving its tailfin – which, luckily, helped Sven to get closer.

'Dad! Watch out!' Sven screamed, while wading towards them. He got a hold of the sideboard and attempted to climb back on. But, with every kick off the muddy bottom, he only sank deeper.

When Cod of Thunder opened its jaw wide, right in front of Roar, its next move became obvious: barbecue Roar to death. Instinctively, Roar leant backwards and pushed one of his legs into the roof of the Cod of Thunder's mouth. The lightning discharged directly onto his leg, setting it alight.

'Aargghhh!' Even though it was the artificial leg that was getting ruined, the phantom limb pain made Roar scream in anguish. This horrific sequence reminded him of the first, nightmarish encounter with Wolferring that was deeply rooted in his memory. 'Sven! Get the spear gun!' Quickly, the feeling of agony switched to urgency. He ripped the burning leg off the knee joint and stuffed it deeper into the creature's mouth – an action which gave him a few seconds longer to survive.

Finally, Sven was able to reach over the boat's edge and rummage through their belongings on the floor. The point of an arrow was poking out from underneath Jaaku. With bleeding hands, Sven grabbed hold of the tip and managed to rip the entire gun out.

'Hurry!' Roar screamed, while watching in terror how Cod of Thunder had finished smoking his fake leg like a real cigar. *That one it can have. But the second one, I'd rather keep myself.*

The immense pressure, however, wasn't helping Sven to work out how to operate the spear gun. Therefore, he just randomly pointed it at Cod of Thunder and pulled the trigger.

But nothing happened. He looked pleadingly at Roar for any advice, but Roar's confused and fearful expression didn't help – neither of them had fished with such a gadget before.

'Put the release down.' Jaaku's quiet, quivering voice came from the bottom of the boat. He couldn't see Sven, but assumed that he may have struggled to shoot since nothing had happened within the first seconds – that felt like minutes.

Sven started pulling, turning and twitching any part of the gun he could get a hold of – apart from the trigger – and hoped that one of them was the 'release'. Once the gun clicked convincingly, he pressed the tip of the arrow to Cod of Thunder's neck and pulled the trigger. The arrow that was released shot through the fish's skin. It snarled in agony. Green liquid splashed out of the hole that the shot created, as if it was bleeding. It rolled over on the empty backseat, releasing Jaaku from underneath. With great effort, he climbed over the edge and fell in the water.

Now it was Sven's turn to face the monster. Like father, like son. Was he going to lose a real limb? Or his life? He put the spear gun between him and the cod.

But the fish was too fast for him. Its lightning strike set the gun on fire in Sven's hands. Panicking, he threw the burning weapon into Cod of Thunder's open mouth. 'Eat this!'

As the fish closed its mouth, the spear gun fired by itself, the tip of the arrow pushing through the Cod of Thunder's cheekbone.

But it didn't stop coming after Sven. He thought this was his last cry for help before he'd become Arctic kebab.

'The axe! Dad!? Use the axe!'

Roar heard Sven's despairing voice. This was not the rematch he was hoping for. Losing his only son, in front of his eyes, would be too much of a burden for him to carry. As he went through his soaked rucksack, of course, there was no axe – it was floating away, still stuck in the late Wolferring's forehead. Instead, he went for Sven's bag and took out a wet lump of newspaper, which he unfolded, revealing the leftovers of the Lord of Herrings' broken fishing rod. Perhaps, Psalmon had warned not to use just any rod, but this magical one. Roar carefully looked at it, but feared to use it, since it had been dormant after it had snapped during the battle against Mooses. He doubted he had the skills to utilise its powers anymore.

'Here, son, try this.'

'What am I gonna do with it?' Sven caught the wand seconds before the next lightning strike.

'Say a palindrome. Anything, as long as it's a palindrome.'

'Ööö... *Abba*?' Sven muttered, naturally thinking about the famous herring brand.

'No! Something longer. It has to be a sentence.'

'Right.' Sven focused. He was tempted to throw the wand in Cod of Thunder's open mouth, like everything else so far. However, he resisted. Instead, he brought the stick up like a proper wizard, drew an elaborate circle of eight in the air and, with some hesitation, began pronouncing the following native incantation, '*Oi... muumi! Yhtäällä tuli hätään...*'

'That's very good! Go on,' Roar shouted encouragingly.

'*...alipaine, meni apila. Niitä... hilu tallaat. Hyi muumio!*'

'GRRAAALLJUUUU!' Cod of Thunder released an alien-like scream and threw its head back, while discharging lightning randomly up into the sky. It was as if they had cleansed evil spirit from its body, mind and soul. Then, Cod of Thunder dropped down on the boat, stretching on its full length from bow to stern. Its back was slowly rising and lowering to the beat of its panting lungs. Saliva dripped from its mouth, mixing with the water in the pond.

'There you have it, you satanic fish!' Roar yelled, adrenaline pumping through his veins. He turned to face Sven. 'That's my boy. I knew you could do it.'

Sven breathed heavily. He had just performed magic, without any knowledge of being under any spell or having such a skill. *Was it hereditary?*

He slid the wand into his jacket pocket and rushed to assist Jaaku, who was still in the water, leaving Cod of Thunder to suffer alone. With Sven holding Jaaku steady in one arm and Roar in the other, all three men stopped to have a last look at the crime scene in which they had tamed the devil.

Yet, Roar didn't think it was over. 'We can't leave it like that.'

'Yes. We should finish it off,' Jaaku grunted, while coughing in pain.

'That's not what I meant.'

Sven wanted to believe the worst was behind them. The final execution of a seemingly defenceless cod was neither necessary, nor would it bring Carl, Christian, Roar's leg or any of those lost fishes back.

'Does it look different? Less harmful?' Roar made a similar observation that supported Sven's gut feeling.

'Well, we beat the crap out of it,' Jaaku smirked. 'What else can you expect?' It was obvious that Sven and Roar did not intend to hurt it anymore – which made Jaaku run out of patience. Someone had to be the judge in this passive court and sentence Cod of Thunder to death. 'Sorry it has to end this way. We've only just met.' Jaaku pushed Sven to the side, waded back to the boat and yanked the rifle from its stock – which was partly visible underneath the fish's limp body.

Roar shook his head, and smirked. 'Do you think that rifle is really going to work?'

'What if it does?' Jaaku pointed the barrel between Cod of Thunder's softened eyes. As he cocked the rifle, a lonely teardrop fell along its bloody gill. 'We're hunters and fishermen after all, right?' Jaaku grunted.

'No!' Sven launched himself towards Jaaku.

But the intervention came too late. Jaaku managed to pull the trigger before Sven landed on him. However, the rifle malfunctioned, with a few drops of water spraying out of the barrel, washing Cod of Thunder's face.

And then Sven pulled Jaaku beneath the surface of the water.

Meanwhile, Roar stayed ringside due to his missing leg, trying to get a glimpse of this underwater wrestling match between the two friends. Soon, though, he feared Sven would drown Jaaku.

'That's probably enough.' Like an injured referee, Roar limped in between and split the two wet brawlers.

Jaaku took support from the edge of the boat, where he came face to face with the defeated Cod of Thunder. It looked convincingly unthreatening and repentant. Jaaku bit his teeth together, while nodding his head.

'Fine. Do as you want with it.' Lips trembling, he waded towards the shore. 'I need to get out of this freezing water.'

'Should we set it free?' Relieved, Roar proposed something unexpected. 'Let it swim away. After all, it's meant to be strongly religious, like Psalmon, doing lots of good work underwater.'

At any time preceding Sven's moment of magic, saving

Cod of Thunder's life would have sounded the most insane and outrageous thing to do. But, so soon minds can change.

'Well, we can't release it here, because it may not be able to swim upstream and back to the river,' Sven said.

'What are you suggesting?' asked Roar. 'That we pull it up the stream?'

'We have to drag the Yolla up, anyway. It would just be a little heavier with Cod of Thunder on it.'

'A little?' Jaaku grunted from the shore, shivering on a tree stomp. 'The fish weighs... like a ton!'

'You're exaggerating.' Sven grabbed the rope of the boat with one hand, and offered his other hand to support Roar. 'Besides, there are three of us.'

'Or two and a half,' said Roar, referring to his limited physique.

'Before we do anything, we should create fire and warm ourselves up.' In despair, Jaaku looked around at the wet forest and ground. It was ironic how all of Pihtamo was boiling under hot lava, yet they seemed to be in the most humid and moist environment of all, with no resources whatsoever to create even the tiniest of sparks.

The boat and its only passenger looked like a tired whale on a watersleigh, as Sven and Roar pulled it to the shore. Roar immediately began examining the loose branches on the ground and planks fallen from the wreck. But everything was soaked.

'I spent years alone in the wild,' he said. 'I learnt a few survival techniques.'

Jaaku sighed, shivering. 'Or, we just leave Cod of Thunder here to rot and go away? At least rowing and fishing would keep us warm.'

Then Roar remembered the last resort, which they had already tested once. 'Sven, do you still have it on you? You know what I mean.'

Sven's eyes lit up. He knew exactly what *it* meant. He pulled the wand out of his pocket.

'Go for it,' Roar said, confident of his son's new skill. 'Anything is possible. Create us fire.'

'No. You do it.' Sven offered the wand to Roar. 'I know you want to.'

'Could one of you just do it?' Jaaku grunted.

With Sven's balancing support, Roar took the stance and lifted the stick up in the air, like he had done hundreds of times. As his sleeve retrieved, a tattoo of a flying reindeer with wings drawn inside a circle or a globe, appeared on his forearm. He lowered that hand again to point at the remains of the wooden Viking vessel.

With a quiet chuckle, Jaaku ridiculed Roar's pompous attempt, whereas Sven remained trustful and serious. Relying on magic was all they had. If there was no fire, they would have to abandon the weak Cod of Thunder in the pond and make a move before hypothermia got them.

'I'm sorry. It's been a while.' Roar cleared his throat, while thinking about the most suitable incantation. '*Ei tällä reput raahaa, lasikallo polla! Kisa laahaa, retuperällä tie.*'

Immediately, sparks hit the wreck and, in the next few seconds, the wet planks were in flames. The burst of bright fire in the darkness momentarily blinded the men. Not that it mattered, as long as the heat was rising.

Roar limped nearer to the burning vessel, the short stump of a wand acting as his walking stick. Sven rushed to assist him on the unsteady ground. However, Roar pulled away. For that brief moment, he wanted to feel powerful again. He had just created fire out of nowhere. He was in charge of nature.

Chapter 52

HARD FEELINGS

The group were together again, forced to evacuate to the same bedroom, ridden with volatile personal relationships: two mothers from opposite social classes and belief-systems; two women who used to love the same man; two ex-lovers; and a dominant madam with her submissive housemaid. The chances to escape one another to different sections of the bunker had been deprived of them, when the lava engulfed both front and meeting rooms. Sometimes, though, when faced with an imminent danger, the human race can unite, leaving old grudges behind. On the contrary, the pressurised situation can only make relations worse, further distancing the ones involved. From now on, their ability to forget the past and bury the hatchets was being truly tested.

Voluntarily, Birgget had decided to avoid confrontation by retreating to the en-suite bathroom – the only alternative left where she could gain some privacy. She lay in the bathtub, fully clothed. By isolating herself, she could stay away from Sophia and Irmeli, who were still going on about Tuppervaara products. Unfortunately, though, she could still hear them talking.

'It is such a shame the party had to end like this.' Irmeli's pretentious voice penetrated the wall.

It was obvious to Birgget that Irmeli was also from a lower social class, who, in the company of Sophia, tried to act more aristocratic. However, any character analysis of Irmeli and her behaviour partly came from Birgget's insecurity and jealousy.

'There will be more to come.' Sophia's hesitating response had less positivity.

Another reason for Birgget's withdrawal from the bedroom was the uncomfortable chemistry between Christian and Ida. He had settled to rest on the bedcover beside Ida and the baby.

Sophia, on the other hand, seemed to admire the trio. Despite their scruffiness and dirtiness from spending hours in the humidity and dust, she saw them as picture-perfect, like some blond and blue-eyed mining family from Australia's Mount Isa who were getting ready for a family portrait. It was a heart-warming sight that Sophia had always wanted to see, but somehow the union had never materialised – no matter how much she had tried to support, or sometimes arrange it. Unfortunately, though, Ida had chosen against her mother's will and married Sven, a fisherman with limited prospects to provide. Nevertheless, if it took a volcanic eruption to bring a more favourable partner candidate within her daughter's reach, so be it.

'I'd be happy to help organise the next party,' Irmeli meaninglessly blabbered.

Sophia turned to face the abandoned kitchen containers and wooden utensils on the floor. *How did they come to this?* Tuppervaara had been the centre of her life for so many years and one of the remaining driving forces keeping her sane after losing Gustav. She always believed that her parties would go on 'no matter what', until today when the natural world outside showed its powers.

For the first time in her life, Sophia felt so small and entrapped. In a few, ground-breaking moments, she had been taken as far as possible from her comfort zone. She was locked up in the same tiny space as these people of lesser value, like her housemaid. Suddenly, they had to share the same bathroom, towels, food scraps, drinking water.

The eruption had stripped away everything she had ever relied on: her big house, estate, money and status. Once those materialistic and hierarchal factors were taken out of reach from this small group of 'prisoners', they came closer to being equals.

It was a disturbing change to the ones who lost, and empowering to the ones with nothing to lose. Ultimately, money did buy the construction of such a place as this – which was something they should be thankful for – but anyone using the facility in times of crises, like this, were in the same boat, despite their race, religion, nationality or social class. Suddenly, essentials mattered over sales skills and blagging. Mastering either capitalism or ice fishing became irrelevant, whereas individuals with expertise in health care, first aid, survival tactics, geography, science, psychological skills, physical and mental stamina suddenly had the upper hand, and they became the ones that were listened to and relied on.

A few of them had recently experienced another catastrophe of a different kind – the tsunami. However, even that hadn't made them any more prepared or confident. Circumstances and consequences in every conflict and disaster were always unpredictable. There were no guidebooks to help anyone trapped, whether on the post office roof surrounded by flood waters or in the basement buried under lava. Thus, common sense ruled, like using energy sparingly, consuming food and drink as little as possible, waiting, and praying.

And, *carpe diem*, Christian thought, when he used the opportunity to hold Ida closer – even if it was the last thing he would do.

Taken by the moment, Ida didn't resist. Not that she needed any more warmth as such, since the bedroom was well heated by the surrounding lava, yet the physical contact and energy radiating from another human being provided some relief.

Discreetly, Irmeli glanced at them, wanting to be where Ida was, being held by Christian. Irmeli may have been old enough to be Christian's mother, yet she only felt half her age – that age when she'd had her affair with young Roar. She met Roar on the ice fishing circuit. It was a passion they both shared. Whether it was the thrill of lust that brought them together, or only the common interest that they confused with love, were questions left unresolved when Roar decided to return to his family. Yet, part of Irmeli was still stuck in that careless, yet heart-breaking period of her life.

When Christian went to place his hand on Ida's thigh, he

knew he was crossing the line. But he did it, anyway.

Despite the rising heat, Ida got the chills and pulled away. She could feel all those poorly disguised, intriguing stares from her mother and Irmeli. She turned her back to everyone, facing the bedside table and its half-open drawer with the letter inside. *Would this be the right time?*

At first, she had thought about sharing its content only with Sophia once they had been rescued. But, since the survival was becoming more unlikely and time was running short, she decided to take the envelope out and reveal the piece of paper from inside. After all, the text would hopefully answer some of their questions about the bunker. No one was paying attention to Ida's deeds anymore, until she stood up in the middle of the bedroom and cleared her throat.

'I found this letter earlier from that drawer. I would like to read it to you all. It's... from my father, Gustav.'

Dumbstruck, Sophia stared at her. Even Birgget shuffled herself behind the bathroom door where she could hear better. Christian took the baby in his arms. They were all ears.

'Dear Survivors. I am knocking on my mahogany desk while writing because I hope that this letter won't be read in my and Sophia's lifetime, or even after our daughters and their children and descendants take over the estate. However, in the most unfortunate event, I want you, the reader, to know that the safety of my family and friends has always been the number one priority of mine. Hence, I started building this... nuclear bomb and lava-proof bunker for us to hide, survive, and keep striving and continuing our family name.

'The volcano of Saalamaa hasn't erupted for over five hundred years. But, inevitably, it will happen at some point in the future. The past records show that there was even a period, supposedly, eight to nine hundred years ago, when the volcano erupted six times in a century. After the last eruption, however, there has been a long period of dormancy and it was believed it would not erupt for another five to eight centuries, if ever.

'Hence, our ancestors felt safe to settle in the area, farming the fertile land and growing crops that, today, have become our empire. Nevertheless, if there were ever to be an external threat, whether a volcanic eruption, flash flooding, nuclear disaster or attack, I hope and pray that my family members will be protected and saved by this secure bunker that I'm building for them, with all my heart, strength and knowledge I currently hold.

'My wish is that the structure will withstand the pressures asserted upon it by any disastrous condition. My deepest apologies and regrets if it doesn't. Because, I can assure you I have done my utmost with planning and executing the building plan based on today's best knowledge and the highest investment available.

'I understand that this is a rather unusual gift from a father to his family. Anyone who has to use this facility, I hope you can appreciate my effort. This has been my most sincere, yet somewhat unusual and clumsy, way to show how much I care and love the people close to me. It hasn't always been easy to display those emotions in everyday life, and I wish this deed would compensate for some of that. I understand that I will never be fully forgiven for always being absent. Yet, my dearest wish would be, wherever I am, when the need arises to use this secure bunker, you, the survivors, would feel my presence and the absolute fact that I am thinking about you.

'Due to a high cadmium exposure to my liver for over-consumption of elk meat, I have been diagnosed with a deadly cancer. I haven't got much time left on this earth, and it is most likely that I will no longer exist when this message is discovered. Therefore, I wish every survivor strength, positivity and hope. The daylight will come and your saviours will find you, sooner or later.

'I would like to end with a famous quote from one my inspirations, Roar Swensson, who was the greatest fisherman Lake Pihtamo has ever had. I never met him personally, but his well-known persistence, wisdom and passion always drove me on. "There is always hope even when the hope is gone." Forever yours, Gustav.'

Ida lowered the letter away from her face, exposing her watery eyes. She stared at her mother, stunned by the enormity of secrets Gustav had kept. 'This is unbelievable. Did you know about his illness?'

Sophia's gaze wandered. 'I thought it was in the early stages, that it was curable. We didn't want to stress you. You had your own life.'

'He did this for all of us, while himself suffering,' Christian said in awe. 'What a great man.'

The letter certainly proved Gustav's good deeds. He wanted to save his family, like many fathers would do. Sophia already knew about this 'softer' side of Gustav, which became obvious in the message; whereas, for Ida, it was a completely new revelation of her father's otherwise controversial character.

In spite of all the negativity she had felt about his methods of bringing them up, the letter was a reminder that there was a loving father hidden somewhere deep inside. Unfortunately, though, Ida had rarely seen this side of him and the distance between them had always been palpable. He had a way of making her feel that she wasn't 'good enough' to carry the majestic family name. The last straw was her marriage to Sven, of which he never approved, either – even though, as it turned out now, he himself was secretly an admirer of Sven's father.

Nevertheless, there she was again unconditionally saved, carried on and kept alive by her estranged father. It was another demonstration of the vast influence Gustav had.

Even though Birgget was touched by the message, she couldn't help but think how unpleasantly Gustav would turn in his grave if he knew that she, their own housemaid and a poor fisherwoman were amongst the survivors. After all, he was the man who had never approved of her son as an addition to his family. Even though Gustav had referred in the text to 'anyone using the facility', she was certain that the privileged few who were truly allowed entrance – if it was up to Gustav – wouldn't include most of the current individuals.

Nevertheless, for Ida's sake, Birgget tried not to let her disapproval show. 'Quite a remarkable story,' she said in a flat tone.

Ida nodded uncomfortably, knowing how the reality had been far from rosy. Unfortunately, all that time Gustav had spent away from his family for various reasons, couldn't simply be compensated for constructing this exclusive basement.

Not only Gustav, but many parents try to buying their way

into their children's affection. Getting the latest gadgets on the market can achieve results and happiness in the short term, yet no toy can replace the time of genuinely and unconditionally being present in each other's lives. Ida, for instance, didn't really know her father, and she never would. She had been largely raised by the many housemaids and nannies her parents had hired over the years. The current housemaid probably knew her the best – even better than Sophia did.

Neither did Sophia really appreciate Gustav's expensive efforts to save them – which, anyway, seemed to be failing. Keeping a secret of this magnitude bothered her the most. She could never forgive him.

Irmeli, however, sobbed, genuinely touched. 'Ida, you're so lucky to have had such a wonderful father. I wish I'd known him better.'

'We all know how that would have turned out,' Birgget scoffed.

'And, what's that supposed to mean?' Irmeli replied, fuming.

'You know very well. Wasn't destroying one marriage enough?'

'I didn't destroy anything! It was you and your Latino lover, Lumbardi, who ruined everything!' Irmeli grunted.

'The chef?' Christian gasped, not being able to see the appeal the old Lumbardi had had over women. He only knew Lumbardi as he was today: a tired-looking man, heavy smoker and unhealthily overweight.

Ida pressed her finger on Christian's lips – a male interruption was not required, as the women were busy having a go at each other.

Birgget carefully contemplated in which direction to take the argument. Being rowdy and straightforward was not in her nature, especially in front of this intimate crowd. However, it felt like this was their final battle and one that she was not willing to lose. If today was to be their last chance to speak to one another, they might as well lay out all the facts – or what they believed was the truth.

She knew that the misery in their marriage was both her and Roar's fault. They were not sure, even now, who had cheated first. But she was certain that Irmeli had made efforts to pursue him – the kind of behaviour she was portraying even these days.

'No!' Birgget continued. 'I blame you for it. You lured Roar into something that he wouldn't have normally done. You're the worst bait there is!' Her life spent surrounded by fishermen became obvious in the way she fought in jealousy.

However, Irmeli was no stranger to Birgget's vocabulary filled with fishing terminology. 'How dare you, you bream!'

Once Irmeli finished her sentence, the two women were all over each other, wrestling in the middle of the bedroom. All the years spent holding back anger, frustration and jealousy exploded at once. The long-awaited confrontation had escalated to this defining moment. The bout between the two was far from a cat fight though, but rather like a second volcanic eruption.

The furniture around them trembled, while both women, both past their menopauses, kept throwing surprisingly strong punches and high kicks at one another. There was definitely still something left in both of their 'basements', so to speak. The aging hadn't worn either of them out, but the opposite, making them even fiercer and tougher. They had that no-nonsense attitude. There was nothing, a problem at work, domestic issue, illness, or a man, that could bring them down – except, perhaps, another woman from the same era.

Christian and Ida jumped in between them, whereas Sophia and the housemaid hesitated, not knowing which side to take. Christian got a hold of Irmeli and Ida managed to contain Birgget. Meanwhile, the housemaid went to console the crying baby. While Irmeli sought consolation in the arms of Christian, Birgget ripped herself free from Ida's hold. Birgget's nose was bleeding.

Sophia, however, only noticed the blood stain on the floor. She snapped her fingers to the housemaid. 'Hey Sanni, clean that right away.'

The housemaid nodded submissively, as she had done for decades. She left the baby for Ida to hold, and disappeared into the bathroom.

Now, it was Ida's turn to lecture her mother as her patience had reached limits. 'She's not the housemaid anymore. Do you understand? There is no house!'

'What do you mean? Of course she is,' Sophia said, trying to sound innocent.

As Sanni returned with a pile of toilet paper, Ida grabbed it off her and threw it all onto Sophia's lap.

'No!' cried Ida. 'From now on, we're all the same. We're about to die and all you care about is a blood stain on the floor, and you're making someone else clean it for us – in your last living moment?!' She looked at her mother in disbelief. 'I just don't understand how we can be so different. You didn't let Sanni inside the bunker in the first place. We had to bring her in. How can you be so cruel?'

'No... That's not true,' Sophia stuttered uncomfortably, as another conflict had arisen, exposing more truths.

In the middle of it all, Sanni could only awkwardly shrug her shoulders and let out a subtle smile – exactly what she had always done while serving the rich and powerful. Of course, she agreed with Ida a hundred per cent. Yet, having been submissive most of her life, she hadn't developed strength and confidence needed to express her opinions.

Out of the corner of her eye, Ida saw Irmeli's hand sliding under Christian's shirt and stroking his abdominals. 'And by the way, Birgget, perhaps you were right about Irmeli.' Ida's sharp words made Irmeli immediately pull her away from him.

In awe, the baby observed how this friction between adults evolved – something, unfortunately, she would also get to take part in one day – if they had a future.

The tension in the room was palpable. No one was talking anymore. The heat kept rising.

Eventually, the standstill became too much for the housemaid to bear. She had always done something, on her feet, serving. Hence, she went to Ida and gently requested to have the toilet paper back.

'May I?' she asked politely. 'I'm sorry, ma'am, but I have served your household for many years. This is all I know.'

Ida sighed and let go, so that Sanni could immerse herself in her work on the floor. To everyone's shock, however, Sophia went and knelt beside her. She took some of the paper off Sanni and began wiping the blood as well.

The ones still standing couldn't believe their eyes. Maybe the times were changing – if only there was more time.

Chapter 53

A GHOST TOWN

As the men reached the centre of New Pihtamo, the empty shops and roads were coated with the same dark grey blanket of dust. It was as if they had been dropped in the middle of the wild west. They could almost anticipate someone dashing out of the bar with guns blazing, to finish off a pistol duel on the deserted high street.

But no one came out. There wasn't a single soul in sight. Presumably, everyone had fled. In which direction, though, they couldn't tell. It was as if the town had been swept barren by a sudden virus pandemic or a radiation leak from some nuclear plant. The only noise was the occasional gust of wind whistling inside the rain collectors, or the loosely hanging ropes flapping against flag posts. Fractions of sulphur were still detectable in the air.

Roar parted from the trio, and went to draw a circle on the dusty window of his restaurant. As he peered inside, he sighed in relief. Everything was still in one place and untouched.

'The stream has flown on the other side,' said Sven, gazing in the opposite direction.

'Thank God,' Jaaku said hesitatingly. 'If the bar is still open, we should celebrate our success.'

'You call this night a "success"?' Sven grunted.

As Roar heard them talking, he turned away from the window. 'It's too early to say. We can assume that Cod of Thunder has been tamed. But only time will tell whether it was the right choice to release it back in the river.'

'Do you think we should've killed it?' Sven asked.

'Saving it felt like the right thing to do,' Roar replied. 'At that moment by the pond, I wouldn't have had the heart to kill it once it began behaving like a normal fish. After all, it has a religious calling. I don't want to end up in hell – although, I might anyway, for what I have done in life.'

Sven also cast doubts on whether they had done the right thing or not. 'Cod of Thunder was so weak and defenceless when we abandoned it. Eventually, some lucky fisher might catch it and make a big meal out of it.'

However, the further away from the lake they travelled, the less he thought about it, since other concerns surfaced, like the safety of his family. With his own eyes, he had to see that everything was fine.

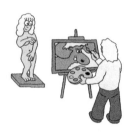

Chapter 54

HIS MUSE

'You have two new voicemails. The first message, on 20th April at one thirty-five pm. Beep... Hi, honey. I hope you're safe. You must be rowing somewhere by now, since I can't get a hold of you. I'm gonna be meeting Birgget soon and we'll take this Tuppervaara party to my mum's place. The boiler just broke down and, because it's Sunday, the engineer can only come tomorrow. How annoying! I was so looking forward to hosting this party at ours... Well, at least we didn't have to cancel. If it's gonna run late, I might stay the night in Örebröre... By the way, there's some mustard herring and potatoes in the fridge, if you're hungry when you come back. Love you. Bye... Beep...

'The second message, on 20th April at nine twenty-eight pm. Beep... Honey! Please, pick up the phone. We've just left Örebröre and we're heading back to New Pihtamo, but every route is being blocked by the lava stream. We may have to go back... Ugh! I'm scared... God... Beep... No more messages. Press two to...'

Sven hung up the phone, breathing heavily.

Indeed, their house felt much colder than normal. He got off the sofa and went to the kitchen where the boiler was. He switched it on, but it showed no signs of life. Assumingly, the engineer never made it. Neither had Ida returned after her departure, which seemed like an urgent one. The kitchen sink was filled with the same dirty dishes from when he'd left the house to meet Roar.

He took a more careful look around the house, and discovered how Ida's wardrobe in the bedroom was left wide open, and there were pieces of clothing scattered on the bed and the floor.

He tried to ring her, but her phone was switched off. He wanted to go out and find her, but his body was too tired. He hadn't slept for over forty-eight hours. He sat on the edge of the bed, then stretched himself out on top of Ida's clothes. He could smell her perfume in them. He pulled one of her furry winter coats over him like a blanket, and closed his eyes. In just a few seconds, he was fast asleep, dreaming about being a wild bull moose, racing through the forest searching for his muse.

Chapter 55

DARKNESS WILL FOLLOW

The baby wondered, baffled, why no grown-up was playing with her anymore. The last ray of hope twinkled in her sparkling eyes, while the adults glazed lifelessly ahead. In spite of her limited life experience, she could sense the anxiety around her. Both the bathroom tap and the broken toilet flush, dripping murky and brown volcanic liquid, added to their despair. Their sustenance reserve was running low: about half a litre bottle of water, a can of tuna and a couple of sheets of toilet paper were all that was left for them to share – not quite the Easter meal they had hoped for.

Ida lay on the bed, staring at the ceiling. 'It's so quiet. Maybe the worst is over?'

'For those lucky ones,' Irmeli sighed, slouched on the floor in the corner.

'At least Gustav got something right.' Bitterly, Sophia observed the durable bedroom door, that, so far, stood firmly as the final seal between their destruction and survival. Neither her nor the others' expertise in building materials was sufficient to understand the reason behind this miracle. What made this one room so special? Or had the stream finally weakened by the doorstep? Those were minor consolations, though, since there was no escape route. The only, seemingly secure, part of the bunker, the bedroom, had become their prison with a death sentence.

'How long have we been here?' Ida asked, while coughing

dust.

'Some days,' Christian guessed, with his weakened voice.

'Too many,' Sophia said, and rested her tired head against Sanni's shoulder. It was the first time ever she acknowledged the housemaid for any other purpose than cooking and cleaning. This simple, but intimate, gesture demonstrated that, after all, there was some humanity left inside Sophia's otherwise cold public persona.

Sanni leant her cheek against the top of Sophia's head. The mistress and her servant had finally found something in common: they were two people with no future.

'They will never find us. We're gonna die here.' Once Ida started sobbing, the baby cried with her. It was as if there was an invisible link between the two, which hadn't disappeared even after cutting of the umbilical cord.

Christian could only console them with another embrace. Just like on the post office roof, he would have wanted to be the hero, the man who comes up with the solution. Yet, he felt as helpless as everyone else. He could have chosen differently in the first place and not sought help from Örebröre, but somewhere, anywhere else. He was trapped again, because of his obsession to get close to Ida. Destiny always brought them together, but only this far, in the most difficult circumstances. Maybe they weren't meant to be.

Meanwhile, Irmeli had to use the bathroom, even though she knew who and what was waiting there.

Birgget, who lay at the bottom of the tub, however, was too weak to make a move. 'Would it bother you if I stay here?' she said.

Irmeli slid the shower curtain between them. 'Whatever.' She pulled her trousers down and sat on the bowl.

I hope it's not number two, Birgget thought regretfully.

Her fear was unnecessary, though. As a result of the minimal diet they were forced to endure the past few days, their digestive systems were empty – even though they still experienced the 'need to go'. Also, the awareness of Birgget sharing the same space made it difficult for Irmeli to fully relax.

Birgget recognised Irmeli's silhouette through the curtain.

She was way past feeling of awkward or anger towards Irmeli for what she had done to her marriage. More serious issues had occupied her mind, such as their survival. Any earthly quarrel suddenly lost its meaning once they were forced to question their own immortality.

'Irmeli... I always wanted to say... that I admire what you've done to the ice fishing community.'

Irmeli's jaw dropped after hearing the most unexpected compliment directly from her nemesis.

'It must've been tough for you,' Birgget continued, seeking that long-desired consensus. 'Young girls look up to you.'

'It wasn't always easy,' Irmeli sighed. 'There were no women before me. I was the first.'

'You are very brave. I understand well what Roar saw in you.'

Irmeli couldn't detect any sarcasm in Birgget's voice. 'Me too, in you,' she replied. 'You radiate kindness and warmth like no other. Roar was lucky to have you. He only loved you and meant no harm, to you, or Sven. Neither did I mean to hurt anyone. We were just young and foolish.'

Birgget sobbed bittersweet tears. If only she could give Sven and Roar, the men in her life, at least that one final embrace.

When Irmeli finally felt like she could fully relax on the bowl, the remaining lights in both rooms went off. It was pitch dark.

In the bedroom, completely blinded, Sophia reached for the rope hanging off the ceiling to switch the light on, while Ida felt for the lamp on the bedside table. However, neither of the lights worked. Meanwhile, in the bathroom, Irmeli quickly pulled her trousers up and went to the light switch. But nothing. The power had been cut off.

Their end had just begun.

Chapter 56

DISASTER ZONE

Sven arrived at the edge of the solidified magma. He followed parallel to the channel that had knocked over, burnt and buried everything in its path. The downward stream gradually widened, disturbingly towards Örebröre. The smell of sulphur intensified again. He pondered if the surface was solid enough to walk on, rather than the soggy levees. As he carefully stepped on the crust, it immediately cracked under his weight. From the foot-size hole he created, a gush of hot steam shot upwards, melting the sole of his boot. Grunting, he pulled the boot and sock off. He hopped aside, and stomped his bright red foot against the dry moss, wishing all the snow hadn't melted away.

'Hey! You shouldn't be here.' A commanding male voice echoed from the bottom of the slope. Three men, wearing protective clothing and gas masks, climbed towards him alongside the stream. The man in the middle continued shouting, 'It's not safe to be here. You must go back the same way you came from.'

'But... I live here,' Sven stuttered lies, while balancing on his one foot. He pointed ahead. 'There.'

The man in the middle was the first to reach Sven. He pushed a gas mask against his chest. 'First things first: you should wear one of these.'

Sven did as he was being told. He removed his hat, and pulled the straps of the gas mask around his head.

'Secondly, what on earth were you trying to do?' said the man. 'That stream is still dangerously hot. You can't walk on it. Unless you want to turn into a piece of exploding leather.'

'I can already feel that,' Sven said. 'My shoe and foot almost became one. Shame I didn't run into you earlier, or see the warning signs.'

'Our plan is to cordon off the whole area.'

The other two men in hazmat suits also lined up in front of Sven. The rescue workers might as well have been those three astronauts who reached the moon – even though one of them never really came outside with the other two.

'How far has it spread?' Sven asked. 'To Örebröre?'

The man on the right nodded. 'Is that where you live?'

'Ööö... Yes.'

'Unfortunately, that area is going to be inaccessible for quite some time. Clearing an eruption this big and making every place accessible again can take several days.'

'Or weeks, largely depending on the weather,' said another of the men. 'If we get a lot of rain or snow, then lava cools and solidifies quicker, which makes our work easier.'

'Did you leave anyone behind?' The man in the middle asked.

'I may have.' Sven stared, concerned, into the direction he believed the estate was.

'You're not sure?'

Sven shook his head.

'Have you got a place to go?'

Sven nodded, his eyes still fixed to the horizon.

The three men exchanged looks, until the one on the right took a pen and notepad from his pocket. 'Meanwhile, we can take your details and let you know as soon as we know more.'

'Of course,' Sven said promptly, turned around and started hopping back to where he had come from.

'Where are you going? We need your name and contact details.'

'Are you sure you can walk?' the man on the left asked.

'Don't worry about me. I'll only take small steps for a man,' Sven wittily replied, while attempting to take painfully giant leaps considering his recent injury.

Apart from the three rescue workers, the sight around him seemed lifeless indeed. Only one, weirdly subtropical and exotic plant, with its stripy green and longish sword-like leaves, protruded incongruously from the midst of the volcanic rocks.

Chapter 57

THE MOTHER-IN-LAW'S TONGUE

For the first time ever, Sven paid attention to the loud and unsettling noise of their clock on the living room wall. Agitated, he took it down and pulled the batteries out. He opened its glass cover and pulled the hands back, wishing this exercise could take him back in time to the day he saw Ida for the last time. Yet, again, he had chosen the fishing community over her; the greater good instead of family.

In the corner, the cot haunted him with its emptiness. A colourful plush fish and a rattling toy were reminders of its lost resident. Even the cats and the rabbit felt her absence, as they lay unmotivated on the floor.

Ignorance truly had been Sven's bliss until he entered parenthood. He used to be fearless and didn't know loneliness. Even the loss of his father didn't change his carefree attitude to life. Roar's spirit and legend kept following and guiding him, even during the years he was gone. Of course, Sven was saddened by the loss. But having a caring mother by his side was another blessing. He knew she'd always be there for him.

However, the challenge he faced today was insurmountable. The agony caused by his burning foot was nothing compared to the aching of his heart. All three females in his life were gone in one strike, without them having a chance to say goodbyes. Was he doomed to spend years, or the rest of his life, chattering with made-up family members who were no longer there? He was left again with unanswered questions about the destiny of his loved ones. The feeling of déjà vu was unavoidable.

He dropped the clock and its loose batteries on the sofa, and plodded to the kitchen. He wanted to drink something cold, but found nothing but a half-empty jar of garlic herring, squashed tube of mustard and a sack of unbaked potatoes in the fridge. He had to settle for lukewarm tap water. It was ironic how, in such a cold climate, the drinking water was never cold. He had a tiny sip, and poured the rest on a plant decorating the kitchen table. It was also the first time in his life he'd watered a plant or a flower – it was always something Ida must've done, since all greens seemed miraculously to survive in their household. But now, with nothing but time on his hands, he suddenly became more aware of the space around him.

It was *Dracaena trifasciata*, also known as the snake plant. He couldn't have known the name by heart, but there was a small tag left on a saucer explaining the product details, together with care instructions. Even though, through his saddened eyes, everything in life seemed dull and grey, the long leaves of the plant in front of him were shining green, trying to shed new hope – exactly like that lonely species growing through the solidifying lava.

Chapter 58

A BURNING SENSATION

The flower pot slid along the bar top, stopping at Jaaku's hand that was holding a bottle. He recognised the plant. 'For cleaning the air?' he said, positively surprised to see Sven in the bar so soon after the disaster.

'I've just discovered that we have plants and flowers in the house.' Sven limped towards him, occasionally taking support from the bar chairs. 'I also found lavender soap in the bathroom, a white fur rug in front of the footboard of our bed, a black and white painting on the living room wall of a couple dancing in clothes that looked like they could be from the nineteen twenties, and a wooden hedgehog outside by the entrance to wipe the snow off our feet.'

He has finally gone mad, Jaaku thought, worried about how Sven had dealt with the grief. 'What happened to your leg?'

'That's the least of my worries,' Sven sighed, and sat next to him.

Jaaku didn't know where to start a conversation with someone who had recently lost so much. 'So, all these items in your house, do you... like them?' he asked, and then gestured for another glass from the bartender.

'I don't know. I've never paid any attention to them. I wouldn't necessarily decorate like that, but...'

'I never realised you were into decorating,' Jaaku interrupted.

'I'm not. It always came more naturally from her.'

348

The more Jaaku listened to him, the more he realised how they both needed a drink. The second glass arrived right when needed, so that Jaaku could start filling it.

But Sven's mind was elsewhere. 'Örebröre has been worst hit. I had to go there to have a look, many times, tried various routes, despite all the warnings from the authorities. But it's completely inaccessible and sealed off.'

'Did you see anything?'

'Only from the distance.' Sven's eyes grew watery as he spoke. 'The house was a ruin. Only a couple of support pillars were standing. And lots of rubble. I thought I'd seen a burnt metal frame of a kicksled or two, but I'm not sure. It was too far away.' He pushed the shot glass to the side. His desire to drink had disappeared with the loss of his family. Suddenly, any pressure to run away from life's responsibilities to alcohol was overtaken by a feeling of emptiness, which no amount of substance could fill. 'The worst thing is not knowing.'

Jaaku wanted to console him, but couldn't find anything intelligent to say or do. 'Finish your drink, mate. That should help,' he blurted out.

Sven thoughtfully gazed through the transparent, tinted liquid. 'Nothing will ease this pain.'

'I met Börje and Kalle again,' Jaaku interrupted Sven's sobbing. 'They spoke to me about the basement.'

This sudden change in subject caused Sven to compose himself. 'You're still hanging out with those losers?'

Jaaku sighed. 'I can hunt because my future family have to survive. I don't necessarily agree with everything the other hunters say or do. Or I can't say that I like Börje and Kalle particularly that much. There must be some fishermen out there you don't get along that great with, either? Christian, for example. He was not your best friend, was he?'

'But Kalle tried to kill us!'

A few heads in the bar turned when Sven raised his voice. They were again receiving undesired attention. Therefore, Jaaku brought his face closer to Sven's.

'I've seen you and Christian trying to kill each other. How is that different?'

'It is. I don't want to spend time with him.'

'Sometimes we cross paths with people we don't like,' said Jaaku. 'It becomes ever harder to avoid those few idiots who practise the same craft and share the same passion. Wasn't that exactly how your dad came across his worst enemy, Carl? By coincidence? They both just happened to be fishing at the same time and ended up chasing the same catch.'

'Please, don't drag him into this.' Sven started breathing heavily.

'I'm just saying...'

'Is this why you wanted to see me then?'

'Yes. Börje and Kalle knew about Gustav's basement. Apparently, Gustav hosted the hunting society's monthly meetings there.'

'Tell me something new,' Sven grunted.

'They also said that Gustav was building something other than just a secret meeting space. It was meant to be a highly secure bunker made of durable materials, like titanium and tungsten.'

Suddenly, Sven became more attentive. 'Could that mean the bunker is secure enough... to last a volcanic eruption?'

'I wouldn't know about that.'

'Ida said, in her last voicemail, something about going back to the house. Could she have meant Örebröre?'

'There's only one way to find out.'

'There isn't. It's impossible to access the ruins.' Sven stood up, accidentally putting weight on his burnt foot, making him flinch. 'And, by the time anyone gets there, it will be too late.'

'Why not take your magic rod with you?' Jaaku smirked. 'I thought you'd be unstoppable now.'

'Me and Dad decided to throw it in with the flaming Viking boat. It was an era that was bound to end. We thought that was the perfect moment.'

'Are you crazy?' Jaaku grunted, causing some heads to turn again. He lowered his voice. 'That was the perfect weapon.'

'Exactly. And neither I nor my father want to have that sort of responsibility. No one should have, and no one will.' Hesitatingly, Sven took support from the bar top and turned away.

For the first time ever, he noticed the new fireplace flickering on the other side of the room. He had never seen it being used. Both the uncomfortable sensation in his foot and the burning flames in the distance reminded him of that one brief and peculiar moment in the animal sanctuary, when Yetilag put its feet in the bonfire and kept them there, for who knows how long, and couldn't feel a thing.

While Sven's eyes were fixated on the bright fireplace, he reached for the shot glass. He downed the drink, put the empty glass upside down on the top and began limping away.

'What about the plant, then?' Jaaku asked.

'You can keep it. Marjukka will be pleased.'

Chapter 59

A HAIRY HERO

From the distance, it seemed like someone was doing one of those banned elephant rides during the wet season. The rain had been pouring almost non-stop for the past week or so. In the midst of the rising steam, Sven's head appeared, popping above the half-burnt tree trunks. He was travelling on the shoulders of Yetilag, whose saggy and dry, but thick, neck skin was solid enough to hold. The night was dark and the trek had been long, yet it was one of the last desperate options worth trying.

The odds of anyone surviving in the basement for this long were non-existent. If they weren't to make this journey, however, Sven's other choice would've been, to wallow in uncertainty and wait for the official rescue team to do something.

He had to react. *What if the hunters were right?*

Every time Yetilag's durable feet broke the solid crust, an ample source of rainwater gushed through the cracks and joints in the ground, absorbing heat from the lava. More steam shot up from the ground. So far, Sven felt confident in his chosen form of transportation, as Yetilag sailed reasonably smoothly in these harsh conditions, not minding the rising gases or sharp and uneven edges. Only a helicopter could do a better job.

However, one of Sven's biggest worries was Yetilag's constant tiredness, and whether it would stay awake until the end – whenever that would be. It was an unusual creature - as if it was constantly travelling on a long-haul. And, apparently, to get the best out of it, it was meant to be kept that way: sleep deprived. That was one if its many uncommon features.

What if Yetilag's constant jetlag becomes too much for it to bear? Was there a breaking point? Annoyingly, Sven kept pulling its hair, tickling its ears and poking its neck – just to make sure it didn't fall asleep and make them dive head first to the steaming ground.

Like a navigator sitting high above, he got a good view over the heart-breaking scenery that was mostly painted with musky dark grey colours. All the greenness of the pine and spruce needles had burnt black. It was like witnessing an aftermath of a big battle scene where too many flamethrowers, fire arrows and Molotov cocktails were being used. In the distance, the corrugated iron gates to Ida's family estate still stood upright, but alone and coated with charcoal.

Every now and then, Yetilag nearly threw Sven off the saddle, when it bent down to clear their path from the biggest lava rocks. Their bumpy ride was like being on a stormy lake – a movement pattern Sven was actually quite used to. Simultaneously, he had to keep a constant eye on any security staff who might have a problem with them entering the area prematurely and without permission. Showing Yetilag in public was another one of his many concerns. They had to be fast and discreet.

They went through the charred gates, and reached the end of the driveway beside the ruins. There was nothing familiar that Sven could recognise from his two brief visits to the house. Almost everything had been flattened. The lava stream had covered all three acres of the garden. A stack of deformed metal objects next to them could been burnt snow vehicles parked in front of a square slab of stone – which, most likely, used to stage the main entrance to the mansion.

They stepped on this half-melted concrete. There was a large pile of unrecognisable rubble ahead that could have been the house and its contents. Only one pillar stood alone in the middle.

'I hardly ever came here – or was invited.' Sven tried to remember which room was which and how they had accessed the basement. He had only been to the ground floor once and, even then, he had only secretly broken in with Jaaku when it was dark.

'Yaaawwnnn!' Yetilag said.

'I wish I'd know what that means.' Sven regretted not bringing Pole Vole with them to translate. But he didn't want any extra weight on Yetilag's shoulders, or anyone else to take valuable space. On the other hand, Pole Vole could've probably sat inside his pocket. 'Hello! Is anyone here?' he randomly spoke to the ruins.

However, the only response came from the wind whistling through and against the rubble. Yetilag took a brave step on the ruins, its leg sinking knee deep in the floor structures.

'Carefully!' said Sven. 'We don't know what's down there.'

Apologetically, Yetilag stopped moving. A solitary crow flew over them and landed on top of that one remaining pillar. It kept staring at them deeply, as if being the silent messenger of destruction. The black bird matched perfectly with the surrounding grim landscape. There was irony in the fact that volcanic soil was supposed to be so fertile, while, at the same time, all things living had just been robbed from the area due to volcanic activity. *How can something so deadly also give life to so many things?*

Yetilag stretched its long arm and pointed at the rubble.

'If you wanna do some digging, please do it gently.'

Yetilag's nod almost shot Sven off the saddle again.

'Gently, I said!' He wrapped his arms tightly around its neck.

Slowly, Yetilag leant over and started shifting the first layer of rocks and burnt planks aside. As its gigantic hands dug deeper through the solid magma, it seemed that everything underneath had moulded together as one mixed compound.

'Ida? Sophia?' Sven called out names, not getting any responses, though. He couldn't tell anymore where the ground floor ended and the basement began. He had to rely on his intuition, and point at random directions. 'Maybe try over there. Or there.'

After about an hour of rummaging through the remains without any discoveries, Yetilag stopped working. It stretched its back straight, while miserably looking away.

Sven wasn't able to see Yetilag's face, but could share the same disappointment. They had come to a dead end. Perhaps, after all, he had wrongly interpreted Ida's last voicemail and she never reached the house, or it was not even her intention.

He couldn't fight back the tears anymore. Was this again the world's cruel and unfair way to keep everything in a constant, bittersweet balance? He had gotten his father back, only to lose everything else. As much as he loved Roar and joyfully welcomed him into his life, he would've preferred things the other way around.

It was another sad but painfully honest thought that deepened his guilt. If he'd only known that the last moment he got to share with Ida and the baby were those days between her waking up in the hospital and him leaving to hunt for Wolferring – that last fishing trip he shouldn't have taken. And, even the time preceding his departure to the lake and the river, he mostly spent training with Roar, rather than paying attention to Ida and the baby. There may have been a window of opportunity to go and save his family, when they came across Jaaku who was running away from the hunters' bullets. Jaaku, obviously, wanted to escape out on the lake, whereas Sven's gut was telling him the opposite: to stay ashore. But he wasn't strong enough to stand his ground.

Sheepishly, Yetilag pressed its head down, knowing it had failed on this perfectly assigned mission – it had been brought there specifically because of its unique qualities. It even managed to help them before, when guiding Sven on Viljo's motorboat, that, eventually, reunited Sven and Ida on the roof of the flooded post office. Yet, it wasn't able to repeat its success. *It's hard to be the hero, twice.*

'Let's go, then.' Sven mumbled the words that sounded so final.

Defeated, Yetilag began sluggishly transporting them away from the site. Its heavy feet kept fracturing the ground, yet neither of them were really bothered or concerned anymore about what lay underneath. The hope was gone.

Against all odds, the rain stopped at their lowest point when the worst downpour was usually meant to begin. Once the sound of the falling rain muted, the whistles of the wind became more audible. It was even more high pitched. Then came a loud, short squeal. And a muffled cry.

Sven ushered Yetilag to stand still, so they could listen. It definitely wasn't the sound of the forest, but something more human.

'Is that... a crying baby?'

Instantly, however, the sobbing they thought they heard, ended. Yetilag shrugged its shoulders, making Sven bounce up and down in the air. Autonomously, it decided to continue rambling ahead on the uneven crust.

'Maybe not, then,' Sven sighed.

However, the mysterious noise returned, and this time a notch louder and repetitively.

'It's definitely a baby!' Sven forcefully pulled Yetilag's neck hair. Interestingly, no barrier was enough to seal the ear-shattering wailing of a tiny human being.

'Yaaawwnnnn!' Yetilag growled from both pain and excitement.

'I'm sorry...' Sven panted so hard that he couldn't get a word out. He looked all around, trying to locate the baby's cry, which now became consistent. He pointed at the middle of the ruin. 'It's coming from somewhere there.'

Yetilag scanned the site with its tired eyes and, with careful steps, took them closer to the source. Now, the baby's loud cry was backed up by other, more muffled, voices coming from underground.

'We're coming! It's Sven and Yetilag!'

Yetilag started by clearing some burnt elements away – that could've been the remains of the bookcase and its contents. Then it ploughed the ground smoothly, like a gardener digging soil. An unbearable stench rose directly in both their nostrils. Fortunately, Yetilag had grown immune to it, whereas Sven struggled to fight back nausea. Even though there were no style points given for their performance, he didn't want to be seen vomiting in front of the rescued.

'We're down here.' A faint male voice from underneath the crust joined the cry for help.

'Christian?' Sven gasped.

But the only response to that was a baby's loud howling.

Layer by layer, Yetilag peeled away the blackened pieces of rock and soggy lava, revealing the two front rooms of the bunker that were completely collapsed. Then, a flat surface of solid titanium and a top edge of a door, that seemed to stand solid, became visible to them in the midst of all the destruction.

'Please let us out!' A quivering female voice travelled through the door.

'Yaaawwnnn!' Yetilag dug the door clear, and yanked its hot handle. But it remained shut.

'Release the lock! Or something,' Sven yelled.

Clunking, rattling and intense chattering was heard from behind the door. 'Try again,' the same male voice spoke.

Sven nodded approvingly to Yetilag. 'Watch out! Stand back!'

Neither of them knew what was to happen. Perhaps the rubble, hot rocks and magma would gush inside and over the entrapped people once the door opened.

This time, though, only a gentle pull from Yetilag was enough to open the door slightly, so the survivors could try and squeeze themselves out. Once the dust had settled, a tip of blond hair popped out.

It was Christian, smiling victoriously.

'You're... alive?' Sven sighed, barely hiding his disappointment.

'Glad to see you, too,' Christian snorted, and popped his head back in. After a few seconds, another face from the dungeon came into sight.

'Irmeli?' Sven said in disbelief. 'Quite a team you have down there.'

'Are you gonna help us out or not?' she grunted, until she saw Yetilag. 'What is that monster?'

'It's a friendly one,' Sven said calmly. 'You need to trust me on this one.'

From inside, Birgget gave an affirming nod to Irmeli.

'Yaaaawwnnnn!' Yetilag showed initiative by shifting Sven across to its right shoulder. Then it leant over, wrapped its long arm firmly around Irmeli's waist and, working like a long hoist, lifted her up and dropped her onto its left shoulder. Once both passengers were securely seated, the towering Yetilag looked ahead for a secure place to drop off the first load.

'We'll come back. Don't go anywhere,' Sven yelled towards the doorway, as Yetilag started carrying them towards the edge of the forest – the nearest evacuating point far enough from the heat, fumes and sketchy ground.

As Yetilag lowered them down to a patch of green grass, it gave Sven an enquiring look.

'No. You go alone.' Sven hopped off. 'You need all your strength to carry the survivors. We don't know how many are there.' He turned to Irmeli. 'How many are there?'

However, she was occupied coughing her lungs out. There was blood mixed in her spit. She dropped down to her knees.

Sven knelt beside her. Even though she was in obvious pain, she tried to smile bravely. He looked up, and gestured to Yetilag to go and take care of business.

'Yaaawwnnn!' Yetilag trotted back by the bedroom door, where Christian's head was visible again. One by one, he assisted Sophia and Birgget into Yetilag's strong arms.

Sven could recognise the two mothers being carried towards him, like royalties transported on a palanquin – another controversial method to abuse those poor elephants. The women took support by holding each other's hands. Whether they did it for a sheer bonding or only to keep balance, wasn't clear to him. Not that it mattered. The sight only proved that two people so different can unite and find common ground – but only when times get this volatile.

Once Birgget's feet touched the safety of the wet grass, she rushed to embrace Sven. 'So glad to see you.' Her voice was weak. She was barely able to stand without support. Sven held her up, despite his own burnt foot. In the moment, he forgot about the pain.

He assisted her mother to sit on a tree stump beside Irmeli – another pair he would never see spending time together, unless being forced to do so. Now, though, the two women huddled together for comfort, without any signs of their bitter past and heartaches they may have caused one another.

Meanwhile, Sophia was distraught to witness the complete destruction of her family home. Decades worth of memories flashed through her mind – many she thought she had forgotten. But the intense shock brought them back from the depths of her heart. It felt like part of her died with the estate being ruined. She suddenly remembered only nice and positive things from the past, like them being young and in love, Gustav not being so busy, family eating dinners together, the general warmth of the house, the near perfection of their family life – which, in the end, was so unattainable. A single teardrop ran down on her dirty cheek.

A big shadow flashed by her peripheral vision. It was Yetilag stumping for another rescue mission. Sven squinted his eyes, trying to get a better look at the next survivor.

'Who is that with Christian?'

'Our housemaid,' Sophia said. 'Sanni is her name.'

'Why aren't they bringing the baby? It was her crying, right?' Disconcerted, Sven turned to face Birgget.

She nodded her heavy head. 'They are both safe.'

A stone fell off Sven's heart. He took a step forward to welcome the next survivors arriving to the safe zone.

'Why couldn't you let Ida and the baby come before you?' he snorted to Christian, even before he was off Yetilag's shoulder.

Patiently, Christian let Yetilag drop them down first before responding. 'She wants to ride with you.'

'With me?' Sven asked with a lump in his throat.

'Who else?' Christian grunted, and walked past him to join the others.

Overwhelmed, Sven climbed on Yetilag's shoulder to fetch the remaining survivors: his small family.

At the halfway point to the bunker, though, an unknown voice shouted from the distance. 'You're not supposed to be there!'

Sven clocked two of the three same rescue workers in the distance – known as 'the astronauts' – waving their arms. He couldn't recognise which two, as they were fully covered from head to toe. They were trotting through the hazard area towards the ruins. This time, they carried black oblong violin cases –

which seemed odd.

'Don't mind them,' said Sven, and urged Yetilag to speed up to the bunker door.

Once they were at the blackened vault, Yetilag reached out its enormous hand again, and pulled out the little baby wrapped in a turquoise blanket. The baby glowed in Yetilag's palm, like a tiny jewel in the centre of a freshly opened clam. She travelled straight into Sven's arms, abounding him in joy.

Lastly, out came Ida, unharmed yet weakened, scruffy and stained with spots of ash and dirt all over her clothes and skin. Yetilag hoisted her up and placed her on the other shoulder, to complete the three-piece puzzle.

When Yetilag was halfway through its last lap as the beast of burden, the roof of the bunker bedroom collapsed. The sealed door and its solid frame may have been the last elements holding the structure together, until giving in under the enormous weight of the rubble. A black dust cloud rose behind them as they left the ruins.

The baby happily chuckled after being reunited with her father. In awe, she stared at the thick, elephant-like skin of Yetilag. Maybe she thought it was their new living room rug with legs.

Sven took Ida's weak hand, while simultaneously trying to find the most fascinating first words to say at such a special reunion.

'I... watered the plants.' He felt utterly disappointed in himself, after spurting out such a mundane opening line.

Surprisingly, though, hearing him speak any words, gave Ida enough strength to respond. 'I've always wanted you to do that.'

'Okay. Great,' Sven replied, confused and delighted at the same time.

Proud of itself, Yetilag dropped the family to the greenery with the others. Immediately, Sven took Ida and the baby into his tight embrace. With the woman he loved in one arm and their creation in the other, he felt on top of the world again.

The special moment was cut short, however, by the approaching rescue workers. 'What's going on in here?' one of them shouted.

Sven turned to face Yetilag. 'I think it's time for you to go. Those men don't need to see you. Or, well, they already have. But, you know what I mean.'

'Yaaawwnnn.' Yetilag fully understood Sven's concern. At this point, too much human attention wasn't necessarily good for its well-being. It had already exposed itself today to six new people: Sophia, Irmeli, Sanni, the baby and the two rescue workers. It was only a matter of time before the world would know about the existence of the intellect animals.

Yetilag patted – as softly as it possibly could – on Sven and Ida's shoulders. Then, with its fingertip, it gently tapped the top of the baby's head, before turning away and trotting off towards the deep forest.

Simultaneously, Elma, Ida's white horse, appeared from her hiding place, fully intact.

'Look!' Ida rejoiced.

Once Yetilag was out of sight, the rescue workers suddenly shifted their interest away from the survivors. Instead, they went after Yetilag, also disappearing into the woods.

'Exactly what I've been afraid of,' Sven said worriedly.

'What did you say that thing was again?' Irmeli asked in awe. 'A big snowman?'

'An angel,' Ida said, and leant against Sven's shoulder. 'One big, hairy angel.'

Chapter 60

DOUBTS

The recurring wintry weather made it possible for Sven, Ida and the baby to plan their first kicksled ride as a complete family.

'We shouldn't be long, Mum. There are some reindeer burgers in the fridge,' Ida said over her shoulder, while rummaging through their wardrobe in the corridor. They had to reintroduce some of the thickest and warmest clothing for their upcoming journey – all of which they had packed away to wait for next season.

'Okay,' Sophia replied from the sofa, her legs comfortably tucked under the warmth of a woollen blanket. She sipped her warm coffee. The cats purred on the floor by the fireplace. The bunny came to flop on his side next to her. A real *Hygge* moment – whatever that really means.

Sophia had asked a few of her so-called friends from Tuppervaara circles to temporarily accommodate her after losing her home, but their responses were vague and confusing. She learnt the hard way that these acquaintances she had cherished over the years were nothing else but business associates, and only kept in touch for one common purpose: to sell and make more money. However, once a genuine request for help came, everyone turned their backs – except her own daughter, who offered this modest roof over her head.

Yet, losing her home was just the beginning of Sophia's hardship. The volcanic eruption damage cover on the insurance policy for their house in Örebröre had expired around the time of Gustav's death, and hadn't been renewed since. While grieving the loss of his death, Sophia had forgotten, or not realised, to take over the responsibilities of all the utilities that were under his name. The unpaid bills with interest had stacked up during the past months.

In addition, the hectares of land they owned had become largely engulfed by lava, with the swede plantations completely ruined. It could take years, or decades, for the area to be resurveyed, if someone was to consider resettling and rebuilding there. Therefore, despite some personal cash savings she had, Sophia was up against another challenge: looming poverty.

It had taken Sophia a natural disaster and a personal bankruptcy to finally come and visit Ida and Sven's little home. She still couldn't fathom, though, how three people were able to survive in such a contained space. There was only one bathroom for all of them to share; no kitchen island; no ice cube maker; and an outdoor sauna that only fitted three people at one time, if being sat skin-on-skin.

Nevertheless, the most recent, humbling of experiences had forced her to keep any strong opinions to herself. She couldn't afford to set any demands – this was the new normal she had to settle with for the time being.

Ida stepped into the living room, almost unrecognisable under all the layers of winter clothing. 'Is everything alright?'

'I was just... admiring this plant,' Sophia muttered.

'Of course.' Ida knew well that her mother being so detached had nothing to do with the snake plant, but something else. 'Everything's going to be fine.'

'It can't get much worse,' Sophia sighed.

'That's the Mother–in–Law's Tongue.' Sven stepped into the room, proudly demonstrating his knowledge of house plants. The baby was in his arms, fully dressed for the adventure.

'Please,' Ida hushed Sven.

Or, maybe it can get worse, Sophia thought, while rolling her eyes.

Sven, however, wasn't going to allow Sophia's negativity to take him down with her. 'It's a good thing. A snake plant gave me hope that there could be life in Örebröre. I saw leaves of one of those sticking through the lava rocks and black magma when I visited the disaster area for the first time. It seemed so out of place.'

'Birgget's plant!' Ida gasped. 'She accidentally dropped it on our way to that Tuppervaara party. She was meant to bring it to you, Mum.'

After hearing this, Sophia spoke more softly to Sven. 'She's alright, your mother.'

'She's quite something,' Sven said proudly. He pulled two tiny, knitted plush suitcases from his pocket, and gave them for the baby to hold. 'She even made her these; to complete the set.'

'And she's very skilled, too,' Sophia added.

'Those go perfectly together with the plush Yetilag.' Ida went by the cot. When she leant over and reached out for the soft toy, a piece of paper fell out of her trouser pocket. She quickly grabbed the sheet and crumpled it inside her palm. 'Shall we go then?'

'What about the toy?' Sven asked dumbfounded, while noticing her swift move to hide the paper.

'Why don't you take it? I'll meet you outside,' Ida said suspiciously. 'Take care, Mum. See you later.'

His hands full with the baby and her toys, Sven followed Ida outside, where she was already sitting on the front seat of his kicksled. The ground was covered with a solid layer of snow – it could have been September again. Although, after such a long winter, their eyes had got used to the bright white colours of the nature. Therefore, seeing snow in the springtime didn't seem as exciting, like the arrival of the first flakes of the season. This was usually a time when people, with open arms, welcomed the drier and warmer, yet much shorter summer season.

In silence, they travelled through the forest, leading to the centre of New Pihtamo. The baby sat calmly on Ida's lap while Sven steered. The ash coating of the buildings had been cleaned, or covered by snow. The businesses were open as usual. The area had survived yet another disaster and, this time, with less damage. The path of the eruption led only to Örebröre. Fortunately, there were no recorded casualties. However, the financial losses, especially those impacting Sophia's life, were insurmountable. It was the end of an era in their family's long tradition of generating wealth by farming. The future generations, like Ida, her two sisters and their descendants, had to 'make it' on their own, without the support or possible inheritance from the family.

The loss of money didn't bother Ida. She was set in her ways, the black sheep of the family, who chose to live and raise a child with a fisherman without fish. Only time would tell if their austere situation, lack of money and modest living standards would start causing problems. So far, there was enough love to keep them going.

Once they reached the town limits, Sven couldn't keep quiet anymore. 'So... about that thing you dropped?'

Ida sighed. 'It's probably better we pull over.'

He didn't have a good feeling about this. The morning had begun so well, so it was about time that some bad news arrived.

She handed the letter to him. 'It's a message my dad left in the bunker for anyone who ever needed to use it. He wasn't such an evil man after all. I didn't want to talk about this in my mother's presence and keep reminding her of him.'

Sven read the message to himself. His head kept nodding up and down, as if assenting to the content. His calm expression only changed once he reached the end of the sheet.

He audibly repeated the last sentence. 'There is always hope even when the hope is gone...' His eyes got watery either from a gust of wind, or from reading that famous quote of Roar's that seemed to touch anyone and everyone.

'I know.' Ida smiled, equally teary. 'My father must have appreciated something Roar had done.'

In disbelief, Sven stared at the letter. A filthy rich, privileged hunters' leader had used his arch enemy's quote in his emotional letter addressed to potential users of his secret bunker. Those people would, most likely, have been his family, closest friends and associates, and their descendants, and certainly not anyone who had anything to do with fishing and exactly that despicable lifestyle Roar represented.

The two men, Gustav and Roar, couldn't have been much

further from each other in terms of background, wealth, life choices they made, and personal and career interests they may have had. Yet, a devoted passion to do the right thing, and be the best in their chosen paths, were common denominators between the two – and the fact that they both had hidden superpowers like no other.

'Maybe... our fathers were not so different after all.'

'That's a mild way of putting it,' said Ida. 'My dad looked up to yours.'

'Then, why was me going out with you such a big problem for him?'

'Honey, none of that matters anymore. He is gone. Whatever he thought of us being together is irrelevant. The only thing this letter shows is that: he had a heart, he wanted to do the right thing, and he had respect towards your father. It means that, he did, or would've, respected you as well, had he been here to see you going from one success to another. Perhaps, we just never gave him a chance before time ran out.' Ida swallowed her tears and took the letter back. 'Shall we go on before it gets too late?'

'Sure.' He hopped back on the rails and pushed them to motion.

The wind was almost non-existent on the flat terrain. Another subtle snowfall began, dropping soft flakes slowly, as if they were floating in the air. After a brief moment of peace, he broke the silence again with another mind-boggling question.

'So... how did you guys spend all your days in the bunker?'

'Surviving,' she replied. 'Eating tuna and drinking water. My mum desperately tried to run her Tuppervaara party almost until the end. She's crazy.'

He responded with a sigh. She wouldn't give him the information he was looking for. 'What about... Christian? How was he?'

'Why?'

'Don't get me wrong. It's not what you think.' He was worried that she might think he was jealous – which was true. 'I'm just interested about his disappearance. He just showed up from nowhere?'

'Ah. That is quite an amazing story. He was so lucky.'

'I bet he was,' Sven snorted.

'What does that mean?'

'Well...' He hesitated, wondering whether he should go first and tell about their findings by the pond, or wait until he had heard Christian's version. He settled for the latter, and let her explain. 'Nothing. What's the story?'

She gave him a suspicious glance over her shoulder. Yet, she decided to go first. 'Christian was attacked by Wolferring at the river...'

'Was he really? At the river?' he interrupted.

'Can I tell the story or not?' she grunted.

'Sorry. Go on.'

'So, apparently, he lost his boat and ended up living in the forest for weeks, until coincidentally ending up near Örebröre.'

'Coincidentally?' he scoffed. 'Did he say anything specific about his boat? Or any other fish?'

'His boat? Not really. About Wolferring, yes. He ended up fighting against it, until some other fish came to intervene,' she explained enthusiastically.

Yet, Sven responded to Christian's claims with suspicion. 'I think he's been feeding you willow rope! We found his belongings by the pond, not by the river. Wolferring's rotten body was there, with only grilled sideburns attached to its face.'

Ida's sudden chuckle interrupted him. 'The sideburns were true, then?'

'Yes!' he grunted, concerned he would never get to the end of the story. His right foot kicked off the ground in faster intervals. They were speeding.

'You're scaring me. And the baby.'

'Listen! The pond was empty of all the fish, because someone, or something, had emptied it. And, there was this wreck of an old Viking vessel on the shore that looked exactly like the one the Lord of Herrings had.'

'Roar's boat?'

'No. That got destroyed and sank in the middle of the lake by Psalmon's preaching after Mooses's attack.' He brought them to a sudden halt. 'Christian's belongings were inside the wreck, including the map to the pond Roar drew for him, and some of his restaurant menus.'

Ida went speechless, while they both thought about exactly the same thing. *Was Christian telling them everything?*

However, to the very end, she wanted to believe that Christian was a man of high moral standards, hence truthful. 'Maybe this cod killed Wolferring and then...'

'Makes sense. But it still doesn't explain the boat, or Christian's involvement?'

Not exactly in the mood they had wished for, they continued the journey. There were doubts, too many unanswered questions and loose ends. Christian's story didn't quite add up. What really happened to all the fish? Where did that Viking vessel come from? How did Psalmon get so fat? And where was Yetilag?

Printed in Great Britain
by Amazon